GREAT IRISH
DRINKING STORIES

Also edited by Peter Haining in the same series

GREAT IRISH STORIES OF THE SUPERNATURAL (1992)
GREAT IRISH DETECTIVE STORIES (1993)
GREAT IRISH TALES OF FANTASY (1994)
GREAT IRISH TALES OF HORROR (1995)
GREAT IRISH HUMOROUS STORIES (1995)
GREAT IRISH STORIES OF CHILDHOOD (1997)
GREAT IRISH STORIES OF MURDER AND MYSTERY (1999)

GREAT IRISH DRINKING STORIES

The Craic's the Thing

Edited by
Peter Haining

SOUVENIR PRESS

First published 2002 by
Souvenir Press Ltd,
43 Great Russell Street, London WC1B 3PD

ISBN 0 285 63659 6

Photoset by Rowland Phototypesetting Ltd,
Bury St Edmunds, Suffolk
Printed in Great Britain by
Creative Print and Design Group (Wales), Ebbw Vale

For
Robert and Rachel
To stir up a few happy memories of Ireland

Work is the curse of the drinking classes.
OSCAR WILDE

CONTENTS

Introduction   11

1   THE CRAIC'S THE THING: Tales of Revelry
After the Wake *by Brendan Behan*   19
Irish Revel *by Edna O'Brien*   26
Gold at Night *by Peter Tremayne*   49
St Patrick's Day in the Morning *by Robert J. Martin*   75
The Hen Party *by Eamonn Sweeney*   94
Teresa's Wedding *by William Trevor*   104
We Are Green! We Are White! *by Roddy Doyle*   115

2   IN FINNEGAN'S WAKE: Pub Stories
Grace *by James Joyce*   123
Ding-Dong *by Samuel Beckett*   146
Peter McCabe's Bargain *by Patrick Kavanagh*   152
The Heat of the Sun *by Sean O'Faolain*   157
The Boils of Thomas Gully *by Patrick McCabe*   172
An Unusual Request *by Glenn Patterson*   183
The First Singles Bar *by Malachy McCourt*   189

3   THE DRINKS' INTERVAL: A Round of Dramas
Christy Mahon's Story *by J. M. Synge*   199
Tim Haffigan *by Bernard Shaw*   207
The Bull of Bashan *by Sean O'Casey*   215
Thirst *by Flann O'Brien*   226
The Diviner *by Brian Friel*   239

4 HOLDING THE HOUR: Drinkers' Tall Stories
The Geography of an Irish Oath *by William Carleton* 255
The Keg of Poteen *by Lynn Doyle* 275
The Drunkard *by Frank O'Connor* 286
The Guinness Goddess *by Marian Keyes* 298
The Rocky Road to Dublin *by Shane MacGowan* 308
Just Visiting *by Bernard Mac Laverty* 312

Acknowledgements 335

INTRODUCTION

Ballybunion, the fabled little town, once the stronghold of the O'Bannions at the mouth of the Shannon, is the source of a number of classic drinking stories. Several of these have been recorded by John B. Keane, the publican from nearby Listowel, who is known far and wide as a prolific storyteller and something of an Irish institution. Blessed with a wonderful sense of humour and a vivid imagination, John has contributed hundreds of short pieces to newspapers and magazines about the state of his community and the nation in general. Indeed, all human life is to be found in his writing and many of the remarkable characters who walk, amble or stagger through his prose have, in all probability, stood at his bar at one time or another.

The Irish love of drinking and conversation is, of course, proverbial. It has helped to earn them a reputation as the most talkative and entertaining folk on earth. They even have a special term for it—the *craic*—which they have turned into an art form. It is said the *craic* contains more than a hint of mockery—in the case of visitors the hope is that the target is the Irish themselves—but no one can ever be *quite* sure.

Certainly, the Irish drinking culture is famous all over the world. It has been said that the main product of Dublin is talk, and a meeting with friends for a drink and a chat is the national pastime. The invitation to take a 'glass of stout' or 'a ball of malt' [whiskey] is an expression as frequently heard as enquiring about someone's health or the weather. More often than not proposed as an antidote to either!

There is one particular Irish expression I heard years ago that had me thinking seriously about the country's drinking tradition and how it had evolved. I was in the bar at the Shelbourne Hotel, if memory serves me correctly, although it could just as easily have been in any of the other little pubs in the neighbourhood which are such a delight to visit. The expression I overheard about a hungover man in the corner by his friend while buying a drink at the bar went like this: 'Aaagh, the stale dregs of yesterday's whiskey have put yer man in a humour that would make a dog bite its father!'

Although it is not my intention to deliver a history lesson on the tradition here, a few facts may be of interest. It is curiously true, for instance, that whiskey is actually quite a modern invention. Celtic historian Peter Berresford Ellis—with whom I've shared many a glass over the years—says that the first mention of it is to be found in the *Irish Annals* of AD 1405 where it is noted that a certain Risteard Mac Rannell, the Chief of Muinter Eolais, turned his toes up after an over-indulgence of *uisge beatha*—i.e. 'water of life' or whiskey.

Of course the Irish were at the ale long before this—as stories from mythology bear lugubrious witness. According to Dioscorides in the first century AD, *coirm*, a brew distilled from barley, was the staple drink. From this evolved the word for an alehouse, *Coirmthhech*, and the ancient Brehon Laws of the time decreed that all such places had to be licensed and all brewers needed to seek legal approval. It was as well for the man who ran a *Coirmthhech* to make sure his drink was of a good quality because complaints from customers could result in him having to pay compensation.

These laws also took a tough line on drunkenness. There are numerous references to the treatment of drunks and how brawls in ale houses were to be dealt with. They were specific, too, on how drunkenness was to be defined in order to spare the innocent from punishment. One rule of thumb was not being able to remember the events of the night before.

Any ordinary working man was allowed to drink up to six pints of ale with his evening meal, the law said. The clergy, however, were not so lucky. *Three* pints was the maximum for the men of the cloth—presumably to stop them from getting drunk and neglecting their duties.

The great St Patrick apparently frowned on drinking. When he was in Connacht on one occasion, he is said to have met a certain intoxicated king and prophesied that his descendants would be drunks and lose their kingdom—which it seems they did. It is perhaps surprising in the light of this that the patron saint had his own brewer: a priest significantly called Mescan.

Connacht was also the home of Medb (Maeve), the legendary warrior queen, whose name translates as 'she who intoxicates' and has been given to the drink known as mead. A glass of this brew which is primarily made from honey was the tipple of the nobility for many centuries. It was mainly brewed in the south of Ireland until the early years of the nineteenth century, but is now coming back into fashion once again.

Stout—Guinness in particular—is probably the most famous Irish drink and, as sampling will prove, certainly tastes better in Ireland than anywhere else. The brewing of the ideal pint—hoppy and rich with lurking fruity flavours, a soft, creamy head and no after-taste—has developed from what was once a cottage indus-try. It was in 1759 that Arthur Guinness used an inheritance to buy a small ale brewery in County Kildare, moved to Dublin, and from 1799 began to produce exclusively the stout that bears his trademark.

Yer man's name is also to be found on one of the biggest selling books in the world, *The Guinness Book of Records*, which is generally accepted as the last word when it comes to settling arguments in pubs. Which is just as it should be because that is why the idea for the annual publication came about. Sir Hugh Beaver, a famous civil engineer and the inventor of the Mulberry moveable harbours used in the D-Day landings, was the boss of Guinness in the years after the Second World War. In 1951, while shooting in Co. Wexford, his party of guns missed a flight of golden plover. Sir Hugh immediately began to wonder whether the plover was Europe's fastest game bird. But where could he find out?

The Guinness boss tried every reference book and encyclopae-dia he could lay his hands on without any luck and grumbled: 'It *ought* to be in a book.' He felt certain such a volume would be invaluable in pubs where there were often disagreements about 'which cow yielded the most milk' and similar topics. Guinness would sponsor the project and it was two brothers, Norris and Ross McWhirter, who turned the idea into a multi-million copy best-seller.

The pub is not just the place for settling arguments, of course. It is somewhere for the telling of stories, tall and otherwise: a platform for the *gleg-tongued*—to use a Belfast expression for those fluent of speech—to spin their yarns. Like many another visitor, I've been surprised to learn that the most Irish of songs, 'Danny Boy' is not a native ballad at all—it was actually written in 1911 by Fred Weatherley, a Bristol lyric writer, to the tune of *The Londonderry Air*, composed by Rory Dall O'Cahan in the seventeenth century—but that creations like the tractor, the ejector seat and barbed wire were all invented in Ireland.

In truth, though, nothing should ever really surprise you about Ireland—especially not where drink and drinking is concerned. Pubs are the fulcrum of social life everywhere and when first-time visitors have got over the shock of realising that references to *craic* are nothing to do with illicit drugs but the delightful opium of good conversation and uninhibited banter, they will find any invitation to join in the fun is given wholeheartedly.

I offer the same with this collection of Irish tales from the scribes of days gone by to today's new generation of storytellers— all of them intoxicated by the nation's drinking culture. I recall the widow of W. B. Yeats insisting that poets wrote best when 'squiffy' and many a writer's wife has complained that it was expected of them to come to the pub at closing time and 'escort yer tottering man of genius home'. Brendan Behan, probably the most famous of all Ireland's literary boozers—'the drinker with writing problems', as he was once described—had a phrase for the whole experience: 'To eat is an accomplishment; to get drunk is a victory.'

In my selection I have tried to feature the varied aspects of this culture. The authors are some of Ireland's best known: very few of whom have been averse to the occasional drink, while some have actually helped to make their reputations because of it. For quite a few, as you will discover, fame came in pint form.

All in all, the brew is one of pleasures and pitfalls, joy and pathos, enlightenment and intoxication, offered in the same spirit of generosity as a young barman showed to my wife and me on holiday in Kinsale a few years ago. Arriving at the bar ten minutes before it was due to open, the young fellow apologised to us and offered a table by the window to enjoy the harbour view while we waited. Less than a minute later, yer man was back.

'Sure, and where are my manners,' he said apologetically in a lilting Cork accent. 'Would you be after having a drink while you're waiting?'

*Gura fada faoi bhláth thú gan easpa ar do shláinte!**

Peter Haining,
April 2002.

* May you prosper long without loss of your health!

1

THE CRAIC'S THE THING

Tales of Revelry

AFTER THE WAKE

Brendan Behan

A wake is described in most dictionaries as 'a vigil beside a corpse', but in Ireland the addition of the words 'often with revelry' is essential. The best of them create just the right balance between the solemn and the ridiculous, though they tend to remain essentially chauvinistic with the male guests settling down to drink and the womenfolk preparing food in the kitchen. Death is, though, generally treated as another cause for a celebration by the Irish, although the motives can be as diverse as the charac-ter of the recently departed. 'After the Wake' is a tale of such a vigil for a young wife who has died of cancer and focuses on the narrator's ambivalent relationship with both her and her husband. Their friendship, regularly augmented with alcohol and interminable conversations, is movingly described in the story that also deals with the intimacies of marriage and hints of homosexuality. It is, perhaps, a surprising short story from the pen of a man famed for his hard-hitting works about prison life and the IRA and his roistering, first-hand accounts of drink and drinkers in Dublin and London. Like the early stories of several of his exiled contemporaries who appear in this book including James Joyce and Samuel Beckett, 'After the Wake' was first published in Paris, in a small literary magazine, Points, *in 1950.*

Born in Dublin, the son of a house painter, Brendan Behan (1923–64) grew up in an Irish Republican family and during his teens served two years in detention for 'complicity in acts of terrorism'. While in Borstal, he began to write and then, following several penniless years in Dublin and Paris, became an overnight sensation with the opening of his play, The Quare Fellow, *about life in prison, in 1956. Two years later came his bestselling book,* Borstal Boy, *which was followed by the memorable* Hold Your Hour and Have Another (1963) *and* Confessions of an Irish Rebel (1965). *In the interim, Behan's irreverent, chaotic and boozy lifestyle kept him forever in the newspaper headlines, although several critics had no hesitation in putting his work in the same literary league as Sean O'Casey, Frank O'Connor and Sean O'Faolain, the later of whom had published some of his early stories. By the time of his tragic death, Brendan Behan was widely known as Ireland's 'roaring boy' and his legend both as a drinker and writer has never diminished.*

*   *   *

When he sent to tell me she was dead, I thought that if the dead live on—which I don't believe they do—and know the minds of the living, she'd feel angry, not so much jealous as disgusted, certainly surprised.

For one time she had told me, quoting unconsciously from a book I'd lent him, 'A woman can always tell them—you kind of smell it on a man—like knowing when a cat is in a room'.

We often discussed things like that—he, always a little cultured, happy, and proud to be so broad-minded—she, with adolescent pride in the freedom of her married state to drink a bottle of stout and talk about anything with her husband and her husband's friend.

I genuinely liked them both. If I went a week without calling up to see them, he was down the stairs to our rooms, asking what they'd done on me, and I can't resist being liked. When I'd go in she'd stick a fag in my mouth and set to making tea for me.

I'd complimented them individually and together, on their being married to each other—and I meant it.

They were both twenty-one, tall and blond, with a sort of English blondness.

He, as I said, had pretensions to culture and was genuinely intelligent, but that was not the height of his attraction for me.

Once we went out to swim in a weir below the Dublin Mountains.

It was evening time and the last crowd of kids too shrimpish, small, neutral cold to take my interest—just finishing their bathe.

When they went off, we stripped and, watching him, I thought of Marlowe's lines which I can't remember properly: 'Youth with gold wet head, through water gleaming, gliding, and crowns of pearlets on his naked arms'.

I haven't remembered it at all, but only the sense of a Gaelic translation I've read.

When we came out we sat on his towel—our bare thighs touching—smoking and talking.

We talked of the inconveniences of tenement living. He said he'd hated most of all sleeping with his brothers—so had I, I'd felt their touch incestuous—but most of all he hated sleeping with a man older than himself.

He'd refused to sleep with his father which hurt the old man very much, and when a seizure took his father in the night, it left him remorseful.

'I don't mind sleeping with a little child,' he said, 'the snug way they round themselves into you—and I don't mind a young fellow my own age'.

'The like of myself,' and I laughed as if it meant nothing. It didn't apparently, to him.

'No, I wouldn't mind you, and it'd be company for me, if she went into hospital or anything,' he said.

Then he told me what she herself had told me sometime before, that there was something the matter with her, something left unattended since she was fourteen or so, and that soon she'd have to go into hospital for an operation.

From that night forward, I opened the campaign in jovial earnest.

The first step—to make him think it manly, ordinary to manly men, the British Navy, 'Porthole Duff', 'Navy Cake' stories of the Hitler Youth in captivity, told me by Irish soldiers on leave from guarding them; to remove the taint of 'cissiness', effeminacy, how the German Army had encouraged it in Cadet Schools, to harden the boy-officers, making their love a muscular clasp of friendship, independent of women, the British Public Schools, young Boxers I'd known (most of it about the Boxers was true), that Lord Alfred Douglas was son to the Marquess of Queensberry and a good man to use his dukes himself, Oscar Wilde throwing old 'Q' down the stairs and after him his Ballyboy attendant.

On the other front, appealing to that hope of culture—Socrates, Shakespeare, Marlowe—lies, truth and half-truth.

I worked cautiously but steadily. Sometimes (on the head of a local scandal) in conversation with them both.

After I'd lent him a book about an English schoolmaster, she'd made the remark about women knowing, scenting them as she would a cat in a dark, otherwise empty room.

Quite undeliberately, I helped tangle her scents.

One night we'd been drinking together, he and I, fairly heavily up in their rooms.

I remember when he'd entered and spoken to her, he said to me: 'Your face lights up when you see her'. And why wouldn't it? Isn't a kindly welcome a warming to both faith and features?

I went over and told her what he'd said.

'And my face lights up when I see yours,' she said, smiling up at me in the charming way our women have with half-drunk men.

The following morning I was late for work with a sick head.

I thought I'd go upstairs to their rooms and see if there was a bottle of stout left that would cure me.

There wasn't, and though she was in, he was out.

I stopped a while and she gave me a cup of tea, though I'd just finished my own down below in our place.

As I was going she asked me had I fags for the day. I said I had—so as not to steal her open store, as the saying has it—and went off to work.

She, or someone, told him I'd been in and he warned me about it the next time we were together. He didn't mind (and I believed him) but people talked, etc.

From that day forward I was cast as her unfortunate admirer, my jealousy of him sweetened by my friendship for them both.

She told me again about her operation and asked me to pray for her. When I protested my unsuitability as a pleader with God, she quoted the kindly, highly heretical Irish Catholicism about the prayers of the sinner being first heard.

The night before she went into hospital we had a good few drinks—the three of us together.

We were in a singing house on the Northside and got very sob-gargled between drinking whiskey and thinking of the operation.

I sang *My Mary of the Curling Hair* and when we came to the Gaelic chorus, '*siúil, a ghrá*' ('walk, my love'), she broke down in sobbing and said how he knew as well as she that it was to her I was singing, but that he didn't mind. He said that indeed he did not, and she said how fearful she was of this operation, that maybe she'd never come out of it. She was not sorry for herself, but for him, if anything happened to her and she died on him, aye, and sorry for me too, maybe more sorry, 'Because, God help you,' she said to me, 'that never knew anything better than going down town half-drunk and dirty rotten bitches taking your last farthing'.

Next day was Monday, and at four o'clock she went into the hospital. She was operated on on Thursday morning and died the same evening at about nine o'clock.

When the doctor talked about cancer, he felt consoled a little. He stopped his dry-eyed sobbing and came with me into a public-house where we met his mother and hers and made arrangements to have her brought home and walked in her own place.

She was laid out in the front room on their spare single bed which was covered in linen for the purpose. Her habit was of blue satin and we heard afterwards that some old ones considered the colour wrong—her having been neither a virgin nor a member of the Children of Mary Sodality.

The priest, a hearty man who read Chesterton and drank pints, disposed of the objection by saying that we were all Children of Mary since Christ introduced St John to our Lady at the foot of the Cross—Son, behold thy Mother; Mother, behold Thy Son.

It is a horrible thing how quickly death and disease can work on a body.

She didn't look like herself, any more than the brown parch-ment-thin shell of a mummy looks like an Egyptian warrior; worse than the mummy, for he at least is dry and clean as dust. Her poor nostrils were plugged with cotton-wool and her mouth hadn't closed properly, but showed two front teeth, like a rabbit's. All in all, she looked no better than the corpse of her granny, or any other corpse for that matter.

There was a big crowd at the wake. They shook hands with him and told him they were sorry for his trouble; then they shook hands with his and her other relatives, and with me, giving me an understanding smile and licence to mourn my pure unhappy love.

Indeed, the old one, far gone in Jameson, said she was looking down on the two of us, expecting me to help him bear up.

Another old one, drunker still, got lost in the complications of what might have happened had he died instead of her, and only brought herself up at the tableau—I marrying her and he blessing the union from on high.

At about midnight, they began drifting away to their different rooms and houses and by three o'clock there was only his mother left with us, steadily drinking.

At last she got up a little shakily on her feet and, proceeding to knock her people, said that they'd left bloody early for blood relatives, but seeing as they'd given her bloody little in life it was the three of us were best entitled to sit waking—she included me and all.

When his mother went, he told me he felt very sore and very drunk and very much in need of sleep. He felt hardly able to undress himself.

I had to almost carry him to the big double bed in the inner room.

I first loosened his collar to relieve the flush on his smooth cheeks, took off his shoes and socks and pants and shirt, from the supply muscled thighs, the stomach flat as an altar boy's, and noted the golden smoothness of the blond hair on every part of his firm white flesh.

I went to the front room and sat by the fire till he called me.

'You must be nearly gone yourself,' he said, 'you might as well come in and get a bit of rest.'

I sat on the bed, undressing myself by the faint flickering of the candles from the front room.

I fancied her face looking up from the open coffin on the Americans who, having imported wakes from us, invented morticians themselves.

IRISH REVEL

Edna O'Brien

Every Irish child dreams of their first party. For many, like farmer's daughter, Mary, the experience has to wait until she is well into her teens, by which time her thoughts are a whirl of anticipation and anxiety. So what is she going to find at the party she has been invited to at the Commercial Hotel? Her mother has warned her not to touch a drop of alcohol and to be wary of men with the gift of the gab. Especially those who are drunk. But when the day of the party finally arrives, it provides more surprises than even Mary could have imagined.

Edna O'Brien (1932–) has been alternately described as 'the most banned author in Ireland after James Joyce' and 'the patron saint of sadness'. What is beyond dispute is that she is among the finest modern Irish writers and has made something of a speciality of writing about the deeply entrenched attitudes and stern religious outlook of the people of rural Ireland where she grew up. Like Mary, the central character in this story, she was born on a farm in Twamgraney in County Clare. Her family was opposed to anything to do with literature; she has recalled, and described the village where she grew up as 'enclosed, fervid and bigoted'. She was educated at the Convent of Mercy at Loughrea in County Galway and then went to Dublin to study to be a pharmacist. During her time as a student, her mother found a book by Sean O'Casey in her suitcase which she wanted to burn. O'Brien's driving ambition was, though, already set on becoming a writer, and between 1960 and 1964 she published 'The Country Girls Trilogy' which became bestsellers around the world—except in Ireland where they were banned for 'smear-

ing Irish womanhood'. Since this successful beginning, she has produced a large number of highly acclaimed short stories and novels including House of Splendid Isolation *(1995) that was awarded the European Prize for Literature. O'Brien has written about the effects of alcohol on the Irish in a number of her stories—including 'The Bachelor' and 'The Small Town Lovers'—and notably in her play,* Our Father *(1999), about a drunken, destructive rural father and his abused family. 'Irish Revel' was first published as 'Come into the Drawing Room, Doris' in the* New Yorker *in 1968.*

*   *   *

Mary hoped that the rotted, front tyre would not burst. As it was, the tube had a slow puncture, and twice she had to stop and use the pump, maddening, because the pump had no connection and had to be jammed on over the corner of a handkerchief. For as long as she could remember she had been pumping bicycles, carting turf, cleaning outhouses, doing a man's work. Her father and her two brothers worked for the forestry, so that she and her mother had to do all the odd jobs—there were three children to care for, and fowl and pigs and churning. Theirs was a mountainy farm in Ireland, and life was hard.

But this cold evening in early November she was free. She rode along the mountain road, between the bare thorn hedges, thinking pleasantly about the party. Although she was seventeen this was her first party. The invitation had come only that morning from Mrs Rodgers of the Commercial Hotel. The postman brought word that Mrs Rodgers wanted her down that evening, without fail. At first, her mother did not wish Mary to go, there was too much to be done, gruel to be made, and one of the twins had earache, and was likely to cry in the night. Mary slept with the year-old twins, and sometimes she was afraid that she might lie on them or smother them, the bed was so small. She begged to be let go.

'What use would it be?' her mother said. To her mother all outings were unsettling—they gave you a taste of something you couldn't have. But finally she weakened, mainly because Mrs Rodgers, as owner of the Commercial Hotel, was an important woman, and not to be insulted.

'You can go, so long as you're back in time for the milking in the morning; and mind you don't lose your head,' her mother warned. Mary was to stay overnight in the village with Mrs Rodgers. She plaited her hair, and later when she combed it it fell in dark crinkled waves over her shoulders. She was allowed to wear the black lace dress that had come from America years ago and belonged to no one in particular. Her mother had sprinkled her with Holy Water, conveyed her to the top of the lane and warned her never to touch alcohol.

Mary felt happy as she rode along slowly, avoiding the potholes that were thinly iced over. The frost had never lifted that day. The ground was hard. If it went on like that, the cattle would have to be brought into the shed and given hay.

The road turned and looped and rose; she turned and looped with it, climbing little hills and descending again towards the next hill. At the descent of the Big Hill she got off the bicycle— the brakes were unreliable—and looked back, out of habit, at her own house. It was the only house back there on the mountain, small, whitewashed, with a few trees around it, and a patch at the back which they called a kitchen-garden. There was a rhubarb bed, and shrubs over which they emptied tea-leaves and a stretch of grass where in the summer they had a chicken run, moving it from one patch to the next, every other day. She looked away. She was now free to think of John Roland. He came to their district two years before, riding a motor-cycle at a ferocious speed; raising dust on the milk-cloths spread on the hedge to dry. He stopped to ask the way. He was staying with Mrs Rodgers in the Commercial Hotel and had come up to see the lake, which was noted for its colours. It changed colour rapidly—it was blue and green and black, all within an hour. At sunset it was often a strange burgundy, not like a lake at all, but like wine.

'Down there,' she said to the stranger, pointing to the lake below, with the small island in the middle of it. He had taken a wrong turning.

Hills and tiny cornfields descended steeply towards the water. The misery of the hills was clear, from all the boulders. The cornfields were turning, it was midsummer; the ditches throbbing with the blood-red of fuchsia; the milk sour five hours after it had been put in the tanker. He said how exotic it was. She had no interest in views herself. She just looked up at the high sky and saw that a hawk had halted in the air above them. It was like a pause in her life, the hawk above them, perfectly still; and just then her mother came out to see who the stranger was. He took off his helmet and said 'Hello', very courteously. He introduced himself as John Roland, an English painter, who lived in Italy.

She did not remember exactly how it happened, but after a while he walked into their kitchen with them and sat down to tea.

Two long years since; but she had never given up hoping— perhaps this evening. The mail-car man said that someone special in the Commercial Hotel expected her. She felt such happiness. She spoke to her bicycle, and it seemed to her that her happiness somehow glowed in the pearliness of the cold sky, in the frosted fields going blue in the dusk, in the cottage windows she passed. Her father and mother were rich and cheerful; the twin had no earache, the kitchen fire did not smoke. Now and then, she smiled at the thought of how she would appear to him—taller and with breasts now, and a dress that could be worn anywhere. She forgot about the rotted tyre, got up and cycled.

The five street lights were on when she pedalled into the village. There had been a cattle fair that day, and the main street was covered with dung. The townspeople had their windows protected with wooden half-shutters and make-shift arrangements of planks and barrels. Some were out scrubbing their own piece of footpath with bucket and brush. There were cattle wandering around, moo-ing, the way cattle do when they are in a strange street, and drunken farmers with sticks were trying to identify their own cattle in dark corners.

Beyond the shop window of the Commercial Hotel, Mary heard

loud conversation, and men singing. It was opaque glass so that she could not identify any of them, she could just see their heads moving about, inside. It was a shabby hotel, the yellow-washed walls needed a coat of paint as they hadn't been done since the time De Valera came to that village during the election campaign five years before. De Valera went upstairs that time, and sat in the parlour and wrote his name with a penny pen in an autograph book, and sympathized with Mrs Rodgers on the recent death of her husband.

Mary thought of resting her bicycle against the porter barrels under the shop window, and then of climbing the three stone steps that led to the hall door, but suddenly the latch of the shop door clicked and she ran in terror up the alley by the side of the shop, afraid it might be someone who knew her father and would say he saw her going in through the public bar. She wheeled her bicycle into a shed and approached the back door. It was open, but she did not enter without knocking.

Two townsgirls rushed to answer it. One was Doris O'Beirne, the daughter of the harness-maker. She was the only Doris in the whole village, and she was famous for that, as well as for the fact that one of her eyes was blue and the other a dark brown. She learnt shorthand and typing at the local technical school, and later she meant to be a secretary to some famous man or other in the Government, in Dublin.

'God, I thought it was someone important,' she said when she saw Mary standing there, blushing, pretty and with a bottle of cream in her hand. Another girl! Girls were two a penny in that neighbourhood. People said that it had something to do with the lime water that so many girls were born. Girls with pink skins, and matching eyes, and girls like Mary with long, wavy hair and good figures.

'Come in, or stay out,' said Eithne Duggan, the second girl, to Mary. It was supposed to be a joke but neither of them liked her. They hated shy mountainy people.

Mary came in carrying cream which her mother had sent to Mrs Rodgers, as a present. She put it on the dresser and took off her coat. The girls nudged each other when they saw the dress. In the kitchen was a smell of cow dung and fried onions.

'Where's Mrs Rodgers?' Mary asked.

'Serving,' Doris said in a saucy voice, as if any fool ought to know. Two old men sat at the table eating.

'I can't chew, I have no teeth,' said one of the men, to Doris. ''Tis like leather,' he said, holding the plate of burnt steak towards her. He had watery eyes and he blinked childishly. Was it so, Mary wondered, that eyes got paler with age, like bluebells in a jar?

'You're not going to charge me for that,' the old man was saying to Doris. Tea and steak cost five shillings at the Commercial.

''Tis good for you, chewing it,' Eithne Duggan said, teasing him.

'I can't chew with my gums,' he said again, and the two girls began to giggle. The old man looked pleased hat he had made them laugh, and he closed his mouth and munched once or twice on a piece of fresh, shop bread. Eithné Duggan laughed so much that she had to put a dish-cloth between her teeth. Mary hung up her coat and went through to the shop.

Mrs Rodgers came from the counter for a moment to speak to her.

'Mary, I'm glad you came, that pair in there are no use at all, always giggling. Now first thing we have to do is to get the parlour upstairs straightened out. Everything has to come out of it except the piano. We're going to have dancing and everything.'

Quickly, Mary realized that she was being given work to do, and she blushed with shock and disappointment.

'Pitch everything into the back bedroom, the whole shootin' lot,' Mrs Rodgers was saying as Mary thought of her good lace dress, and of how her mother wouldn't even let her wear it to Mass on Sundays.

'And we have to stuff a goose too and get it on,' Mrs Rodgers said, and went on to explain that the party was in honour of the local Customs and Excise Officer who was retiring because his wife won some money in the Sweep. Two thousand pounds. His wife lived thirty miles away at the far side of Limerick and he lodged in the Commercial Hotel from Monday to Friday, going home for the weekends.

'There's someone here expecting me,' Mary said, trembling with the pleasure of being about to hear his name pronounced by someone else. She wondered which room was his, and if he was likely to be in at that moment. Already in imagination she had climbed the rickety stairs and knocked on the door, and heard him move around inside.

'Expecting you!' Mrs Rodgers said, and looked puzzled for a minute. 'Oh, that lad from the slate quarry was inquiring about you, he said he saw you at a dance once. He's as odd as two left shoes.'

'What lad?' Mary said, as she felt the joy leaking out of her heart.

'Oh, what's his name?' Mrs Rodgers said, and then to the men with empty glasses who were shouting for her. 'Oh all right, I'm coming.'

Upstairs Doris and Eithne helped Mary move the heavy pieces of furniture. They dragged the sideboard across the landing and one of the castors tore the linoleum. She was expiring, because she had the heaviest end, the other two being at the same side. She felt that it was on purpose: they ate sweets without offering her one, and she caught them making faces at her dress. The dress worried her too in case anything should happen to it. If one of the lace threads caught in a splinter of wood, or on a porter barrel, she would have no business going home in the morning. They carried out a varnished bamboo whatnot, a small table, knick-knacks and a chamber-pot with no handle which held some withered hydrangeas. They smelt awful.

'How much is the doggie in the window, the one with the waggledy tail?' Doris O'Beirne sang to a white china dog and swore that there wasn't ten pounds' worth of furniture in the whole shibeen.

'Are you leaving your curlers in, Dot, till it starts?' Eithne Duggan asked her friend.

'Oh def.,' Doris O'Beirne said. She wore an assortment of curlers—white pipe-cleaners, metal clips, and pink, plastic rollers. Eithne had just taken hers out and her hair, dyed blonde, stood out, all frizzed and alarming. She reminded Mary of a moulting hen about to attempt flight. She was, God bless her, an unfortunate girl with a squint, jumbled teeth and almost no lips; like something put together hurriedly. That was the luck of the draw.

'Take these,' Doris O'Beirne said, handing Mary bunches of yellowed bills crammed on skewers.

Do this! Do that! They ordered her around like a maid. She dusted the piano, top and sides, and the yellow and black keys; then the surround, and the wainscoting. The dust, thick on everything, had settled into a hard film because of the damp in that room. A party! She'd have been as well off at home, at least it was clean dirt attending to calves and pigs and the like.

Doris and Eithne amused themselves, hitting notes on the piano at random and wandering from one mirror to the next. There were two mirrors in the parlour and one side of the folding fire-screen was a blotchy mirror too. The other two sides were of water-lilies painted on black cloth, but like everything else in the room it was old.

'What's this?' Doris and Eithne asked each other, as they heard a hullabulloo downstairs. They rushed out to see what it was and Mary followed. Over the banisters they saw that a young bullock had got in the hall door and was slithering over the tiled floor, trying to find his way out again.

'Don't excite her, don't excite her I tell ye,' said the old, toothless man to the young boy who tried to drive the black bullock out. Two more boys were having a bet as to whether or not the bullock would do something on the floor when Mrs Rodgers came out and dropped a glass of porter. The beast backed out the way he'd come, shaking his head from side to side.

Eithne and Doris clasped each other in laughter and then Doris drew back so that none of the boys would see her in her curling pins and call her names. Mary had gone back to the room, downcast. Wearily she pushed the chairs back against the wall and swept the linoleumed floor where they were later to dance.

'She's bawling in there,' Eithne Duggan told her friend Doris. They had locked themselves into the bathroom with a bottle of cider.

'God, she's a right-looking eejit in the dress,' Doris said. 'And the length of it!'

'It's her mother's,' Eithne said. She had admired the dress before that, when Doris was out of the room, and had asked Mary where she bought it.

'What's she crying about?' Doris wondered, aloud.

'She thought some lad would be here. Do you remember that lad stayed here the summer before last and had a motor-cycle?'

'He was a Jew,' Doris said. 'You could tell by his nose. God, she'd shake him in that dress, he'd think she was a scarecrow.' She squeezed a blackhead on her chin, tightened a curling pin which had come loose and said, 'Her hair isn't natural either, you can see it's curled.'

'I hate that kind of black hair, it's like a gipsy's,' Eithne said, drinking the last of the cider. They hid the bottle under the scoured bath.

'Have a cachou, take the smell off your breath,' Doris said as she hawed on the bathroom mirror and wondered if she would get off with that fellow O'Toole, from the slate quarry, who was coming to the party.

In the front room Mary polished glasses. Tears ran down her cheeks so she did not put on the light. She foresaw how the party would be; they would all stand around and consume the goose, which was now simmering in the turf range. The men would be drunk, the girls giggling. Having eaten, they would dance, and sing, and tell ghost stories, and in the morning she would have to get up early and be home in time to milk. She moved towards the dark pane of window with a glass in her hand and looked out at the dirtied streets, remembering how once she had danced with John on the upper road to no music at all, just their hearts beating, and the sound of happiness.

He came into their house for tea that summer's day and on her father's suggestion he lodged with them for four days, helping

with the hay and oiling all the farm machinery for her father. He
understood machinery. He put back doorknobs that had fallen
off. Mary made his bed in the daytime and carried up a ewer of
water from the rain-barrel every evening, so that he could wash.
She washed the check shirt he wore, and that day, his bare back
peeled in the sun. She put milk on it. It was his last day with
them. After supper he proposed giving each of the grown-up
children a ride on the motor-bicycle. Her turn came last, she felt
that he had planned it that way, but it may have been that her
brothers were more persistent about being first. She would never
forget that ride. She warmed from head to foot in wonder and
joy. He praised her as a good balancer and at odd moments he
took one hand off the handlebar and gave her clasped hands a
comforting pat. The sun went down, and the gorse flowers blazed
yellow. They did not talk for miles; she had his stomach encased
in the delicate and frantic grasp of a girl in love and no matter
how far they rode they seemed always to be riding into a golden
haze. He saw the lake at its most glorious. They got off at the
bridge five miles away, and sat on the limestone wall, that was
cushioned by moss and lichen. She took a tick out of his neck
and touched the spot where the tick had drawn one pin-prick of
blood; it was then they danced. A sound of larks and running
water. The hay in the fields was lying green and ungathered, and
the air was sweet with the smell of it. They danced.

'Sweet Mary,' he said, looking earnestly into her eyes. Her
eyes were a greenish-brown. He confessed that he could not love
her, because he already loved his wife and children, and anyhow
he said, 'You are too young and too innocent.'

Next day, as he was leaving, he asked if he might send her
something in the post, and it came eleven days later: a black-and-
white drawing of her, very like her, except that the girl in the
drawing was uglier.

'A fat lot of good, that is,' said her mother, who had been
expecting a gold bracelet or a brooch. 'That wouldn't take you
far.'

They hung it on a nail in the kitchen for a while and then one
day it fell down and someone (probably her mother) used it to

sweep dust on to, ever since it was used for that purpose. Mary
had wanted to keep it, to put it away in a trunk, but she was
ashamed to. They were hard people, and it was only when someone died that they could give in to sentiment or crying.

'Sweet Mary,' he had said. He never wrote. Two summers
passed, devil's pokers flowered for two seasons, and thistle seed
blew in the wind, the trees in the forestry were a foot higher.
She had a feeling that he would come back, and a gnawing fear
that he might not.

'Oh it ain't gonna rain no more, no more, it ain't gonna rain no
more; How in the hell can the old folks say it ain't gonna rain
no more.'

So sang Brogan, whose party it was, in the upstairs room of
the Commercial Hotel. Unbuttoning his brown waistcoat, he sat
back and said what a fine spread it was. They had carried the
goose up on a platter and it lay in the centre of the mahogany
table with potato stuffing spilling out of it. There were sausages
also and polished glasses rim downwards, and plates and forks
for everyone.

'A fork supper' was how Mrs Rodgers described it. She had
read about it in the paper; it was all the rage now in posh houses
in Dublin, this fork supper where you stood up for your food
and ate with a fork only. Mary had brought knives in case anyone
got into difficulties.

'Tis America at home,' Hickey said, putting turf on the smoking fire.

The pub door was bolted downstairs, the shutters across, as
the eight guests upstairs watched Mrs Rodgers carve the goose
and then tear the loose pieces away with her fingers. Every so
often she wiped her fingers on a tea-towel.

'Here you are, Mary, give this to Mr Brogan, as he's the guest
of honour.' Mr Brogan got a lot of breast and some crispy skin
as well.

'Don't forget the sausages, Mary,' Mrs Rodgers said. Mary
had to do everything, pass the food around, serve the stuffing,
ask people whether they wanted paper plates or china ones. Mrs

Rodgers had bought paper plates, thinking they were sophis-
ticated.

'I could eat a young child,' Hickey said.

Mary was surprised that people in towns were so coarse and
outspoken. When he squeezed her finger she did not smile at all.
She wished that she were at home—she knew what they were
doing at home; the boys at their lessons; her mother baking a
cake of wholemeal bread, because there was never enough time
during the day to bake; her father rolling cigarettes and talking
to himself. John had taught him how to roll cigarettes, and every
night since he rolled four and smoked four. He was a good man,
her father, but dour. In another hour they'd be saying the Rosary
in her house and going up to bed: the rhythm of their lives never
changed, the fresh bread was always cool by morning.

'Ten o'clock,' Doris said, listening to the chimes of the landing
clock.

The party began late; the men were late getting back from the
dogs in Limerick. They killed a pig on the way in their anxiety
to get back quickly. The pig had been wandering around the road
and the car came round the corner; it got run over instantly.

'Never heard such a roarin' in all me born days,' Hickey said,
reaching for a wing of goose, the choicest bit.

'We should have brought it with us,' O'Toole said. O'Toole
worked in the slate quarry and knew nothing about pigs or farm-
ing; he was tall and thin and jagged. He had bright green eyes
and a face like a greyhound; his hair was so gold that it looked
dyed, but in fact it was bleached by the weather. No one had
offered him any food.

'A nice way to treat a man,' he said.

'God bless us, Mary, didn't you give Mr O'Toole anything to
eat yet?' Mrs Rodgers said as she thumped Mary on the back to
hurry her up. Mary brought him a large helping on a paper plate
and he thanked her and said that they would dance later. To him
she looked far prettier than those good-for-nothing townsgirls—
she was tall and thin like himself; she had long black hair that
some people might think streelish, but not him, he liked long
hair and simple-minded girls; maybe later on he'd get her to go

into one of the other rooms where they could do it. She had funny eyes when you looked into them, brown and deep, like a bloody bog-hole.

'Have a wish,' he said to her as he held the wishbone up. She wished that she were going to America on an aeroplane and on second thoughts she wished that she would win a lot of money and could buy her mother and father a house down near the main road.

'Is that your brother the Bishop?' Eithne Duggan, who knew well that it was, asked Mrs Rodgers, concerning the flaccid-faced cleric over the fireplace. Unknown to herself Mary had traced the letter J on the dust of the picture mirror, earlier on, and now they all seemed to be looking at it, knowing how it came to be there.

'That's him, poor Charlie,' Mrs Rodgers said proudly, and was about to elaborate, but Brogan began to sing, unexpectedly.

'Let the man sing, can't you,' O'Toole said, hushing two of the girls who were having a joke about the armchair they shared; the springs were hanging down underneath and the girls said that at any minute the whole thing would collapse.

Mary shivered in her lace dress. The air was cold and damp even though Hickey had got up a good fire. There hadn't been a fire in that room since the day De Valera signed the autograph book. Steam issued from everything.

O'Toole asked if any of the ladies would care to sing. There were five ladies in all—Mrs Rodgers, Mary, Doris, Eithne, and Crystal the local hairdresser, who had a new red rinse in her hair and who insisted that the food was a little heavy for her. The goose was greasy and undercooked, she did not like its raw, pink colour. She liked dainty things, little bits of cold chicken breast with sweet pickles. Her real name was Carmel, but when she started up as a hairdresser she changed to Crystal and dyed her brown hair red.

'I bet you can sing,' O'Toole said to Mary.

'Where she comes from they can hardly talk,' Doris said.

Mary felt the blood rushing to her sallow cheeks. She would not tell them, but her father's name had been in the paper once, because he had seen a pine-marten in the forestry plantation; and they ate with a knife and fork at home and had oil cloth on the kitchen table, and kept a tin of coffee in case strangers called. She would not tell them anything. She just hung her head, making clear that she was not about to sing.

In honour of the Bishop O'Toole put 'Far away in Australia' on the horn gramophone. Mrs Rodgers had asked for it. The sound issued forth with rasps and scratchings and Brogan said he could do better than that himself.

'Christ, lads, we forgot the soup!' Mrs Rodgers said suddenly, as she threw down the fork and went towards the door. There had been soup scheduled to begin with.

'I'll help you,' Doris O'Beirne said, stirring herself for the first time that night, and they both went down to get the pot of dark giblet soup which had been simmering all that day.

'Now we need two pounds from each of the gents,' said O'Toole, taking the opportunity while Mrs Rodgers was away to mention the delicate matter of money. The men had agreed to pay two pounds each, to cover the cost of the drink; the ladies did not have to pay anything, but were invited so as to lend a pleasant and decorative atmosphere to the party, and, of course, to help.

O'Toole went around with his cap held out, and Brogan said that as it was *his* party he ought to give a fiver.

'I ought to give a fiver, but I suppose ye wouldn't hear of that,' Brogan said, and handed up two pound notes. Hickey paid up, too, and O'Toole himself and Long John Salmon—who was silent up to then. O'Toole gave it to Mrs Rodgers when she returned and told her to clock it up against the damages.

'Sure that's too kind altogether,' she said, as she put it behind the stuffed owl on the mantelpiece, under the Bishop's watchful eye.

She served the soup in cups and Mary was asked to pass the cups around. The grease floated like drops of molten gold on the surface of each cup.

'See you later, alligator,' Hickey said, as she gave him his; then he asked her for a piece of bread because he wasn't used to soup without bread.

'Tell us, Brogan,' said Hickey to his rich friend, 'what'll you do, now that you're a rich man?'

'Oh go on, tell us,' said Doris O'Beirne.

'Well,' said Brogan, thinking for a minute, 'we're going to make some changes at home.' None of them had ever visited Brogan's home because it was situated in Adare, thirty miles away, at the far side of Limerick. None of them had ever seen his wife either, who it seems lived there and kept bees.

'What sort of changes?' someone said.

'We're going to do up the drawing-room, and we're going to have flower-beds,' Brogan told them.

'And what else?' Crystal asked, thinking of all the lovely clothes she could buy with that money, clothes and jewellery.

'Well,' said Brogan, thinking again, 'we might even go to Lourdes. I'm not sure yet, it all depends.'

'I'd give my two eyes to go to Lourdes,' Mrs Rodgers said.

'And you'd get 'em back when you arrived there,' Hickey said, but no one paid any attention to him.

O'Toole poured out four half-tumblers of whiskey and then stood back to examine the glasses to see that each one had the same amount. There was always great anxiety among the men, about being fair with drink. Then O'Toole stood bottles of stout in little groups of six and told each man which group was his. The ladies had gin and orange.

'Orange for me,' Mary said, but O'Toole told her not to be such a goody, and when her back was turned he put gin in her orange.

They drank a toast to Brogan.

'To Lourdes,' Mrs Rodgers said.

'To Brogan,' O'Toole said.

'To myself,' Hickey said.

'Mud in your eye,' said Doris O'Beirne, who was already unsteady from tippling cider.

'Well we're not sure about Lourdes,' Brogan said. 'But we'll get the drawing-room done up anyhow, and the flower-beds put in.'

'We've a drawing-room here,' Mrs Rodgers said, 'and no one ever sets foot in it.'

'Come into the drawing-room, Doris,' said O'Toole to Mary, who was serving the jelly from the big enamel basin. They'd had no china bowl to put it in. It was red jelly with whipped egg-white in it, but something went wrong because it hadn't set properly. She served it in saucers, and thought to herself what a rough-and-ready party it was. There wasn't a proper cloth on the table either, just a plastic one, and no napkins, and that big basin with the jelly in it. Maybe people washed in that basin, downstairs.

'Well someone tell us a bloomin' joke,' said Hickey, who was getting fed up with talk about drawing-rooms and flower-beds.

'I'll tell you a joke,' said Long John Salmon, erupting out of his silence.

'Good,' said Brogan, as he sipped from his whiskey glass and his stout glass alternately. It was the only way to drink enjoyably. That was why, in pubs, he'd be much happier if he could buy his own drink and not rely on anyone else's meanness.

'Is it a funny joke?' Hickey asked of Long John Salmon.

'It's about my brother,' said Long John Salmon, 'my brother Patrick.'

'Oh no, don't tell us that old rambling thing again,' said Hickey and O'Toole, together.

'Oh let him tell it,' said Mrs Rodgers who'd never heard the story anyhow.

Long John Salmon began, 'I had this brother Patrick and he died; the heart wasn't too good.'

'Holy Christ, not this again,' said Brogan, recollecting which story it was.

But Long John Salmon went on, undeterred by the abuse from the three men:

'One day I was standing in the shed, about a month after he was buried, and I saw him coming out of the wall, walking across the yard.'

'Oh what would you do if you saw a thing like that,' Doris said to Eithne.

'Let him tell it,' Mrs Rodgers said. 'Go on, Long John.'

'Well it was walking toward me, and I said to myself, "What

do I do now?''; 'twas raining heavily, so I said to my brother Patrick, "Stand in out of the wet or you'll get drenched."' '

'And then?' said one of the girls anxiously.

'He vanished,' said Long John Salmon.

'Ah God, let us have a bit of music,' said Hickey, who had heard that story nine or ten times. It had neither a beginning, a middle nor an end. They put a record on, and O'Toole asked Mary to dance. He did a lot of fancy steps and capering; and now and then he let out a mad 'Yippee'. Brogan and Mrs Rodgers were dancing too and Crystal said that she'd dance if anyone asked her.

'Come on, knees up Mother Brown,' O'Toole said to Mary, as he jumped around the room, kicking the legs of chairs as he moved. She felt funny: her head was swaying round and round, and in the pit of her stomach there was a nice, ticklish feeling that made her want to lie back and stretch her legs. A new feeling that frightened her.

'Come into the drawing-room, Doris,' he said, dancing her right out of the room and into the cold passage where he kissed her clumsily.

Inside Cystal O'Meara had begun to cry. That was how drink affected her; either she cried or talked in a foreign accent and said, 'Why am I talking in a foreign accent?' This time she cried.

'Hickey, there is no joy in life,' she said as she sat at the table with her head laid in her arms and her blouse slipping up out of her skirtband.

'What joy?' said Hickey, who had all the drink he needed, and a pound note which he slipped from behind the owl when no one was looking.

Doris and Eithne sat on either side of Long John Salmon, asking if they could go out next year when the sugar plums were ripe. Long John Salmon lived by himself, way up the country, and he had a big orchard. He was odd and silent in himself; he took a swim every day, winter and summer, in the river, at the back of his house.

'Two old married people,' Brogan said, as he put his arm

round Mrs Rodgers and urged her to sit down because he was out of breath from dancing. He said he'd go away with happy memories of them all, and sitting down he drew her on to his lap. She was a heavy woman, with straggly brown hair that had once been a nut colour.

'There is no joy in life,' Crystal sobbed, as the gramophone made crackling noises and Mary ran in from the landing, away from O'Toole.

'I mean business,' O'Toole said, and winked.

O'Toole was the first to get quarrelsome.

'Now ladies, now gentlemen, a little laughing sketch, are we ready?' he asked.

'Fire ahead,' Hickey told him.

'Well, there was these three lads, Paddy th'Irishman, Paddy th'Englishman, and Paddy the Scotsman, and they were badly in need of a . . .'

'Now, no smut,' Mrs Rodgers snapped, before he had uttered a wrong word at all.

'What smut?' said O'Toole, getting offended. 'Smut!' And he asked her to explain an accusation like that.

'Think of the girls,' Mrs Rodgers said.

'Girls,' O'Toole sneered, as he picked up the bottle of cream—which they'd forgotten to use with the jelly—and poured it into the carcass of the ravaged goose.

'Christ's sake, man,' Hickey said, taking the bottle of cream out of O'Toole's hand.

Mrs Rodgers said that it was high time everyone went to bed, as the party seemed to be over.

The guests would spend the night in the Commercial. It was too late for them to go home anyhow, and also Mrs Rodgers did not want them to be observed staggering out of the house at that hour. The police watched her like hawks and she didn't want any trouble, until Christmas was over at least. The sleeping arrangements had been decided earlier on—there were three bed-rooms vacant. One was Brogan's, the room he always slept in. The other three men were to pitch in together in the second big

bedroom, and the girls were to share the back room with Mrs
Rodgers herself.

'Come on, everyone, blanket street,' Mrs Rodgers said, as she
put a guard in front of the dying fire and took the money from
behind the owl.

'Sugar you,' O'Toole said, pouring stout now into the carcass
of the goose, and Long John Salmon wished that he had never
come. He thought of daylight and of his swim in the mountain
river at the back of his grey, stone house.

'Ablution,' he said, aloud, taking pleasure in the world and in
thought of the cold water touching him. He could do without
people, people were waste. He remembered catkins on a tree
outside his window, catkins in February as white as snow; who
needed people?

'Crystal, stir yourself,' Hickey said, as he put on her shoes
and patted the calves of her legs.

Brogan kissed the four girls and saw them across the landing
to the bedroom. Mary was glad to escape without O'Toole notic-
ing; he was very obstreperous and Hickey was trying to control
him.

In the bedroom she sighed; she had forgotten all about the
furniture being pitched in there. Wearily they began to unload
the things. The room was so crammed that they could hardly
move in it. Mary suddenly felt alert and frightened, because
O'Toole could be heard yelling and singing out on the landing.
There had been gin in her orangeade, she knew now, because
she breathed closely on to the palm of her hand and smelt her
own breath. She had broken her Confirmation pledge, broken her
promise; it would bring her bad luck.

Mrs Rodgers came in and said that five of them would be too
crushed in the bed, so that she herself would sleep on the sofa
for one night.

'Two of you at the top and two at the bottom,' she said, so
she warned them not to break any of the ornaments, and not to
stay talking all night.

'Night and God bless,' she said, as she shut the door behind
her.

'Nice thing,' said Doris O'Beirne, 'bunging us all in here; I wonder where she's off to?'

'Will you loan me curlers?' Crystal asked. To Crystal, hair was the most important thing on earth. She would never get married because you couldn't wear curlers in bed then. Eithne Duggan said she wouldn't put curlers in now if she got five million for doing it, she was that jaded. She threw herself down on the quilt and spread her arms out. She was a noisy, sweaty girl but Mary liked her better than the other two.

'Ah me old segotums,' O'Toole said, pushing their door in. The girls exclaimed and asked him to go out at once as they were preparing for bed.

'Come into the drawing-room, Doris,' he said to Mary, and curled his forefinger at her. He was drunk and couldn't focus her properly but he knew that she was standing there somewhere.

'Go to bed, you're drunk,' Doris O'Beirne said, and he stood very upright for an instant and asked her to speak for herself.

'Go to bed, Michael, you're tired,' Mary said to him. She tried to sound calm because he looked so wild.

'Come into the drawing-room, I tell you,' he said, as he caught her wrist and dragged her towards the door. She let out a cry, and Eithne Duggan said she'd brain him if he didn't leave the girl alone.

'Give me that flower-pot, Doris,' Eithne Duggan called, and then Mary began to cry in case there might be a scene. She hated scenes. Once she hard her father and a neighbour having a row about boundary rights and she'd never forgotten it; they had both been a bit drunk, after a fair.

'Are you cracked or are you mad?' O'Toole said, when he perceived that she was crying.

'I'll give you two seconds,' Eithne warned, as she held the flower-pot high, ready to throw it at O'Toole's stupefied face.

'You're a nice bunch of hard-faced aul crows, crows,' he said. 'Wouldn't give a man a squeeze,' and he went out cursing each one of them. They shut the door very quickly and dragged the sideboard in front of the door so that he could not break in when they were asleep.

They got into bed in their underwear; Mary and Eithne at one end with Crystal's feet between their faces.

'You have lovely hair,' Eithne whispered to Mary. It was the nicest thing she could think of to say. They each said their prayers, and shook hands under the covers and settled down to sleep.

'Hey,' Doris O'Beirne said a few seconds later, 'I never went to the lav.'

'You can't go now,' Eithne said, 'the sideboard's in front of the door.'

'I'll die if I don't go,' Doris O'Beirne said.

'And me, too, after all that orange we drank,' Crystal said. Mary was shocked that they could talk like that. At home you never spoke of such a thing, you just went out behind the hedge and that was that. Once a workman saw her squatting down and from that day she never talked to him, or acknowledged that she knew him.

'Maybe we could use that old pot,' Doris O'Beirne said, and Eithne Duggan sat up and said that if anyone used a pot in that room she wasn't going to sleep there.

'We have to use something,' Doris said. By now she had got up and had switched on the light. She held the pot up to the naked bulb and saw what looked to be a hole in it.

'Try it,' Crystal said, giggling.

They heard feet on the landing and then the sound of choking and coughing, and later O'Toole cursing and swearing and hitting the wall with his fist. Mary curled down under the clothes, thankful for the company of the girls. They stopped talking.

'I was at a party. Now I know what parties are like,' Mary said to herself, as she tried to force herself asleep. She heard a sound as of water running, but it did not seem to be raining outside. Later, she dozed, but at daybreak she heard the hall door bang, and she sat up in bed abruptly. She had to be home early to milk, so she got up, took her shoes and her lace dress, and let herself out by dragging the sideboard forward, and opening the door slightly.

There were newspapers spread on the landing floor and in the lavatory, and a heavy smell pervaded. Downstairs, porter had flowed out of the bar into the hall. It was probably O'Toole who had turned on the taps of the five porter barrels, and the stone-floored bar and sunken passage outside was swimming with black porter. Mrs Rodgers would kill somebody. Mary put on her high-heeled shoes and picked her steps carefully across the room to the door. She left without even making a cup of tea.

She wheeled her bicycle down the alley and into the street. The front tyre was dead flat. She pumped for a half-an-hour but it remained flat.

The frost lay like a spell upon the street, upon the sleeping windows, and the slate roofs of the narrow houses. It had magically made the dunged street white and clean. She did not feel tired, but relieved to be out, and stunned by lack of sleep she inhaled the beauty of the morning. She walked briskly, sometimes looking back to see the track which her bicycle and her feet made on the white road.

Mrs Rodgers wakened at eight and stumbled out in her big nightgown from Brogan's warm bed. She smelt disaster instantly and hurried downstairs to find the porter in the bar and the hall; then she ran to call the others.

'Porter all over the place; every drop of drink in the house is on the floor—Mary Mother of God help me in my tribulation! Get up, get up.' She rapped on their door and called the girls by name.

The girls rubbed their sleepy eyes, yawned, and sat up.

'She's gone,' Eithne said, looking at the place on the pillow where Mary's head had been.

'Oh, a sneaky country one,' Doris said, as she got into her taffeta dress and went down to see the flood. 'If I have to clean that, in my good clothes, I'll die,' she said. But Mrs Rodgers had already brought brushes and pails and got to work. They opened the bar door and began to bail the porter into the street. Dogs came to lap it up, and Hickey, who had by then come down, stood and said what a crying shame it was, to waste all that drink. Outside it washed away an area of frost and revealed the dung of yesterday's fair day. O'Toole the culprit had fled since the night; Long John Salmon was gone for his swim, and upstairs in bed Brogan snuggled down for a last-minute warm and deliberated on the joys that he would miss when he left the Commercial for good.

'And where's my lady with the lace dress?' Hickey asked, recalling very little of Mary's face, but distinctly remembering the sleeves of her black dress which dipped into the plates.

'Sneaked off, before we were up,' Doris said. They all agreed that Mary was no bloody use and should never have been asked.

'And 'twas she set O'Toole mad, egging him on and then disappointing him,' Doris said, and Mrs Rodgers swore that O'Toole, or Mary's father, or someone, would pay dear for the wasted drink.

'I suppose she's home by now,' Hickey said, as he rooted in his pocket for a butt. He had a new packet, but if he produced that they'd all be puffing away at his expense.

Mary was half-a-mile from home, sitting on a bank.

If only I had a sweetheart, something to hold on to, she thought, as she cracked some ice with her high heel and watched the crazy splintered pattern it made. The poor birds could get no food as the ground was frozen hard. Frost was general all over Ireland; frost like a weird blossom on the branches, on the river-bank from which Long John Salmon leaped in his great, hairy nakedness, on the ploughs left out all winter; frost on the stony fields, and on all the slime and ugliness of the world.

Walking again she wondered if and what she would tell her mother and her brothers about it, and if all parties were as bad. She was at the top of the hill now, and could see her own house, like a little white box at the end of the world, waiting to receive her.

GOLD AT NIGHT

Peter Tremayne

At many of the great Irish Festivals in the past, drinking contests between the clans were regular events. At these gatherings, champion imbibers would be pitted one against another to see who would first succumb to intoxication. The man left standing was declared the winner. The honour of a clan was very much at stake on these occasions as the jugs of ale were quaffed by the contestants, each roared on by their inebriated supporters. 'Gold At Night' is the story of just such a contest in the seventh century held at the Feast of Lugnasadh, in which Ruisin, the famous champion of the Osraige is pitted against mighty Cronan of the Fidh Gabha. Instead of a victor, though, death intrudes into the celebrations and presents the well-known dalaigh, *Sister Fidelma with one of her most baffling mysteries.*

Sister Fidelma, a crime-fighting advocate, who has been described by the Irish Post *as 'fast becoming a world ambassador for ancient Irish culture', has to date appeared in ten novels (the first,* Absolution by Murder, *in 1994) and almost twice that number of short stories. The success of these tales set in a dangerous historical world owes much to their authenticity which is based on years of research into Celtic history by Peter Tremayne, the pen name of the Irish scholar and historian, Peter Berresford Ellis (1943–). The son of a Cork journalist, Ellis has a master's degree in Celtic studies and has published a number of seminal works on the subject as well as an impressive body of fiction. The stories about the shrewd and resourceful advocate with her mastery of the Brehon laws have been published in America and translated into several European languages as well as inspiring the International Sister Fidelma Society. 'Gold At Night' with its unique slant on Celtic revelry has been especially written for this collection.*

*　　*　　*

'By this time tomorrow, thanks be to God, it will be all over for another three years. I have to admit that I am quite exhausted.'

Sister Fidelma smiled at her companion as they walked along the banks of the broad river of Bearbha. Abbot Laisran of Durrow was a portly man, short of stature, with silver hair and a permanent air of jollity about him. He had been born with a rare gift of humour and a sense that the world was there to provide enjoyment to those who inhabited it. In this he was in contrast with many of his calling.

But in spite of his statement, he looked far from fatigued.

Fidelma and Laisran paused a while to watch some boys fishing in the river, the abbot watching their casts with a critical eye.

'Was it worth your coming?' he suddenly asked.

Fidelma considered the question before answering. She did not like to give glib answers for the sake of politeness.

'The great Fair of Carman is an experience not to be missed,' she relied with studied reflection.

The Aenach or Fair of Carman was held once every three years over the days of the Feast of Lugnasadh, the first days of what the Romans called the month of Augustus and it was one of the two major fairs held within the kingdom of Laighin. It was attended in person by Fáelán of the Uí Dúnláinge, King of Laighin, and no less than forty-seven of his leading nobles. During the period of the fair, there were games, contests in sports and the arts. Poets would declaim their verses and strong men would contest with one another in all manner of feats of skill as well as strength. So would women because there were special times set aside for contests between women. In addition to the entertainment, there were markets for all manner of livestock, produce and goods.

In fact, Laisran had been telling Fidelma how he had to chase

a stall keeper from the fairground because the man had been
selling potions for destroying pests such as foxes and wolves.
But the very noxious brews that would kill a fox or a wolf could
kill other animals and, as such, were prohibited from sale at the
Fair. Yet it was true that many wonderful and curious things
were to be found on sale in the stalls of the Aenach Carman.

But there was also a serious side to the Aenach Carman, unlike
the Aenach Lifé, which was Laighin's other great fair and devoted
to horse racing.

During the days of the Aenach Carman, the assembly of the
kingdom met. All the nobles, the chiefs of clans, the Brehons
and lawyers, the professional men and women gathered to discuss
the laws. On the first day, the men and women of the kingdom
held separate councils at which the other sex was not allowed to
enter. The women's council admitted no man and the men's
council admitted no women. Each council met and decided matters pertaining to their sex and elected representatives to go forward to attend the formal meetings of the Great Assembly of
Laighin. Both sexes attended this and matters pertaining to all
the people were discussed and decided upon. The King, his Brehons, or judges, and representatives of all the people would discuss any necessary amendment to the laws and agree the fiscal
policies of the kingdom for the next three years.

While Fidelma was from the neighbouring kingdom of Muman,
and therefore not qualified to voice any opinion in the councils
nor Assembly, she had been invited by the women's council to
attend and speak to them as their guest. She was asked to advise
them on certain laws in her own kingdom and how they might
be applicable to Laighin. For while the great law system applied
equally in all five kingdoms, there was a section of laws called
the *Urrdas Law* which were the minor variations that applied
from kingdom to kingdom. But now such serious matters were
over and one more day of festivity would end the fair.

Fidelma had been delighted, although not surprised, to find her
distant cousin and friend, Laisran, Abbot of Durrow, the great
teaching college, attending the fair. Not only attending it, but
being present as advisor to the Great Assembly. It had been

Laisran who had persuaded her to join the nearby abbey of Brigid at the Church of the Oaks, not far from the plain by the river Bearbha on which the Aenach Carman was held. But Fidelma had long since left the abbey of Brigid to return to her own land.

'What did you think of the competence of our law-makers?' Laisran was asking. 'Do we pass good laws and have good government?'

Fidelma chuckled.

'Did not Aristotle say that good laws, if they are not obeyed, do not constitute good government?'

Laisran answered his young cousin's infectious humour.

'I might have expected that from a lawyer,' he said. 'Seriously, have you enjoyed the Aenach Carman?'

Fidelma agreed but added: 'Although I have often wondered why it is so called. Wasn't Carman a malevolent female figure who had three sons and didn't they blight all the crops in Éireann until the children of Danu defeated them and drove them into exile? How, then, does it come about that the people of Laighin do honour to her by naming their principal festival after her?'

Laisran's eyes had a twinkle.

'Well, if I were to tell you . . .'

'My lord!'

A man who came running towards them cut his words short. He was well dressed and wore a chain of office.

'Lígach, chieftain of the Laisig,' whispered Laisran in quick explanation. 'The Laisig are the hereditary organisers and stewards of the fair.'

The man halted somewhat breathlessly before the abbot. He was clearly disturbed about something.

'My lord abbot . . .' He began breathlessly and then had to pause to gulp some air.

'Calm yourself Lígach. Catch your breath and then state calmly the matter that is troubling you.'

The chieftain paused and took several breaths.

'We need your services. Ruisín is dead. I have sent for an apothecary but we cannot find one on the field. I know you are not without some medical skills, lord Abbot.'

'Ruisín dead? How did he die?'

'Ruisín?' intervened Fidelma, interested by Laisran's concern. 'Who is he?'

Laisran replied immediately.

'He is . . . he was,' he corrected, 'a champion of the Osraige.' He turned back to Lígach. 'What has happened? An accident?'

Lígach shook his head.

'We think a surfeit of alcohol has killed him.'

Fidelma raised an eyebrow in query. Lígach saw the look and answered.

'He was taking part in a challenge. Crónán, the champion of the Fidh Gabhla, had challenged him as to how much ale each of them could consume. Suddenly, with no more than the first jug taken, Ruisín collapsed, was carried to his tent but when we laid him down we found his pulse no longer beat.'

'A drinking contest?' Fidelma's features twisted into a grimace of disapproval. Drink in moderation, wine with a meal, there was nothing better. But to drink to destroy the senses was pathetic, something she could never understand.

Lígach was defensive.

'There are often such contests between the champions of the clans. A clan can loose all honour if their champion fails.'

She sniffed in distaste.

'Far be it for me to condemn anyone when a man lays dead but my mentor, the Brehon Morann, always said that alcohol is lead in the morning, silver at noon and gold at night and lead always follows the period of gold. So excessive drinking is merely a pursuit of fool's gold.'

'Please, my lord,' urged Lígach, ignoring her, 'come, confirm his death and perform the last rite of the Faith. Ruisín's wife Muirgel is with the body and is in distress.'

'Lead me to his tent, then,' Laisran said, and then glancing at Fidelma. 'Perhaps you would like to accompany me, Fidelma? You might be able to formulate some words to the widow for I feel myself inadequate to utter comfort in such circumstances.'

Reluctantly, Fidelma fell in step with the abbot. She, too, could not think what might be said to comfort someone who drank him or herself into an early grave for the sake of a wager. They followed the nervous chieftain to the area of the field where the tents of those participating in the fair were raised. A small group stood outside one tent which marked it off as the one in which Ruisín's body had been lain. The group of men and women parted before them.

Lígach went in before them.

Inside a woman was kneeling beside the body of a man. She was young and fairly attractive. She glanced up as they entered. Fidelma noticed that her face wore an almost bland expression. The eyes were large and round and dry. There was no discernible grief in the face, not tearful lines of one struck by sudden grief.

'This is Muirgel,' Lígach said quickly.

The young woman regarded them curiously. She seemed almost a somnambulant. It was as if she was not quite cognisant of her surroundings.

'Muirgel, this is Abbot Laisran and Sister . . . Sister . . . ?'

'Fidelma,' supplied Laisran, bending down to the body.

Fidelma glanced down. The man whose body lay there had been a big, broad shouldered man with a shock of red curling hair and a beard that covered most of his barrel chest. He had obviously been a strong man.

A thought struck Fidelma.

'What work did this man do?' she asked Lígach quietly.

'He was a blacksmith, Sister,' replied the chieftain.

'Didn't you say that he collapsed after the first jug of ale had been consumed?'

'I did so.'

Laisran, kneeling beside the body, suddenly expelled the air from his lungs with a hiss.

'The man is, indeed, dead. I am sorry for this anguish that has been visited upon you Muirgel. Lígach, would you take Muirgel outside for a moment?'

Fidelma frowned at the studied seriousness of Laisran's voice.

Lígach hesitated and then reached forward to help Muirgel to her feet. She did not actually respond willingly but she offered no resistance. It was as if she had no will of her own. She allowed Lígach to lead her out of the tent without a word.

'Shock, perhaps,' Fidelma commented. 'I have seen death take people so.'

Laisran did not seem to hear her.

'Take a look at the man's mouth, Fidelma,' he said quietly. 'The lips, I mean.'

Puzzled a little, Fidelma bent down. She found that the man's beard was so full and wiry that she had to pull it back a little to view his mouth and the lips. Her brows came together. The lips were a bright purple colour. Her eye travelled to the skin. She had not noticed it before. It was mottled as if someone had painted a patterning on the man.

She looked up.

'This man has not died from an excess of alcohol,' Laisran said, anticipating her conclusion.

'Poison?'

'Some virulent form,' agreed Laisran. 'I have not practised the apothecary's art for some time, so I would not be able to identify it. Death was not from excessive alcohol, that is obvious. He was young, strong and fit, anyway. And if it was poison that caused his death, then . . .'

'Then it was either an accident or murder,' concluded Fidelma.

'And no poison would enter a jug in a drinking contest by mere accident.'

'Murder?' Fidelma paused and nodded slowly. 'The local Brehon must be summoned.'

There was a movement behind them. Lígach had re-entered the tent unnoticed by them. He had heard their conclusion.

'Are you sure that Ruisín has been murdered?' he demanded, aghast.

Laisran confirmed it with a quick nod of his head.

'And are you Fidelma of Cashel?' Lígach added, turning to Fidelma. 'I heard that you were attending the Fair. If so, please undertake the task of inquiring how Ruisín came by his death for I have heard great things of you. As organiser of the Fair, this is my jurisdiction and I willingly grant you the right to pursue these inquiries. If we do not clear this matter up then the reputation of the Aenach Carman will be blighted for it will be said, murder can be done within the king's shadow and the culprit can escape unknown and unpunished.'

Before Fidelma could protest, Laisran had agreed.

'There is none better than Fidelma of Cashel to dissect any web of intrigue that is woven around a murder.'

Fidelma sighed in resignation. It seemed that she had no choice. It was time to be practical.

'I would like another tent where I may sit and examine the witnesses to this matter.'

Lígach was smiling in his relief.

'The tent next to this one is at your disposal. It is my own.'

'Then I shall want all involved in this matter to be gathered outside, including the widow, Muirgel. I will tarry a moment more with the body.'

Lígach hastened off while Laisran stood awkwardly as Fidelma bent down to examine the body of Ruisín very carefully.

'What should I do?' he asked.

Fidelma smiled briefly up at him.

'You will witness my inquiry,' she replied, 'for I would not like to be accused of interference by the Chief Brehon of Laighin.'

'I will guarantee that,' confirmed Laisran.

Fidelma was carefully examining the body of the dead man.

'What are you looking for?' the abbot asked after a while.

'I do not know. Something. Something out of the ordinary.'

'The extraordinary thing is the fact that the man was poisoned, surely?'

'Yet we have to be sure that we do not miss anything.' She rose to her feet. 'Now, let us question the witnesses.'

Fidelma and Laisran seated themselves on camp stools within Lígach's tent. There was a table and a scribe had been sent for to record the details. He was a young, nervous man, who sat huddled over his inks and leaves of imported papyrus.

'Who shall I bring in first, Sister?' asked Lígach.

'Who organised this drinking contest?'

'Rumann, who was Ruisín's friend, and Cobha, who supplied the ale.;

'Bring in Rumann first.'

First through the tent door came a young, eager terrier, its ears forward, his jaws slightly opened, panting and its neck straining against a rope. The animal hauled a burly man into the tent who was clutching the leash. It leapt towards Fidelma in its excitement but in a friendly fashion with short barks and its tail wagging furiously.

The man on the end of the leash snapped at it and tugged the animal to obedience at his heel. Then he gestured apologetically.

Rumann was almost the twin image of Ruisín, but with brown tousled hair. He was burly man who also had the look of a smithy about him. Indeed, such was the craft he pursued.

'Sorry, Sister, but Cubheg here is young and excitable. He won't harm you.'

He turned to a tent post and tied the rope around it. The dog continued to tug and pull forward, Rumann glanced round.

'With your permission, Sister?' he indicated a bowl on the table. There was a jug of ale nearby. He poured some ale in the bowl and set it down before the animal which began to noisily lap at it with great relish. 'Cubheg likes a drink of ale. I can't deny him. Now, how can I help you?'

'This contest: whose idea was it?' demanded Fidelma without preamble.

'Crónán of the Fidh Gabhla issued the challenge.'

'For what purpose?'

Rumann shrugged.

'The rivalry between the Fidh Gabhla and the Osraige is generations old.'

'This is so,' whispered Abbot Laisran at her side.

'During the games these last few days, there have been several contests and the Osraige have held their own with the Fidh Gabhla,' went on Rumann. 'Crónán then challenge my friend, Ruisín, to a contest which would finally decide who were the greater at this fair, Osraige or the Fidh Gabhla.'

Fidelma's mouth turned down in disapproval.

'A clan made great simply by whoever could drink the most?'

'Sister, you must know that it is an old contest known in many lands? Whoever can drink most and still remain on their feet is the champion. This was to be the last great contest between us at the Aenach Carman.'

'Why was Ruisín chosen to take part?'

'He was our champion. And he was a great drinker,' Rumann said boastfully. 'He would drink a barrel of ale and still lift the empty barrel above his head at the end of it.'

Fidelma hid her cynicism.

'So the challenge was to him or to the Osraige?'

'Ruisín was champion of Osraige. It was the same thing.'

'So explain what happened at this contest.'

'Ruisín and Crónán met at the tent of Cobha the ale maker. He supplied the ale. And . . .'

'And which side was Cobha on?' queried Fidelma sharply.

'He was from the Fidh Gabhla. But the supplier of the ale in these contests is supposed to maintain neutrality.'

'Was there an impartial referee?'

'We were all referees. The men of Osraige and the men of Fidh Gabhla were there to see fair play.'

'No women?'

Rumann looked pained.

'It was not a contest that appealed to women,' he said.

'Quite so,' replied Fidelma grimly. 'So a crowd was gathered round?'

'Cobha poured two jugs of ale . . .'

'From the same barrel?'

Rumann frowned and thought.

'I think so. One jug apiece. Each man took up positions at each end of a wooden table on which the jugs were set. At a word from Cobha, they began to drink. Each man drained the first jug without a problem. Cobha bought the second jug . . . my friend, Ruisín had picked up the second jug when he staggered. He dropped the jug and he suddenly fell back. How the men of the Fidh Gabhla jeered, but I saw him writing on the ground. I knew he was ill. Within a moment he was dead. That is all I know.'

Fidelma was quiet for a moment.

'You say that Ruisín was your friend?'

'He was.'

'He was a smith?'

'Like myself. We often worked together when our chieftain needed two pairs of bellows instead of one.'

'Would you say that Ruisín was a strong man, a healthy man?'

'I have known him since he was a boy. There was never a stronger man. I refuse to believe that a surfeit of alcohol would kill him. Why, just one jug of ale and he went down like a cow at the slaughter.'

Fidelma sat back and gazed at the man with interest.

'Did your friend have enemies?'

'Enemies? Why, was he not our champion and being challenged by the Fidh Gabhla? The Fidh Gabhla had enough motive to ensure that their man should win.'

'But in these circumstances, there would be no victory.'

Rumann pursed his lips as though he had no thought of that fact.

'Did he have any other enemies?'

Rumann shook his head.

'He was regarded a first class craftsman, had plenty of work. He was happily married to Muirgel and no other cares in the world except how to enjoy his life more fully. No one would wish him harm . . .'

'Except?' Prompted Fidelma as his voice trailed away and the cast of thought came into his eyes.

'Only the men of the Fidh Gabhla,' he replied shortly. Fidelma knew that he had thought of something and was hiding it.

Crónán, the drinking champion of the Fidh Gabhla, was shown in next; a surly man with a mass of dark hair and bright blue eyes which flickered nervously as if seeking out potential danger.

'We have had many a drinking contest in the past, Ruisín and I. We were rivals. Our clans were rivals. But we were friends.'

'That's not what Rumann seems to imply,' Fidelma pointed out.

'Rumann has his own way of looking at things. Sometimes it is not a reality.'

'Why would anyone put poison into Ruisín's drink during this contest?'

Crónán raised his chin defiantly.

'I did not, that you may take as the truth. I swear that by the Holy Cross.'

'I would need more than an oath if I were to attempt to use it as evidence in court. You were both given separate jugs. I am told that the ale was poured from the same barrel.'

'It was. There were many witnesses to that. Cobha opened a new barrel so that the measure could be strictly witnessed.'

'What were the jugs?'

'The usual pottery jugs, they contained two *meisrin* each. We watched Cobha filled them and we all watched carefully so that the measure was equal. We had to double check because of Rumann's damned dog.'

'His dog?' Fidelma frowned.

'That young excitable terrier. He broke loose from Rumann just when Cobha was pouring the second jug for me. He had set the first on the table while he poured the second. Then the dog went between his legs and nearly had him over. Rumann was apologetic and tied the dog up for the rest of the contest. I and Lennán, who was my witness, had to double check to make sure that Cobha had poured an equal measure for me.'

'And when you had ensured that he had . . . ?'

'He brought it to the table and placed them before us. The signal was given. We took them and downed the contents, each being equal in time to the other.'

'Cobha then filled a second pair of jugs?'

The man shook his head.

'No he retrieved the empty jugs from us and refilled them with the same measure, no more than two *meisrin* each. He put the jugs on the table before us as before. The signal was given and I began to drink mine. It was then that I noticed that while Ruisín had picked up his jug, he held it loosely, staggered and then fell back dropping it.'

'Did it break?'

'What?'

'The jug, I mean. Did it break?'

'I think so. Yes, it cracked on the side of the table. I remember now, the damned dog ran forward to try to lap at the contents and Rumann had to hauled him away with a good smack on the nose.'

Fidelma turned to Lígach.

'Can the broken pieces of the jug be found?'

The man went off about the task.

'Tell me, on this second time of filling, Crónán, I presume the same jugs were returned to you both? The jug that you first drank from was returned to you and the jug Ruisín drank out of was returned to him? Can you be sure?'

'Easy enough to tell. The jugs had different coloured bands around them, the colours of the Fidh Gabhla and Osraige.'

'What craft do you follow, Crónán?' asked Fidelma suddenly.

'Me? Why, I am a hooper.'

'You make barrels?'

'I do indeed.'

Lígach returned. The broken jug could not be found. A more than diligent assistant to Cobha the ale keeper had apparently cleaned the area and taken the pieces to a rubbish dump where the results of several days of broken jugs and clay goblets were discarded in such manner that it was impossible to sort them out at all.

'I thought it best to take the broken jug to the rubbish dump immediately,' the assistant said defensively when summoned. 'It was dangerous. Broken pieces and jagged. Rumann had difficulty dragging his dog away from it. He was very perturbed that the animal would injure itself. There were sharp edges.'

When Cobha entered to give his account, Fidelma had to disguise her instant dislike of the man. He was tall, thin, exceedingly thin so that he gave the appearance of someone on the verge of starvation. His looks were sallow and the eyes sunken filled with suspicion. The only touch of colour was the thin redness of his lips. He came before Fidelma with his head hanging like someone caught in a shameful act. His speech was oily and apologetic.

His account basically confirmed what had been said before.

'Did you examine the jugs before you poured the measure?' asked Fidelma.

Cobha looked puzzled.

'Were they clean?' Fidelma was more specific.

'Clean? I would always provide clean drinking vessels to my customers,' Cobha said, with an air of ingratiation. 'I have been coming to the Fair of Carmen for two decades and no one has ever criticised my ale . . . nor died of it.'

'Until today,' Abbot Laisran could not help but add, showing he, too, disapproved of the ale-man's character.

'My ale was not to blame.'

'Do you have any idea what or who might be to blame?'

Cobha shook his head.

'Ruisín was not liked by everyone.'

Fidelma leant forward quickly.

'Is that so? Who did not like him?'

'Lennán, for example. He hated Ruisín.'

'Why?'

'Because of his sister.'

'Explain.'

'He once told me that his sister was having an affair with Ruisín. He disliked that.'

'Who is his sister and who is Lennán?' asked Fidelma. 'He has been mentioned before as being Crónán's witness.'

'Lennán is a farmer. His farm straddles the borders of Osraige and the lands of the Fidh Gabhla. His sister is Uainiunn. Lennán hated Ruisín but, to be honest, I think Lennán was trying to find an excuse for his hate. I have seen Uainiunn and Muirgel together and they were close friends.'

Fidelma sat back thoughtfully.

'And Lennán was Crónán's witness today?'

Cobha nodded.

'Let us go back to the jugs. How did you decide which jug to give to whom?'

'Easy enough. One jug had a yellow band on it, the colour for Osraige. The other jug had a red band for the Fidh Gabhla.'

'Who put the colour bands on them?'

'I did.'

'Before the contest?'

'About half an hour before.'

'And where did the jugs stand while the contestants readied themselves and you finally took up the jugs to fill?'

'On the table by the cask.'

'I want you to think clearly. Did you examine the jugs before you began to fill them?'

This time Cobha thought more carefully.

'I looked into them to make sure that they were still clean and nothing had crept it, a fly or some such creature.'

'And they were clean?'

Cobha nodded emphatically.

'I would not serve ale, even in such circumstances as this contest, in dirty vessels. I have my licence to consider. My ale-house has always been *dligtech* for it has passed the three tests according to law.'

Fidelma was looking puzzled.

'The contestants were standing with the table between them. Is that so?'

'It is.'

'How near were the onlookers?'

Cobha rubbed his jaw thoughtfully.

'Gathered around,' he said with a shrug.

'Such as? Who was, say, near, Crónán? I presume this witness, Lennán?'

'Lennán was next to him.' Cobha agreed and added. 'Lennán would not miss an opportunity to see Ruisín worsted.'

'That he certainly saw,' commented Fidelma dryly.

Cobha suddenly looked nervous.

'I did not mean to imply that ... I only meant to say ... You asked me where Lennán was.'

'And you told me,' agreed Fidelma. 'Who else was there?'

Cobha compressed his lips for a moment then shrugged.

'Uainiunn was with her brother.'

'I thought Rumann said that there were no women present?' frowned Fidelma.

Cobha shrugged indifferently.

'She was the only woman present apart from Muirgel. Perhaps that is what Rumann meant?'

Fidelma's eyebrows shot up.

'Muirgel as well? Where was she standing? You say that Uainiunn stood by her brother, Lennán? So they were close to Crónán?'

'That is so. Rumann and Muirgel were standing at the opposite end of the table on either side of Ruisín.'

'And you were the only person to pour the ale and place the jugs on the table?'

'True enough.'

She gestured for him to withdraw and turned with a fretful expression to Abbot Laisran.

'So far as I can see, there are only two possibilities. One possibility is that the poison was introduced into the jug destined for Ruisín between the time of it being poured and the time of his drinking it.'

'That surely meant that Cobha is chief suspect for if anyone else had introduced the poison then they would surely be seen?' replied Laisran. 'But I fail to see the second possibility?'

'That would involve introducing the poison to Ruisín before the contest so that it would affect him later?'

Laisran immediately shook his head.

'I know of no such poison that could have such a long-term affect as had been described. By all accounts Ruisín was well until the second jug was placed before him.'

'Importantly, we are told that he did not drink from it. So the poison must have been in the first jug.'

There was a moment of silence between them.

'It seems an impossible crime for it was carried out in front of so many witnesses,' Laisran sighed. 'We don't even know how the crime was committed let alone who committed it. Although a young *dálaigh* I knew would say, solve the one and find the other.'

Fidelma shook her head with a wry smile.

'That young *dálaigh* was being a little glib,' she confessed.

'You were correct then. The principle is also correct now.'

'Let us see what Lennán has to say,' she sighed. 'At least he is the only person who seems to have had some dislike for Ruisín.'

She called to Lígach to bring in the man.

Lennán was another of those people that she felt should be distrusted on sight. Shifty, weak eyes, constantly flickering here and there, but never focusing on the person he was addressing. His face was not thin but wiry; the mouth seemed malleable and he had a weak jaw. Nothing seemed firm about him. A vivid white line curved across his forehead, the scar of some terrible wound. The aura he gave out was intangible; that was the word Fidelma came up with. There seemed nothing substantial about the man that would even give a reason for her feeling of distrust.

'Well, Lennán,' she began sharply. 'We understand that you did not like Ruisín.'

The man actually cringed before her. It was not a pleasant sight.

'With good reason, Sister. With good reason,' he whined.

'And what good reason?'

'He was having an affair with my sister and he being married to Muirgel. It is a matter of her honour.'

'How did you know Ruisín was having an affair with your sister?'

'How do I know the midday sun is bright?' retorted the man.

'Sometimes the midday sun is obscured by grey cloud,' Fidelma pointed out dryly. 'I ask again, how did you know this?'

'She was always going to Ruisín's house.'

'But isn't that naturally explained. Ruisín's wife was her friend.'

Lennán sniffed in annoyance, the closest gesture he came in defiance of her.

'Ruisín's wife was an excuse. It was not Muirgel that she was going to see.'

'I still cannot see how you can be so sure. I presume you asked her?'

'She denied it.'

'Did you ask Ruisín?'

'He also denied it.'

'So did you kill Ruisín?'

The question was put in the same tone and without pause so that Lennán was about to answer before he realised what he was being asked. He frowned in annoyance.

'I would have done so if I had the chance,' he replied in a surly tone.

'That seems honest enough,' admitted Fidelma. 'You take your sister's honour seriously. I think you take it more seriously than she does. I wonder why?'

The man said nothing.

'You can offer no facts about this affair between your sister and Ruisín?'

'I don't need facts. I base my knowledge on logic.'

'Ah, logic. My mentor, Brehon Morann once said that anything could be demonstrated by logic. By logic we can prove whatever we wish to. Very well. During this contest, I am told you were standing at the table next to Crónán?'

'I was. My sister was beside me, mooning across the table at that oaf, Ruisín.'

'And you saw no one interfere with the drinking vessels?'

'I would not stoop to poison, Sister. If I reached the point where I wished to kill Ruisín, my weapon would be a sword or axe.'

Abbot Laisran was smiling in satisfaction when Lennán left the tent.

'That is our man, Fidelma. A whole *screpall* on it. That's worth a good barrel of Gaulish wine.'

'I think you are a little free with your money, Laisran,' she smiled,. 'Before taking the wager, let us have a word with his sister, Uainiunn.'

Uainiunn looked nothing like her brother. She was fleshy; almost voluptuous with an animal magnetism and a provocative way of looking at one, from under half closed eyelids. She was dark of hair and eyes with full red lips.

'I understand that you attended this drinking contest.'

'With my brother. He insisted.'

'He insisted?'

'He wanted to see Ruisín beaten by Crónán.'

'And you?'

The girl shrugged.

'It was a matter of indifference to me.'

Fidelma examined her closely.

'Why would that be so?' she asked.

Uainiunn sniffed.

'What entertainment is there is watching men drink themselves senseless?'

'True enough, but didn't you want to see Ruisín win the contest?'

'Not particularly. I am sad for Muirgel, though. The loss of Ruisín is going to be a heavy blow for her. However, I do not doubt that she will find another man to take care of her. Rumann for example. It might stop Rumann chasing me. He does not interest me.'

'Ruisín's death does not affect you in any way?' demanded Abbot Laisran, slightly outraged at the seeming callousness of the girl.

Uainiunn frowned.

'Only inasmuch as it affects my friend, Muirgel.'

'It sounds as though you did not care much for Ruisín,' Fidelma reflected.

'She was my friend's husband, that is all.'

'I understand that is not what your brother thought.'

The girl's eyes blazed for a moment. It was like a door opening suddenly and for a moment Fidelma glimpsed something equivalent to the hot fires of hell beyond. Then they snapped shut.

'I am not responsible for what Lennán thinks,' she snapped.

'So you would deny his claim that you were having an affair with Ruisín?'

The girl threw back her head and laughed. Yet it was not a pleasant sound. There was no need to press her further on her opinion.

'Very well,' Fidelma said quietly. 'You may leave us.'

Abbot Laisran turned eagerly after she left.

'You think that she did it? She is callous enough.'

Fidelma raised an eyebrow.

'Are you about to place another wager, another *screpall* on it?' she asked.

Laisran flushed.

'Perhaps either one of them did it,' he countered.

Fidelma did not reply directly. She turned to Lígach.

'Let Muirgel come in.'

Laisran looked slightly crushed and sat back. He whispered stubbornly.

'No, she didn't do it. A *screpall* on Lennán. He's your man, I am now certain. After all, he confessed that he wanted to murder Ruisín.'

'But says that he did not. If he were guilty of the fact, he would surely have attempted to hide his intention?' replied Fidelma.

'A subtle way of deflecting you from the truth. He has motive and . . .'

'And opportunity? How so? He was with Crónán on the far side of the table.'

Laisran shook his head.

'This is worse than the mystery you had to solve in my abbey, when Wulfstan was found stabbed to death in his cell which had been locked from the inside. Do you remember?'

'I remember it well,' agreed Fidelma.

'No one could have entered nor left—so who had killed Wulfstan? Here we have a similar problem.'

'Similar?'

'There is Ruisín. He is in full view of a large number of people and he is poisoned. No one can have administered the poison without being seen.'

Fidelma smiled softly.

'Yet someone did.'

Muirgel came in; her face was still mask-like, displaying no emotion. Fidelma pointed to a chair and invited her to sit down.

'We will not keep you long.'

The woman raised a bland face to them as she sat.

'The gossip is that my husband did not die from excess of drink but was poisoned.'

'It is a conclusion that we have reached.'

'But why? There was no reason to kill him.'

'There obviously was and we require your help in discovering that reason. What enemies did he have?'

'None except . . .' she suddenly looked nervous and paused.

'Lennán?'

'You know about him?'

'I know only that he hated your husband.'

Muirgel sat silently.

'Was your husband having an affair with Uainiunn?' demanded Fidelma brutally.

At once Muirgel shook her head vehemently.

'What makes you so positive?' pressed Fidelma.

'Uainiunn is my friend. I have known her longer than Ruisín. But I also know Ruisín. You cannot live in close proximity with a man day in and day out without knowing whether he is seeing another woman, especially if the woman is your best friend.'

Fidelma grimaced. She had known women who had been fooled as well as men come to that. But she did not comment further. Then another thought occurred to her.

'Rumann was your husband's friend?'

'He was.'

'And your friend also?'

The woman frowned.

'Of course.'

'Rumann is not married?'

'He is not.'

Fidelma was watching the woman's expression intently when she posed the questions with their subtle implication. But there was no guile there. Nothing was hidden.

'I suppose that you and Ruisín, Rumann and Uainiunn were often together?'

Again, Muirgel looked puzzled.

'Uainiunn was my friend. Rumann was Ruisín's friend. It was inevitable that we would be together from time to time.'

'What of Uainiunn's brother—Lennán? Was he in your company?'

Muirgel looked annoyed.

'I thought we had cleared up that matter. He was never in our company.'

Fidelma nodded with a sigh.

'You see, I would like to understand why Lennán has developed this idea about his sister and your husband?'

'If you can peer through a person's skull, through into the secrets of their mind, then you find the answer. All I know is that Lennán was not so extreme until after he returned from the cattle raid against the Uí Néill.'

'You will have to explain that.'

'Over a year ago Lennán decided to join a raiding party to retrieve some cattle stolen by the one of Uí Néill clans. When he came back he was a changed man. You saw the scar across his forehead?'

'He was wounded?'

'The rest of the raiding party did not return,' went on Muirgel. 'Only he returned out of the score of men who went off.'

'Did he explain what had happened to them?'

'An ambush. A fight. He was, indeed, wounded, and left for dead. A hill shepherd cared for him until he was well enough and then he returned. That was when he became suspicious of everyone and when he began to make those silly accusations against Ruisín.'

Fidelma leaned forward a little with interest.

'So this started only after his return. And you say there was no reason that you knew of?'

'Perhaps he had become deranged.'

'Did you speak about this to Uainiunn?'

Muirgel grimaced.

'Of course. Lennán was her brother.'

'And what comment did she make?'

'That we should ignore him. She said that most people knew

he had become a changed man since his return from the cattle raid. No one would take him seriously.' Muirgel suddenly paused and her eyes widened as she gazed at Fidelma. 'Lennán? Do you suspect Lennán of killing Ruisin? How? He was standing on the far side of the table when the contest started. How could he have killed my husband?'

'You've no idea who killed your husband?' Fidelma asked, ignoring her question.

'None.'

'That is all then.'

Muirgel rose and went to the flap of the tent.

'Oh, just one question more,' called Fidelma softly.

The woman turned expectantly.

'You were not having an affair with Rumann, were you?'

Muirgel's eyes widened for a moment in shock and then a cynical smile slowly crossed her face. She made a sound, a sort of suppressed chuckle and shook her head.

'I am not. And Rumann is too interested in Uainiunn to bother with me and I would have discouraged him. I loved Ruisín.'

Fidelma nodded and gestured her to leave.

Abbot Laisran was staring at Fidelma in surprise.

'That was surely an insensitive question to ask of a newly widowed woman?' He spoke in a tone of stern rebuke.

'Sometimes, Laisran, in order to get to firm ground one has to tread through bogland, through mire,' she replied.

'Do you really suspect that Muirgel poisoned her husband because she was having an affair with his friend, Rumann?'

'Every question I ask is for a purpose. You should know my methods by now, Laisran.'

'I am still at a loss. I thought it was clear that Lennán must be the culprit. But your question to Muirgel . . . ?'

Fidelma had turned to Lígach who had entered the tent again. The chieftain bent down and whispered in her ear. She nodded firmly.

'Bring Rumann back,' she ordered.

Rumann came it with his dog again but this time immediately tied it to the tent post so that it would not leap up.

'Well, Sister? Have you found out who killed my friend?'

Fidelma regarded him with grave, chill eyes.

'I think I have a good idea, Rumann. You did.'

The man froze. He tried to form a sentence but the words would not come out. He managed a nervous laugh.

'You are joking, of course?'

'I never joke about these matters, Rumann.'

'How could I have done such a thing?'

'Is that a practical question or a philosophical question?'

Rumann stood defiantly before her having regained his composure. He folded his arms across his chest.

'You must be mad.'

'I think that you will find that you have been the victim of madness but that does not emanate from me. How did you do it? The drinking contest had been arranged. Early in the fair you saw the stall which sold poisons. Abbot Laisran had told me how he had to chase the stallholder away because the noxious brews that he was selling to control pests could also be used to kill other animals. They would also kill human beings. You acquired some of that brew before Abbot Laisran forced the stall to close.'

For the first time Rumann looked nervous.

'You are guessing,' he said uncertainly. 'And am I supposed to have slipped this poison into his drink in full view of everyone gathered to watch the contest?'

'Supposed to and did so,' agreed Fidelma. 'It was very simple. You were standing by his side. Your terrier is always with you. It seems to like ale. As Cobha had poured the first jug, and each jug was marked for the individual contestant, you let slip the leash of your dog who ran to Cobha just after he set down Ruisín's jug and while he was filling the jug for Crónán. The immediate concern was to save Crónán's jug that he was filling. No one noticed that you slipped the phial of poison into Ruisín's jug while people fussed over whether Cobha had filled a proper measurement in the other jug.'

Rumann was silent.

'You retrieved your dog and tied it to a post. When Ruisín

fell dead and his jug shattered to pieces, your dog sprang forward to lap the ale in the broken pieces. You don't mind your dog lapping at ale. I asked myself why you were so concerned to draw your dog away from the ale in those broken pieces. A fear that the beast might injured himself on the broken pieces? Dogs have more sense. You thought some residue of the poison might be left, didn't you? You didn't want your dog to be poisoned.'

Rumann was still silent. Fidelma glanced towards the open tent flap.

'I could bring forth the stallholder who sold you the poison but I am sure you won't want to give us that trouble,' mused Fidelma softly.

Laisrean went to say something and then put a hand in front of his features and coughed noisily. Rumann did not seem to notice him and his jaw came up defiantly.

'Even if I admitted that I purchase poison from that stall, you have yet to argue a good cause why I would want to kill my friend, Ruisín.'

Fidelma shook her head.

'Sadly, that is not difficult. It is a cause, if you would call it so, that is as old as time itself. Jealously.'

'I? Jealous of Ruisín's wife? Ridiculous!'

'I did not say who you were jealous of. It was not Ruisín's wife. You are desperately in love with Uainiunn although she does not appear to care for you. In your justification for this, you came to believe the stories that Lennán was putting about—that his sister was having an affair with Ruisín. She was not. But you chose to believe Lennán because you could not accept that Uainiunn was simply not interested in you. Your jealousy knew no bounds. Pitifully, you believed if you killed Ruisín, that Uainiunn would turn to you. It is not love that is blind, Rumann, but, jealousy.'

'I loved Uainiunn. Ruisín stood in my way,' replied the smith firmly.

'He did not. That was no more than a deranged mind's fantasy which a frustrated and suspicious ear picked up and was then nurtured among the gall of rejection. The bitter fruits of this harvest have destroyed minds as well as lives. Love that is fed only on jealousy dies hard. So it will die in you, Rumann.'

She gestured to Lígach to remove the man from the tent.

Abbot Laisran was wiping the sweat from his brow.

'I swear that you had been worried there, Fidelma. A *dálaigh* is not supposed to tell an untruth to force a confession. What if Rumann had called your bluff and demanded that you bring in that stallholder that I chased from here?'

Fidelma smiled wanly.

'Then I would have asked him to come in. As soon as I saw that poison was involved, I remembered what you said and asked Lígach to find the man. You did not think that an entrepreneur would meekly depart from such a good source of revenue as this fair ground just because you chased him away from his stall? He had not gone very far at all.'

'I think I shall need a drink after this, but an amphora of good Gaulish wine—' Laisran shuddered. 'Certainly not ale!'

Fidelma looked cynical.

'What was it that you were going to wager with me—a *screpall*? A barrel of Gaulish wine? Lucky for you I did not accept it. You'll find wine is sweet but sour its payment.'

'I'm willing to fulfil my obligation,' the abbot said defensively.

Fidelma shook her head.

'A share of the amphora will do. You are not searching for the gold at night, surely? Tomorrow will only bring lead.'

Abbot Laisran grimaced wryly.

'Poor Ruisín found lead earlier than most. Moderation, Fidelma. I agree. I invite you to the hospitality of the abbey.'

'And is it not an old saying that it is not an invitation to hospitality without a drink?' smiled Fidelma.

ST PATRICK'S DAY IN
THE MORNING

Robert J. Martin

St Patrick's Day—17 March—probably amounts to the most famous Irish revel in the world—a day of noise and parapher-nalia, drinking and craic, *which countless millions elsewhere do their best to emulate, whether of Irish extraction or not. Curi-ously, though, St Patrick, the Patron Saint of Ireland, was* not *actually Irish. He was the son of a Romano-British town council-lor in Wales, was born around 390 and named Maewyn. The chances are that he probably did not die on 17 March either, and did not touch a drop of the hard stuff that features so largely in the celebration named after him. Nor did St Patrick drive all the snakes out of Ireland (there were none there in the first place) and the claim that he earned his reputation by explaining the mysteries of the Holy Trinity with the aid of the three-leafed Shamrock is hotly disputed by scholars. But, then, the Irish have never let the facts spoil a good story. Interestingly, too, St Patrick's Day was not designated as a public holiday in Ireland until 1901, although it has been used as the excuse for a monu-mental annual celebration in places like Boston, Chicago and New York where for more than 200 years the people have turned the rivers and the beer green to make the occasion. Throughout Ireland, street parties and processions, pub drinking sessions and house parties show the rest of the world—in the words of a former tourist minister, Jim McDaid—'that the Irish know how to celebrate'.*

'St Patrick's Day in the Morning' is the hilarious account of

one such celebration—and its aftermath. The author, Robert Jasper Martin (1845–1905) is best known as the author of 'Bally-hooley' one of the most popular music halls songs of the nineteenth century. Born in Dublin, he was the eldest brother of Violet Florence Martin who, under her pseudonym 'Martin Ross', wrote the Irish classic, Some Experiences of an Irish RM *(1899) with her cousin, Edith Somerville. Accounts of Robert Martin's life describe him as a 'charming man who liked to pose as a stage Irishman'. He wrote poems, songs and stories of Irish life for the* Globe, *the best of which were collected in* Bits of Blarney *(1899). Sadly, it seems, he ended his life in penury, rather like Dermot Blake, the owner of ramshackle Ballyblake Castle, in 'St Patrick's Day in the Morning'. Blake has, however, been recommended to go to Australia to make his fortune and thereby restore the family estate. With this in mind, he invites twenty of his friends and neighbours to a magnificent St Patrick's Night revel to seek their advice. But the arrival of a motley collection of comically inept waiters hired for the occasion—plus an unexpected guest—lead to an uproarious night with Dermot's plans taking an unexpected detour, first via the local court . . .*

*　　*　　*

I

It took place in the evening of course. Anybody acquainted with Ireland knows that the morning of St Patrick's Day consists of the night of the 17th of March, flavoured strongly with the morning of the 18th. Whoever else is ignorant of the fact, it was well known to the twenty true men, who on Patrick's evening many years ago answered to the invitation of Dermot Blake to drown the Shamrock at Ballyblake Castle. Dermot Blake was the youthful proprietor of that piece of family bankruptcy, known as the Ballyblake estate. His father left the world and his debts behind him when Dermot was twenty-two years of age, and for four years the new owner has been giving demonstration to the world at large that he was a true son of his father, a chip off the old block,

or, as Tim, the butler and ruler of the establishment, put it 'an
honest transaction.' Dermot kept hounds, retainers, and his word
like an Irish gentleman. His bills were as long as his pedigree, but
of their length and general appearance Dermot was an indifferent
judge—he met them so seldom. His stables and larder were frequently not as full as he might wish, but Tim, the butler, had
only to pass the word, and the 'tinantry' saw that put to rights.
Indeed, once when bailiffs were rash enough to seize the Blake
stud, the 'tinantry' were all day long sorting out the horses they
had lent the 'masther'—the men of the law had to depart emptyhanded, and with several proofs on their heads that the Blake
retainers were not in the same condition. But for all that, things
were not going too well at Ballyblake Castle. The advance of
civilisation was making every day the work of the sheriff's
officers an easier matter. Dermot sought the advice of his father's
old friend, Harry Fitzgibbon. A staunch and true man was Harry,
between fifty and sixty years of age; but, as the Clerk of the
Crown had said in proposing Harry's health at a grand jury dinner,
'Time had not left a bother on him.'

'Dermot, my boy,' said Harry, 'you're doing no good where
you are. The ways and traditions of your ancestors are throttling
you, and will soon be jumping on your chest. I have had an
opening offered to me for a young fellow in Australia. Take it,
my boy; go out and try it at all events, and leave the management
of the estate to me. I hold the first mortgage on it, and while you
are away I will do the best I can with the creditors. I tried hard
to save your father, my boy, and failed. Now give me a chance
of saving his son.'

Dermot went home pondering on this sage advice. Harry he
knew was the only man with money and sense in the country,
and so Dermot cogitated, and the result of his cogitations was
the Patrick's Night dinner, of which I am about to invite my
readers to be spectators.

But before dinner could be got ready, Tim, the butler, had to
give his permission, and that was not easily got. 'Dinner for
twenty—dinner for twenty, indeed! And what sort of a twenty
is it? Divil a dinner they'll have! Whiskey and ''spoiled five''

is good enough for the likes of them. I know what your dinners is, Masther Dermot. You'll be slaughtering everything from Kerry bulls to pea-hens, and putting them into mouths that are so hardened from whisky that they wouldn't know a mince-pie from a gizzard. Well, have yer own way; I'd rather be giving them my opinion of them than champagne.'

But in the end Dermot had his own way, and on St Patrick's Night were twenty of the best of Dermot's neighbours and friends at Ballyblake Castle. At the last minute Tim's equanimity received a deadly blow. Dermot had sent into the nearest city, Gartnacoppal, for any waiters that could be procured, and Tim had nothing but curses for the strangers that had arrived.

'Damned stragglers from the sayside,' he called them, and he would have sacked them there and then had not the introduction of the guests called away his attention.

First to arrive was Sarsfield O'Callaghan, of Ballyshillelagh.

'I've got the brush, Dermot, my boy,' was his remark; 'first man up.'

'Not yet awhile, my lad,' said the master; 'we haven't found yet awhile, not to talk of the death, but you're heartily welcome, Sarsfield.'

Then came Peter Maher, of Skelp-ma-gower, six foot four horizontal or perpendicular, *i.e.* before or after dinner. Then Father John Flannery, a real good old priest of the old school, a good man to hounds and a good man to parishioners, with a taste for saying good-natured things, and playing 'spoiled five.' Sir Dennis O'Loghlin, the foreman of the Grand Jury, a lover of good stories and old claret. Colonel Dominick O'Flynn, of Leenane Artillery, a regiment whose big-gun practice was spoken of, but seldom seen. The Hon. Charlie Morgan, brother of Lord Menlo, a death-or-glory boy, bald, bankrupt, beautiful. Andy Brannigan, of Towrow, a determined thruster, who could earn a post-mortem over a stone wall—so he declared—as well as any man in Ireland. Sir Valentine Galway, a sixteen-tumbler man full of patriotic sentiment and thirst, and many others, arriving in quick succession.

Dinner was thus announced by Tim: 'Gentlemen, I am prepared to strip,' an allusion to the removal of dish-covers, which was speedily grasped by the company, who filed in to dinner. But on he way into the dining-room a new and unexpected visitor arrived—a smooth-faced man, not in evening clothes, but neatly dressed, was announced as Mr John M'Elligott.

'You'll excuse me, Mr Blake,' he said. 'I have come to see you on very important business. I, of course, had no idea you had a dinner party.'

'Mr M'Elligott, you are a stranger to me,' said Dermot, 'and, therefore, welcome to Ballyblake. D——n business! dinner is what we are going for. It's St Patrick's Day, my lad, so you stay here to-night and talk business in the morning. Another place for Mr M'Elligott, Tim,' and thus was an uninvited guest added to the company.

The beginning of the feast was remarkable for excursions and alarms on the part of Tim against the hired waiters, who certainly appeared anything but practised attendants.

'If you'd only told me, ye vagabond,' whispered Tim to his master, 'the divil a bit of the ould silver would have been taken out of the hole where it was hidden from the bailiffs. These dirty hounds are consthructed for larceny, divil a ha'porth else of use in them! Go asy with the soup, there, ye fool with two left legs, or ye'll be putting it over the Honourable Charles' bald head.'

But these little *contretemps* were held of no account by the company, in fact added to the enjoyment, and as the champagne went round, and the lively conversation flowed fast and faster, every Irishman's heart began to fully recognise that it was Patrick's Day 'in the morning.'

'Sherry and soup, only an affair of out-posts,' said Colonel O'Flynn, as the soup tureens were removed and a magnificent salmon was placed one end of the table and a turbot at the other.

'All over the first fence,' said Sarsfield O'Callaghan, 'and there'll be no refusals at this one.'

'Are you fond of fishing, Andy?' said Charlie Morgan.

'Indeed I am, Charlie, with a net; but rod-fishing is as tedious as claret.'

'What's the best bait for salmon?' said M'Elligott, trying to get into the conversation somehow.

'Parsley and butter,' said Andy.

'Or one of Andy's stories,' said Charlie Morgan. 'No salmon could swallow that without its sticking in its throat.'

'It all depends,' said Sir Valentine, 'on whether you see the salmon or not. If you see it, do you know the best thing to do?'

'Hook it,' said Charlie, and then the discussed fish filled the mouths of the talker. Dinner proceeded, with hilarity travelling alongside of it; but there were two whom joviality did not seem to have reached. One was M'Elligott, who gave early symptoms of being a bit out of his depth, from a social point of view: the other was the host. Not that Dermot did not talk and laugh—he did both loudly, and yet mirth had found no place in either his conversation or laughter. He seemed to be at enmity with himself for not being jolly.

'Drink that champagne, Sir Dennis,' he said; 'there isn't a headache in a hogshead of it. The wine is dry, see that the bottle is the same.'

'The shamrock never met a watery grave in better,' said Sir Dennis.

'Watery, be hanged!' shouts Sir Valentine. 'Strong waters are the only bits of wet that will smother the vegetable,' and he proceeded to illustrate his remark.

The joints were numerous, and varied enough to justify Tim's description—all varieties of beast and bird known to the cook were distinctly visible, and ample justice was done to them by the guests. Tim's preliminary engagement with the hirelings had developed into a battle all along the line, but the visitors were too intent in their struggle with food and drink to recognise the combat, which had got to a critical state. Tim dotted the eye of one of his attendants with the soup ladle; and then Dermot, order having been partially restored, rose to his feet.

'Gentlemen,' he said, 'Dermot Blake rises in his father's hall to drink to St Patrick and the emblem he gave us' (*loud applause*).

Dermot had got thus far when he found M'Elligott, who was evidently loaded with drink to the brim, standing also.

'Say that about your father's hall again!' shouts M'Elligott.

'As often as you like, Mr M'Elligott,' said Dermot; 'but as you are my guest, may I claim the right to say a word or two?' M'Elligott was pulled down by men around him, and Dermot continued: 'Gentlemen, old friends, friends of my father and myself, there is here a true shamrock—landlord, tenant, and clergy, never forgetting they grow on a common stem—pride in the old land to which they belong—pride in the land to which they may leave, but which they will never forget. Well, gentlemen, this takes me on to what I have to say to you. This is the last Patrick's Day in the morning I shall for a long time spend among you.'

'Dermot, my boy,' said Sir Dennis, rising, 'what is this?'

'Sit down!' shouts M'Elligott, 'he's talking sense.'

'I'll leave you without sense to talk anything if you don't shut your mouth!' said Andy Brannigan.

'What's the matter, Dermot?'

'Why, this,' said the host, speaking with difficulty. 'This hunting season is over, and for the last run of the season the Master is the fox. The Hard Times Hounds will soon run him from scent to view, and there is nothing for him but to look for another country for some seasons to come. Across the water a place for him has been found, but, please God, in a few years' time I shall meet once again one and all under this old roof, and we shall drink once more to Patrick's Day in the morning.'

'Do you mean this for good-bye, Dermot? You, the boy we all have known all your life!' says Sir Dennis. 'Don't let the want of the money take you from us.'

'Take him from us, my boy!' shouts Tim, going on his knees, and taking Dermot by the hand; 'never, while Tim Murphy can raise a hand!'

'We all will stand by you!' shouts Sir Valentine, amidst loud cheers.

'Then, do so,' said M'Elligott, rising.

'Who the deuce are you who dare to interrupt?' shouts Sir Dennis and Sarsfield O'Callaghan simultaneously.

'I will tell you,' answers M'Elligott. 'I came here to this table on Mr Blake's invitation—it was his wish, not mine. Had I announced my business it would have spoiled your banquet. As it is, I have no desire to stop it even now, and so, gentlemen, I drink with our host Patrick's Day in the morning.'

'You half-hatched thief!' shouts Andy. 'Who are you?'

'I wish to tell you,' was the answer, 'the waiters around you are sheriff's officers, and I am the man in possession.'

A shout, a crash, and down went M'Elligott from the blow of a decanter fired by Tim. Two of Tim's foes, the supposed waiters, pinned him from behind, more men rushed in from various parts, whereupon Andy Brannigan, hurling over lights and tables, soon left the room in darkness, and the feast of St Patrick's was at an end.

II

It was 'Coort' day, and the drowning of the shamrock was nearly a fortnight old. The interim had been employed at Ballyblake in discovering how matters stood, and why heroes fell, and neither of the investigations were entirely satisfactory. The first thing to be done was to remove the stain placed on the memory of St Patrick by an execution and sheriff's officers having interfered with the funeral of his emblem, and the twenty good men and true who were the guests that memorable evening, saw to that. It was only a hundred pounds after all.

'The coroner's curse on the blackguards!' said Sir Valentine Galway, while combining the ingredients of his twelfth tumbler, 'let us each pay a quarter of it, and let the hunt give the balance.'

'Let us start with ten pounds a-piece,' said Sarsfield O'Callaghan, and see how much that comes to.'

And this suggestion was adopted, as there was a general feeling that after twelve o'clock at night it was better to rely on whisky than arithmetic. And so, within two days, M'Elligott and his myrmidons had to take their battered features from the old home of the Blakes, and Tim, the butler, resumed his throne in the pantry. The operation which Tim had performed, for the purpose of testing M'Elligott's strength of head, had not been altogether successful, and the external application of bottles generally had been productive of nothing more beautifying than sticking-plaister on the summits of the myrmidons of the law.

'Out you go, ye left leg of an informer!' shouts Tim, in triumph, as M'Elligott and his band started from Ballyblake Hall door. 'Bad cess to the whole crew of yees! I'd set the dogs at yees, only the bastes might die of poison if they tasted the like of bailiffs! The Devil will never be asy till ye are dancing on nothing from the end of his fishing-rod—that's the gallows!'

'Never you mind, my lad,' shouts M'Elligott. 'You had a shot at me with the bottle; I'll have a shot at you which will stir you up.' And he was as good as his word, for, within two days, arrived a summons to attend the 'Coort' at Gornacoppal, and answer there, to the justices assembled, the complaint of Paul Peter M'Elligott. It having been decided that none of the magistrates present at the dinner should adjudicate, the bench consisted of the following—'Ould John,' as he was always called, the father of Andy Brannigan; 'Boghole Burke,' so nicknamed because he had a brass knocker on his door; Sir John O'Hooligan, of Castle Ballyflannigan, and Captain MacTartan, the stipendiary (a foreigner from Londonderry).

'The Queen against Timothy Murphy,' says the Petty Sessions Clerk.

'And he's not one ha'porth afraid of her,' says a voice in Court.

'Silence!' said the police sergeant, shaking the wrong man by the collar, and then the clerk calls Paul Peter M'Elligott. M'Elligott, with a scared look, goes into the box, as a sort of moan of execration goes through the audience at the back; he takes the Book in his hand, repeats the oath, and raises the Testament towards his lips.

'He's kissing his thumb, not the book!' says a voice at the back of the Court, whereupon a constable turned out a deaf old woman for uproar.

M'Elligott proceeds then to give his evidence; how he had accepted Dermot's ill-bestowed hospitality, and when he did his duty, and announced that he was there in the Queen's name, he was anointed with a bottle, which was bounteously bestowed on him by the hand of Timothy Murphy. Mr Costigan, Timothy's solicitor, rose to cross-examine, and Sarsfield O'Callaghan and Andy Brannigan, sitting behind him, beamed on the Court for the first time. The audience by this time had got over the interruption stage, and was eager for the baiting of a bailiff.

'M'Elligott,' said Costigan, scratching his head from mere force of habit, as he wore a wig, 'you have been a sheriff's officer for some years. What were you before you adopted this honourable profession?'

'A man,' said M'Elligott.

'Were you?' said Costigan, coaxingly. 'Then you yourself have noticed the change that has come over you? But what used you to do with yerself in the days you were a man?'

'No matter what I did,' said M'Elligott, 'that's no rason why Tim Murphy should part my hair with a bottle.'

'Answer the question,' said 'Ould John'.

'Don't mind him, Ould John,' said a voice. 'Lave him to Costigan, he'll cooper him.'

And then every one shouted 'Silence!' including the man who made the remark.

'Come, sir,' said Costigan, 'where did you get the name of M'Elligott?'

'How do I know?' said the witness uneasily.

'I can tell you, M'Elligott,' said Costigan: 'you got it from a policeman after you turned informer in the case of——'

'I rise to object,' said the counsel on the other side, hastily; 'the question is not from whom he got his name, but from whom he got the blow on his head.'

'We don't deny, your worships, that in the hurry-scurry of the moment, when he made himself known,' said Costigan, 'the butler forgot to hand M'Elligott the wine with all the courtesy which he should have shown to a guest in his master's house. But, remember this, that this man had palmed himself off on the company as an ordinary visitor, and his conduct amounts to this— that, having eaten a man's dinner, he collared the forks and spoons. His whole performance was one of mean, sneaking fraud. Waiters are imported who are his minions, and if M'Elligott got a bit more hospitality than he bargained for, why, serve him right!'

'I should like to ask M'Elligott the cost of the sticking-plaister, because I think he is fully entitled to that,' said Boghole Burke— a remark in which Sir John O'Hooligan and Ould John fully agreed.

But not so Captain MacTartan.

'M'Elligott,' he remarked, 'was the Queen's officer in the execution of his duty, and was entitled to protection from the law.'

'I don't know about the execution of his duty,' said Ould John, 'but I shouldn't mind the duty of his execution.'

And then the whole Court cheered, and Captain MacTartan demanded that the magistrates should retire and consider the matter. And retire they did, and returned shortly into Court again, when Sir John O'Hooligan, interrupted by grunts of approval from Ould John and Boghole, and snorts of dissent from the Captain, gave judgment: 'By three to one we have arrived at this decision: St Patrick is our national saint, his day must be honoured, and his shamrock drowned. He saved us from snakes, but he left us bailiffs, for whom Captain MacTartan claims the protection of the law. There are laws of the land and laws of hospitality, and M'Elligott wants the protection of both in order that he may take Dermot Blake's plate and furniture. Well, he has got his money, and if we pay him five shillings for the amount of money he is out of pocket by the sticking-plaister, well, that's enough for him. Five shillings and costs, gentlemen, by three to one.'

Then arose a yell; over the benches came the mob, and for a minute or two there was a bit of difficulty in finding anybody in particular.

'Half a crown from me!'—'And me!' shout Andy and Sarsfield.

'Costs from me!' cries Dermot, and Tim is carried aloft on men's shoulders through the town. Needless to say, he was carried from one house of call to another. Enthusiasm for Sir John ran so high that the O'Hooligan tenantry met there and then and agreed that they would pay him his rent—with a reduction—on the next gale day. Finally, it became no longer safe to carry Tim; it took most of them all their time to carry their load of the whisky. And then it was remembered that M'Elligott had not received all the sticking-plaister they wished for, and so they started to look for him. But whether it was that their enthusiasm had interfered with their eyesight, or the object of their search had been removed by the prudent forethought of the police, as Micky Doolan remarked: 'M'Elligott was as hard to find as to-morrow's newspaper.'

'It's St Patrick's day in the morning all over again,' said Dermot to Sir Dennis O'Loghlin.

'Not a fear of it, Dermot, my boy!' said Sir Dennis. 'It's the same old St Patrick's day in the morning, only it has taken a fortnight to finish it.'

'Well, it's over now,' said Dermot, 'and my time here is nearly the same. You know I have waited for this trial, and to-night I leave for London.'

They were sitting in the private dining-room of the Blake Arms.

'Boys,' said Dermot, rising, 'I must ask from you "Slantha." If I have to go to Australia, it is to make me able to come back to stay. You will hunt the hounds without me, but my heart will be with you wherever I may be, but my heart will be with you wherever I may be, and counting the days till we are riding over the country together again!'

'Dermot, my boy, my boy!' cries Sir Dennis, 'may life be given me to see you back again!'

Dermot rose.

'Boys, one last favour; harden your hearts, and see me through this parting without flinching. Andy, a song.'

And then Andy rose and sung in his rich voice—

> THE KING SHALL ENJOY HIS OWN AGAIN
> 'We are losing our leader—our hearts all sad—
> Our captain in many a bygone fray;
> But we'll fill up a bumper to him, my lad,

And wish him good luck when he's far away:
For hope's lying hidden to-night in the cup,
And its music will steal through the old refrain
So I give you a toast—ev'ry man stand up—
That the King may enjoy his own again.

CHORUS.

'Again, again, the old refrain,
While comrades true take up the strain,
And the world will be bright with a vanished light
When the King will enjoy his own again.

'To-night we are sitting to reckon the cost
Of the foes without and the foes within,
But we drink to the King who has fought and lost
For we know he's going to fight and win.
Yes, the darkest hour is the herald of light,
It is hope that whispers 'Regret is vain';
And as sure as the day must follow the night
The King will enjoy his own again.

'Good-bye, good-bye, with a stifled sigh,
The hills re-echo the old refrain,
But the bells will ring when our only King
Comes back to enjoy his own again.'

And then, as evening closed in, they gathered round their old friend. At the station were gathered the peasants and the gentry, all crowding round to give a real Irish good-bye. Dermot steps into the carriage, and then are heard three ringing view holloas as the whistle sounds, while there rings out the chorus of the song, 'The King shall enjoy his own again,' and the train rushes away, bearing Dermot on the first stage of his journey from his old home to the new.

III

It was ten years after, and things had not gone rosily with the estate of Ballyblake in the meantime. The incursion of M'Elligott was, after all, only a preliminary skirmish, for, as the story went round, creditors from all parts came to look after their forlorn hopes. The consequence was that the law, with its army of bailiffs and men in possession, daily put chalk marks on poor Dermot's property, and Tim had to confess that all strategical measures which he had taken for the purpose of keeping out the foe were of no more use than a child's squire to a bonfire. Andy Brannigan and Sarsfield O'Callaghan discussed the position with Harry Fitzgibbon.

'Begad, Harry,' said Andy, 'it comes to this: our ancestors had all the one kind of legacy to leave their families. There never was a Blake, not to mention a Bodkin or a Burke, that was fairly happy until he made his descendants snug and warm by leaving them a mortgage or two.'

'True for you, Andy,' says Sarsfield; 'and they were leaving them and leaving them till they are as thick as Ballyblake as the holes in a beggarman's trousers, or, you might say, a landing-net.' Sarsfield's strong point was simile. 'And sure a landing-net is nothing but holes tied together with string. Well, it all comes of belonging to an old family. Every Blake that has died for the last seven hundred years has had to keep up the honour of the family and leave a mortgage, until at last poor Dermot was that full of mortgage that there was no room for himself.'

'True, indeed,' added Andy, 'it is often the will of God that too much pudding should choke a dog.'

'There is no use in discussing reasons when we have to face facts,' said Harry Fitzgibbon. 'When long ago I saw that the smash must come, I tried to give a loophole for Dermot to escape from his difficulties. I bought up the first mortgage on his property, and now I can put my foot down, and I will. Dermot is away, and has left the management of the property to me. I mean to step in and assert my rights. I shall put a receiver over Ballyblake and see what can be done.'

So a receiver was put over Ballyblake, and the house and place were let to an Englishman of the name of Simpkins, who came to Ireland full of English remedies for Irish grievances.

'You may be sure of one thing, Mr Simpkins,' said Sir Dennis

O'Loghlin, 'that you are not going the right way about the country-people.'

'But you don't understand, Sir Dennis,' said the confident Simpkins; 'it is you Irishmen who have made the mistake with your peasantry. They are lazy and dirty. I am determined to make them clean and industrious. They are not altogether truthful; I shall employ none but those who are incapable of lying, and I shall do so that the family of Blake will not know their tenantry when they return.'

'They won't, sure enough,' said Sir Dennis, 'if you make them all this. But you ought to know, first of all, two peculiarities about every Irish grievance. The first is, that it doesn't exist, and the second is, that no Englishman can cure it,' and, so saying, the Irishman left the Saxon to carry out his improvements.

Needless to say that Mr Simpkins' experiments were not very satisfactory. He began, after spending much money, and meeting with many disappointments, to find out that the same suit of clothes won't fit everybody, and that English ideas were only accepted by the Hibernians as long as they could get any good out of them. White-washing their cottages was all very well as long as Simpkins did the white-washing. A window, too, was a luxury, but panes of glass were simply put there to be broken, and replaced with brown paper, or a wisp of straw. His most unpopular movement, though, was an attempt to dislodge the pig from his position under the bed, where he was installed by the universal consent of the household, and any endeavour to remove the gentleman who pays the rent to suffer from the cold indignity of a pig-stye, was looked upon as one of the greatest injustices to Ireland imaginable.

So Simpkins was not beloved of those whom he meant to benefit. He found, to his astonishment, that the Blake tenantry mourned for their missing master, and longed for his return, and had put bare toleration for Simpkins, whom they looked upon as his Saxon supplanter. Of course with the new *régime* Tim Murphy was butler no more at Ballyblake.

'It is no use taching an ould fox-hound bull-dog's tricks,' said Tim, 'and you shall never make a Saxon butler of Tim Murphy.'

And so he went—went 'to his boy,' as he called him—to Dermot across the sea, and of him and his young master, little was heard by the peasants, who mourned for them and wished them every day 'home again.'

The kennels were closed, the hounds were sold, and the sport enjoyed by Simpkins was, though good, not of much use to the country generally. He had prosecuted several men for poaching, and had insisted on their being severely fined, and the consequence was, that the tenants who had been Dermot's gamekeepers were of no use whatever to Simpkins, stamped on partridge eggs, and took no interest in his shooting parties—while the fact that he shot foxes made him so unpopular with the gentry, that Simpkins was obliged to confess that he was no more use as an Irish gentleman than a sick headache. And so, when his tenancy of seven years came to an end, and Simpkins went back to his native land, he carried with him few regrets and little good-will from those whom he was leaving, and he had to own that for some reason or other Simpkins' infallible cures for the Irish race were of no earthly use whatever. And then came the worst and the most dreaded. Harry Fitzgibbon had been in failing health, for the care he had devoted to the struggle for Dermot's rights had been too much for him. He had fought against the second and third mortgagees, but an English assurance company had brought these charges up, and was determined that if interest due were not paid, Ballyblake should come to the hammer.

Meanwhile the news from Dermot Blake was not of the brightest. He had gone in largely for sheep-farming in Australia, and had been on the very brink of a big fortune, when, just at the time that the money seemed in his hands and the game won, the price of wool went down, a terrible drought played havoc with his flocks, and just when the money was wanted to save the old place and the old name, Dermot found himself nearly as poor as when he began.

A law-suit was threatened between Harry Fitzgibbon and the English company, and, to the horror of all, the latter triumphed, and insisted on sending down as head manager of Ballyblake, Mr M'Elligott, the uninvited guest at the Patrick's Day banquet I have described. Then began bad times for all. The tenants were processed, writted, and evicted by the ruthless M'Elligott, who had not forgotten their jubilation on the day of Tim Murphy's trial, and policemen had to guard M'Elligott day and night.

And then the last blow fell on the county. Ballyblake Castle, the home of the Blakes for seven hundred years, was sold to a stranger! No details were given, but Harry Fitzgibbon issued an invitation to the surrounding gentry to meet him and the new landlord in Ballyblake Castle on Patrick's Day in the morning, that is to say, at 7.30 P.M., on the 17th of March. Thither came to our old friends once more. Harry Fitzgibbon had sent in his own cook and servants, and had seen to the banquet being prepared. As he walked up the steps leaning on the arm of Sir Valentine Galway, he was confronted by M'Elligott.

'I wish to know, Mr Fitzgibbon, by what right you have come here this evening?' he said.

'Right!' said Harry, looking him straight in the face; 'by a right which even the law will have to respect. Stand aside! You will be seen in your true colours to-night, and not as the masquerader you were ten years ago.'

'If you don't want your eyes put in mourning, out of the way,' said Andy, stepping up, and then M'Elligott slunk away.

They were all there—all those who sat down in the same hall ten years ago—all except one, and that one was in every one's thoughts, though no one mentioned him.

It was, indeed, the full cast of 'Hamlet' with the part of the Prince of Denmark left out.

'Bad luck to it!' said Sir Valentine, 'that damned fellow Simpkins has left a taste in this room which seems to have driven joviality out of it. Sir Dennis, a glass of wine with you; the same with you, Charlie Morgan; the same to all of you gentlemen; and remember the real Irish question: What's two bottles of whisky among one?'

They drank with Sir Val; but, someway, as Sarsfield put it, 'there was a hole in the bellows somewhere.'

'We somehow feel more or less like as if we had no right to

be here without some one to bid us welcome,' whispered Sir
Dennis to Colonel O'Flynn; 'but, after all, we shall be able to
have our drink out this evening without M'Elligott.'

'I don't know that,' said the Colonel, repeating a remark which
he always made when in a difficulty; 'the thief is about, so I
don't know that.'

Dinner over, Harry Fitzgibbon rose on his legs. 'Gentlemen,
I am filling a position here to-night which should not be mine to
fill. I had hoped that the new owner of Ballyblake would have
been here, but he has a long way to come, and, in coming down
to have the pleasure of making your acquaintance, he has missed
his train. You all know how I have fought to keep the old place for
the old family. (Loud cheers, and a remark from Andy Brannigan:
'There ought to be twins of every man like you.') My efforts
have failed, the old place is sold—(a sort of moan went round)—
and the new owner is——'

A sound of wheels is heard without.

'It's the new man late for dinner,' shouts Andy.

A fire shines in Harry Fitzgibbon's eyes; he stands erect with
a gleam of triumph unmistakable looking younger than he has
done since Dermot left Ireland. 'Gentlemen,' he cries, 'the toast
is——'

The door opens, and there goes up a shout from a voice known
and loved by all. 'Patrick's Day in the morning!' and Dermot
Blake stands once more amongst his old friends, who have not
got one dry eye amongst them all.

'What is this?' shouts M'Elligott, rushing in.

'Why, this,' said Tim, the butler, seizing him by the collar,
'out you go. There is the ould master in the ould place, thanks
be to God!'

'Amen!' says Harry Fitzgibbon, and as M'Elligott goes from
the room, assisted by Tim's toe, they gather round Dermot and
hear his wonderful story.

After all, his as a story well known to our colonists, of a man
nearly bankrupt who had found gold on his claim—gold enough
to pay off every debt that the Blake ancestry had bequeathed to

posterity, and then he came back to tell the same old friends of his, as he had told them years before the story of his ruin.

'And it's all owing to Harry,' said Dermot, as he went down and kissed his hand; 'he *would* have it kept a secret till I was able to tell it to you all myself on Patrick's Day in the morning.'

Shouts are heard without, the tenants have heard the news, bonfires light up the scene, cheers ring out for the new master, who is the old. And by-and-by, through the open windows of Ballyblake, is heard the old song:—

> 'Now the winter has gone with its frosts and dearth,
> We are nearing the comforts that Time will bring,
> When the sunshine will come to gladden the earth,
> And carpet the world with flowers of spring.

> 'Then the summer will bring us its kindly aid,
> With its leafy shelters and golden grain.
> For the light it will live, though the light may fade,
> And the King will enjoy his own again.

> 'Good-bye, good-bye, to the griefs that fly
> When they list to the sound of the old refrain,
> For the night is past, it is day at last,
> And the King will enjoy his own again.'

THE HEN PARTY

Eamonn Sweeney

The Irish revel described by Edna O'Brien has given way to a very different scene at the turn of the twentieth century, as the author has herself admitted. Writing in 1986, she said: 'There are a lot of young people who are irreligious, or less religious. They are aping English and American mores—if I went to a dance hall in Dublin now I would feel as alien as in a disco in Oklahoma.' It is this new world which is reflected in 'The Hen Party' taking place in a disco-cum-pub called the Dandy Diner. The party—once unthinkable for young Irish girls before their wedding—is for Mary Colreavy and her friends who are planning to go as wild and get as drunk as any of the boys. The girls are, however, in for a number of surprises during the evening— including a 'stripogram'—the prelude to the party suddenly dis- integrating into terrible violence.

Eamonn Sweeney (1968–) is one of the most exciting new talents in Irish literature. Born in Sligo, he worked in London for a number of years before returning to live in Ireland. Based in Dublin he began contributing short stories to several periodicals including the Sunday Tribune *and* Raconteur, *and in 1994 won the* Raconteur *Short Story Competition. His first novel,* Waiting for the Healer *was published in 1997 and immediately received praise from critics on both sides of the Atlantic. A graphically violent study of pub manager Paul Kelly's reluctant return from London for the funeral of his brother who has been killed in the small town underworld of Rathbawn, it is told in a wild, drunken narrative voice which critic Colm Toibin has described as 'Irish filthy realism, original, violent, full of pain'. Sweeney has fol-*

lowed this impressive debut with The Photographer *(2000). 'The Hen Party' is an extract from* Waiting for the Healer *and is recounted by the omnipresent Kelly*...

*   *   *

The Dandy Diner must have been cursed at one stage by someone who knew how to curse. A Nevin or a McDonagh. Whoever owned it always put a ridiculous name on it. Once it had been the Nashville Rooms. Another time Kades Kounty. At one stage it was even Nijinsky's Nite Spot. That name would have delighted the Gay Swimming Club who came into the King William every Thursday night for a few pints after leaving the Lido.

A space opened up in front of us when we walked in. It developed into a funnel which fed us straight through to the bar even though the joint was wedged. Two of a Kind were playing. I got jammed against a pillar. A poster threatened to fall on my head.

OKEY DOKEY KARAOKE. EVERY MONDAY NIGHT WITH P.J. AND MARGARET. SUBSTANTIAL CASH PRIZES.

The hen party sat in one corner of the pub with their chairs drawn round in a circle. Mary Colreavy in the middle had a party hat on her head and streamers waterfalling from her shoulders. I wondered if Lydia's hen had been like this. It struck me I'd never asked her about it.

Clinger arrived and hovered over my shoulder. He reached to shake hands with me.

—All right.

—All right. I'll buy a pint. I reckoned you must be broke when you didn't show up in Donoghue's.

He winked at me and extended his leg so it touched the pillar. Then he reached towards his shoe.

—I have a few pound put away, see. And if we'd gone to Donoghue's the quare one would have known I had it and I'd have to give her some.

Clinger took off his shoe and reached into a blue sock that covered all of his left foot except for the big toe that poked out of a frayed hole and wriggled around frantically like it was trying to dig into sand as the tide went out. A black circle covered the top end of the nail.

—The oul sock, you see, it's the only safe place in the end.

He took out two tenners and brushed some flakes of skin off their surface. I still bought the first round. We talked about football.

I bought the next round as well. And put on a chaser for myself. Beetlejuice was there when I got back from the bar. His hands shook a lot. He lifted his pint to his mouth and left it down a couple of times without taking more than a sup. When he spoke his lips shook too.

—I'm nervous, Paul, I just am. I have this feeling and it's the same feeling I had the night Johnny was killed. I know something's going to happen.

Beetlejuice stuttered through most of the words. He reached his hand out for his pint and pulled it back before it got there.

—That fuck. That fuck, him, he's up to something.

An old man loitered at the bottom of the stairs. He was hopping a thick brown walking stick off the floor. The pub was at basting temperature but he was rigged out in a thick pair of specs, a tweed cap and a long coat buttoned to the top.

—He's at something. I'll skull him.

—He's a fucking oul man. What could he be at?

—I'm going to fucking skull him.

Beetlejuice got to within a couple of yards of the old geezer before Richie Fee caught him. They had a few words. Beetlejuice had stopped shaking when he came back.

—Richie told me the score, boys. It's all copacetic. Jesus, such a crack, wait till you see it.

A couple of the hens walked up to the stage. Two of a Kind launched straight away into an instrumental. The one they play on telly at the end of the World Snooker Championship when they show the funny shots. A big movement from our side of the pub over to the chair where Mary Colreavy was. Beetlejuice pulled my arm.

—Come over. The crack is starting.

The band started to run through the tune a second time. People were standing on chairs now and looking into the circle of hens. It reminded me of the time in the Horse and Groom a squaddie bet he'd be able to drink a pint of sick.

—Wait till you see this for crack.

Beetlejuice was happy. The band looked down the pub like they were waiting for some sort of signal. The pub went silent as the old man dondered towards Mary Colreavy. He leaned heavily on his stick. I half expected him to drop before he got to her. He peered at her through his double-glazed glasses.

—Are you the girleen who's getting married? Sure you'll give us a biteen of an oul kiss.

His lips puckered out about half a mile in front of his face. Mary looked around for some assistance but there wasn't any. Belinda Greer was breaking her heart laughing. Beetlejuice snickered. The old guy put his arm around Mary's neck and planted a big slimy kiss on her lips before jumping into the air and clicking his heels together. He threw the tweed cap on the floor.

—*Hasta la vista*, baby.

The glasses, the coat, the cap and the stick were all on the floor within ten seconds of that spake and the old geezer was now a young guy with muscles on him that looked like they were going to burst. All he had on was a deep suntan and a pair of boxer shorts. A noise sprinted round the pub.

—Woooo.

Even the barmen stopped what they were doing and looked over at the ex-old man sitting on Mary's knee. Belinda bent double with laughing. Mary looked terrified. Her new pal planted another kiss on her lips and got a roar from the hens as he flexed the muscles on his arm. They shone under the lights. He looked like a chicken covered in cooking oil.

—A lot of them bucks is queer, said someone a couple of yards behind me.

It was a man's voice. Not one of the women had touched a drink since bucko shed his coat and fifty years. Missus Fee looked like one of those Charismatics who have just been possessed by the Spirit of the Lord. But she wasn't speaking in tongues.

—You're lovely, you're lovely. Go on and show us what you've got.

The stripper jumped off Mary's lap and gave a little bow before pulling a string which disintegrated his boxers into a heap on the floor. For a second everyone thought he didn't have anything at all on. His arse was bare. But there was a little string running around the front and an orange pouch for him to cram his tackle into. He bent down to his coat and took out a piece of paper. The chest muscles got another flex before he started declaiming.

> Hello Mary here I am
> Your saucy sexy stripogram
> Please be good you know you should
> Let's get on this could be good
> I've got a present I thought would suit
> Now I want you to suck my . . .

He paused. A couple of people bellowed:
—Flute.
He waited a couple more seconds before he took the banana out of his coat.
—Fruit.
—You've some fucking body on you.
A woman's shout from the balcony. I held my breath and tried to hold in my stomach. I wouldn't say I was the only one imagining what I'd look like in front of a pub of women with my kit off. You could jog, I suppose. And there's American exercises that get you in shape in just ten minutes a day and you end up only having to do them three times a week. You could go on the Scarsdale Diet. Fuck it. He probably wasn't happy in his life.

Belinda got hold of him by the pouch. His lad popped out but he just grinned and flicked it expertly back in with his left hand. All the men were disappointed it was a good size. He arranged the banana so it protruded from his pouch.
—Suction. It must be, said a voice full of awe.
The woman clattered the tables. The stripper pushed Mary's head towards his groin. She shied her head away at first. The buck she was marrying was in the army with 0800. He'd been

going out with Mary for six years and he bursted anyone who
looked crooked at her. I was fierce sorry he wasn't in the Dandy
Diner. Someone should have asked him to come along.

A drum-roll from Two of a Kind. Snap. Mary's head came
up. She had the top half of the banana in her mouth. A dozen
flashes went off at once and the stripper threw on his coat and
got the fuck out of there. He was just past the table when Missus
Fee got him a pinch on the arse you could nearly feel just from
seeing it. Another woman grabbed him by the kecks and tried to
yank them off. He bolted for the door with a gang of women
after him. Screaming. I'd never heard screaming like it. He nearly
knocked down the barman who was bringing down a cake in the
shape of a muscle-man.

Someone grabbed me around the waist and the next thing I
knew I was in a circle twirling around the floor with Two of a
Kind playing the can-can and of course there's always one header
who levers himself up on his neighbour's shoulders and does a
wild kick with both of his feet up in the air and falls down then
and nearly brings everyone else with them and it was Beetlejuice
naturally enough. He was gone fucking hyper.

Mary opened a package. Belinda helped her. They removed
the wrapping and took out a pair of big Y-fronty knickers about
the size of two wigwams.

—Woooo.

The Jordan woman who used to be a midwife crammed a big
slice of the muscle-man cake into her mouth. Oozy black cherries
dangled from it. She picked them off and put them into the
ashtray. A few of Mary's buddies stood her up and put her legs
into the knickers. Belinda planted a kiss that left a ruby smear
of lipstick on Mary's face.

The can-can stopped and myself and Missus Fee were left
leaning awkwardly against each other and trying to remember
what the weather had been like so we could talk about it.

Two of a Kind played a Country song about honky-tonks
and broken hearts. Beetlejuice hugged Mary Colreavy. He was
enjoying himself like . . . No. Like nothing. You think of these
things later. More significance. More Columbo. He stuck his legs

into the giant underpants. First the left. Then the right. He put his arms around Mary and they danced. Suspended in their giant nappy with green balloons flying over their heads. Myself, Clinger and Dalton stood in a circle and headed a balloon to each other. Each determined not to be the first to let it hit the ground or float away.

—Fuck's sake. Another one of these lads, they're gone mad on them altogether.

Clinger controlled the balloon with his shoulder.

—Handball.

Myself and Dalton at the same time. The guitarist in Two of a Kind did one of those long, twiddly-bit, Jesus-I'm-Eddie-Van-Halen-can't-you-nearly-see-the-smoke-rising-off-me-fingers solos. I couldn't make out what the song was because he was gone so much to town on it.

—What's that song, boys?

—Jesus. It's a bit much now all the same, a second lad, it nearly knocks the good out of it.

—What? I didn't catch you right.

—One of those stripogram bucks again.

—What's the name of that song?

A tall man in a long black coat, wearing a plastic gorilla false face topped by a baseball cap, pushed his way through the crowd. A dancing arm clipped the side of his head and knocked his cap skew-ways. He stopped and straightened it very deliberately with his left hand. Then he patted the cap down on his nut to make sure it was properly balanced. With his left hand again. He held his right arm under his coat like it was broken and suspended in a sling. The cap was a Utah Jazz one. You had to laugh at this grinning gorilla face making its way across the pub. People smile and stood back to let him through.

—Beetlejuice. Beetlejuice Reilly. Noelie Reilly.

The voice came from underneath the mask. Beetlejuice and Mary were still jumping up and down.

—Beetlejuice Reilly. Is that you?

Beetlejuice tried to turn round. The upper half of his body swivelled but his legs stayed facing Mary Colreavy.

—Away we go, said the false face.

A revolver came out from under the coat. Beetlejuice's gob was fixed in a toothy smile when the gun blew it away. He staggered and the man stepped forward and shot him in the back of the head. A tiny burst of flame seemed to jump from the gun. The gorilla's hand was rock-steady.

Mary Colreavy's face was covered in blood and goo. She screeched as Beetlejuice fell and dragged her to the floor. Both of them were still trapped in those monster Y-fronts. Nothing was left of Beetlejuice's head only a sight of blood. Mary was in hysterics. Two of a Kind stopped playing. The singer crouched down behind one of the amps. People knocked over tables and chairs as they tried to get out of the pub.

Beetlejuice wasn't moving. Mary kicked like mad to try and disentangle herself from him. Belinda shoved through the crowd and bent down to her. The gunman aimed carefully and put a third shot through Beetlejuice's head. I heard the sound of something soggy falling on a concrete path from a great height. Beetlejuice's body jerked. Mary's body had to make the same movement. She was gone pure white in the face. She looked past Belinda who had pulled her head off the floor and was cradling her.

Mary's face and neck and the front of her little black dress were all covered with whatever comes out when someone's head explodes. She slipped out of Belinda's arms and lay on the floor again. Blood seeped out of what used to be Beetlejuice.

—What's my name, what's my name.

The gunman's words were all muffled by the plastic mask. He turned and walked towards the door like he didn't give a breeze. I tried to shrink back into one of the alcoves. I had a feeling he'd want to shoot me if he knew I was in the pub. Clinger and Dalton started after him.

—Get the cunt. Stop him.

Have-a-go heroes. He turned and fired a couple of shots at them. They seemed like noisier shots. The Dandy Diner filled up with the sound of firecrackers let off in a small space. Clinger was on the ground with blood soaking through his shirt. Dalton was plugged in the arm. The gunman did a little dance.

—How you like me now, motherfuckers. How you like me now.

It was a fake American accent but it wouldn't have fooled anyone except maybe for one of those women who refused to believe that Big Tex and the Rangers were a gang of lads from Sheepwalk who worked in the abattoir. He let off a couple more shots but his hand was jumping around now. A hole appeared in one of the windows. Glasses tinkled. He walked out the side door of the Dandy Diner.

A car revved up and took off. It left two perky blasts of a horn behind it in the night air. The killer had been wearing those Converse basketball boots with the star at the side of them. It's funny what you think of. I couldn't take in much else.

Mary lay stock-still in a corner with a gang of her friends screaming at everybody to do something. Clinger had dragged himself up on to a chair. He leaned back with his shirt open and blood slowly trickling down in different streams. Richie Fee walked Dalton out the door. Dalton's arm hung down like it wasn't really attached to him.

Blood all over the gaff. Little specks in the ashtrays. Splotches on the walls. Long streaks on the glass of the alcoves. Spots of it soaked through the cheap paper Dandy Diner beer mats. The late Noel Reilly lay face down in a big pool of the stuff with the woman of the Jordans who'd been a midwife hunkered down beside him. She shook her head.

I was left on my own in my alcove when everyone else moved on to the street. There I was, looking at what was left of Beetle-juice lying there like an old Guy Fawkes fucked into an estate lift in the middle of November. Rag and bone. Stupid bastard. Friend of my brother. The late John Kelly. Whatever the fuck the story was, someone had it in for them big time.

The light show outside. Ambulances and squads and the street-lamps. And the noise of the sirens adding to it. Except you couldn't hardly hear them. You could hear the crying in the street a bit better. But what you could hear most was the screaming of the women. It kept at the same pitch and level until they sounded like they were going hoarse and then it'd stop for an instant and start again. Back at the same level and pitch.

The husband-to-be had arrived by the time they got Mary Colreavy to her feet. He hammered his way through the cops at the door and put his arms out to her. I don't know did she see him. She just screamed. I never heard screaming like it.

The cops brought me into the street and asked did I want a lift home. I didn't answer them. I just pretended to myself I was a night on the road in the middle of a journey. And kept thinking if it hadn't been for me going to a party on the night of my brother's funeral none of this would have happened and everyone would have been safe. You couldn't have luck.

TERESA'S WEDDING

William Trevor

The Irish Wedding is pretty unique among celebrations of marriage. The mixture of highly charged religious feelings and alcohol makes it an unforgettable experience for all the participants— sometimes in the most unexpected ways, as this next story demonstrates. The reception for Teresa's weeding in Swanton's lounge bar is, in certain respects, like many another in Ireland: a gathering packed with relatives and friends and fuelled with generous amounts of alcohol. It is a time when old memories as well old enmities surface in the babble of conversation among people whose tongues have been loosed and their inhibitions lowered. 'Teresa's Wedding' is a classic of what has been described by the Times *as the 'wild and often wicked territory' that William Trevor has made his own.*

Trevor (1928–) was born William Trevor Cox, the son of a bank manager in Mitchelstown, County Cork, and spent an itinerant childhood as his father was moved from one position to another around the country. This unsettled existence, he thinks, gave him his abiding interest in the human condition and helped to develop his keen eye at observing the effects of poverty, stress, sex and particularly drink on men and women in any number of different situations. William Trevor has won widespread acclaim for his fiction: he has been short-listed for the Booker Prize on several occasions, won the Hawthornden Prize in 1964 and was twice awarded the Whitbread Prize for his novels, The Children of Dynmouth *(1976) and* Fools of Fortune *(1983). There are a number stories about drink to be found in his eight collections of brilliantly crafted short tales, but none, I think, is more charged with alcohol, poignancy and ultimate heart-break than 'Teresa's Wedding'* . . .

*   *   *

The remains of the wedding-cake were on top of the piano in Swanton's lounge-bar, beneath a framed advertisement for Power's whiskey. Chas Flynn, the best man, had opened two packets of confetti: it lay thickly on the remains of the wedding-cake, on the surface of the bar and the piano, on the table and the two small chairs that the lounge-bar contained, and on the tattered green-and-red linoleum.

The wedding guests, themselves covered in confetti, stood in groups. Father Hogan, who had conducted the service in the Church of the Immaculate Conception, stood with Mrs Atty, the mother of the bride, and Mrs Cornish, the mother of the bride-groom, and Mrs Tracy, a sister of Mrs Atty's.

Mrs Tracy was the stoutest of the three women, a farmer's widow who lived eight miles from the town. In spite of the jubilant nature of the occasion, she was dressed in black, a colour she had affected since the death of her husband three years ago. Mrs Atty, bespectacled, with her grey hair in a bun, wore a flowered dress—small yellow-and-blue blooms that blended easily with the confetti. Mrs Cornish was in pink, with a pink hat. Father Hogan, a big red-complexioned man, held a tumbler containing whiskey and water in equal measures; his companions sipped Winter's Tale sherry.

Artie Cornish, the bridegroom, drank stout with his friends Eddie Boland and Chas Flynn, who worked in the town's bacon factory, and Screw Doyle, so called because he served behind the counter in McQuaid's hardware shop. Artie, who worked in a shop himself—Driscoll's Provisions and Bar—was a freckled man of twenty-eight, six years older than his bride. He was heavily built, his bulk encased now in a suit of navy-blue serge, similar to the suits that all the other men were wearing that morning in Swanton's lounge-bar. In the opinion of Mr Driscoll, his employer, he was a conscientious shopman, with a good

memory for where commodities were kept on the shelves. Customers occasionally found him slow.

The fathers of the bride and bridegroom, Mr Atty and Mr
Cornish, were talking about greyhounds, keeping close to the
bar. They shared a feeling of unease, caused by being in the
lounge-bar of Swanton's, with women present, on a Saturday
morning. 'Bring us two more big ones,' Mr Cornish requested
of Kevin, a youth behind the bar, hoping that this addition to his
consumption of whiskey would relax matters. They wore white
carnations in the buttonholes of their suits, and stiff white collars
which were reddening their necks. Unknown to one another, they
shared the same thought: a wish that the bride and groom would
soon decide to bring the occasion to an end by going to prepare
themselves for their journey to Cork on the half-one bus. Mr Atty
and Mr Cornish, bald-headed men of fifty-three and fifty-five,
had it in mind to spend the remainder of the day in Swanton's
lounge-bar, celebrating in their particular way the union of their
children.

The bride, who had been Teresa Atty and was now Teresa
Cornish, had a round, pretty face and black, pretty hair, and was
a month and a half pregnant. She stood in the corner of the lounge
with her friends, Philomena Morrissey and Kitty Roche, both of
whom had been bridesmaids. All three of them were attired in
their wedding finery, dresses they had feverishly worked on to
get finished in time for the wedding. They planned to alter the
dresses and have them dyed so that later on they could go to
parties in them, even though parties were rare in the town.

'I hope you'll be happy, Teresa,' Kitty Roche whispered. 'I
hope you'll be all right.' She couldn't help giggling, even though
she didn't want to. She giggled because she'd drunk a glass of
gin and Kia-Ora orange, which Screw Doyle had said would
steady her. She'd been nervous in the church. She'd tripped twice
on the walk down the aisle.

'You'll be marrying yourself one of these days,' Teresa whispered, her cheeks still glowing after the excitement of the cere-
mony. 'I hope you'll be happy too, Kit.'

But Kitty Roche, who was asthmatic, did not believe she'd

ever marry. She'd be like Miss Levis, the Protestant woman on
the Cork road, who'd never got married because of tuberculosis.
Or old Hannah Flood, who had a bad hip. And it wasn't just that
no one would want to be saddled with a diseased wife: there was
also the fact that the asthma caused a recurrent skin complaint
on her face and neck and hands.

Teresa and Philomena drank glasses of Babycham, and Kitty
drank Kia-Ora with water instead of gin in it. They'd known
each other all their lives. They'd been to the Presentation Nuns
together, they'd taken First Communion together. Even when
they'd left the Nuns, when Teresa had gone to work in the Medical Hall and Kitty Roche and Philomena in Keane's drapery,
they'd continued to see each other almost every day.

'We'll think of you, Teresa,' Philomena said. 'We'll pray for
you.' Philomena, plump and pale-haired, had every hope of marrying and had even planned her dress, in light lemony lace, with
a Limerick veil. Twice in the last month she'd gone out with
Des Foley the vet, and even if he was a few years older than he
might be and had a car that smelt of cattle disinfectant, there was
more to be said for Des Foley than for many another.

Teresa's two sisters, much older than Teresa, stood by the
piano and the framed Power's advertisement, between the two
windows of the lounge-bar. Agnes, in smart powder-blue, was
tall and thin, the older of the two; Loretta, in brown, was small.
Their own two marriages, eleven and nine years ago, had been
consecrated by Father Hogan in the Church of the Immaculate
Conception and celebrated afterwards in this same lounge-bar.
Loretta had married a man who was no longer mentioned because
he'd gone to England and had never come back. Agnes had
married George Tobin, who was at present sitting outside the
lounge-bar in a Ford Prefect, in charge of his and Agnes's three
small children. The Tobins lived in Cork now, George being the
manager of a shoe-shop there. Loretta lived with her parents, like
an unmarried daughter again.

'Sickens you,' Agnes said. 'She's only a kid, marrying a goop
like that. She'll be stuck in this dump of a town for ever.'

Loretta didn't say anything. It was well known that Agnes's

own marriage had turned out well: George Tobin was a teetotaller and had no interest in either horses or greyhounds. From where she stood Loretta could see him through the window, sitting patiently in the Ford Prefect, reading a comic to his children. Loretta's marriage had not been consummated.

'Well, though I've said it before I'll say it again,' said Father Hogan. 'It's a great day for a mother.'

Mrs Atty and Mrs Cornish politely agreed, without speaking. Mrs Tracy smiled.

'And for an aunt too, Mrs Tracy. Naturally enough.'

Mrs Tracy smiled again. 'A great day,' she said.

'Ah, I'm happy for Teresa,' Father Hogan said. 'And for Artie, too, Mrs Cornish; naturally enough. Aren't they as fine a couple as ever stepped out of this town?'

'Are they leaving the town?' Mrs Tracy asked, confusion breaking in her face. 'I thought Artie was fixed in Driscoll's.'

'It's a manner of speaking, Mrs Tracy,' Father Hogan explained. 'It's a way of putting the thing. When I was marrying them this morning I looked down at their two faces and I said to myself, "Isn't it great God gave them life?"'

The three women looked across the lounge, at Teresa standing with her friends Philomena Morrissey and Kitty Roche, and then at Artie, with Screw Doyle, Eddie Boland and Chas Flynn.

'He has a great career in front of him in Driscoll's,' Father Hogan pronounced. 'Will Teresa remain on in the Medical Hall, Mrs Atty?'

Mrs Atty replied that her daughter would remain for a while in the Medical Hall. It was Father Hogan who had persuaded Artie of his duty when Artie had hesitated. Mrs Atty and Teresa had gone to him for advice, he'd spoken to Artie and to Mr and Mrs Cornish, and the matter had naturally not been mentioned on either side since.

'Will I get you another glassful, Father?' inquired Mrs Tracy, holding out her hand for the priest's tumbler.

'Well, it isn't every day I'm honoured,' said Father Hogan with his smile, putting the tumbler into Mrs Tracy's hand.

At the bar Mr Atty and Mr Cornish drank steadily on. In their

corner Teresa and her bridesmaids talked about weddings that
had taken place in the Church of the Immaculate Conception in
the past, how they had stood by the railings of the church when
they were children, excited by the finery and the men in serge
suits. Teresa's sisters whispered, Agnes continuing about the
inadequacy of the man Teresa had just married. Loretta whispered
without actually forming words. She wished her sister wouldn't
go on so because she didn't want to think about any of it, about
what had happened to Teresa, and what would happen to her
again tonight, in a hotel in Cork. She'd fainted when it had
happened to herself, when he'd come at her like a farm animal.
She'd fought like a mad thing.

It was noisier in the lounge-bar than it had been. The voices
of the bridegroom's father were raised; behind the bar young
Kevin had switched on the wireless. '*Don't get around much
anymore*,' cooed a soft male voice.

'Bedad, there'll be no holding you tonight, Artie,' Eddie
Boland whispered thickly into the bridegroom's ear. He nudged
Artie in the stomach with his elbow, spilling some Guinness. He
laughed uproariously.

'We're following you in two cars,' Screw Doyle said. 'We'll
be waiting in the double bed for you.' Screw Doyle laughed also,
striking the floor repeatedly with his left foot, which was a habit
of his when excited. At a late hour the night before he'd told
Artie that once, after a dance, he'd spent an hour in a field with
the girl whom Artie had agreed to marry. 'I had a great bloody
ride of her,' he'd confided.

'I'll have a word with Teresa,' said Father Hogan, moving
away from Teresa's mother, her aunt and Mrs Cornish. He did
not, however, cross the lounge immediately, but paused by the
bar, where Mr Cornish and Mr Atty were. He put his empty
tumbler on the bar itself, and Mr Atty pushed it towards young
Kevin, who at once refilled it.

'Well, it's a great day for a father,' said Father Hogan. 'Aren't
they a tip-top credit to each other?'

'Who's that, Father?' inquired Mr Cornish, his eyes a little
bleary, sweat hanging from his cheeks.

Father Hogan laughed. He put his tumbler on the bar again, and Mr Cornish pushed it towards young Kevin for another refill.

In their corner Philomena confided to Teresa and Kitty Roche that she wouldn't mind marrying Des Foley the vet. She'd had four glasses of Babycham. If he asked her this minute, she said, she'd probably say yes. 'Is Chas Flynn nice?' Kitty Roche asked, squinting across at him.

On the wireless Petula Clark was singing 'Downtown'. Eddie Boland was whistling 'Mother Macree'. 'Listen, Screw,' Artie said, keeping his voice low although it wasn't necessary. 'Is that true? Did you go into a field with Teresa?'

Loretta watched while George Tobin in his Ford Prefect turned a page of the comic he was reading to his children. Her sister's voice continued in its abuse of the town and its people, in particular the shopman who had got Teresa pregnant. Agnes hated the town and always had. She'd met George Tobin at a dance in Cork and had said to Loretta that in six months' time she'd be gone from the town for ever. Which was precisely what had happened, except that marriage had made her less nice than she'd been. She'd hated the town in a jolly way once, laughing over it. Now she hardly laughed at all.

'Look at him,' she was saying. 'I doubt he knows how to hold a knife and fork.'

Loretta ceased her observation of her sister's husband through the window and regarded Artie Cornish instead. She looked away from him immediately because his face, so quickly replacing the face of George Tobin, had caused in her mind a double image which now brutally persisted. She felt a sickness in her stomach, and closed her eyes and prayed. But the double image remained: George Tobin and Artie Cornish coming at her sisters like two farmyard animals and her sisters fighting to get away. 'Dear Jesus,' she whispered to herself. 'Dear Jesus, help me.'

'Sure it was only a bit of gas,' Screw Doyle assured Artie. 'Sure there was no harm done, Artie.'

In no way did Teresa love him. She had been aware of that when Father Hogan had arranged the marriage, and even before that, when she'd told her mother that she thought she was pregnant and had then mentioned Artie Cornish's name. Artie Cornish was much the same as his friends: you could be walking along a road with Screw Doyle or Artie Cornish and you could hardly tell the difference. There was nothing special about Artie Cornish, except that he always added up the figures twice when he was serving you in Driscoll's. There was nothing bad about him either, any more than there was anything bad about Eddie Boland or Chas Flynn or even Screw Doyle. She'd said privately to Father Hogan that she didn't love him or feel anything for him one way or the other: Father Hogan had replied that in the circumstances all that line of talk was irrelevant.

When she was at the Presentation Convent Teresa had imagined her wedding, and even the celebration in this very lounge-bar. She had imagined everything that had happened that morning, and the things that were happening still. She had imagined herself standing with her bridesmaids as she was standing now, her mother and her aunt drinking sherry, Agnes and Loretta being there too, and other people, and music. Only the bridegroom had been mysterious, some faceless, bodiless presence, beyond imagination. From conversations she had had with Philomena and Kitty Roche, and with her sisters, she knew that they had imagined in a similar way. Yet Agnes had settled for George Tobin because George Tobin was employed in Cork and could take her away from the town. Loretta, who had been married for a matter of weeks, was going to become a nun.

Artie ordered more bottles of stout from young Kevin. He didn't want to catch the half-one bus and have to sit beside her all the way to Cork. He didn't want to go to the Lee Hotel when they could just as easily have remained in the town, when he could just as easily have gone in to Driscoll's tomorrow and continued as before. It would have been different if Screw Doyle hadn't said he'd been in a field with you: you could pretend a bit on the bus, and in the hotel, just to make the whole thing go. You could pretend like you'd been pretending ever since Father Hogan had laid down the law, you could make the best of it like Father Hogan had said.

He handed a bottle of stout to Chas Flynn and one to Screw Doyle and another to Eddie Boland. He'd ask her if it was true. For all he knew the child she was carrying was Screw Doyle's child and would be born with Screw Doyle's thin nose, and everyone in the town would know when they looked at it. His mother had told him when he was sixteen never to trust a girl, never to get involved, because he'd be caught in the end. He'd get caught because he was easy-going, because he didn't possess the smartness of Screw Doyle and some of the others. 'Sure, you might as well marry Teresa as anyone else,' his father had said after Father Hogan had called to see them about the matter. His mother had said things would never be the same between them again.

Eddie Boland sat down at the piano and played 'Mother Macree', causing Agnes and Loretta to move to the other side of the lounge-bar. In the motor-car outside the Tobin children asked their father what the music was for.

'God go with you, girl,' Father Hogan said to Teresa, mentioning Kitty Roche and Philomena away. 'Isn't it a grand thing that's happened, Teresa?' His red-skinned face, with the shiny false teeth so evenly arrayed in it, was close to hers. For a moment she thought he might kiss her, which of course was ridiculous, Father Hogan kissing anyone, even at a wedding celebration.

'It's a great day for all of us, girl.'

When she'd told her mother, her mother said it made her feel sick in her stomach. Her father hit her on the side of the face. Agnes came down specially from Cork to try and sort the matter out. It was then that Loretta had first mentioned becoming a nun.

'I want to say two words,' said Father Hogan, still standing beside her, but now addressing everyone in the lounge-bar. 'Come over here alongside us, Artie. Is there a drop in everyone's glass?'

Artie moved across the lounge-bar, with his glass of stout. Mr Cornish told young Kevin to pour out a few more measures. Eddie Boland stopped playing the piano.

'It's only this,' said Father Hogan. 'I want us all to lift our
glasses to Artie and Teresa. May God go with you, the pair of
you,' he said, lifting his own glass.

'Health, wealth and happiness,' proclaimed Mr Cornish from
the bar.

'And an early night,' shouted Screw Doyle. 'Don't forget to
draw the curtains, Artie.'

They stood awkwardly, not holding hands, not even touching.
Teresa watched while her mother drank the remains of her sherry,
and while her aunt drank and Mrs Cornish drank. Agnes's face
was disdainful, a calculated reply to the coarseness of Screw
Doyle's remarks. Loretta was staring ahead of her, concentrating
her mind on her novitiate. A quick flush passed over the rough-
ened countenance of Kitty Roche. Philomena laughed, and all
the men in the lounge-bar, except Father Hogan, laughed.

'That's sufficient of that talk,' Father Hogan said with contrived severity. 'May you meet happiness halfway,' he added,
suitably altering his intonation. 'The pair of you, Artie and
Teresa.'

Noise broke out again after that. Father Hogan shook hands
with Teresa and then with Artie. He had a funeral at half past
two, he said: he'd better go and get his dinner inside him.

'Goodbye, Father,' Artie said. 'Thanks for doing the job.'

'God bless the pair of you,' said Father Hogan, and went away.

'We should be going for the bus,' Artie said to her. 'It wouldn't
do to miss the old bus.'

'No, it wouldn't.'

'I'll see you down there. You'll have to change your clothes.'

'Yes.'

'I'll come the way I am.'

'You're fine the way you are, Artie.'

He looked at the stout in his glass and didn't raise his eyes
from it when he spoke again. 'Did Screw Doyle take you into a
field, Teresa?'

He hadn't meant to say it then. It was wrong to come out with
it like that, in the lounge-bar, with the wedding-cake still there
on the piano, and Teresa still in her wedding-dress, and confetti

everywhere. He knew it was wrong even before the words came out; he knew that the stout had angered and befuddled him.

'Sorry,' he said. 'Sorry, Teresa.'

She shook her head. It didn't matter: it was only to be expected that a man you didn't love and who didn't love you would ask a question like that at your wedding celebration.

'Yes,' she said. 'Yes, he did.'

'He told me. I thought he was codding. I wanted to know.'

'It's your baby, Artie. The other thing was years ago.'

He looked at her. Her face was flushed, her eyes had tears in them.

'I had too much stout,' he said.

They stood where Father Hogan had left them, drawn away from their wedding guests. Not knowing where else to look, they looked together at Father Hogan's black back as he left the lounge-bar, and then at the perspiring, naked heads of Mr Cornish and Mr Atty by the bar.

At least they had no illusions, she thought. Nothing worse could happen than what had happened already, after Father Hogan had laid down the law. She wasn't going to get a shock like Loretta had got. She wasn't going to go sour like Agnes had gone when she'd discovered that it wasn't enough just to marry a man for a purpose, in order to escape from a town. Philomena was convincing herself that she'd fallen in love with an elderly vet, and if she got any encouragement Kitty Roche would convince herself that she was mad about anyone at all.

For a moment as Teresa stood there, the last moment before she left the lounge-bar, she felt that she and Artie might make some kind of marriage together because there was nothing that could be destroyed, no magic or anything else. He could ask her the question he had asked, while she stopped there in her wedding-dress: he could ask her and she could truthfully reply, because there was nothing special about the occasion, or the lounge-bar all covered in confetti.

WE ARE GREEN!
WE ARE WHITE!

Roddy Doyle

Watching televised football matches in pubs has now become something of a national obsession in Ireland—as it has, of course, in many other parts of the world. The elation and despair that comes with the sport is, though, perhaps more deeply felt by the Irish than many others—especially when they are playing the 'auld enemy', England. The excitement, consumption of alcohol and general revelry are in direct relation to the fortunes of their side and some past matches remain forever engrained in the national psyche along with the memory of monumental hangovers. Such a game is the Republic of Ireland v. England match immortalised in this next story by Roddy Doyle, one of the country's most enthusiastic football lovers as well as one of its best-selling contemporary authors.

Roddy Doyle (1958–) was a teacher of English and Geography in his native Dublin before becoming one of the highest profile Irish writers with his 'Barrytown Trilogy', The Commitments (1987), The Snapper (1990) *and* The Van (1991) *all set in the Kilbarrack area where he grew up. He has won the Booker prize (in 1993 with* Paddy Clarke Ha Ha Ha), *seen his work translated into over 20 languages and the trio of Barrytown sagas filmed. His own childhood as the son of a printer was unruffled and happy without the problems of drink, violence and dysfunction that he has often portrayed in his books—notably* The Woman who Walked into Doors *(1996) about the brutality inflicted on an alcoholic woman by her husband. Roddy Doyle does enjoy the occasional drink, however, and apart from supporting the Republic is also a fan of the London club, Chelsea FC. 'We Are Green! We Are White!' is a wildly Rabelaisian episode from* The Van.

*　　*　　*

——Sheedy gets it back——and Sheedy shoots!

The place went fuckin' mad!

Ireland had got the equaliser. Jimmy Sr grabbed Bimbo and nearly broke him in half with the hug he gave him. Bertie was up on one of the tables thumping his chest. Even Paddy, the crankiest fucker ever invented, was jumping up and down and shaking his arse like a Brazilian. All sorts of glasses toppled off the tables but no one gave a fuck. Ireland had scored against England and there was nothing more important than that, not even your pint.

—Who scored it!? Who scored it?

—Don't know. It doesn't fuckin' matter!

They all settled down to see the action replay but they still couldn't make out who'd scored it, because they all went wild again when the ball hit the back of the net from one, two, three different angles, and looking at poor oul' Shilton trying to get at it, it was a fuckin' panic.

Word came through from the front.

—Sheedy.

—Sheedy got it.

—Kevin Sheedy.

—WHO PUT THE BALL IN THE ENGLISH NET—

SHEEDY—

SHEEDY—

God, it was great; fuckin' brilliant. And the rest of the match was agony. Every time an Irishman got the ball they all cheered and they groaned and laughed whenever one of the English got it; not that they got it that often; Ireland were all over them.

—Your man, Waddle's a righ' stick, isn't he?

—Ah, he's like a headless fuckin' chicken.

A throw-in for Ireland.

—MICK—MICK—MICK—MICK—MICK—

They all cheered when they saw Mick McCarthy coming up to take it. And there was Paddy Mick-Mick-Micking out of him and only an hour ago he'd been calling Mick McCarthy a fuckin' liability.

—OLÉ——OLÉ olé olé—

—OLÉ

—OLÉ—

There was ten minutes left.

—Ah Jaysis, me heart!

—No problem, compadre.

Jimmy Sr was about ten yards away from where he'd started when Sheedy's scored. He didn't know how that had happened. He tried to get back to his pint.

—'Xcuse me.——Sorry there;—thanks.——'Xcuse me.—— Get ou' o' me way, yeh fat cunt.

His pint was gone, on the floor, or maybe some bollix had robbed it. He looked over at the bar. He'd never get near it; it was jammered. Anyway, Leo the barman was ignoring all orders; he was looking at the big screen and praying; he was, praying.

—Look it, Jimmy Sr pointed him out to Bimbo.

He had his hands joined the way kids did, palm against palm, like on the cover of a prayer book, and his lips were moving. When everyone else cheered Leo just kept on praying.

—How much is there left?

—Five, I think.

—Fuck.

He looked around him. There were a lot of young ones in the pub. They hadn't been paying much attention to the match earlier but they were now. There was one of them, over near the bar; she was in a white T-shirt that you could see her bra through it and—

There was a big groan. Jimmy Sr got back to the match.

—What's happenin'?

—They have it.

Gascoigne got past two of the Irish lads and gave it to someone at the edge of the box and he fired—Jimmy Sr grabbed Bimbo's arm—but it went miles over the bar.

They cheered.

—Useless.

—How much left now?

—Two.

—Take your time, Packie!

—ONE PACKIE BONNER

THERE'S ONLY ONE PACKIE BONNER—

—Up them steps, Packie!

—Ah, he's a great fuckin' goalkeeper.

—ONE PACKIE BOHHHH-NER—

—He's very religious, yeh know. He always has rosary beads in his kit bag.

—He should strangle fuckin' Lineker with them, said Jimmy Sr, and he got a good laugh.—How much now, Bimbo?

Before Bimbo answered the Olivetti yoke came up on the screen and answered his question; they were into time added on.

They cheered.

—Come on, lads; go for another one!

—Ah, Morris; you're fuckin' useless.

—Fuck up, you. He's brilliant.

—ONE GISTY MORRIS

THERE'S ONLY ONE GISTY MORRIS—

—Blow the fuckin' whistle, yeh cunt yeh!

They laughed.

Jesus, the heat. You had to gasp to get a lungful; that and the excitement. He couldn't watch; it was killing him.

—OLÉ——OLÉ olé olé—

Jimmy Sr was looking over at the young one again when he got smothered by the lads. They went up—the ref had blown the whistle—and he stayed down. But he grabbed a hold of Bimbo and hung on. Everyone was jumping up and down, even Leo blessing himself. The tricolours were up in the air. He wished he had one. He'd get one for the rest of the matches.

Bertie was back up on the table doing his Norwegian commentator bit.

—Maggie Thatcher!—Winston Churchill!—

—WHO PUT THE BALL IN THE ENGLISH NET—

SHEEDY—SHEEDY—

—Queen Elizabeth!—Lawrence of Arabia!—Elton John! Yis can all go an' fuck yourselves!

They cheered.

Jimmy Sr was bursting; not for a piss, with love. He hugged Bimbo. He hugged Bertie. He hugged Paddy. He even hugged Larry O'Rourke. He loved everyone. There was Sharon. He got over to her and hugged her, and then all her friends.

—Isn't it brilliant, Daddy?

—Ah, it's fuckin' brilliant; brilliant.

—I love your aftershave, Mister Rabbitte.

—OLÉ—OLÉ olé olé—

—Jaysis, said Jimmy Sr when he got back to Bimbo.—An' we only fuckin' drew. Wha' would happen if we'd won?

Bimbo laughed.

Everyone in the place sang. Jimmy Sr hated the song but it didn't matter.

—GIVE IT A LASH JACK

GIVE IT A LASH JACK

NEVER NEVER NEVER SAY NO

IRELIN'—IRELIN'—REPUB-ILIC OF IRELIN'

REV IT UP AN' HERE WE GO—

—It's a great song, isn't it? said Bimbo.

—Ah, yeah, said Jimmy Sr.

It was that sort of day.

—We'd better get goin', I suppose, said Bimbo.

—Fair enough, said Jimmy Sr.

He was raring to go.

—Red alert, he shouted.—Red alert.

They came charging out of the pub, the two of them. Jimmy Sr let go of a roar.

—Yeow!!

His T-shirt was wringing. Fuck it though, he was floating.

Bimbo got the back door open and hopped in; really hopped now; it was a fuckin' gas.

Jimmy Sr stopped.

—Listen, he said.

They could hear loads of cars honking. And there were people out on the streets, they could hear them as well.

WE ARE GREEN—WE ARE WHI'E

WE ARE FUCKIN DYNAMI'E

2

IN FINNEGAN'S WAKE

Pub Stories

GRACE

James Joyce

*Davy Burne's in Duke Street, Dublin is one of the most famous
Irish pubs in the world, renowned for its selections of beer,
whiskey and wine. History and Literature intermingle amidst its
riot of Art Deco and murals including a series of pictures by the
artist and poet Cecil ffrench Salkeld and a cartoon entitled 'The
Passing of the Holy Hour' which marks the ending of afternoon
closing time. Legends about the place proliferate. Michael Collins
is said to have written a telegraph there to Davy Byrne during
the lengthy negotiations about the Irish Free State in London in
the 1920s: 'Send over a bottle of brandy and a soda siphon to
settle the Irish question'; while Brendan Behan got involved in
a fight outside the bar in 1954 to which half the drinking popu-
lation of Dublin claim to have been eye-witnesses. James Joyce
was for a time a regular, too, and there is a memorable scene
in* Ulysses *in which Leopold Bloom steps into Byrne's for a glass
of wine and 'strips of sandwich with pungent mustard and the
feety savour of green cheese' during the course of his twenty-four-
hour perambulating odyssey on 16 June [1904]. This next story,
'Grace' was also inspired by the pub, but it should be noted by
anyone who goes looking, that the establishment has changed
somewhat since Joyce's time.*

*James Joyce (1882–1941) was educated at the National Uni-
versity of Ireland, studied medicine in Paris, and for a time took
up voice-training for a concert-platform career. He was then
employed as a tutor of English in Trieste before revolutionising
modern literature with his unique prose style. A collection of
short stories,* Dubliners (1914), *was followed by* Portrait of the

Artist as a Young Man *in 1917, his masterpiece* Ulysses *first published in Paris five years later, and* Finnegans Wake (1939). *In these works he translated to the art of writing the conception and technique of the art of musical composition—with varying degrees of success according to which authorities are consulted. 'Grace' is the story of a classic situation: a drink-inspired discussion about whiskey and religion beginning with Joyce's inimitable introduction of his central character, the 'peloothered' Tom Kernan . . .*

*   *   *

Two gentlemen who were in the lavatory at the time tried to lift him up: but he was quite helpless. He lay curled up at the foot of the stairs down which he had fallen. They succeeded in turning him over. His hat had rolled a few yards away and his clothes were smeared with the filth and ooze of the floor on which he had lain, face downwards. His eyes were closed and he breathed with a grunting noise. A thin stream of blood trickled from the corner of his mouth.

These two gentlemen and one of the curates carried him up the stairs and laid him down again on the floor of the bar. In two minutes he was surrounded by a ring of men. The manager of the bar asked everyone who he was and who was with him. No one knew who he was, but one of the curates said he had served the gentleman with a small rum.

'Was he by himself?' asked the manager.

'No, sir. There was two gentlemen with him.'

'And where are they?'

No one knew; a voice said:

'Give him air. He's fainted.'

The ring of onlookers distended and closed again elastically. A dark medal of blood had formed itself near the man's head on the tessellated floor. The manager, alarmed by the grey pallor of the man's face, sent for a policeman.

His collar was unfastened and his necktie undone. He opened his eyes for an instant, sighed and closed them again. One of the gentlemen who had carried him upstairs held a dinged silk hat in his hand. The manager asked repeatedly did no one know who the injured man was or where had his friends gone. The door of the bar opened and an immense constable entered. A crowd which had followed him down the laneway collected outside the door, struggling to look in through the glass panels.

The manager at once began to narrate what he knew. The constable, a young man with thick immobile features, listened. He moved his head slowly to right and left and from the manager to the person on the floor, as if he feared to be the victim of some delusion. Then he drew off his glove, produced a small book from his waist, licked the lead of his pencil and made ready to indite. He asked in a suspicious provincial accent‘

'Who is the man? What's his name and address?'

A young man in a cycling suit cleared his way through the ring of bystanders. He knelt down promptly beside the injured man and called for water. The constable knelt down also to help. The young man washed the blood from the injured man's mouth and then called for some brandy. The constable repeated the order in an authoritative voice until a curate came running with the glass. The brandy was forced down the man's throat. In a few seconds he opened his eyes and looked about him. He looked at the circle of faces and then, understanding, strove to rise to his feet.

'You're all right now?' asked the young man in the cycling-suit.

'Sha, 's nothing,' said the injured man, trying to stand up.

He was helped to his feet. The manager said something about a hospital and some of the bystanders gave advice. The battered silk hat was placed on the man's head. The constable asked:

'Where do you live?'

The man, without answering, began to twirl the ends of his moustache. He made light of his accident. He spoke very thickly.

'Where do you live?' repeated the constable.

The man said they were to get a cab for him. While the point was being debated a tall agile gentleman of fair complexion, wearing a long yellow ulster, came from the far end of the bar. Seeing the spectacle, he called out:

'Hallo, Tom, old man! What's the trouble?'

'Sha, 's nothing,' said the man.

The newcomer surveyed the deplorable figure before him and then turned to the constable, saying:

'It's all right, constable. I'll see him home.'

The constable touched his helmet and answered:

'All right, Mr Power!'

'Come now, Tom,' said Mr Power, taking his friend by the arm. 'No bones broken. What? Can you walk?'

The young man in the cycling-suit took the man by the other arm and the crowd divided.

'How did you get yourself into this mess?' asked Mr Power.

'The gentleman fell down the stairs,' said the young man.

'I' 'ery 'uch o'liged to you, sir,' said the injured man.

'Not at all.'

'' 'an't we have a little . . . ?'

'Not now. Not now.'

The three men left the bar and the crowd sifted through the doors into the laneway. The manager brought the constable to the stairs to inspect the scene of the accident. They agreed that the gentleman must have missed his footing. The customers returned to the counter, and a curate set about removing the traces of blood from the floor.

When they came out into Grafton Street, Mr Power whistled for an outsider. The injured man said again as well as he could:

'I' 'ery 'uch o'liged to you, sir. I hope we'll 'eet again. 'y na'e is Kernan.'

The shock and the incipient pain had partly sobered him.

'Don't mention it,' said the young man.

They shook hands. Mr Kernan was hoisted on to the car and, while Mr Power was giving directions to the carman, he expressed his gratitude to the young man and regretted that they could not have a little drink together.

'Another time,' said the young man.

The car drove off towards Westmoreland Street. As it passed the Ballast Office the clock showed half past nine. A keen east wind hit them, blowing from the mouth of the river. Mr Kernan was huddled together with cold. His friend asked him to tell how the accident had happened.

I 'an't 'an,' he answered, ''y 'ongue is hurt.'

'Show.'

The other leaned over the wheel of the car and peered into Mr Kernan's mouth but he could not see. He struck a match and, sheltering it in the shell of his hands, peered again into the mouth which Mr Kernan opened obediently. The swaying movement of the car brought the match to and from the opened mouth. The lower teeth and gums were covered with clotted blood and a minute piece of the tongue seemed to have been bitten off. The match was blown out.

'That's ugly,' said Mr Power.

'Sha, 's nothing,' said Mr Kernan, closing his mouth and pulling the collar of his filthy coat across his neck.

Mr Kernan was a commercial traveller of the old school which believed in the dignity of its calling. He had never been seen in the city without a silk hat of some decency and a pair of gaiters. By grace of these two articles of clothing, he said, a man could always pass muster. He carried on the tradition of his Napoleon, the great Blackwhite, whose memory he evoked at times by legend and mimicry. Modern business methods had spared him only so far as to allow him a little office in Crowe Street, on the window blind of which was written the name of his firm with the address—London, EC. On the mantelpiece of this little office a little leaden battalion of canisters was drawn up and on the table before the window stood four or five china bowls which were usually half full of a black liquid. From these bowls Mr Kernan tasted tea. He took a mouthful, drew it up, saturated his palate with it and then spat it forth into the grate. Then he paused to judge.

Mr Power, a much younger man, was employed in the Royal Irish Constabulary Office in Dublin Castle. The arc of his social rise intersected the arc of his friend's decline, but Mr Kernan's decline was mitigated by the fact that certain of those friends who had known him at his highest point of success still esteemed him as a character. Mr Power was one of these friends. His inexplicable debts were a byword in his circle; he was a debonair young man.

The car halted before a small house on the Glasnevin Road and Mr Kernan was helped into the house. His wife put him to bed, while Mr Power sat downstairs in the kitchen asking the children where they went to school and what book they were in. The children—two girls and a boy, conscious of their father's helplessness and of their mother's absence, began some horseplay with him. He was surprised at their manners and at their accents, and his brow grew thoughtful. After a while Mrs Kernan entered the kitchen, exclaiming:

'Such a sight! Oh, he'll do for himself one day and that's the holy alls of it. He's been drinking since Friday.'

Mr Power was careful to explain to her that he was not responsible, that he had come on the scene by the merest accident. Mrs Kernan, remembering Mr Power's good offices during domestic quarrels, as well as many small, but opportune loans, said:

'O, you needn't tell me that, Mr Power. I know you're a friend of his, not like some of the others he does be with. They're all right so long as he has money in his pocket to keep him out from his wife and family. Nice friends! Who was he with to-night, I'd like to know?'

Mr Power shook his head but said nothing.

'I'm so sorry,' she continued, 'that I've nothing in the house to offer you. But if you wait a minute I'll send round to Fogarty's, at the corner.'

Mr Power stood up.

'We were waiting for him to come home with the money. He never seems to think he has a home at all.'

'O, now, Mrs Kernan,' said Mr Power, 'we'll make him turn over a new leaf. I'll talk to Martin. He's the man. We'll come here one of these nights and talk it over.'

She saw him to the door. The carman was stamping up and down the footpath, and swinging his arms to warm himself.

'It's very kind of you to bring him home,' she said.

'Not at all,' said Mr Power.

He got up on the car. As it drove off he raised his hat to her gaily.

'We'll make a new man of him,' he said. 'Good night, Mrs Kernan.'

Mrs Kernan's puzzled eyes watched the car till it was out of sight. Then she withdrew them, went into the house and emptied her husband's pockets.

She was an active, practical woman of middle age. Not long before she had celebrated her silver wedding and renewed her intimacy with her husband by waltzing with him to Mr Power's accompaniment. In her days of courtship, Mr Kernan had seemed to her a not ungallant figure: and she still hurried to the chapel door whenever a wedding was reported and, seeing the bridal pair, recalled with vivid pleasure how she had passed out of the Star of the Sea Church in Sandymount, leaning on the arm of a jovial well-fed man, who was dressed smartly in a frock-coat and lavender trousers and carried a silk hat gracefully balanced upon his other arm. After three weeks she had found a wife's life irksome and, later on, when she was beginning to find it unbearable, she had become a mother. The part of mother presented to her no insuperable difficulties and for twenty-five years she had kept house shrewdly for her husband. Her two eldest sons were launched. one was in a draper's shop in Glasgow and the other was clerk to a tea-merchant in Belfast. They were good sons, wrote regularly and sometimes sent home money. The other children were still at school.

Mr Kernan sent a letter to his office next day and remained in bed. She made beef-tea for him and scolded him roundly. She accepted his frequent intemperance as part of the climate, healed him dutifully whenever he was sick and always tried to make him eat a breakfast. There were worse husbands. He had never been violent since the boys had grown up, and she knew that he would walk to the end of Thomas Street and back again to book even a small order.

Two nights after, his friends came to see him. She brought them up to his bedroom, the air of which was impregnated with a personal odour, and gave them chairs at the fire. Mr Kernan's tongue, the occasional stinging pain of which had made him somewhat irritable during the day, became more polite. He sat propped up in the bed by pillows and the little colour in his puffy cheeks made them resemble warm cinders. He apologized to his guests for the disorder of the room, but at the same time looked at them a little proudly, with a veteran's pride.

He was quite unconscious that he was the victim of a plot which his friends, Mr Cunningham, Mr M'Coy, and Mr Power had disclosed to Mrs Kernan in the parlour. The idea had been Mr Power's, but its development was entrusted to Mr Cunningham. Mr Kernan came of Protestant stock, and, though he had been converted to the Catholic faith at the time of his marriage, he had not been in the pale of the Church for twenty years. He was fond, moreover, of giving side-thrusts at Catholicism.

Mr Cunningham was the very man for such a case. He was an elder colleague of Mr Power. His own domestic life was not very happy. People had great sympathy with him, for it was known that he had married an unpresentable woman who was an incurable drunkard. He had set up house for her six times; and each time she had pawned the furniture on him.

Everyone had respect for poor Martin Cunningham. He was a thoroughly sensible man, influential and intelligent. His blade of human knowledge, natural astuteness particularized by long association with cases in the police courts, had been tempered by brief immersions in the waters of general philosophy. He was well informed. His friends bowed to his opinions and considered that his face was like Shakespeare's.

When the plot had been disclosed to her, Mrs Kernan had said: 'I leave it all in your hands, Mr Cunningham.'

After a quarter of a century of married life, she had very few illusions left. Religion for her was a habit, and she suspected that a man of her husband's age would not change greatly before death. She was tempted to see a curious appropriateness in his accident and, but that she did not wish to seem bloody-minded, she would have told the gentlemen that Mr Kernan's tongue would not suffer by being shortened. However, Mr Cunningham was a capable man; and religion was religion. The scheme might do good and, at least, it could do no harm. Her beliefs were not extravagant. She believed steadily in the Sacred Heart as the most generally useful of all Catholic devotions and approved of the sacraments. Her faith was bounded by her kitchen, but, if she was put to it, she could believe also in the banshee and in the Holy Ghost.

The gentlemen began to talk of the accident. Mr Cunningham said that he had once known a similar case. A man of seventy had bitten off a piece of his tongue during an epileptic fit and the tongue had filled in again, so that no one could see a trace of the bite.

'Well, I'm not seventy,' said the invalid.

'God forbid,' said Mr Cunningham.

'It doesn't pain you now?' asked Mr M'Coy.

Mr M'Coy had been at one time a tenor of some reputation. His wife, who had been a soprano, still taught young children to play the piano at low terms. His line of life had not been the shortest distance between two points and for short periods he had been driven to live by his wits. He had been a clerk in the Midland Railway, a canvasser for advertisements for *The Irish Times* and for *The Freeman's Journal*, a town traveller for a coal firm on commission, a private inquiry agent, a clerk in the office of the Sub-Sheriff, and he had recently become secretary to the City Coroner. His new office made him professionally interested in Mr Kernan's case.

'Pain? Not much,' answered Mr Kernan. 'But it's so sickening. I feel as if I wanted to retch off.'

'That's the booze,' said Mr Cunningham firmly.

'No,' said Mr Kernan. 'I think I caught cold on the car. There's something keeps coming into my throat, phlegm or—'

'Mucus,' said Mr M'Coy.

'It keeps coming like from down in my throat; sickening thing.'

'Yes, yes,' said Mr M'Coy, 'that's the thorax.'

He looked at Mr Cunningham and Mr Power at the same time with an air of challenge. Mr Cunningham nodded his head rapidly and Mr Power said:

'Ah, well, all's well that ends well.'

'I'm very obliged to you, old man,' said the invalid.

Mr Power waved his hand.

'Those other fellows I was with—'

'Who were you with?' asked Mr Cunningham.

'A chap. I don't know his name. Damn it now, what's his name? Little chap with sandy hair . . .'

'And who else?'

'Harford.'

'Hm,' said Mr Cunningham.

When Mr Cunningham made that remark, people were silent. It was known that the speaker had secret sources of information. In this case the monosyllable had a moral intention. Mr Harford sometimes formed one of a little detachment which left the city shortly after noon on Sunday with the purpose of arriving as soon as possible at some public house on the outskirts of the city where its members duly qualified themselves as *bona-fide* travellers. But his fellow-travellers had never consented to overlook his origin. He had begun life as an obscure financier by lending small sums of money to workmen at usurious interest. Later on he had become the partner of a very fat, short gentleman, Mr Goldberg, in the Liffey Loan Bank. Though he had never embraced more than the Jewish ethical code, his fellow-Catholics, whenever they had smarted in person or by proxy under his exactions, spoke of him bitterly as an Irish Jew and an illiterate, and saw divine disapproval of usury made manifest through the person of his idiot son. At other times they remembered his good points.

'I wonder where did he go to,' said Mr Kernan.

He wished the details of the incident to remain vague. He wished his friends to think that had been some mistake, that Mr Harford and he had missed each other. His friends, who knew quite well Mr Harford's manners in drinking, were silent. Mr Power said again:

'All's well that ends well.'

Mr Kernan changed the subject at once.

'That was a decent young chap, that medical fellow,' he said. 'Only for him—'

'O, only for him,' said Mr Power, 'it might have been a case of seven days, without the option of a fine.'

'Yes, yes,' said Mr Kernan, trying to remember. 'I remember now there was a policeman. Decent young fellow, he seemed. How did it happen at all?'

'It happened that you were peloothered, Tom,' said Mr Cunningham gravely.

'True bill,' said Mr Kernan, equally gravely.

'I suppose you squared the constable, Jack,' said Mr M'Coy.

Mr Power did not relish the use of his Christian name. He was not strait-laced, but he could not forget that Mr M'Coy had recently made a crusade in search of valises and portmanteaux to enable Mrs M'Coy to fulfil imaginary engagements in the country. More than he resented the fact that he had been victimized, he resented such low playing of the game. He answered the question, therefore, as if Mr Kernan had asked it.

The narrative made Mr Kernan indignant. He was keenly conscious of his citizenship, wished to live with his city on terms mutually honourable and resented any affront put upon him by those whom he called country bumpkins.

'Is this wha we pay rates for?' he asked. 'To feed and clothe these ignorant bostooms . . . and they're nothing else.'

Mr Cunningham laughed. He was a Castle official only during office hours.

'How could they be anything else, Tom?' he said.

He assumed a thick, provincial accent and said in a tone of command:

'65, catch your cabbage!'

Everyone laughed. Mr M'Coy, who wanted to enter the conversation by any door, pretended that he had never heard the story. Mr Cunningham said:

'It is supposed—they say, you know—to take place in the depot where they get these thundering big country fellows, omadhauns, you know, to drill. The sergeant makes them stand in a row against the wall and hold up their plates.' He illustrated the story by grotesque gestures.

'At dinner, you know. Then he has a bloody big bowl of cabbage before him on the table and a bloody big spoon like a shovel. He takes up a wad of cabbage on the spoon and pegs it across the room and the poor devils have to try and catch it on their plates: 65, *catch your cabbage.*'

Everyone laughed again: but Mr Kernan was somewhat indignant still. He talked of writing a letter to the papers.

'These yahoos coming up here,' he said, 'think they can boss the people. I needn't tell you, Martin, what kind of men they are.'

Mr Cunningham gave a qualified assent.

'It's like everything else in this world,' he said. 'You get some bad ones and you get some good ones.'

'O yes, you get some good ones, I admit,' said Mr Kernan, satisfied.

'It's better to have nothing to say to them,' said Mr M'Coy. 'That's my opinion!'

Mrs Kernan entered the room and, placing a tray on the table, said:

'Help yourselves, gentlemen.'

Mr Power stood up to officiate, offering her his chair. She declined it, saying she was ironing downstairs, and, after having exchanged a nod with Mr Cunningham behind Mr Power's back, prepared to leave the room. Her husband called out to her:

'And have you nothing for me, duckie?'

'O, you! The back of my hand to you!' said Mrs Kernan tartly.

Her husband called after her:

'Nothing for poor little hubby!'

He assumed such a comical face and voice that the distribution of the bottles of stout took place amid general merriment.

The gentlemen drank from their glasses, set the glasses again on the table and paused. Then Mr Cunningham turned towards Mr Power and said casually:

'On Thursday night, you said, Jack?'

'Thursday, yes,' said Mr Power.

'Righto!' said Mr Cunningham promptly.

'We can meet in M'Auley's,' said Mr M'Coy. 'That'll be the most convenient place.'

'But we mustn't be late,' said Mr Power earnestly, 'because it is sure to be crammed to the doors.'

'We can meet at half-seven,' said Mr M'Coy.

'Righto!' said Mr Cunningham.

'Half-seven at M'Auley's be it!'

There was a short silence. Mr Kernan waited to see whether he would be taken into his friends' confidence. Then he asked:

'What's in the wind?'

'O, it's nothing,' said Mr Cunningham. 'It's only a little matter that we're arranging about for Thursday.'

'The opera, is it?' said Mr Kernan.

'No, no,' said Mr Cunningham in an evasive tone, 'it's just a little . . . spiritual matter.'

'O,' said Mr Kernan.

There was silence again. Then Mr Power said, point-blank:

'To tell you the truth, Tom, we're going to make a retreat.'

'Yes, that's it,' said Mr Cunningham, 'Jack and I and M'Coy here—we're all going to wash the pot.'

He uttered the metaphor with a certain homely energy and, encouraged by his own voice, proceeded:

'You see, we may as well all admit we're a nice collection of scoundrels, one and all. I say, one and all,' he added with gruff charity and turning to Mr Power. 'Own up now!'

'I own up,' said Mr Power.

'And I own up,' said Mr M'Coy.

'So we're going to wash the pot together,' said Mr Cunningham.

A thought seemed to strike him. He turned suddenly to the invalid and said:

'D'ye know what, Tom, has just occurred to me? You might join in and we'd have a four-handed reel.'

'Good idea,' said Mr Power. 'The four of us together.'

Mr Kernan was silent. The proposal conveyed very little meaning to his mind, but, understanding that some spiritual agencies were about to concern themselves on his behalf, he thought he owed it to his dignity to show a stiff neck. He took no part in the conversation for a long while, but listened, with an air of calm enmity, while his friends discussed the Jesuits.

'I haven't such a bad opinion of the Jesuits,' he said, intervening at length. 'They're an educated order. I believe they mean well, too.'

'They're the grandest order in the Church, Tom,' said Mr Cunningham, with enthusiasm. 'The General of the Jesuits stands next to the Pope.'

'There's no mistake about it,' said Mr M'Coy, 'if you want a thing well done and no flies about, you go to a Jesuit. They're the boyos have influence. I'll tell you a case in point . . .'

'The Jesuits are a fine body of men,' said Mr Power.

'It's a curious thing,' said Mr Cunningham, 'about the Jesuit Order. Every other order of the Church had to be reformed at some time or other, but the Jesuit Order was never once reformed. It never fell away.;

'Is that so?' asked Mr M'Coy.

'That's a fact,' said Mr Cunningham. 'That's history.'

'Look at their church, too,' said Mr Power. 'Look at the congregation they have.'

'The Jesuits cater for the upper classes,' said Mr M'Coy.

'Of course,' said Mr Power.

'Yes,' said Mr Kernan. 'That's why I have a feeling for them. It's some of those secular priests, ignorant, bumptious—'

'They're all good men,' said Mr Cunningham, 'each in his own way. The Irish priesthood is honoured all the world over.'

'O yes,' said Mr Power.

'Not like some of the other priesthoods on the Continent,' said Mr M'Coy, 'unworthy of the name.'

'Perhaps you're right,' said Mr Kernan, relenting.

'Of course I'm right,' said Mr Cunningham. 'I haven't been in the world all this time and seen most sides of it without being a judge of character.'

The gentlemen drank again, one following another's example. Mr Kernan seemed to be weighing something in his mind. He was impressed. He had a high opinion of Mr Cunningham as a judge of character and as a reader of faces. He asked for particulars.

'O, it's just a retreat, you know,' said Mr Cunningham. 'Father Purdon is giving it. It's for business men, you know.'

'He won't be too hard on us, Tom,' said Mr Power persuasively.

'Father Purdon? Father Purdon?' said the invalid.

'O, you must know him, Tom,' said Mr Cunningham, stoutly. 'Fine, jolly fellow! He's a man of the world like ourselves.'

'Ah . . . yes. I think I know him. Rather red face; tall.'

'That's the man.'

'And tell me, Martin . . . Is he a good preacher?'

'Munno . . . It's not exactly a sermon, you know. It's just a kind of a friendly talk, you know, in a common-sense way.'

Mr Kernan deliberated. Mr M'Coy said:

'Father Tom Burke, that was the boy!'

'O, Father Tom Burke,' said Mr Cunningham, 'that was a born orator. Did you ever hear him, Tom?'

'Did I ever hear him!' said the invalid, nettled. 'Rather! I heard him . . .'

'And yet they say he wasn't much of a theologian,' said Mr Cunningham.

'Is that so?' said Mr M'Coy.

'O, of course, nothing wrong, you know. Only sometimes, they say, he didn't preach what was quite orthodox.'

'Ah! . . . he was a splendid man,' said Mr M'Coy.

'I heard him once,' Mr Kernan continued. 'I forget the subject of his discourse now. Crofton and I were in the back of the . . . pit, you know . . . the—'

'The body,' said Mr Cunningham.

'Yes, in the back near the door. I forgot now what . . . O yes, it was on the Pope, the late Pope. I remember it well. Upon my word it was magnificent, the style of the oratory. And his voice! God! hadn't he a voice! *The Prisoner of the Vatican*, he called him. I remember Crofton saying to me when we came out—'

'But he's an Orangeman, Crofton, isn't he?' said Mr Power.

''Course he is,' said Mr Kernan, 'and a damned decent Orangeman, too. We went into Butler's in Moore Street—faith, I was genuinely moved, tell you the God's truth—and I remember well his very words. *Kernan*, he said, *we worship at different altars*, he said, *but our belief is the same*. Struck me as very well put.'

'There's a good deal in that,' said Mr Power. 'There used always be crowds of Protestants in the chapel where Father Tom was preaching.'

'There's not much difference between us,' said Mr M'Coy. 'We both believe in—'

He hesitated for a moment.

'. . . in the Redeemer. Only they don't believe in the Pope and in the mother of God.'

'But, of course,' said Mr Cunningham quietly and effectively, 'our religious is *the* religion, the old, original faith.'

'Not a doubt of it,' said Mr Kernan warmly.

Mrs Kernan came to the door of the bedroom and announced:

'Here's a visitor for you!'

'Who is it?'

'Mr Fogarty.'

'O, come in! come in!'

A pale, oval face came forward into the light. The arch of its fair trailing moustache was repeated in the fair eyebrows looped above pleasantly astonished eyes. Mr Fogarty was a modest grocer. He had failed in business in a licensed house in the city because his financial condition had constrained him to tie himself to second-class distillers and brewers. He had opened a small shop on Glasnevin Road where, he flattered himself, his manners would ingratiate him with the housewives of the district. He bore himself with a certain grace, complimented little children and spoke with a neat enunciation. He was not without culture.

Mr Fogarty brought a gift with him, a half-pint of special whisky. He inquired politely for Mr Kernan, placed his gift on the table and sat down with the company on equal terms. Mr Kernan appreciated the gift all the more since he was aware that there was a small account for groceries unsettled between him and Mr Fogarty. He said:

'I wouldn't doubt you, old man. Open that, Jack, will you?'

Mr Power again officiated. Glasses were rinsed and five small measures of whisky were poured out. This new influence enlivened the conversation. Mr Fogarty, sitting on a small area of the chair, was specially interested.

'Pope Leo XIII,' said Mr Cunningham, 'was one of the lights of the age. His great idea, you know, was the union of the Latin and Greek Churches. That was the aim of his life.'

'I often heard he was one of the most intellectual men in Europe,' said Mr Power. 'I mean, apart from his being Pope.'

'So he was,' said Mr Cunningham, 'if not *the* most so. His motto, you know, as Pope, was *Lux upon Lux—Light upon Light*.'

'No, no,' said Mr Fogarty eagerly. 'I think you're wrong there. It was *Lux in Tenebris*, I think—*Light in Darkness*.'

'O yes,' said Mr M'Coy, '*Tenebrae*.'

'Allow me,' said Mr Cunningham positively, 'it was *Lux upon Lux*. And Pius IX his predecessor's motto was *Crux upon Crux*— that is, *Cross upon Cross*—to show the difference between their two pontificates.'

The inference was allowed. Mr Cunningham continued.

'Pope Leo, you know, was a great scholar and a poet.'

'He had a strong face,' said Mr Kernan.

'Yes,' said Mr Cunningham. 'He wrote Latin poetry.'

'Is that so?' said Mr Fogarty.

Mr M'Coy tasted his whisky contentedly and shook his head with a double intention, saying:

'That's no joke, I can tell you.'

'We didn't learn that, Tom,' said Mr Power, following Mr M'Coy's example, 'when we went to the penny-a-week school.'

'There was many a good man went to the penny-a-week school with a sod of turf under his oxter,' said Mr Kernan sententiously. 'The old system was the best: plain honest education. None of your modern trumpery . . .'

'Quite right,' said Mr Power.

'No superfluities,' said Mr Fogarty.

He enunciated the word and then drank gravely.

'I remember reading,' said Mr Cunningham, 'that one of Pope Leo's poems was on the invention of the photograph—in Latin, of course.'

'On the photograph!' explained Mr Kernan.

'Yes,' said Mr Cunningham.

He also drank from his glass.

'Well, you know,' said Mr M'Coy, 'isn't the photograph wonderful when you come to think of it?'

'O, of course,' said Mr Power, 'great minds can see things.'

'As the poet says: *Great minds are very near to madness*,' said Mr Fogarty.

Mr Kernan seemed to be troubled in mind. He made an effort to recall the Protestant theology on some thorny points and in the end addressed Mr Cunningham.

'Tell me, Martin,' he said. 'Weren't some of the Popes—of course, not our present man, or his predecessor, but some of the old Popes—not exactly . . . you know . . . up to the knocker?'

There was a silence. Mr Cunningham said:

'O, of course, there were some bad lots . . . But the astonishing thing is this. Not one of them, not the biggest drunkard, not the most . . . out-and-out ruffian, not one of them ever preached *ex cathedra* a word of false doctrine. Now isn't that an astonishing thing?'

'That is,' said Mr Kernan.

'Yes, because when the Pope speaks *ex cathedra*,' Mr Fogarty explained, 'he is infallible.'

'Yes,' said Mr Cunningham.

'O, I know about the infallibility of the Pope. I remember I was younger then . . . Or was it that—?'

Mr Fogarty interrupted. He took up the bottle and helped the others to a little more. Mr M'Coy, seeing that there was not enough to go round, pleaded that he had not finished his first measure. The others accepted under protest. The light music of whisky falling into glasses made an agreeable interlude.

'What's that you were saying, Tom?' asked Mr M'Coy.

'Papal infallibility,' said Mr Cunningham, 'that was the greatest scene in the whole history of the Church.'

'How was that, Martin?' asked Mr Power.

Mr Cunningham held up two thick fingers.

'In the sacred college, you know, of cardinals and archbishops and bishops there were two men who held out against it while

the others were all for it. The whole conclave except these two
was unanimous. No! They wouldn't have it!'

'Ha!' said Mr M'Coy.

'And they were a German cardinal by the name of Dolling . . .
or Dowling . . . or—'

'Dowling was no German, and that's a sure five,' said Mr
Power, laughing.

'Well, this great German cardinal, whatever his name was, was
one; and the other was John MacHale.'

'What?' cried Mr Kernan. 'Is it John of Tuam?'

'Are you sure of that now?' asked Mr Fogarty dubiously. 'I
thought it was some Italian or American.'

'John of Tuam,' repeated Mr Cunningham, 'was the man.'

He drank and the other gentlemen followed his lead. Then he
resumed:

'There they were at it, all the cardinals and bishops and archbishops from all the ends of the earth and these two fighting dog
and devil until at last the Pope himself stood up and declared
infallibility a dogma of the Church *ex cathedra*. On the very
moment John MacHale, who had been arguing and arguing
against it, stood up and shouted out with the voice of a lion:
''*Credo!*'''

'*I believe!*' said Mr Fogarty.

'*Credo!*' said Mr Cunningham. 'That showed the faith he had.
He submitted the moment the Pope spoke.'

'And what about Dowling?' asked Mr M'Coy.

'The German cardinal wouldn't submit. He left the Church.'

Mr Cunningham's words had built up the vast image of the
Church in the minds of his hearers. His deep, raucous voice had
thrilled them as it uttered the word of belief and submission.
When Mrs Kernan came into the room, drying her hands, she
came into a solemn company. She did not disturb the silence,
but leaned over the rail at the foot of the bed.

'I once saw John MacHale,' said Mr Kernan, 'and I'll never
forget it as long as I live.'

He turned towards his wife to be confirmed.

'I often told you that?'

Mrs Kernan nodded.

'It was at the unveiling of Sir John Gray's statue. Edmund Dwyer Gray was speaking, blathering away, and here was this old fellow, crabbed-looking old chap, looking at him from under his bushy eyebrows.'

Mr Kernan knitted his brows and, lowering his head like an angry bull, glared at his wife.

'God!' he exclaimed, resuming his natural face, 'I never saw such an eye in a man's head. It was as much as to say: *I have you properly taped, my lad.* He had an eye like a hawk.'

'None of the Grays was any good,' said Mr Power.

There was a pause again. Mr Power turned to Mrs Kernan and said with abrupt joviality:

'Well, Mrs Kernan, we're going to make your man here a good holy pious and God-fearing Roman Catholic.'

He swept his arm round the company inclusively.

'We're all going to make a retreat together and confess our sins—and God knows we want it badly.'

'I don't mind,' said Mr Kernan, smiling a little nervously.

Mrs Kernan thought it would be wiser to conceal her satisfaction. So she said:

'I pity the poor priest that has to listen to your tale.'

Mr Kernan's expression changed.

'If he doesn't like it,' he said bluntly, 'he can . . . do the other thing. I'll just tell him my little tale of woe. I'm not such a bad fellow—'

Mr Cunningham intervened promptly.

'We'll all renounce the devil,' he said, 'together, not forgetting his works and pomps.'

'Get behind me, Satan!' said Mr Fogarty, laughing and looking at the others.

Mr Power said nothing. He felt completely out-generalled. But a pleased expression flicked across his face.

'All we have to do,' said Mr Cunningham, 'is to stand up with lighted candles in our hands and renew our baptismal vows.'

'O, don't forget the candle, Tom,' said Mr M'Coy, 'whatever you do.'

'What?' said Mr Kernan. 'Must I have a candle?'

'O yes,' said Mr Cunningham.

'No, damn it all,' said Mr Kernan sensibly, 'I draw the line there. I'll do the job right enough. I'll do the retreat business and confession, and ... all that business. But ... no candles! No, damn it all, I bar the candles!'

He shook his head with farcical gravity.

'Listen to that!' said his wife.

'I bar the candles,' said Mr Kernan, conscious of having created an effect on his audience and continuing to shake his head to and fro. 'I bar the magic-lantern business.'

Everyone laughed heartily.

'There's a nice Catholic for you!' said his wife.

'No candles!' repeated Mr Kernan obdurately. 'That's off!'

The transept of the Jesuit Church in Gardiner Street was almost full; and still at every moment gentlemen entered from the side door and, directed by the lay-brother, walked on tiptoe along the aisles until they found seating accommodation. The gentlemen were all well dressed and orderly. The light of the lamps of the church fell upon an assembly of black clothes and white collars, relieved here and there by tweeds, on dark mottled pillars of green marble and on lugubrious canvases. The gentlemen sat in the benches, having hitched their trousers slightly above their knees and laid their hats in security. They sat well back and gazed formally at the distant speck of red light which was suspended before the high altar.

In one of the benches near the pulpit sat Mr Cunningham and Mr Kernan. In the bench behind sat Mr M'Coy alone: and in the bench behind him sat Mr Power and Mr Fogarty. Mr M'Coy had tried unsuccessfully to find a place in the bench with the others, and, when the party had settled down in the form of a quincunx he had tried unsuccessfully to make comic remarks. As these had not been well received, he had desisted. Even he was sensible of the decorous atmosphere and even he began to respond to the religious stimulus. In a whisper, Mr Cunningham drew Mr Kernan's attention to Mr Harford, the moneylender, who sat some distance off, and to Mr Fanning, the registration agent and mayor maker of the city, who was sitting immediately under the pulpit beside one of the newly elected councillors of the ward. To the right sat old Michael Grimes, the owner of three pawnbroker's shops, and Dan Hogan's nephew, who was up for the job in the Town Clerk's office. Farther in front sat Mr Hendrick, the chief reporter of *The Freeman's Journal*, and poor O'Carroll, an old friend of Mr Kernan's, who had been at one time a considerable commercial figure. Gradually, as he recognized familiar faces, Mr Kernan began to feel more at home. His hat, which had been rehabilitated by his wife, rested upon his knees. Once or twice he pulled down his cuffs with one hand while he held the brim of his hat lightly, but firmly, with the other hand.

A powerful-looking figure, the upper part of which was draped with a white surplice, was observed to be struggling up into the pulpit. Simultaneously the congregation unsettled, produced handkerchiefs and knelt upon them with care. Mr Kernan followed the general example. The priest's figure now stood upright in the pulpit, two-thirds of its bulk, crowned by a massive red face, appearing above the balustrade.

Father Purdon knelt down, turned towards the red speck of light and, covering his face with his hands, prayed. After an interval, he uncovered his face and rose. The congregation rose also and settled again on its benches. Mr Kernan restored his hat to its original position on his knee and presented an attentive face to the preacher. The preacher turned back each wide sleeve of his surplice with an elaborate large gesture and slowly surveyed the array of faces. Then he said:

'For the children of this world are wiser in their generation than the children of light. Wherefore make unto yourselves friends out of the mammon of iniquity so that when
you die they may receive you into everlasting dwellings.'

Father Purdon developed the text with resonant assurance. It was one of the most difficult texts in all the Scriptures, he said, to interpret properly. It was a text which might seem to the casual observer at variance with the lofty morality elsewhere preached by Jesus Christ. But, he told his hearers, the text had seemed to him specially adapted for the guidance of those whose lot it was to lead the life of the world and who yet wished to lead that life not in the manner of worldlings. It was a text for business men and professional men. Jesus Christ, with His divine understanding of every cranny of our human nature, understood that all men were not called to the religious life, that by far the vast majority were forced to live in the world, and, to a certain extent, for the world: and in this sentence He designed to give them a word of counsel, setting before them as exemplars in the religious life those very worshippers of Mammon who were of all men the least solicitous in matters religious.

He told his hearers that he was there that evening for no terrifying, no extravagant purpose; but as a man of the world speaking to his fellow-men. He came to speak to business men and he would speak to them in a businesslike way. If he might use the metaphor, he said, he was their spiritual accountant; and he wished each and every one of his hearers to open his books, the books of his spiritual life, and see if they tallied accurately with conscience.

Jesus Christ was not a hard taskmaster. He understood our little failings, understood the weakness of our poor fallen nature, understood the temptations of this life. We might have had, we all had from time to time, our temptations: we might have, we all had, our failings. But one thing only, he said, he would ask of his hearers. And that was: to be straight and manly with God. If their accounts tallied in every point to say:

'Well, I have verified my accounts. I find all well.'

But if, as might happen, there were some discrepancies, to admit the truth, to be frank and say like a man:

'Well, I have looked into my accounts. I find this wrong and this wrong. But, with God's grace, I will rectify this and this. I will set right my accounts.'

DING-DONG

Samuel Beckett

The Palace Bar off Westmoreland Street is also famous through-
out Dublin for its association with Ireland's leading journalists
and a coterie of literary figures including James Joyce and
Samuel Beckett whose portraits hang on the walls behind the
wood-panelled bar with its array of old casks and serving jugs.
Due to its close proximity to the Irish Times, *it has a reputation*
as a meeting place for newspapermen and for years there was a
corner of the bar known as the 'Intensive Care Unit' where
reporters were given their assignments for the day. The Palace
is also very popular with students and was one of the calling
places of Beckett's indolent and lascivious young man, Belacqua
Shulah, who appeared in some of his very first stories written in
the 1930s. These tales and their preoccupation with language, and
the failure of human beings to communicate, undoubtedly reflects
his own Dublin background and experiences as a young man.

Samuel Barclay Beckett (1906–89) was born into a comfort-
able middle-class Protestant family in Foxrock, near Dublin, and
studied at the city's Trinity College where he read English,
French and Italian. After teaching English and French abroad
for several years, he settled in Paris and published his first novel,
Murphy, *in 1938. International fame came several years later*
with the staging of his play, Waiting for Godot, *in Paris in*
January 1953. Thereafter Beckett became regarded as one of the
leading avant-garde authors of the day, writing his work first in
French and then translating it into English himself. 'Ding-Dong'
is an episode from his first collection of short stories, More Pricks
Than Kicks (1934), *in which Belacqua wanders listlessly from*

*Westmoreland Street along Pearse Street and then enters a pub
in Lombard Street. Here his quiet drink is about to be interrupted
by a strange woman selling 'Seats in Heaven' . . .*

*   *   *

Belacqua turned left into Lombard Street, the street of the sanitary
engineers, and entered a public-house. Here he was known, in
the sense that his grotesque exterior had long ceased to alienate
the curates and make them giggle, and to the extent that he was
served with his drink without having to call for it. This did not
always seem a privilege. He was tolerated, what was more, and
let alone by the rough but kindly habitués of the house, recruited
for the most part from among dockers, railwaymen and vague
joxers on the dole. Here also art and love, scrabbling in dispute
or staggering home, were barred, or, perhaps better, unknown.
The aesthetes and the impotent were far away.

These circumstances combined to make of this place a very
grateful refuge for Belacqua, who never omitted, when he found
himself in its neighbourhood with the price of a drink about him,
to pay it a visit.

When I enquired how he squared such visits with his anxiety
to keep on the move and his distress at finding himself brought
to a standstill, as when he had come out of the underground in
the mouth of College Street, he replied that he did not. 'Surely'
he said 'my resolution has the right to break down.' I supposed
so indeed. 'Or' he said 'if you prefer, I make the raid in two hops
instead of non-stop. From what' he cried 'does that disqualify me,
I should very much like to know.' I hastened to assure him that
he had a perfect right to suit himself in what, after all, was a
manœuvre of his own contriving, and that the raid, to adopt his
own term, lost nothing by being made in easy stages. 'Easy!' he
exclaimed, 'how easy?'

But notice the double response, like two holes to a burrow.

Sitting in this crapulent den, drinking his drink, he gradually
ceased to see its furnishings with pleasure, the bottles, rep-
resenting centuries of loving research, the stools, the counter,

the powerful screws, the shining phalanx of the pulls of the beer-engines, all cunningly devised and elaborated to further the relations between purveyor and consumer in this domain. The bottles drawn and emptied in a twinkling, the casks responding to the slightest pressure on their joysticks, the weary proletarians at rest on arse and elbow, the cash-register that never complains, the graceful curates flying from customer to customer, all this made up a spectacle in which Belacqua was used to take delight and chose to see a pleasant instance of machinery decently subservient to appetite. A great major symphony of supply and demand, effect and cause, fulcrate on the middle C of the counter and waxing, as it proceeded, in the charming harmonies of blasphemy and broken glass and all the aliquots of fatigue and ebriety. So that he would say that the only place where he could come to anchor and be happy was a low public-house and that all the wearisome tactics of gress and dud Beethoven would be done away with if only he could spend his life in such a place. But as they closed at ten, and as residence and good faith were viewed as incompatible, and as in any case he had not the means to consecrate his life to stasis, even in the meanest bar, he supposed he must be content to indulge this whim from time to time, and return thanks for such sporadic mercy.

All this and much more he laboured to make clear. He seemed to derive considerable satisfaction from his failure to do so.

But on this particular occasion the cat failed to jump, with the result that he became as despondent as though he were sitting at home in his own great armchair, as anxious to get on the move and quite as hard put to it to do so. Why this was he could not make out. Whether the trituration of the child in Pearse Street had upset him without his knowing it, or whether (and he put forward this alternative with a truly insufferable complacency) he had come to some parting of the ways, he did not know at all. All he could say was that the objects in which he was used to find such recreation and repose lost gradually their hold upon him, he became insensible to them little by little, the old itch and algos crept back into his mind. He had come briskly all the way from Tommy Moore, and now he suddenly found himself sitting paralysed and grieving in a pub of all places, good for nothing but to stare at his spoiling porter and wait for a sign.

To this day he does not know what caused him to look up, but look up he did. Feeling the impulse to do this strong upon him, he forced his eyes away from the glass of dying porter and was rewarded by seeing a hatless woman advancing slowly towards him up the body of the bar. No sooner had she come in than he must have become aware of her. That was surely very curious in the first instance. She seemed to be hawking some ware or other, but what it was he could not see, except that it was not studs or laces or matches or lavender or any of the usual articles. Not that it was unusual to find a woman in that public-house, for they came and went freely, slaking their thirst and beguiling their sorrows with no less freedom than their men-folk. Indeed it was always a pleasure to see them, their advances were always most friendly and honourable, Belacqua had many a delightful recollection of their commerce.

Hence there was no earthly reason why he should see in the advancing figure of this mysterious pedlar anything untoward, or in the nature of the sign in default of which he was clamped to his stool till closing-time. Yet the impulse to do so was so strong that he yielded to it, and as she drew nearer, having met with more rebuffs than pence in her endeavours to dispose of her wares, whatever they were, it became clear to him that his instinct had not played him false, in so far at least as she was a woman of very remarkable presence indeed.

Her speech was that of a woman of the people, but of a gentle-woman of the people. Her gown had served its time, but yet contrived to be respectable. He noticed with a pang that she sported about her neck the insidious little mock fur so prevalent in tony slumland. The one deplorable feature of her get up, as apprehended by Belacqua in his hasty survey, was the footwear—the cruel strait outsizes of the suffragette or welfare worker. But he did not doubt for a moment that they had been a gift, or picked up in the pop for a song. She was of more than average height and well in flesh. She might be past middle-age. But her face, ah her face, was what Belacqua had rather refer to as her countenance, it was so full of light. This she lifted up upon him and no error. Brimful of light and serene, serenissime, it bore no trace of suffering, and in this alone it might be said to be a notable face. Yet she tormented faces that he had seen, like the face in the National Gallery in Merrion Square by the Master of Tired Eyes, it seemed to have come a long way and subtend an infinitely narrow angle of affliction, as eyes focus a star. The feature were null, only luminous, impassive and secure, petrified in radiance, or words to that effect, for the reader is requested to take notice that this sweet style is Belacqua's. An act of expression, he said, a wreathing or wrinkling, could only have had the effect of a dimmer on a headlight. The implications of this triumphant figure, the just and the unjust, etc., are better forgone.

At long last she addressed herself to Belacqua.

'Seats in heaven' she said in a white voice 'tuppence apiece, four fer a tanner.'

'No,' said Belacqua. It was the first syllable to come to his lips. It had not been his intention to deny her.

'The best of seats' she said 'again I'm sold out. Tuppence apiece the best of seats, four fer a tanner.'

This was unforeseen with a vengeance, if not exactly vaudeville. Belacqua was embarrassed in the last degree, but transported also. He felt the sweat coming in the small of his back, above his Montrouge belt.

'Have you got them on you?' he mumbled.

'Heaven goes round' she said, whirling her arm, 'and round and round and round and round.'

'Yes' said Belacqua 'round and round.'

'Rowan' she said, dropping the d's and getting more of a spin into the slogan, 'rowan an' rowan an' rowan.'

Belacqua scarcely knew where to look. Unable to blush he came out in this beastly sweat. Nothing of the kind had ever happened to him before. He was altogether disarmed, unsaddled and miserable. The eyes of them all, the dockers, the railwaymen and, most terrible of all, the joxers, were upon him. His tail drooped. This female dog of a pixy with her tiresome Ptolemy, he was at her mercy.

'No' he said 'no thank you, no not this evening thank you.'

'Again I'm sold out' she said 'an' buked out, four fer a tanner.'

'On those authority . . .' began Belacqua, like a Scholar.

'For yer frien' ' she said 'yer da, yer ma an' yer motte, four fer a tanner.' The voice ceased, but the face did not abate.

'How do I know' piped Belacqua 'you're not sellin' me a pup?'

'Heaven goes rowan an' rowan . . .'

'Rot you' said Belacqua 'I'll take two. How much is that?'

'Four dee' she said.

Belacqua gave her a sixpence.

'Gobbless yer honour' she said, in the same white voice from which she had not departed. She made to go.

'Here' cried Belacqua 'you owe me twopence.' He had not even the good grace to say tuppence.

'Arragowan' she said 'make it four cantcher, yer frien', yer da, yer ma an' yer motte.'

Belacqua could not bicker. He had not the strength of mind for that. He turned away.

'Jesus' she said distinctly 'and his sweet mother preserve yer honour.'

'Amen' said Belacqua, into his dead porter.

Now the woman went away and her countenance lighted her to her room in Townsend Street.

But Belacqua tarried a little to listen to the music. Then he also departed, but for Railway Street, beyond the river.

PETER McCABE'S BARGAIN

Patrick Kavanagh

Patrick Kavanagh was another regular of the Palace Bar and there is a drawing by Alan Reeve entitled 'Dublin Culture' which shows him and a number of other writers including Lynn Doyle, Maurice Walsh and Flann O'Brien at a literary gathering in the 1940s. This pub—and a number of others in the city—are featured in several of Kavanagh's articles, short stories and, especially, his poetry. Among the best of these verses which capture the wayward character of their creator are 'If Ever You Go to Dublin Town,' 'Mermaid Tavern', 'Sensational Disclosures' and the classic, 'The Paddiad; or, The Devil as a Patron of Irish Letters'. This wonderful satire on literary Dublin was clearly modelled on Alexander Pope's 'The Dunciad' and substitutes Irish paddies for the English poet's dunces and a contemporary Dublin pub for the Grub street of eighteenth-century London. The central character Paddy Conscience, who makes fun of a bevy of Irish writers while drinking in the Pearl Bar, is clearly Paddy Kavanagh himself. When published, it infuriated several of the victims and it is not difficult to understand why Frank O'Connor later referred to Kavanagh as 'one of the strayed revellers of the Irish literary revival'.

Despite his fame as a poet and author, Patrick Kavanagh lived much of his life in straitened circumstances, his health blighted by alcoholism. He was born in Inniskeen, County Monaghan, the son of a cobbler-cum-small farmer. Leaving school at the age of twelve he seemed destined to work on the land until some of his poems were spotted by the critic AE (George Russell). These began to appear in Irish and English periodicals, to whom he

*also contributed weekly columns and articles. His first book of
verse,* Ploughman and Other Poems, *appeared in 1938, to be
followed by his autobiographical book,* The Green Fool *(1938).
By Kavanagh's own admission,* The Green Fool *was influenced
by the work of one of his favourite authors, William Carleton,
who hailed from the neighbouring county of Tyrone. The book
was apparently set in Inniskeen, though he changed the name of
many of the places and people who filled the lively chapters about
rural weddings, deaths and religious celebrations. Years after its
publication, Kavanagh confessed, 'I invented so many stories
about myself in* The Green Fool *to illustrate my own unique
character that I don't know myself what's true about me and
what isn't!' In 1948, he published* Tarry Flynn, *also inspired by
Carleton's* Traits and Stories of the Irish Peasantry, *a comical
account of the life of a high-spirited young farmer in the 1930s.
Despite again disguising Inniskeen as Dargan in County Cavan,
the book was banned in Ireland for several weeks until this was
lifted by the Appeal Board. Subsequently,* Tarry Flynn *has been
acknowledged as 'the best and most authentic account of life as
it was lived in Ireland in the first half of the twentieth century'
and reprinted several times in paperback. Among the magazines
to which Kavanagh contributed was* The Bell *for whom he wrote
the following sardonic tale of an outrageous confidence trick in
August 1951. It marks the first republication of the story which
is very reminiscent in some passages to Carleton's* Traits and
Stories . . .

*   *   *

Peter McCabe had in the bank in dry money something around
seven thousand pounds. Most of it he had scraped together but
he had had one lucky break when he bought a little out-of-the-way
pub and re-sold it.

About a mile from Channonsmill on the edge of the parish of
Kilking there was a pub which drew on an average twelve customers each year. It was one of those pubs which had to survive
on the fame of oul' decency. It was a child of what might be

called the quarry or stone-rush when the new railway was being made, and like inns and towns of a loftier coinage dereliction came down upon it when the stoney industry was let overgrow with weeds. Everyone agreed that it was the real oul' timer but it being in off the main roads and in a thinly populated district, since the closing of the quarry where the stones for the railway were got, everyone went for his drinks to the pub in the village.

The widow who owned the place was more than surprised when Peter offered to buy it and—like the horse dealers in their astuteness—she was sure that Peter McCabe was mad. He was acting like one of those rich men who have apparently poor ideas of making a bargain, but the women did not know that that apparent foolishness is one of their most valuable qualifications for the profession of millionaire.

He bought the pub, painted it a bit and then in some remote country newspapers advertised it for sale.

A man who had been a railway stationmaster in Roscommon answered the advertisement. Arrangements were made for him to inspect the premises and Peter in a letter suggested a certain day and hour.

The man called at the appointed hour but was unable to get inside the pub owing to the crowd and was unable to make himself heard to Peter—who was rushing from tap to tap filling pints and half-ones—because of the general bedlam of good fellowship.

'Four pints here, Peter.'

'Can't yous wait, damn yous.'

The man from Roscommon lingered near the door trying to catch the eye of the busy publican but that man was already an expert in the art of ignoring, and so the man at the door had to be content. Eventually Peter saw him and asked him was it a pint he wanted.

'No.'

'What?'

'Another couple here, Peter.'

'I'm the man from Roscommon.'

'What? Oh, will you wait a minute? You can see the hobble I'm in with this crowd that would kill a man for a pint.'

The Roscommon man was brought into a snug where the shoe-maker, Jemmy Papper, Johnie Toal, two of the Kennys and a few others were upholding the respectable end of that pub's trade.

The man was offered a drink but refused; he was a teetotaler.

The Kennys with all their own roguery of heart were anxious to give the man the wink but the cobbler and Jemmy kept the poor man covered. The cobbler was shouting at the top of his voice ridiculous things: 'Luckiest house from here to hell. Terrible great business. A dacent man like you—there's good good-ness in your face—a dacent man like you will do well here . . . Peter, fill them again.' That was the set-up.

Peter left Jemmy and one of the Kennys to take charge of the house while he, the cobbler and the man from Roscommon went in Peter's side-car to the Mill House.

The man was flabbergasted when he saw the splendours of the mill and the Mill House. He knew that the man who owned such property was a safe man to have dealings with.

Peter's wife and children had received curt orders to remove themselves from the conference table.

'Do you see that mill out there?' said Peter. He waited for an answer to show that his question was really important and not a rhetorical one.

'I do,' said the man.

'Barney,' Peter turned to the cobbler, 'tell this man where I made the money to buy that mill.'

'Every penny in that pub up the road,' said Barney faithfully.

After that the selling of the premises was easy. The price arranged was one which was exactly—as the cobbler had learned from the Roscommon man—the total of the stationmaster's life savings.

He was unmarried and this eased whatever conscience the rogues around the table might have had.

He took possession of the pub in a few weeks. He employed a barman—and then waited for the crowds to arrive with thirsts like a steam engine with a leaky boiler.

He waited a week and a month and the only customers he had were three tinkers who offered him tin poringers in lieu of cash. He waited another month and by this time one could see that he was beginning to feel queer. Nobody told him direct that he had been diddled. He might easily have got his money back had he gone to court and proved, as he could, that a gross fraud had been perpetrated. Instead of that he went mad, melancholic. He took to prayer.

Then one night his body was found in the river beyond the Kilking mill. The foreman of the coroner's jury that sat at the inquest was the cobbler, who proposed a rider to the usual verdict of suicide while of unsound mind, that the county council should be asked to erect a paling along the river at this point. Peter McCabe promised to bring the matter up at the next meeting.

THE HEAT OF THE SUN

Sean O'Faolain

Rodger's Pub in this next story is always referred to as 'Uncle Alfie's' because of the barman who runs the place. An imposing figure in his white apron with a bowler hat permanently lodged on his receding red hair, he knows everyone. *And Alfie not only knows his customers and what they like to drink, but all the local gossip and scandal to satisfy their curiosity, too. Rumour has it that the barman has a wife and kids somewhere—although he seems to be anti-women—yet he's always willing to hand out advice to some of the younger men looking for girls. It's what happens when 'Uncle Alfie' is suddenly missing from behind the bar and the drinkers in Rodger's Pub begin to worry they have lost their man, that events take a very unexpected turn.*

    Sean O'Faolain (1900–91), father of Julia O'Faolain, was for years a leading figure in the Irish cultural world and apart from his varied short stories, and fine novels, edited the influential magazine, The Bell. *Born the son of a policeman in Dublin, he grew up in Cork City and worked for the Republican side in the Irish Civil War as publicity officer. He studied at the National University of Ireland and Harvard University, taught at a teacher training college near London, then returned to Ireland. His* Midsummer Night Madness and Other Stories *(1932) and* A Nest of Simple Folk *(1933) received widespread acclaim. O'Faolain also produced several biographies of leading Irish political figures. His short stories, though, are particularly highly regarded for the manner in which they display his deep understanding of the ordinary people of Ireland and the way they go about their everyday lives in homes, communities and pubs. 'The Heat of the Sun' was first published in 1966.*

*   *   *

They never said, 'Let's go down to Rodgers', although it was old Rodgers who owned the pub; they said, 'Let's go down to Uncle Alfie.' A good pub is like that, it is the barman who makes it, not the boss. They gave their custom to Rodgers, they gave their confidence to Alfie. He knew them all, some of them ever since they were old enough to drink their first pint in a pub. He knew their fathers, mothers, brothers, sisters, girls, prospects, wages, hopes, fears and what they were always calling their ideas and their ideals and that he called their ould guff. Always their friend, sometimes their philosopher, he was rarely their guide. Your da gave you money (sometimes) and you hardly thanked him for it. Alfie loaned it. Your da gave you advice and you resented it. Alfie could give you a rap as sharp as lightning, and you accepted it because he gave it as your equal. Your da never had any news. Alfie knew everything. He was your postman, passing on bits of paper with messages in pencil: 'Deirdre was asking for you, try 803222, Hughesy.' Or, 'For Jay's sake leave a half-note for me, Paddywhack.' He might hand you out a coloured postcard with a foreign stamp, taken from the little sheaf stuck behind the cash register. The sheeting around the register was as wall-papered as a Travel Bureau with coloured postcards from all over the world. Best of all, he was there always: his coat off, his shirtsleeves rolled up, his bowler hat always on his balding red head, a monument in a white apron, with a brogue like an echo in an empty barrel.

You pushed the two glass doors in like a king.

'Hi, Alfie!'

'Jazus, Johnny, is that yourself?' With a slap on the shoulder and your drink slid in front of you unasked. 'Fwhere were you this time? Did yoo have a good voyage?'

'Not bad. Same old thing—Black Sea, the Piraeus, Palermo, Naples, Genoa. Crumby dumps!' Your half pint aloft. What's the best port in all creation, Alfie?'

'As if you needed to ask me!'

'Here's to it, and God bless it. *Dublin town, O Dublin Town / That's where I long to be, / With the friends so dear to me, / Grafton Street where it's all so gay. / And the lights of Scotsman's Bay.* Theme-song of every poor bloody exile of Erin. Up the rebels. Long live the Queen of Sheba. How's Tommy? How's Angela? How's Casey, Joanna, Hughesy, Paddywhack? Does my little black-eyed Deirdre still love me?'

'Paddy was in on Chuesday night. He's working with the Gas Company now.'

'Poor old Paddywhack! Has he the gold wristlet still? And the signet ring? Will the poor bugger never get a decent job?'

'His wife had another child. That's six he has now.'

'Sacred Heart!'

'Hughesy is going strong with Flossie.'

(He noticed that Deirdre was being passed over.)

'Sure that line is four years old. When is the bastard going to make an honest woman of her?'

'Is it a busman? She's aiming higher than that. The trouble with yoo young fellows is ye pick gurls beyond yeer means. Yeer eyes are bigger than yeer balls. Leave them their youth. Wedded, bedded and deaded, the world knows it.'

He was anti-woman. Everybody knew he had a wife somewhere, and three kids, separated five years ago. She was before their time—none of them had ever seen her. Poor old Alfie! In hope and in dreams and in insecurity is life. In home and in safety is . . . He should know, he had it every time he came home. Like tonight:

'Oh, no! Johnny! You're not going out from us on your first night home? We haven't seen you for four months! And your father and me looking forward to a nice bit of a chat. About your future, Johnny. About your plans, Johnny. About your prospects. Sit down there now and be talking to us.'

You sat back. They talked. You mumbled. The end of it was always the same. After another half-hour of twitching you said it again.

'I think I'll drop down to Uncle Alfie for an hour to see the boys. I won't be late, Mum. But leave the key under the mat. Don't wait up for me, I'll creep in like a mouse.'

Hating the way they looked at one another, knowing well that you wouldn't be in before one in the morning—if then—shoes in hand, head cocked for the slightest tweak of a bedspring upstairs, feeling a right bastard or, if with God's help, you were tight enough, feeling nothing but your way. Hell roast 'em! Why couldn't they understand that when you cabled, 'Coming home Thursday stop love stop Johnny,' it meant you wanted to see them okay, and you were bringing presents for them, okay, and it would be nice to have your own old room, okay, but what you were really seeing was the gleam of the bottles, and the wet mahogany, and the slow, floating layers of smoke, shoulders pushing, hands shooting, everybody talking at the top of his voice to be heard and old Alfie grinning at ye all like an ape. God Almighty! When a fellow has only seven lousy days' shore leave . . .

It was dry October, the softest twinge of faintest fog, the streets empty, a halo around every light, a right night for a landfall. Tramping downhill, peaked cap slanted, whistling, he foresaw it all. A dollar to a dime on it—Alfie would resume exactly where they left off four months ago:

'Johnny! It is high time yoo thought of settling down.'

'Gimme a chance, Alfie. I'm only twenty-three. I'll settle down some day. Why don't you say that to Loftus or Casey?'

'Loftus will find it hard. With that short leg. Anyway I mean settled down ashore. That wandering life you're leading! It's no life!'

'I'm not ready, Alfie. I want to meet the right girl. I'm mad about Deirdre, but she's always talking about motorcars, and houses in Foxrock, and Sunday morning sherry parties. I'm not sure of her. The right girl is damn hard to find. It's a funny thing, Alfie, all the nice women I meet are married women.'

'An ould shtory. And the ladies tell me all the nice men are married men. I think the truth is that no wan is ready until they know by heart the music that tames the wild bashte—know it and are beginning to forget it. I don't think Deirdre is the right sawrt for you at all, Johnny. She's too expensive for you. She's too ambitious. She's like Flossie—playing with Hughesy, trying to learn the chune on the cheap, as you might say. Johnny! If I were you, I'd choose a woman of experience. What'd suit you, now, down to the ground would be a nice, soft, cosy, widow-woman that knows every chune in the piper's bag.'

'Oh, for God's sake, Alfie! With a wooden leg? And a yellow wig? And a blue band-book? I'm young, Alfie. What I dream about, in the middle watch, looking up at the stars, is a young, beautiful, exquisite, lovely, fond, right-dimensional Irish girl of eighteen. Like my little Deirdre. Pure as the driven snow. Loyal and true. Gentle as the dawn. Deirdre, without the motor-car!'

Alfie would draw up from the counter and make a face as if he was sucking alum.

'You could sing it if yoo had the voice for it. "*She was luvely and fair, as the roase of the Summer, But it was not her beauutye aloane tha-at won me . . .*"'

He would snatch it from him tonight:

'"*Oh no! 'Twas the truth in her eyes ever dawning. That made me love Mary, the Rose of Tra-a-leee.*" A hundred per cent right, Alfie. Lead me to her.'

'I wouldn't give you two pinnies for a gurl of eighteen—she couldn't cook an egg for you. And dimensions are all very fine and dandy, but they don't lasht, boy. They don't lasht! Did I ever tell yoo about the fellow that married the opera singer? She was like an angel out of heaven on the stage. In the bed she was no better to him than an ould shweeping brush. He used to wake her up in the middle of the night and say, "Sing, damn yoor sowl!"'

Aboard ship he had told them that one many times. Always the old deck-hands would nod solemnly and say, 'And e's dead right, chum! Feed me and love me, what more can a man ask for?' Well, if he said it tonight he would be ready for him; drawing himself up, with one hand flat on his top, left, brass button:

'Alfie! In this rotten, cheating, stinking, lousy, modern world my generation is going to *fight* for our ideals!'

Four miles out over the shadow sea the light on the Kish bank winked drowsily. Fog? It was so quiet along the promenade that he could hear the small waves below him sucking into the rocks. Wind soft from the south. The only person he passed was a Civic Guard in a cape. He turned right, then left, passed the Coal Harbour, wheeled right again, left, and there were the lights flowing out on the pavement. He pushed the two glass doors in like a king.

'Hi! . . .'

He stopped. The young barman was staring at him with uplifted eyebrows. He looked around. The place was like a morgue. He recognized old Molly Goosegog, her fat legs spread, soaking it up as usual with the one-armed colonel. Three business types, their hats on, hunched over a table, talking low. In the farthest corner two middle-aged women were drinking gins and bitters. Dyed, dried, skewered and skivered, two old boiling hens, cigarettes dangled from their red beaks. He moved slowly to the counter.

'Where's Alfie?' he asked quietly.

'On leave.'

'Alfie never took leave in his life unless he took leave of his senses.'

'Well, he's on leave now. What can I get you, sir?'

Sir! Sullenly he said, 'A large whiskey,' although he had been planning a night of draught porter. Alfie would have said, 'Johnny! There is no such thing on earth as a *large* whiskey.' Or he might have said nothing but come back with a half pint of draught and said, 'That'll be better for you.'

Was it because it was Thursday night? Nobody much ever came on Thursday night: less even than came on Friday night. Everyone stony. Behold my beeves and fatlings are all killed, and nobody cometh to eat them. Seven lousy nights and the first a flop? Go forth into the highways and by-ways. From pub to pub? The whiskey appeared before him. The barman stood waiting. He looked up.

'Four and sixpence, sir.'

With Alfie, you let it run for a week, for two, for three, for as long as you liked. Then you asked, 'What's on the slate, Alfie?'

and, if you were flush, you paid a half-note over and above for
future credit. Man knoweth not the hour nor the night. He paid
out four shillings and a sixpenny bit. The barman rang it up and
retired down the counter to lean over his *Herald*.

'How long is Alfie going to be on leave?'

The fellow barely glanced up.

'I don't know, I'm only here this past two weeks.'

'Is the boss in?'

'He's gone down to the chapel. The October Devotions.'

Thinking of his latter end. *Dies irae, dies illae.* Back in New-
bridge with the Dominicans. All Souls Night. He glanced at the
door. Would there be anyone down at The Blue Peter? Or in
Mooney's? Maybe in The Purty Kitchen?'

'Any message for me there behind the old cashbox?'

'Name?'

'Kendrick.'

The barman, his back to him, went through the light sheaf.
Without turning he said, 'Nothing,' shoved it back and returned
to his *Herald*. Out of sight out of mind. Bugger the whole lousy
lot of them! And Deirdre along with them! The glass doors
swished open and there were Paddywhack and Loftus. He leaped
from his stool.

'Hi, scouts!'

'Johnny!'

Handshakes all round. Paddy was as hungry-looking as a dis-
placed Arab. His shirtsleeves too long. The gold wristlet. The
signet ring. Loftus, as always, as lean and yellow as a Dane.
Hoppity Loftus with his short leg. He never worked. He was a
Prod and had an English accent, and he lived off his mother. All
he did was to get her breakfast in the morning and have her
supper ready for her at night. She worked in the Sweep.

'Name it, boys! I'm standing!'

Paddy looked thirstily at the glass of whiskey.

'Are you on the hard tack?'

'Naw! Just this bloody place gave me the willies. The usual?'
He commanded the barman. 'Two halfpints. Make it three and
I'll use this as a chaser. God, it's marvellous to see ye! Come

on, come on! Give! Give! Gimme all the dirt. Tell me more, tell
me all. Are you still with the Gas Company, Paddy?'

'I'm with a house-agent now. Looney and Cassidy. In Dame
Street.' He made a fish-face. 'NBG Paid on commission. Just to
tide me over a bad patch.' He laughed cheerfully. 'The wife is
preggers again.'

'Paddy! I dunno how you do it.'

'I'm told,' said Loftus lightly, 'that it's a very simple matter,
really.'

'How's your mother, Loftus?'

A rude question. Loftus shrugged it away. They took their
drinks to one of the round tables. Paddy lifted his glass.

'Johnny! You don't know how lucky you are. A steady job,
cash in your pocket, a girl in every port.'

'And as brown,' said Loftus lifting his glass, 'and as round as
a football.'

'Me round?' he shouted, ripped open the jacket of his uniform
and banged his narrow waist. 'Feel that, go on, feel it! Hard
as iron, boy! Eight stone ten. You,' he said condescendingly,
rebuttoning, 'must be about ten stone eight.' He paused. Then
he had to say it: 'Does Deirdre still love me?'

Loftus's eyes glinted as he proffered the sponge on the spear.

'I saw her two weeks ago in a red Triumph. A medical student
from Trinity, I believe. She looked smashing.'

His heart curdled, his throat tightened, he laughed loudly.

'So the little bitch is betraying me, eh?'

He could see her, with her dark hair curled down on one
shoulder as if she had a monkey on her head. The red lips. The
high bosoms.

'It's just because you're not around much,' Paddy said comfort-
ingly. 'Wait until she hears you're home!'

'How are all those girls of yours?' Loftus smiled. 'In foreign
parts.'

Paddy poured sad oil.

'Too bad about poor Alfie?'

'I heard nothing,' he said sourly. 'Nobody writes to me. Where
is the ould devil!'

'You didn't know! Hospice for the Dying. Cancer. These last three months. It'll be any day now.'

It gagged him. There was a long silence. His first death. The double doors let in Hughesy and Flossie; their oldest and youngest—a blonde mop, black lashes, a good looker, but not a patch on his D. Their welcomes were muted. They sat down stiffly like people who did not mean to stay.

' "Here," ' he chanted mournfully, ' "here, the gang's all here." '

'Not all of us,' Paddy said.

'This is a committee meeting, really,' Hughesy said, taking charge of it at once. 'Well?' he asked Paddywhack and Loftus. 'How much can we raise?'

'We're gathering for Mrs Alfie,' Paddywhack explained. 'She hadn't a sou.'

'I managed to borrow five bob,' Flossie said, taking two half-crowns from inside her glove and laying them on the table.

'That,' said Hughesy, putting down half a crown, 'is all I can manage.'

Paddywhack squirmed and said, 'Six kids and another coming, and Thursday night.'

Loftus showed empty palms. 'Unless I could pop something?'

He felt worse than a wanderer—a stranger.

'Mrs Alfie? How in God's name did ye meet *her*?' he asked Hughesy.

'It was Alfie asked us to keep an eye on her and the kids. I saw him again today,' he told the others.

'How is he?' he asked.

Hughesy looked away.

'Alas, poor Yorick,' Loftus said. 'A skull!'

Flossie began to cry.

'But where's the rest of the gang? Joanna, and Tommy, and Angela and Casey.'

He stopped short of Deirdre. Paddywhack shook his head and made faint gestures.

'I nearly didn't come myself. Can you manage anything, Johnny?'

He took out his pocketbook and planked down a pound note.

'Good man!' said Hughesy, and looked up at the barman standing over them, and down at the pound note. He smiled apologetically at Johnny. 'Any more of that nice stuff?'

'Come on, scouts, I'm standing. If it's to be a wake, for Christ's sake let it be a wake. What's yours, Flossie? Still sticking to the dry sherry? Hughesy? The old pint?' He nodded to the barman, who departed silently. 'Let me in on this. Tell me all about Alfie.'

As the drinks warmed them they walked. A man, by God! A true friend if there ever was one. They don't often come like that nowadays. True from his bald head to the soles of his feet. Tried and true. A son of the soil. A bit of old Ireland. Vanishing down the drain. Not one bit of cold about him. His jokes . . . We shall not look upon his like again. The pound note melted. Paddywhack said, 'Life is a mystery all right. She looks such a nice woman, and she *is* a nice woman, and full of guts, not one word of complaint, and three kids. What in God's name happened to them?' They told him, asking how she lived, that she used to work as a dressmaker. 'Yes, he did!' Loftus answered him. 'After a fashion, he did. He supported her. After a fashion.' Flossie said she would never come to this pub again. They agreed with Hughesy that Dublin wouldn't be the same without him. She said the fact was he had nothing to do with all those . . . They followed her eyes down to Molly Goosegog and the one-armed colonel, and the three business types, and the two boiled hakes with the gins and bitters. Hughesy slapped the table. 'And that's a true bill, Flossie! He was one of us. Old in body but young in heart. You agree, Johnny?' He agreed that Alfie was the only man he ever met who understood them. 'He fought for his ideals.' They talked of understanding, and ideals, and truth, and true love, and how well Alfie understood what it means to be young, and to believe in things, that was it—to believe in things. A second pound was melting, and it was after ten, when Flossie said to Hughesy that she must go home soon.

'Mind your few quid, Johnny,' Hughesy said. 'What's left there will be enough. A dozen bottles of stout, say a dozen and a half. Just to cheer her up. We'll drop around for a minute, Flossie. Just to cheer her up.'

'One for the road,' he insisted, and held them. They leaned back.

It was nearly eleven when they left in a bunch, carrying the three brown-paper bags of stout, out into the dry streets, the nebulous night, under the dim stars and the gathering clouds that were lit by the city's glow. Loftus said it was a fine night for a ramble. Hughesy laughed and said, 'Or for courting.' Two by two, hooting merrily backwards and forwards at one another, they wound up among shaggy, dim-lit squares with names like Albert Gardens, Aldershot Place or Portland Square, all marked on green and white tablets in Irish and English, until they came to a basement door and, stepping down to it, rang and waited in a bunch under a stone arch. In the dark they were suddenly silent, listening. A light went on over the door. She opened it.

Alfie's youth. She was soft and welcoming. All the parts of her face seemed to be running into one another, dissolving like ice-cream in the sun, her mouth melting, her blue-blue eyes swimming. A loose tress of her grey-fair hair flowed over a high forehead. Her voice was as timid as butter. She was not a bad-looking woman, and for a moment a little flame of youth flared up in her when they introduced him to her, and she laughed softly and said, 'So this is Johnny! He said you were the baby of the lot.' She held his hand in her two hands, moist and warm as if she had been washing something, and he remembered a line from a poem they used to read at school, long forgotten, never understood. *Fear no more the heat of the sun* . . .

'Glad to meet you, Mrs Alfie,' he said and realized for the first time that he did not know Alfie's name.

'We brought a few drinks,' Hughesy explained. 'Just to brighten the night.'

'Come in, boys, come in. Talk low,' she begged. 'Jenny is only just gone to sleep.'

The low room was small and untidy, and smelled of soap. The fire was ashen. She had only two glasses. They sat in a circle and drank out of cups, or from the bottle-necks. Moist cloths hung drooping and wet on a line: the stuffing of the chairs tufted out, he saw a toy horse with three legs, torn green paperbacks, a house-of-cards half collapsed on a tray. Staring at her, he heard nothing of their whispering; both surprised and pleased to hear her laugh so often. He became aware that Hughesy and Flossie were fading out, for the last bus. Around midnight Paddywhack said he must give the wife a hand with the kids, and slid away. She put a few bits of sticks in the grate and tried ineffectually to remake the fire. Then Loftus clumped off home to his mother and there were only the two of them in the room, stooping over one flicker in the ashes, whispering, heads together.

Only once again did she mention Alfie; when she said, 'They're a grand bunch. ye are all good boys. Decent young men. It was what he always said about ye.'

'Did you see him often?'

'Hardly at all. He might drop in after he shut the pub. To see the children. He told me he was always at ye to settle down. Hughesy, and Flossie, and Casey, and Loftus and you. Do you like Loftus?'

'He's cold. And bitter.'

'Is Deirdre your girl?'

'Yes. But I think she's letting me down. Did you meet her? She's a smasher.'

'She is a beautiful girl. I don't want to interfere in your life, Johnny, but I would be inclined to think that I would nearly say that she might have a hard streak in her.'

'Not like you?' he smiled.

'I'm not faulting her. A woman must think of her own good.'

There he was off, full-cock, about youth, ideals, loyalty, truth, honesty, love, things that only the gang understood, everybody else talking to you about your future, and good jobs, and making money. 'Ireland is the last fortress. The Noah's Ark of the world. No place like it.' And he should know, an exile! She agreed, she agreed. She said, 'The people here are warm and natural still in spite of all.' He was with her, all the way with her. 'We are not materialists. Not the best of us.' At that they were both off, whispering breaking into louder talk, hushing, glancing fearfully at the door of the bedroom.

The last flicker of the fire died away. They drank the last bottle of stout between them, passing it from mouth to mouth. Her voice grew softer, her hand when she held his was padded like a cat's. The night became a fugitive. Faintly a foghorn in the bay moaned through a muffled blanket. He looked out and up through the window and saw a yellow blur of street light, and the mist that clung wetly to a fogged tree. She got up to make tea. He followed her into the messy kitchen to help and talk. They came back and she put a few more futile chips of sticks on the warm ashes. She laughed at the slightest thing—when the toy horse toppled, or when he told her about the dog, kicked, and beaten, and mangy, that he bought in Palermo, and how it swam ashore back to its Moorish slum. Or that night in Odessa in the YMCA when he got into a fight by pretending the C stood for Communist.

When it was two o'clock he said, 'You must send me away.' She said, 'Listen to the dripping outside. Oh, don't go away, Johnny!' He said, 'You must sleep.' She said, 'I don't know what sleep is,' and held him by his wrist, frightened to be left alone. 'Listen to the drip-drop,' she wheedled. 'And look! It's yellow as mustard outside. Sleep here. Sleep in my bed. We're friends, aren't we? Just lie and sleep. You're a good boy. I know you. Go in there and lie down.' She led him into the bedroom with its unmade bed. He barely made out the child asleep on a camp-bed, one arm hooped around its head. She took her nightgown from a chair and went out.

He hung up his jacket, removed his shoes and lay down, gazing out the door at the yellow blur of the street lamp. It was as cold as the grave in the bed. She came back to her rumpled nightdress, her hair about her shoulders, got in under the clothes beside him and put out the light. The yellow street lamp bleared in through the bedroom door.

'It's bloody cold,' he said.

'We'll soon warm up. You should have taken your clothes off and got under the blankets, sure what does it matter?'

They lay in silence for a while, hearing nothing but their breathing and the faint, far fog-horn. He moved closer and began to whisper into her ear about what it means to be homeless, and she whispered to him about the time she came up to Dublin for the first time from County Cavan, for her honeymoon. She never once went back there. He whispered to her, 'You are a heroine.' She said. 'You're a good lad, Johnny.'

After a while more she said, 'We must sleep,' and he lay on his back, his hands clasped behind his head. After a long while he said, 'Deirdre is a bitch,' and she said, 'She is very young.' After another while he whispered, 'Try to sleep,' and she whispered, 'Yes.' After another long time he said, 'You're not sleeping. You are thinking of him. When will you know?' She said, 'It might be any minute. Then I'll sleep. And sleep. And sleep.'

Sleep stole on him. He woke abruptly, at five o'clock. She was no longer in the bed. He saw her in the front room, a man's overcoat on her shoulders, leaning her elbows on the window-sill staring out. In his stockinged feet he went to her and put his arm around her shoulder.

'You can't sleep?'

She did not stir. Her face had melted completely, her two cheeks were wet. He did not know what to say to her. By the cleansed lamplight outside he saw that the fog had lifted. She whispered. 'It's all over.'

'You can't tell!'

'I know it. I'll go out and ring the hospital at six o'clock. But I know it.' Her face screwed up and more tears oozed from her closed eyes. 'You'd better go, Johnny. Your people may be worrying.'

He dressed, shivering, among the empty bottles of stout on the floor, some of them standing to attention, some of them rolled on their sides. He put on his peaked cap with the white top, patted her hooped back, said, 'God help you,' and went out up the steps to the street level. It was black as night. From the pavement he looked down at the shadow of her face behind the misty glass, lifted a hand and walked away.

When he came to the Coal Harbour he halted on the centre of the railway bridge and leaned his hands on the wet parapet. Six

miles across the level bay the string of orange lights flickered
along the shoreline, and farther west the city's night-glow underlit
its mirror of cloud. The harbour water, dark as oil, held the
riding-light of a coaltub. He drew in deep breaths of the raw air
and blinked his sanded eyes. He said quietly, 'I still love you,
you bitch.' Then he lifted his head, put his two palms about his
mouth like a megaphone, and howled in a long, wild howl across
the bay, 'Do you love me?'

The city lay remote under its dull mirror.

He rubbed the stone and remembered, 'Quiet consummation
have; and renowned be thy grave'—and marched homewards,
arms swinging, chin up, white cap slanted. The water of the main
harbour was inscribed by a slow wheel of light. Far out from the
Kish bank a flight of light beamed and died at regular intervals.
The whole way home the only sound he heard was a faint, faraway
humming like a bee, a dawn-flight out of Dublin across the sea.

As he stole indoors a voice whispered, upstairs, 'Are you all
right, darling?'

'Okay, Mum!'

'Daddy's asleep.'

'Okay, Mum.'

'Sleep well, love.'

'Okay, Mum. I'll sleep. And sleep. And sleep.'

THE BOILS OF THOMAS GULLY

Patrick McCabe

The narrator of this next story, Phildy Hackball, is a regular at the Bridge Bar in Barntrosna where—if he isn't inebriated—he's on the look-out for material for his short stories. He has been writing these tales for several years—mostly appearing in small press anthologies—prior to the publication of his first collection, Mondo Desperado *in 1999. Hackball describes his major interests as 'relaxing with friends' and 'having a few jars', although 'studied eccentricity' might be added to the list as attested to by one visitor to his home who was greeted by yer man wearing a leopard-skin swimsuit and smoking a large cigar. The same visitor was left in a foggy haze after being plied with any number of bottles of whiskey and brandies while his host intoned the story of 'The Boils of Thomas Gully'. Gully is a neighbouring farmer who drinks at Shamus Henley's pub in Barntrosna where he grows ever more maudlin about his inability to find a wife. Until, that is, the night a stunning, perfume-drenched woman sits down next to him at the bar and his world—not to mention his fortunes—are turned upside-down.*

The village of Barntrosna and its inhabitants are the unique creation of Patrick McCabe (1955–). They are featured in a number of stories which have been compared by The Observer *to the best-selling American author, Garrison Keillor's series: 'The place is an unlikely bog-trotter's Lake Wobegon told in the souped-up blarney of one Phildy Hackball.' McCabe himself was born in Clones, County Monaghan and drink featured largely in his childhood as his father died from cirrhosis of the liver when the boy was just seventeen. He always wanted to be a writer and*

*describes his great influence as James Joyce, 'because of his
assault upon language'. McCabe worked initially as a primary
school teacher, writing in his spare time, and published his first
children's book,* The Adventures of Shay Mouse, *in 1985. This
has been followed by an increasingly successful clutch of adult
novels including* Music on Clinton Street *(1986),* Carn *(1989)
and* Butcher Boy *(1992) which was short-listed for the Booker
Prize and filmed by Neil Jordan. The sheer exuberance and
uproarious comedy of 'The Boils of Thomas Gully' surely make
it imperative that Phildy Hackball is encouraged to leave the
Bridge Bar from time to time and set down more tales of this
extraordinary Irish village and its inhabitants.*

*   *   *

Tom Gully is a farmer from Cloonee, which is a small town-land
approximately one mile from the village of Barntrosna. Tom is
a very nice man but he is not really what you would call the
very attractive film-star type. Which he wishes he were but he
knows that it is impossible and has long since resigned himself
to the situation. As he says himself: 'Sure, if I have a few pounds
in my pocket and have the couple of pints at night, what's the
use in complaining?' He is a creature of habit, Tom. Being a
farmer, every morning he drives his tractor into the village to
leave his milk churns to be collected. Then he goes to the post
office to lodge a few shillings into his account and after that it's
into Shamey Henley's for one or two glasses of stout. That's all,
mind, for there are plenty of chores to be done in the afternoon—
groceries, fertilizer to be purchased, boots to be left into the
shoemakers and so on. Then it's off down the high road for
Cloonee once again, with you motoring along in your stuttering
old tractor. But at least with a nice warm glow about your person
that you didn't have when you came in. And which you'd need,
if your name was Tom Gully, at any rate, because when Tom
arrives home and goes inside to his rickety old farmhouse, the
very same sentence always falls from his lips: 'What kind of an
eejit am I that I can't get myself a woman? Everybody else has

one!' Which was not entirely true but there would be no point in disputing it with Tom. It would only end with him slumping into the armchair with his head in his hands, self-consciously tweaking at the boil which had emerged on his forehead at the age of thirty-two, sighing that no matter what you said he hadn't a woman and that was all that mattered. And not much sign of getting one either. O, there had been times all right when it looked as if his prayers were about to be answered—particularly when the young Cooney one from Longfield Cross had agreed to allow him drive her home—even kiss her indeed! But in the end it had all come to nothing and she had married a McGarry from Kilkeerin and was never seen again. There had been another girl too, a Teresa McMenamin who had the most beautiful hair that Tom Gully had ever seen. Hair so soft and clean and fine that it made him want to almost die, such was the feeling of coarseness and crudity it provoked within him as regards the nature of his own rotund and somewhat unkempt physical aspect. A feeling which he went on to experience on many, many occasions, before Teresa finally announced that she was moving to the city of Dublin to further her nursing career and would be ceasing to return home for weekends. All this made Tom sad. He wondered, was it his boil? Or was it just him? Would I be capable of getting myself a girlfriend if I hadn't got the boil, maybe? he would often wonder.

Sometimes when that thought occurred to him, he would just sit in the dark and sob like a big girl. All he could see were the shapes of the kitchen utensils on the table and the random items of furniture throughout the room—so shadowy and indistinct that they often made him wonder, would he be like that too, soon? A silhouette sitting on a chair, no longer of this world? And never in all his time on this earth having known the pleasure of a woman? He felt that he was a disgrace and that it was shameful for him to call himself a man, to even think of doing so. Sometimes when he considered this, Tom Gully would cry. Then his dog Napper would come up to him and whimper and he would try to elucidate his troubles for the animal but, try as he might, he could never seem to find the proper words. Which upset him even more. Because he loved Napper. 'O, Napper,' he wept one day as he hugged the sad-eyed collie's tatty fur, 'I love you so much you'll never know because I am so useless that the words are all tangled up inside me like briars and I can't get at them.'

Once or twice, Tom felt like putting an end to the whole thing. 'It's a waste of time, that's what it is,' he said to himself and paused for a moment to consider the tin of Paraquat weedkiller he knew to be located in the outhouse. But, fortunately, he proceeded no further with this idea, and consequently the following afternoon was to be found sitting, once more, on the high stool in Shamey's, sipping his stout and wondering, in a chin-scratching moment of philosophy, what for the love of God had gotten into Shamey, the way he had destroyed his good pub. An observation which he didn't really in his heart and soul believe—had simply said it, in fact, because all the other farmers did. Because, after all, it had to be admitted that the disco (exotically named RA! RA'S!) brought plenty of women from outside and, with whom—if you played your cards right—well, who knew? The old bar was still the same, of course, with all the faded football photos and boxing stars lined up on the walls as they had been for years—but the back lounge? O, for God's sake, stop! thought Tom to himself, smiling broadly. No wonder he had to be drunk to go into it! They even had films on the walls now (black singers in sunglasses and shiny suits, if you don't mind!) and lights that made you think you had dust all over your jacket! It was just when Tom was thinking this that out of the corner of his eye he saw something that made him remark—silently of course—to himself: 'Jeepers! I think there must be something in this stout. Perhaps I'd better lay off it for a while!'

You have to remember, you see, that as yet it was only one thirty in the afternoon! And, although RA!RA'S! was due to open its doors that night, even the wildest women who came into Barntrosna, from Mullingar and various other places, to drink themselves senseless, didn't usually appear until at least seven thirty! Yet now, here was one of the most stunning, heavily made-up and perfume-drenched women Tom Gully had ever seen in his whole life! Sitting directly across from him and tapping on the glass with long crimson fingernails!

When he was younger, Tom's mother used to say to him: 'When you're big, love, and you find yourself in what you consider a difficult situation—particularly with girls—what I want you to do is say three Hail Marys for holy purity.' Somewhere deep within him, Tom felt sure that that was probably good advice. But somewhere also, quite close to the surface, it seemed, there was a voice that insistently repeated: 'Pay no heed to that old nonsense! Listen to me! Listen to me, Tom Gully! Don't be a fool! It's time to live, my boy! Time to live—and no better time to start!'

If anyone had been curious as to why, for no apparent reason, a great big grin appeared all of a sudden on the face of the heavy-set farmer at that precise moment, they would have found the answer in that very thought. And also in the image that, quite unexpectedly, followed on the heels of it. That of Tom Gully in a pair of dark glasses exactly like those favoured by the dancers in the films they projected on the walls at RA! RA'S! Resulting in his considering leaning over to the young woman to whisper in her ear: 'I was wondering, ma'am? Would you like a bottle of something?' Which Tom, because he knew himself and his own habits so well, was aware that there wasn't a hope in a million of him *actually* saying unless he applied himself with steely diligence to the task of consuming as many bottles of stout accompanied by as many brandy chasers as might be humanly possible. A task towards which he was now spurred on by the undulating curves of perfume that came sailing past directly beneath his nostrils, not to mention the whisper-crash of silk as two legs were once again crossed and a husky voice to the barman cooed: 'Excuse me, darling! May I have another Bacardi, please?'

When he heard this, it was all Tom Gully could do not to splutter the contents of his glass all down the front of his jacket. For in his mind he kept hearing that sentence repeat itself. Deep within him, there was a lighthouse and those were the words it beamed across the water. Over and over across the water. Tom suddenly felt dizzy. Nails! Crimson! And those pants! With spangles all over them, glittering away like glass in the sun. O, but that hair! Oo, that hair! (It was a pageboy cut but Tom didn't know that. And didn't care, either!) All he wanted to do with her hair was kiss it. Kiss it and run his fingers through it and say: 'O ma'am, I love your hair! I love it to bits, I'm telling you!'

Then—a shiver went running through him. He had forgotten his boil! He almost cried out: 'What if she doesn't like my boil?' Instantly he found himself on the verge of weeping and ordered two more brandy chasers. Within seconds, he felt good again. Good? He felt absolutely fantastic! The question he was now asking himself was: 'What boil?' Tom couldn't see any boil. If someone was talking about boils, it must be boils on someone else's poor unfortunate head they were talking about. Just who was the happiest, most contented man in the village of Barntrosna right at that very moment? The answer to that question is: Tom Gully. There could be absolutely no doubt about it. Certainly, he was a big, heavy-set man with a boil on his forehead and a somewhat casual attitude, perhaps, to personal hygiene, but as far as inner peace and feelings of self-worth were concerned, Tom Gully was now a paradigm. Which was why he had no difficulty whatsoever in sliding from one seat to the next to find himself—in Ray-Ban sunglasses no less! (as it now, thanks to the rapidity of his consumption, appeared to him!)—sitting directly opposite a beautiful young lady chipped out of china! Who didn't seem to mind in the least, it has to be said. Affording him, in fact, just the tiniest of approving smiles! Which Tom Gully just could not believe, quite frankly! For he had not—not in a million years—expected it all to be so easy! For a split second he wondered—could it be a trick? And then almost wept when it became clear that it was not. 'Why yes—I think I would rather like another Bacardi,' she softly replied. Tom Gully felt as if he had just been elected President of Ireland. He could not stop himself hoping that the door would open and someone he knew—any-one—would arrive in and see him sitting there. This did not happen but it didn't matter—Tom Gully was still happy. Happy? It is a word which doesn't even come close to describing the state of inner excitement which Tom Gully was experiencing at that moment! He could not for the life of him believe the effect her voice was having on him. The sound of it was a magic melody in his ears. And she seemed so interested in everything! In what was going on around the village, when they had done up Shamey's place, expectations for the coming tourist season, and so on. All of a sudden, Tom found himself transformed into the village spokesman. Which he was more than happy to be. Interesting facts regarding the local area poured from his lips in a torrent. When he went to the toilet, he was terrified on his return that she would be gone. His head was reeling as he searched for her through the haze. 'She's gone! Vanished!' he cried, and then he saw her, tapping ash into the tray. 'Mandy!' he cried in a weak falsetto, for that, she had informed him, was her name.

It was quite amusing when they were leaving the bar and Tom fell across one of the high stools. 'O, now, Tom!' Shamey gently chided him. 'You'll have to mind yourself now, you and them auld brandy chasers!' Tom pawed the air and smiled bashfully as his new companion helped him up. 'Thank you, Mandy!' he said and felt himself melting as she mischievously whispered: 'You great big thing you, Tom Gully!'

Tom was a little bit ashamed to be bringing her back to his crumbly old house but she assured him it didn't matter. In fact he had spent so long apologizing in advance that he was somewhat amazed she hadn't turned around and left him already. Which was why he kept repeating: 'I love you, Mandy,' as he went and stumbled across the step. Having to be assisted by her once again! 'O, you silly!' she said and chuckled. 'I love the way you say that,' he said. And he did! He could have listened to her saying it all night long! 'O, you silly, O you silly,' he said, and they both laughed as they went inside.

Napper was pleased to see them home, jumping up on his master's chest and licking him all over his face. Not knowing, of course, what to make of this new visitor. But not complaining either, because he could see it was perfectly plain she was being kind to his master. Kind? It was as if she had known him for years, for Heaven's sake! Even longer than Napper himself!

What Tom could not for the life of him understand was—why was she so interested in him? Why on earth would a woman so beautiful want to know a thing about Tom Gully? Those were the thoughts running through his mind as Tom lay spreadeagled in the chair, like a gigantic soft toy. How many times had he thus reclined, he asked himself, in that damp and mouldy kitchen, listening to the radio just as they were doing now, and dreaming this very scene, except never in a million years expecting it to be so close and tender? He felt perhaps he was losing his reason. Yes! That was it! He was going exquisitely, beautifully, made in the head!

'So tell me then, Tom,' her voice whispered, 'do you like me? Do you like your little Mandy?'

Tom wanted to press his fingers to his eyes. He wanted to hide as he tried to find the courage to say to her: 'Miss—Miss! Please ask me that again,' because the white nylon blouse with the ruffles on the cuffs she was dangling on the end of her shiny crimson fingernail was distracting him.

Look out, Tom! White flesh! White flesh! flashed a sign inside his mind.

But flesh there wasn't—not as yet. Nothing, only an elegantly sculpted hand that languidly traced its way across the mesh of a brassière's blackest lace.

'O, I feel so hot!' she sighed.

Tom tried frantically to think of news. *Any* news as she began to sway to the rhythm of the music. The music that was made by Margo and the Country Flavour. Except that somehow now it has been transmuted into a primeval, untamed drumbeat in Tom Gully's mind! As she effortlessly slides onto his lap!

O, naughty boy! O, wicked Tom Toms! Who sobs in his night-time lady's arms as out across the fields his cows and sheep go moo and baa. Crimson nails stroking his cheek as Tom Gully shivers with a fear that is so sweet he wants to die of it. Die of it right now as he puts his arms around her neck to kiss her alabaster skin.

'I love you, Mandy!' he says. 'You didn't even remark on my boil.'

'Go away,' she coos, 'naughty boil!'

Tom is quivering like a reed in the breeze. 'Marry me, Mandy!' he says. 'Marry me and I'll give you all my money!'

Already, Tom Toms' peepers are aglow! For she really is considering!

'All the money in the house and all the land I own!' he cries, curling one plump finger around a thumb.

'O, Tom Toms! I couldn't! I really couldn't!' flutters Mandy.

'Here!' cries Tom as a shoal of five-pound notes from a drawer to the ground goes floating.

'Oo! You are serious after all!' coos Mandy.

As ruffly blouse to ceiling it goes sailing and sparkly pants at once come swooshing down!

Now Tom Gully had never been in a situation before where his head it kept banging off the chair and his voice became so high-pitched that you would have easily been confused as to the nature of his gender. Neither had he ever felt, as he did some hours later, as if some enormous vacuum cleaner had come along and sucked from within him all the enzymes and juices and male fluids he had in his life possessed. For the very first time, his cheeks had become so flushed that it was actually impossible to determine where exactly his boil began and his face ended. Why, he was in such a state that it was a miracle he was able to speak at all! Uttering the words: 'Oh my God! What a beautiful woman you are, Mandy! Mandy! God love you!' in the voice of a valiant athlete who has just, against all odds, completed the decathlon. Not that it made any difference, however, for his declarations, sadly, fell on deaf ears, if cold stone floors can be described as having ears. There is a sensation which will be familiar to readers of urban myths and similar tales of travellers in foreign parts who awake in discomfiting surroundings to experience a feeling of mortal dread in the lower regions of the abdomen. Who will discover, to their horror, some time later, that their innermost organs—their kidneys as a rule—have been removed whilst they slept, in the most treacherous of backstreet larcenies. A not dissimilar feeling now overcame Tom Gully, as he repeatedly called out Mandy's name—but in vain, to be answered only by the thin Barntrosna breeze rattling the bolt on the swinging back door of his kitchen. As his weather-beaten hand sank itself deep into the penumbral regions of his trouser pocket, the cold realization dawned on him that they were indeed missing—not his kidneys, but the innumerable five-pound notes which had been, he thought, safely and securely deposited there. He felt like weeping.

'Come back! Come back, you! That money belongs to me!' he cried helplessly as he waved his fist at the night, his only response that provided by the reluctantly turned head of a sleepy-eyed Charolais bull.

Tom Gully was now beside himself. There is no other way of describing it. For three solid hours, we wept copious amounts of tears into the firegrate. 'You idiot, Tom Gully!' he reproached himself remorselessly. 'You stupid silly idiot! For that's all you are! You should have known she was only taking you for a ride! Now look at you! A disgrace! A disgrace to the name Gully, nothing more! Are you surprised you're devastated?'

Which he was—devastated, that is—but not half as much as he was when, only some days later, he stretched before the mirror after a hard day's work, and to his amazement, divined once more upon the flush expanse of his forehead, a shining, almost gloatingly triumphant—boil! A pink-red sphere of flesh that seemed to lean towards him like some eerie red eye and wink: 'Hello there, Tom!'

That was but the beginning. In the days that followed, such lesions were to become commonplace and soon it was as if Tom Gully was similar to some horrible mutation that had—ludicrous as it seems, in a place not noted for covert government research or comparable activity—somehow managed to come into contact with radioactive materials. And, had it not been for the efforts of his physician, Dr Joe McCaffrey, would almost certainly have taken his own life.

'No,' Dr Joe counselled, folding his stethoscope, 'the cause of your ailment is not mysterious radiation or anything like it—as you well know, Tom Gully!'

Dr Joe fixed his patient with a firm but benevolent gaze.

'She stole your money, didn't she?'

It was as if all the unbearable, pent-up fury that had been bottled up inside Tom Gully for weeks came roaring out in a huge tidal wave.

'Yes, doctor!' he cried as he sank his meaty fist into the heart of his palm. 'Every penny! Every last penny I ever earned, she took it off me! It's true! Every word you've spoken is true!'

This was to be the beginning of the healing process for Tom Gully and, years later, whenever he would reflect on his ordeal, that evening in Dr Joe's surgery always featured as the very first point on the journey it had fallen to him to make—the 'long march towards recovery', as it were.

And whenever he would speak of it, to his neighbours, or while having a stout with Shamey in the bar, he would always smile wistfully—but not without a tinge of regret, for what might have been, perhaps—abstractedly fingering his last remaining boil beneath his shirt as he mused: 'Yes! She made a cod of me, and it's been a long road—but it's all over now! And it'll be a long time before she does it again, let me tell you!' before yet again taking his zinc buckets—a regular ritual now!—and heading off down the open road, swinging them gaily as he approached the dairy, meticulously positioning them as he stroked the flanks of the gentle heifer, who went 'moo' in eager anticipation, a contentment the like of which he'd never known settling at last upon Tom Gully as he adjusted his cap and, licking his lips, once more felt a broad proprietorial smile beginning to unwind across his bright, weather-beaten cheeks.

AN UNUSUAL REQUEST

Glenn Patterson

For years, in less troubled times, the bars of Belfast's International Hotel on the south side of Donegall Square were a favourite meeting place for a drink. The place itself was unmissable with its canopy of frosted glass on mosaic pillars thrusting out into the street, with stairs on either side of the main entrance running down to the basement bars. Located just behind City Hall, it had a dual attraction for locals and visitors alike. In June 1966, however, the International made unwanted headlines in the Irish and English press when one of its barmen, Peter Ward, was murdered by the UVF. A little over ten years later, in 1975, the hotel closed and its reputation as one of the city's best watering holes seemed destined to disappear with it. Then in 1999, the brilliant young Irish novelist, Glenn Patterson, used the hotel, its bar-staff and a cast mingling respectable citizens with dodgy characters from the mid-Sixties as the background for the latest of his acclaimed novels, The International.

Glenn Patterson (1961–   ) was born in Belfast and lived there until he went to the University of East Anglia in England to study creative writing under the authors Angela Carter and Malcolm Bradbury. After finishing his degree course with an MA, Patterson lived for a time in Manchester before returning to Northern Ireland in the late Eighties. While working for the Northern Ireland Arts Council as Writer in the Community for Lisburn and Craigavon, he began his first novel, Burning Your Own *(1988). This won him the Betty Trask Award and the Rooney Prize for Irish Literature. His second novel,* Fat Lad *(1992) was short-listed for the GPA Book Award and was greeted by reviewer*

Tom Adair as 'perhaps the finest novel written out of Ulster in twenty five years.' Paterson's use of authentic, colloquial dialogue in his work led the Sunday Tribune *to declare, 'No other novelist has proved as capable of capturing the heart of modern Belfast.' In this episode from* The International, *the narrator, teenage barman Daniel Hamilton, recalls one of the strangest incidents ever to occur at a hotel function . . .*

*   *   *

Jamesie said he had never in all his days working in The International seen anything like it. He had feared the worst when he walked in the door of the Portaferry Room and every head turned towards him, for all the world, he said, as though they were looking for help. Seeing he was just a barman the heads turned away again. And that was when he heard the accordion. It was over on the far side of the room, the Donegall Square side. The drapes were not quite meeting in the middle and the light from the elongated streetlamp—so close you could nearly have leaned out the window and touched it—shone through and for a moment all that Jamesie could make out was this light and the accordion moving as though of its own volition. He had to squint to pin down the accordion player, starting with the fingers and working in. The head was wrinkled and entirely hairless. ('You couldn't go that bald,' Jamesie said, 'you'd have to have been that way from birth.') It bobbed fitfully above the bellows like a balloon left over from a long-ago party. The noise came to an abrupt end. The applause was on the discouraging side of polite.

' "Thank you," your man says in this squeaky wee voice. "That was the Tune the Old Cow Died Of,"—well he might as well have—"And now I'm going to play you some old bollocks of a jig and I'd like to see you all up on your feet." And off he went again. Nobody moved but me. I fucking legged it over to the bar before someone snapped and grabbed the hold of me to dance.'

The bar in the Portaferry Room consisted of trestle tables, pushed together to form three sides of a rectangle and draped with white cloths. Flea Johnston (Flea? Don't ask me, even his wife called him that), who normally worked in the Cocktail Bar, was stood behind here, arms folded across his chest, staring blankly. Jamesie waved a hand before Flea's eyes. He said he still couldn't be sure the start Flea gave was put on.

'Wasn't there supposed to be a wedding here?' Jamesie asked him as the accordion shrieked and wheezed. 'Did the bride not turn up or what?'

Flea nodded towards an unhappy-looking young woman in a plain pale turquoise dress clashing calamitously with the wall-paper's magenta flowers.

('She wasn't bad, herself, like,' Jamesie said. 'I mean I'd've given her one.' Coming from Jamesie, this did little to distinguish her from the broad mass of women between the ages of sixteen and sixty in Belfast.)

The groom—'A fucking glipe,' according to Jamesie—sat beside her patting her hand, possibly in sympathy, possibly in time to the music.

'That there's the minister,' Flea said.

'Who?'

Jamesie was still eyeing up the bride.

'With the accordion.'

'Ah, fuck off.'

'I'm telling you.'

And sure enough when Jamesie looked a second time he saw that the neck beneath the shrivelled head was ringed by a shiny dog collar.

'Apparently he has an LP out.'

'Name of Jesus,' said Jamesie.

'I think that one is already taken.'

The racket went from bad to worse to woeful. The groom's father and mother came out on to the yawning space before the minister and walked around it a couple of times. Two women, handbags, hanging like breeze-blocks from the crooks of their arms, got up and followed them. As they passed Jamesie, he heard one of them counting to the other under her breath.

'One-two-three, one-two-three.'

'That's the way!' the minister shouted, launching into yet another tune. He was enjoying himself. 'Let's see you all out there.'

The two couples sat down. The groom pulled lightly on the bride's hand. She drew it away, sharp. Everyone else was looking at the carpet between their undancing feet. Not a single person came near the bar.

'He has them terrified,' Flea said.

'So what did you need me here for?'

'I'm sorry. The Swinging Vicar went out for a while. I thought he was finished. *They* thought he was finished. For about a quarter of an hour I never stopped. It was mental. Actually, it was great.'

Jamesie stirred with the point of an index finger the paltry collection of coins in the glass ashtray Flea had been using for tips.

'Somebody's going to have to do something,' he said.

Flea Johnston swore blind that Jamesie really did do what he told me he did next.

'I thought, fuck this for a lark, so the next time your man comes to the end of a tune I saunters over.'

'Jamesie, you didn't?'

'Fucking right I did. Saunters over and has a wee word in his ear.'

It was Tuesday before I got a proper chance to talk to Flea.

'It's true,' he said. 'I could hardly believe myself he was going to go through with it. You know Jamesie, most of the time, all mouth. I was half expecting him to swerve out of the way at the last minute and start picking up glasses, but he didn't, he bent down and started whispering. The whole room was staring, they could see the minister frowning, and then Jamesie straightened up and the minister shook his head and leaned forward towards the microphone and says, "I've had a bit of an unusual request." '

'I said it was for the happy couple, for luck,' Jamesie told me. 'I said it was a sort of tradition in The International. He said it was the first he'd heard of it. I told him he could suit himself but that was the way it had always been and by that stage I think he was scared of not believing me, so he just made the announcement and handed me the microphone.'

Jamesie sang. He said he did, Flea said he did.

'I asked the Rev did he know "Love Me Tender". I hummed him a bit. I didn't let on it was Elvis, for fear he'd take a buckle in his eye.'

'Were you not scundered?' I asked. Jamesie twisted his face. 'Ach . . .'

'He was fucking amazing,' Flea told me on Tuesday. 'I would never say it to his face, but he was. "Love Me Tender", "Crying", "Your Cheating Heart".'

'Nobody shouted at me to stop after the first one,' Jamesie said, 'so I thought I might as well carry on. I forgot the words a couple of times, like, but I just went la-la-la until I got on to the ones I knew again. I don't know why people make such a big deal of these pop stars, it's a piece of piss, really.'

The minister, it seems, joined in gamely, even if he never was one hundred per cent convinced he ought to be letting this happen.

'A bit ropy on "Your Cheating Heart",' Jamesie said. 'But, give him his dues, he made a pretty good fist of it. Even called the guests up to dance again.'

Jamesie had by now adopted his normal stance behind the counter of the Blue Bar, right foot a little to the fore of the left, head drawn back and inclined to one side, observing the fawn flow of Guinness into an angled pint glass. I realised that behind the bar or behind a microphone, it was all one to Jamesie. I realised that I hoped one day somebody would tell him he was in fact some sort of star.

'And did they dance?'

'Dance? Fuck! Those people wouldn't have got out of their seats if it had been Elvis himself standing up there in front of them.'

When he had finished his third song he replaced the microphone on its stand and shook the minister's hand.

'They're all yours, Reverend,' he said. 'And good luck to you.'

Jamesie rested the glass on the grid above the slops tray. The last Guinness in turned halfway down and started for the top again.

'I'm telling you,' he said. 'I've never in all my days here seen the like of it.'

THE FIRST SINGLES BAR

Malachy McCourt

Irish theme pubs and bars have become a world-wide craze in recent years—examples are to be found from Berlin to Tokyo and from Abu Dhabi to Rome. Some represent a genuine attempt to recreate the Celtic-style architecture and friendly, sociable atmosphere laced with an edge of wildness that is the genuine Irish tavern; far too many are kitsch monuments to bad taste in both their appearance and the drinks they serve: a world away, in fact, from the essence of the real Irish pub. In many American cities where the Irish have settled, both types of establishment can be found—though among their number few have equalled 'Malachy's' on New York's East Side. In its day, it has attracted several famous Irish celebrities including Richard Harris and Peter O'Toole who came to rub shoulders at the bar with other members of their profession, notably Grace Kelly, Barbra Streisand and Gig Young. A greater claim to fame—according to its founder—is that it was the first singles bar in America.

Malachy McCourt (1932–) is the younger brother of Frank McCourt whose international bestseller and Pulitzer prize-winning book, Angela's Ashes (1996) *told the tragic, occasionally comic story of the family's life in Limerick with their drunken, wastrel father. The children and their mother moved to America in the hope of a better life and there Malachy grew up, working first in the New York docks and then as a bartender. A man of irrepressible good humour, he also managed to find employment in television on the* Tonight *show with Jack Paar and then appeared as an actor on the stage in* Ulysses in Nighttown, *an adaptation of James Joyce's* Ulysses, *and a production of* Play-boy of the Western World. *In 1962, Malachy McCourt appeared with Robert Mitchum in the movie,* Two for the Seesaw. *He has also co-written a play with his brother,* A Couple of Blackguards (1997), *in which two people recall characters they knew in Limerick. Malachy McCourt's own account of a young Irishman growing up in America,* A Monk Swimming (1998), *has been a bestseller like this brother's opus, and was hailed on publication by* The Observer *as 'a drunken, exhilarating version of the American dream'.*

*   *   *

There came a night when a couple of chaps, Roland Martinez and Hal Kemp Jr.—another scion of sorts, whose pater had been a band leader in the thirties and forties—asked if I would meet them, as they had a business proposition to discuss with me. My watchword being 'Sí!' to everything, of course, I agreed.

Roland was an extremely nervous man, constantly on the move, with tics and spasmodic gestures animating his entire corpus. Later, he took to chomping on toothpicks, and the devastation wrought on the rain forests by his consumption of wood cannot be measured.

Hal was a balding, chubby chap, concerned mainly with the club, the thinning hair, and dipping his wick. In all the time I knew him, he searched for a remedy for the excess avoirdupois festooning his frame. A very gentle, good-humored fellow was Hal, and much loved by the ladies of all ages. 'Ooooh,' they would begin, as they hugged the lad. 'You are sooo cuddly.' Hal would agree, and he was fairly successful in persuading them that cuddling *sans culottes* was great fun, too.

Women are always wary of the lounge lizard Lothario, he of teeth and tan, but a roundish, pink, bespectacled chap could pose no danger.

His other quest was for the restoration of the hair to the head, and he rubbed everything into the scalp, from the urine of the pregnant woman to the saliva of the black bear, but still the hair fell, and more scalp showed, and no one loved him any the less because he had too much flesh and too little hair.

Their business proposition was as follows: They wanted to open a saloon on the East Side, and they wanted me to be a partner. They would name it 'Malachy's', my having become a bit of a celebrity, and the money would flow in. For the huge sum of fifteen hundred dollars invested on my part, I would own a twenty-five percent share. Of course, I didn't have fifteen hundred dollars, nor a hope of accumulating it, either. Hal Jr. said that would not present any problem, as he would lend it to me, sans interest.

'Good enough,' sez I, so the search for a suitable premi began, as did the tedious process of securing clearances for the license. The two hurdles in the way of uncorking a bottle and vending its spirituous contents were the ABC and the SLA. These were not organizations devoted to education and terrorism, they were the Alcoholic Beverage Commission and the State Liquor Authority. These were the folk who demanded proof that you were of good character, an upstanding citizen, and that your money source was clean and free from any organized-crime patina. One sign of good citizenship was the flutter of crisp lettuce in the form of one-hundred-dollar bills slipped 'twixt the pages of applications attesting to our honesty and fierce devotion to God and country, and to our promises never to sell a vodka to a dying Communist, even if he promised to convert to capitalism, should he recover.

Those offices were run by hacks, hypocrites, and whores who, whilst accepting bribes to do what they were being paid to do, opening up their arseholes for the biggest pricks in the Mafia, deigned to pass judgment on innocent idiots like Martinez, Kemp, and myself.

It seemed the cleaner you were, the more trouble these agencies gave you. All over the city, you'd see those little *boîtes* springing up: black Formica bar, leather bar stools, spangled walls, fluorescent lights, and men-only staff—barmen and waiters togged out in white shirt, black bow tie, red form-fitting bellboy jackets, black hair, and lots of teeth. These were places patronized by

elderly men of sallow complexion, in dark suits and wide-
brimmed hats, with the flashy pinky ring, accompanied by
sequined young blondes, who shrieked their laughter at every
utterance, to show they were having a 'wunderful' time.

The exigencies of being a crime-free citizen has not yet been
dealt with in literature. At that time—the fifties and sixties—you
had to serve food and prove you had a kitchen. You had to have
a table for every two feet of bar, or something like that. You
could open twenty hours a day, 8 A.M. 'til 4 A.M. the next morning,
except early Sunday morning, when you had to close at 3 A.M.
and not reopen until 1 P.M., to allow people to attend church.

Surely.

You had to have soap in the lavatories, under penalty of law,
and any law enforcer could snaffle your soap and issue a ticket
for same, for which you actually had to go to court. Picture that.
A portion of the criminal justice system had to be given over to
the Case of the Missing Soap!

The lighting had to be of sufficient brightness to allow the
reading of newspaper print. Indeed, I once answered a summons
relating to this matter. In court I said I thought the light in the
bar was sufficient, as I often transacted my business paperwork
there. The surprisingly enlightened judge then called the cop, that
paragon of literacy, to the stand, and asked him the name of the
newspaper he had tried to read in the bar. The *Daily Mirror* was
his reply. The judge said (1) he disapproved of the choice of
reading material, and (2), if the man wanted to read, try the public
library. Case dismissed.

Acquire enough of these violations, though they were nearly
always dismissed, and the SLA would request your presence at
a hearing to determine your suitability as a licensee, operating
on the theory that, where there is smoke, there is a little glowing
conflagration lurking somewhere. Meanwhile, in the wide-open
Mafia Formica fiefdoms, people were shot, garroted, poisoned,
and stabbed, not to mention assaulted and robbed by the open-
thighed ladies who rented their various orifi for a living. Yes,
sir, soap missing from a lavatory in which you cannot read the
Mirror is a serious criminal matter.

Nonetheless, having crossed various palms with silver, we did indeed secure a license to operate a premise between Sixty-third and Sixty-fourth Streets on Third Avenue, previously known as 'O'Rourke's'. It had been a traditional New York Irish saloon, dark and old, the walls mortared with depression and despond. A bit of cream paint, a bit of red carpet on the floor, a bit of housecleaning, and we were ready for biz.

Hal Kemp installed a brightly lit fish tank, which added a nice touch to the place. On the floor waiting tables, in the kitchen cooking burgers, was Earl Walker, a jack-of-all-doings, who came with a pedigree as a hash slinger in a hamburger joint called 'Rikers'. I liked his briskness and his easy way with all kinds of people, so he became an important fixture at Malachy's.

I had neglected to mention to my then-current employer, Frank Clavin, that I was opening a competing premises five blocks away. I needed the continuing income and was a bit scared of the little man, as well, for he had what is known as an uncertain temper. So, there I was, caught between publicizing my new saloon to the congregation each night, and trying to keep it secret from El Toro Clavin and his largish Missus, Marylyn. The matter was resolved the day my partners hoisted a canopy outside the new saloon proclaiming to the world that this was to be Malachy's. It was seen and remarked on by various bods, and when I arrived for the evening duties at Clavin's, I was greeted with torrents of words, including 'treachery', 'robbery', 'Judas', 'Benedict and all the Arnolds', and something about being stabbed in the back.

Now, I'd made a somewhat cursory study of various economic systems, my reading encompassing John Locke, Adam Smith, and *Das Kapital* by K. Marx, and all of that stuff had given me an idea of what constitutes capitalism, a system that seems to operate in the USA. I endeavored to explain to the Clavins that, operating on the theory that competition is essential to economic progress and good for it, I was doing them a favor by opening up next door. My point was not well taken and I was told to shut the fuck up and get the fuck out and forget about the fucking wages, as I couldn't ever hope to make up what I'd cost them.

I would miss the camaraderie of Clavin's, and my conscience was bothered by the deceitful way I'd behaved—I'd had a free hand there, with no restrictions on what I ate or drank, and Frank Clavin was far from stingy with the money—but ambition must be served, and Malachy's must be opened. As the soothsayers say, it came to pass that on the 12th day of May in the Year of our Lord 1958, the maidenhead of the first singles bar in the world was penetrated by the vanguard of the horny hordes trooping in so that they could say, 'I was there in the beginning.'

There may be some who will contradict me when I say that Malachy's was the first singles bar in the United States of America, if not in the world, but it was. It was a happy accident of luck and location, abetted by the Irish historical memory of the Law of Hospitality. Before St Patrick came and ruined a perfectly decent society, Ireland was governed by traditional laws, called the 'Brehon Laws', which covered everything: property, education, medicine, death, succession, inheritance, crime. These included the law of hospitality: not tradition, not rule, but *law* of hospitality. You could disgrace yourself, your family, and your tribe if perchance a stranger were strolling in your part of the country and he were allowed to pass your portals without being offered sustenance for the journey. And not just leavings of the table, but the best of what you had.

So, when the doors of Malachy's opened, it was incumbent on me to put up the Cead Mile Failté, pronounced 'Kade Meela Fallchee,'—'a hundred thousand welcomes to all.'

And I meant to all. At that time, by tradition and by fear, females were not allowed at the bar proper. In Ireland, they had little cubicles known as 'snugs', for ladies with a taste for the stuff, and in the famous El Vino's in London, a hangout for the Fleet Street crowd, women had to sit six feet from the bar. On Third Avenue in the Fifties, any seat would do as long as it was not a bar stool. That was tradition, and the fear part was that a titted person at a bar was there for one reason—to entice the poor, gullible males. This view of bar life was held by police, priests, and politicians, and it was so widespread that there was a general impression that it was the law of the land. Not so. I looked into the matter and found that man or woman, of legal age and sober, and in possession of legal currency, could plonk the arse on the stool and order the refreshing nectar.

As it happened, around the corner at Lexington and Sixty-first Street was the Barbizon Hotel for Women, a large building throbbing with post-pubescent sexuality. We used to fantasize about being let loose in there for a week, and it was proposed and seconded and passed that every man among us would be willing to die at the end of the week if the wish were granted. Second best, and as was the case, the lovely young things learned that at Malachy's, the cute, new place around the corner, there were lots of cute guys and you could go there without a date or escort.

Among those guys were several young actors from Blighty who found the plenitude of pulchritude very much to their liking. Peter O'Toole, Richard Burton, and Alan Bates would stop by, as would Richard Harris, who had grown up in Limerick, not that we associated much there.

Dickie was from the part of Limerick where the gentry lived in the big houses with lawns, trees, shrubbery, and private lavatories within the house. The Harrises were well-to-do; they trooped off to private schools, were well shod, went en masse to the seaside for the yearly holiday season. They played tennis in gleaming whites, and the boys were always togged out nicely for the rugby game.

I only played one game against RH in Limerick. It was an Under Twenty final, the rule being that all players had to be under twenty years old at the beginning of the season. Harris and several members of his team were over twenty when we played— as a matter of fact, he was twenty-one on the very day of the game, October First, 1951. A Jesuit-trained team it was, so you'd expect diligence and honor from these laddies.

When I ran into Harris again, he told me he remembered everyone on my team except me. As a Limerick laner—that's slum kid to you—I was used to people not remembering me, especially Limerick aristocracy.

But now he, along with everyone else, would perform the only civilized act they knew in a pub, which was to offer to buy me a drink, and I, in turn, would reciprocate the civility by accepting. There were times when I'd have a dozen whiskies lined up for attention. All of a sudden, I was King of the Castle, with all kinds of guys punching me lightly on the shoulder, saying, 'How ya doin',' and the dainty young things telling me I was cute and had a cute Irish brogue. I misunderstood that 'cute' business for a while, as in Ireland 'cute' retains its original meaning of sly, cunning, tricky, slippery, but the light soon dawned, and that only helped swell the head a little more.

3

THE DRINKS' INTERVAL

A Round of Dramas

CHRISTY MAHON'S STORY

J. M. Synge

The Irish pub play in which the action and narrative take place almost wholly within the confines of a saloon bar is a long-standing tradition that began almost a century ago with J. M. Synge's The Playboy of the Western World. *This drama about a murderer who holes up in a remote Irish* shebeen *was first performed at the legendary Abbey Theatre in Dublin in January 1907 and provoked riots in the opening week when some members of the audience hurled eggs, potatoes and even a slice of fruit cake at the actors during four performances. Despite the fact that much of the drama must have been difficult to hear because of the uproar—caused by playgoers who felt that some of the lines were an insult to Irish women—*The Playboy of the Western World *was destined to become a classic. The formula which Synge devised of using a bar where drink fires the imaginations and loosens the tongues of the customers proved a source of inspiration for a number of other Irish playwrights who appear in this section.*

John Millington Synge (1871–1909) was born of an old Anglo-Irish family at Rathfarnham in County Dublin, but due to ill-health was educated mainly by private tutors before entering Trinity College, Dublin. He tried unsuccessfully to be a concert violinist and was having an equal lack of success as a writer until he met W. B. Yeats in Paris in 1895. Yeats encouraged Synge to forgo the comfortable life of the French capital and visit the Aran Islands to study the lives of its inhabitants. The mixture of credulity, violence and parochailism that Synge observed and then adapted into a series of plays resulted in him being labelled the greatest of the Irish dramatists of peasant life.

If some of the satiric elements in his plays, Riders to the Sea *(1904),* The Wells of the Saints *(1905) and especially his master-piece,* The Playboy of the Western World, *offended a number of Synge's countrymen, they nevertheless revealed the writer's deep affection for rural communities and assured him of an enduring influence on the theatre. Synge was working as a director at the Abbey Theatre when his life was tragically cut short by cancer. 'Christie Mahon's Story' is an extract from* Playboy *in which the runaway parricide stumbles into Michael James's rough, untidy pub and tells his story to the assembled company: the landlord, a barmaid, Pegeen, her inhibited boyfriend, Shawn, and two of the regulars, Philly Cullen and Jimmy Farrell, both farmers. It is a scene at once dramatic and comic . . . and with the author's postscript, probably among the most remarkable to be staged in a bar.*

*   *   *

[Enter CHRISTY MAHON, a slight young man. He is very tired and frightened and dirty.]

    CHRISTY *[in a small voice]*: God save all here!

    MEN: God save you kindly!

    CHRISTY *[going to the counter]*: I'd trouble you for a glass of porter, woman of the house.

       [He puts down a coin.]

    PEGEEN *[serving him]*: You're one of the tinkers, young fellow, is beyond camped in the glen?

    CHRISTY: I am not; but I'm destroyed walking.

    MICHAEL *[patronizingly]*: Let you come up then to the fire. You're looking famished with the cold.

    CHRISTY: God reward you. *[He takes up his glass and goes a little way across to the left, then stops and looks about him.]* Is it often the polis do be coming into this place, master of the house?

    MICHAEL: If you'd come in better hours, you'd have seen 'Licensed for the Sale of Beer and Spirits, to be Consumed on the Premises', written in white letters above the door, and what would the polis want spying on me, and not a decent house within four miles, the way every living Christian is a bona fide, saving one widow alone?

CHRISTY [*with relief*]: It's a safe house, so. [*He goes over to the fire, sighing and moaning. Then he sits down, putting his glass beside him, and begins gnawing a turnip, too miserable to feel the others staring at him with curiosity.*]

MICHAEL [*going after him*]: Is it yourself is fearing the polis? You're wanting, maybe?

CHRISTY: There's many wanting.

MICHAEL: Many, surely, with the broken harvest and the ended wars. [*He picks up some stockings, etc., that are near the fire, and carries them away furtively.*] It should be larceny, I'm thinking?

CHRISTY [*dolefully*]: I had it in my mind it was a different word and a bigger.

PEGEEN: There's a queer lad. Were you never slapped in school, young fellow, that you don't know the name of your deed?

CHRISTY [*bashfully*]: I'm slow at learning, a middling scholar only.

MICHAEL: If you're a dunce itself, you'd have a right to know that larceny's robbing and stealing. Is it for the like of that you're wanting?

CHRISTY [*with a flash of family pride*]: And I the son of a strong farmer [*with a sudden qualm*], God rest his soul, could have bought up the whole of your old house a while since, from the butt of his tail-pocket, and not have missed the weight of it gone.

MICHAEL [*impressed*]: If it's not stealing, it's maybe something big.

CHRISTY [*flattered*]: Ay; it's maybe something big.

JIMMY: He's a wicked-looking young fellow. Maybe he followed after a young woman on a lonesome night.

CHRISTY [*shocked*]: Oh, the saints forbid, mister; I was all times a decent lad.

PHILLY [*turning on Jimmy*]: You're a silly man, Jimmy Farrell. He said his father was a farmer a while since, and there's himself now in a poor state. Maybe the land was grabbed from him, and he did what any decent man would do.

MICHAEL [*to Christy, mysteriously*]: Was it bailiffs?

CHRISTY: The divil a one.

MICHAEL: Agents?

CHRISTY: The divil a one.

MICHAEL: Landlords?

CHRISTY [*peevishly*]: Ah, not at all, I'm saying. You'd see the like of them stories on any little paper of a Munster town. But I'm not calling to mind any person, gentle, simple, judge or jury, did the like of me.

[*They all draw nearer with delighted curiosity.*]

PHILLY: Well, that lad's a puzzle-the-world.

JIMMY: He'd beat Dan Davies' circus, or the holy missioners making sermons on the villainy of man. Try him again, Philly.

PHILLY: Did you strike golden guineas out of solder, young fellow, or shilling coins itself?

CHRISTY: I did not, mister, not sixpence nor a farthing coin.

JIMMY: Did you marry three wives maybe? I'm told there's a sprinkling have done that among the holy Luthers of the preaching north.

CHRISTY [*shyly*]: I never married with one, let alone with a couple or three.

PHILLY: Maybe he went fighting for the Boers, the like of the man beyond, was judged to be hanged, quartered, and drawn. Were you off east, young fellow, fighting bloody wars for Kruger and the freedom of the Boers?

CHRISTY: I never left my own parish till Tuesday was a week.

PEGEEN [*coming from counter*]: He's done nothing, so. [*To Christy*] If you didn't commit murder or a bad, nasty thing; or false coining, or robbery, or butchery, or the like of them, there isn't anything that would be worth your troubling for to run from now. You did nothing at all.

CHRISTY [*his feelings hurt*]: That's an unkindly thing to be saying to a poor orphaned traveller, has a prison behind him, and hanging before, and hell's gap gaping below.

PEGEEN [*with a sign to the men to be quiet*]: You're only saying it. You did nothing at all. A soft lad the like of you wouldn't slit the windpipe of a screeching sow.

CHRISTY [*offended*]: You're not speaking the truth.

PEGEEN [*in mock rage*]: Not speaking the truth, is it? Would you have me knock the head off you with the butt of the broom?

CHRISTY [*twisting round on her with a sharp cry of horror*]: Don't strike me. I killed my poor father, Tuesday was a week, for doing the like of that.

PEGEEN [*with blank amazement*]: Is it killed your father?

CHRISTY [*subsiding*]: With the help of God I did, surely, and that the Holy Immaculate Mother may intercede for his soul.

PHILLY [*retreating with* JIMMY]: There's a daring fellow.

JIMMY: Oh, glory be to God!

MICHAEL [*with great respect*]: That was a hanging crime, mister honey. You should have had good reason for doing the like of that.

CHRISTY [*in a very reasonable tone*]: He was a dirty man, God forgive him, and he getting old and crusty, the way I couldn't put up with him at all.

PEGEEN: And you shot him dead?

CHRISTY [*shaking his head*]: I never used weapons. I've no licence, and I'm a law-fearing man.

MICHAEL: It was with a hilted knife maybe? I'm told, in the big world, it's bloody knives they use.

CHRISTY [*loudly, scandalized*]: Do you take me for a slaughter-boy?

PEGEEN: You never hanged him, the way Jimmy Farrell hanged his dog from the licence, and had it screeching and wriggling three hours at the butt of a string, and himself swearing it was a dead dog, and the peelers swearing it had life?

CHRISTY: I did not, then. I just riz the loy and let fall the edge of it on the ridge of his skull, and he went down at my feet like an empty sack, and never let a grunt or groan from him at all.

MICHAEL [*making a sign to Pegeen to fill Christy's glass*]: And what way weren't you hanged, mister? Did you bury him then?

CHRISTY [*considering*]: Aye. I buried him then. Wasn't I digging spuds in the field?

MICHAEL: And the peelers never followed after you the eleven days that you're out?

CHRISTY [*shaking his head*]: Never a one of them, and I walking forward facing hog, dog, or divil on the highway of the road.

PHILLY [*nodding wisely*]: It's only with a common weekday kind of a murderer them lads would be trusting their carcase, and that man should be a great terror when his temper's roused.

MICHAEL: He should then. [*To Christy*] And where was it, mister honey, that you did the deed?

CHRISTY [*looking at him with suspicion*]: Oh, a distant place, master of the house, a windy corner of high, distant hills.

PHILLY [*nodding with approval*]: He's a close man, and he's right, surely.

PEGEEN: That'd be a lad with the sense of Solomon to have for a pot-boy, Michael James, if it's the truth you're seeking one at all.

PHILLY: The peelers is fearing him, and if you'd that lad in the house there isn't one of them would come smelling around if the dogs itself were lapping poteen from the dungpit of the yard.

JIMMY: Bravery's a treasure in a lonesome place, and a lad would kill his father, I'm thinking, would face a foxy divil with a pitchpike on the flags of hell.

PEGEEN: It's the truth they're saying, and if I'd that lad in the house, I wouldn't be fearing the loosed khaki cut-throats, or the walking dead.

CHRISTY [*swelling with surprise and triumph*]: Well, glory be to God!

MICHAEL [*with deference*]: Would you think well to stop here and be pot-boy, mister honey, if we gave you good wages, and didn't destroy you with the weight of work?

SHAWN [*coming forward uneasily*]: That'd be a queer kind to bring into a decent, quiet household with the like of Pegeen Mike.

PEGEEN [*very sharply*]: Will you wisht? Who's speaking to you?

SHAWN [*retreating*]: A bloody-handed murderer the like of . . .

PEGEEN [*snapping at him*]: Whisht, I am saying; we'll take no fooling from your like at all. [*To Christy with a honeyed voice*] And you, young fellow, you'd have a right to stop, I'm thinking, for we'd do our all and utmost to content your needs.

CHRISTY [*overcome with wonder*]: And I'd be safe this place from the searching law?

MICHAEL: You would, surely. If they're not fearing you, itself, the peelers in this place is decent, drouthy poor fellows, wouldn't touch a cur dog and not give warning in the dead of night.

PEGEEN [*very kindly and persuasively*]: Let you stop a short while anyhow. Aren't you destroyed walking with your feet in bleeding blisters, and your whole skin needing washing like a Wicklow sheep.

CHRISTY [*looking round with satisfaction*]: It's a nice room, and if it's not humbugging me you are, I'm thinking that I'll surely stay.

JIMMY [*jumps up*]: Now, by the grace of God, herself will be safe this night, with a man killed his father holding danger from the door, and let you come on, Michael James, or they'll have the best stuff drunk at the wake.

MICHAEL [*going to the door with men*]: And begging your pardon, mister, what name will we call you, for we'd like to know?

CHRISTY: Christopher Mahon.

MICHAEL: Well, God bless you, Christy, and a good rest till we meet again when the sun'll be rising to the noon of day.

CHRISTY: God bless you all.

MEN: God bless you.

Note by J. M. Synge: 'The oldest man on the isle of Inishmaan told me about a Connaught man who killed his father with the blow of a spade when he was in a passion, and then fled to this island and threw himself on the mercy of some of the natives with whom he was said to be related. They hid in him a hole— which the old man has shown me—and kept him safe for weeks, though the police came and searched for him, and he could hear their boots grinding on the stones over his head. In spite of a reward which was offered, the island was incorruptible, and after much trouble the man was safely shipped to America.

'This impulse to protect the criminal is universal in the west [of the Aran Islands]. It seems partly due to the association between justice and the hated English jurisdiction, but more directly to the primitive feeling of these people, who are never criminals yet always capable of crime, that a man will not do wrong unless he is under the influence of a passion which is as irresponsible as a storm on the sea. If a man has killed his father, and is already sick and broken with remorse, they can see no reason why he should be dragged away and killed by the law.'

TIM HAFFIGAN

Bernard Shaw

The 'stage Irishman'—comical, irresponsible, verbose and drunken—is a familiar figure in literature and art. The creation of this slick-talking, rollicking figure is generally credited to the Dublin novelist, Charles Lever (1806–72), whose comic tales of Irish life including The Confessions of Harry Lorrequer (1839) and Charles O'Malley (1841), earned him the epithet 'Harry Rollicker' and the friendship of Dickens, Thackeray and Trollope. Although he was resented in some quarters of Irish life for 'making fun of his fellow countrymen', his prototype was to reappear again and again in the works of Flann O'Brien, J. P. Donleavy and, perhaps surprisingly, Bernard Shaw who introduced arguably the most unforgettable 'stage Irishman' into the theatre in his play, John Bull's Other Island, which he wrote in 1904. Tim Haffigan is a conniving, drink-sodden opportunist summoned to the offices of Doyle and Broadbent, civil engineers, to talk to Tom Broadbent, an Englishman infatuated with Ireland, who requires someone to help 'break the ice between me and your warmhearted, impulsive countryman'. The invitation is manna from heaven to someone like Tim Haffigan.

George Bernard Shaw (1856–1950), one of the great playwrights of the twentieth century whose works such as Major Barbara (1905), Pygmalion (1912) and Saint Joan (1923) are still regularly performed around the world, was born in Dublin, the son of an improvident father. He was educated at Wesley College and thereafter worked for almost five years in the Dublin offices of a firm of land-agents, striving all the time to become a writer. In 1876 he moved to London and after several years of impoverishment, *received critical acclaim for his series of* Plays Pleasant and Unpleasant *staged in 1898. His reputation as a dramatist, essayist and critic grew rapidly and in 1904 he was asked to write a play for the Abbey Theatre, creating* John Bull's Other Island *which, as he later wrote, 'proved uncongenial to the whole spirit of the neo-Gaelic movement . . . as a very uncompromising presentment of the real old Ireland'. The play, from which the following extract is taken, was instead produced at the Court Theatre in London and became an immediate success.*

*   *   *

Haffigan is a stunted, shortnecked, smallheaded, redhaired man of about 30, with reddened nose and furtive eyes. He is dressed in seedy black, almost clerically, and might be a tenth-rate schoolmaster ruined by drink. He hastens to shake Broadbent's hand with a show of reckless geniality and high spirits, helped out by a rollicking stage brogue. This is perhaps a comfort to himself, as he is secretly pursued by the horrors of incipient delirium tremens.

HAFFIGAN: Tim Haffigan, sir, at your service. The top o the mornin to you, Misther Broadbent.

BROADBENT [*delighted with his Irish visitor*]: Good afternoon, Mr Haffigan.

TIM: An is it the afthernoon it is already? Begorra, what I call the mornin is all the time a man fasts afther breakfast.

BROADBENT: Havnt you lunched?

TIM: Divil a lunch!

BROADBENT: I'm sorry I couldnt get back from Brighton in time to offer you some; but—

TIM: Not a word, sir, not a word. Sure itll do tomorrow. Besides, I'm Irish, sir: a poor ather, but a powerful dhrinker.

BROADBENT: I was just about to ring for tea when you came. Sit down, Mr Haffigan.

TIM: Tay is a good dhrink if your nerves can stand it. Mine cant. *Haffigan sits down at the writing table, with his back to the*

filing cabinet. Broadbent sits opposite him. Hodson enters
emptyhanded; takes two glasses, a siphon, and a tantalus
from the cupboard; places them before Broadbent on the
writing table; looks ruthlessly at Haffigan, who cannot meet
his eye; and retires.

BROADBENT: Try a whisky and soda.

TIM [*sobered*]: There you touch the national wakeness, sir.
[*Piously*] Not that I share it meself. Ive seen too much of
the mischief of it.

BROADBENT [*pouring the whisky*]: Say when.

TIM: Not too sthrong. [*Broadbent stops and looks enquiringly*
at him]. Say half-an-hour. [*Broadbent, somewhat startled*
by this demand, pours a little more, and again stops and
looks]. Just a dhrain more: the lower half o the tumbler
doesnt hold a fair half. Thankya.

BROADBENT [*laughing*]: You Irishmen certainly do know how
to drink. [*Pouring some whisky for himself*] Now thats my
poor English idea of a whisky and soda.

TIM: An a very good idea it is too. Dhrink is the curse o me
unhappy counthry. I take it meself because Ive a wake heart
and a poor digestion; but in principle I'm a teetoatler.

BROADBENT [*suddenly solemn and strenuous*]: So am I, of
course. I'm a Local Optionist to the backbone. You have
no idea, Mr Haffigan, of the ruin that is wrought in this
country by the unholy alliance of the publicans, the bishops,
the Tories, and The Times. We must close the public-houses
at all costs [*he drinks*].

TIM: Sure I know. It's awful [*he drinks*]. I see youre a good
Liberal like meself, sir.

BROADBENT: I am a lover of liberty, like every true Englishman, Mr Haffigan. My name is Broadbent. If my name were
Breitstein, and I had a hooked nose and a house in Park
Lane, I should carry a Union Jack handkerchief and a penny
trumpet, and tax the food of the people to support the Navy
League, and clamor for the destruction of the last remnants
of national liberty—

TIM: Not another word. Shake hands.

BROADBENT: But I should like to explain—

TIM: Sure I know every word youre going to say before yev said it. *I* know the sort o man yar. An so youre thinkin o comin to Ireland for a bit?

BROADBENT: Where else can I go? I am an Englishman and a Liberal; and now that South Africa has been enslaved and destroyed, there is no country left to me to take an interest in but Ireland. Mind: I dont say that an Englishman has not other duties. He has a duty to Finland and a duty to Macedonia. But what sane man can deny that an Englishman's first duty is his duty to Ireland? Unfortunately, we have politicians here more unscrupulous than Bobrikoff, more bloodthirsty than Abdul and Damned; and it is under their heel that Ireland is now writhing.

TIM: Faith, theyve reckoned up with poor oul Bobrikoff anyhow.

BROADBENT: Not that I defend assassination: God forbid! However strongly we may feel that the unfortunate and patriotic young man who avenged the wrongs of Finland on the Russian tyrant was perfectly right from his own point of view, yet every civilized man must regard murder with abhorrence. Not even in defence of Free Trade would I lift my hand against a political opponent, however richly he might deserve it.

TIM: I'm sure you wouldnt; and I honor you for it. Youre goin to Ireland, then, out o sympathy: is it?

BROADBENT: I'm going to develop an estate there for the Land Development Syndicate, in which I am interested. I am convinced that all it needs to make it pay is to handle it properly, as estates are handled in England. You know the English plan, Mr Haffigan, dont you?

TIM: Bedad I do, sir. Take all you can out of Ireland and spend it in England: thats it.

BROADBENT [*not quite liking this*]: My plan, sir, will be to take a little money out of England and spend it in Ireland.

TIM: More power to your elbow! an may your shadda never be less! for youre the broth of a boy intirely. An how can I help you? Command me to the last dhrop o me blood.

BROADBENT: Have you ever heard of Garden City?

TIM [*doubtfully*]: D'ye mane Heavn?

BROADBENT: Heaven! No: it's near Hitchin. If you can spare half an hour I'll go into it with you.

TIM: I tell you hwat. Gimme a prospectus. Lemme take it home and reflect on it.

BROADBENT: Youre quite right: I will. [*He gives him a copy of Mr Ebenezer Howard's book, and several pamphlets*]. You understand that the map of the city—the circular construction—is only a suggestion.

TIM: I'll make a careful note o that [*looking dazedly at the map*].

BROADBENT: What I say is, why not start a Garden City in Ireland?

TIM [*with enthusiasm*]: Thats just what was on the tip o me tongue to ask you. Why not? [*Defiantly*] Tell me why not.

BROADBENT: There are difficulties. I shall overcome them; but there are difficulties. When I first arrive in Ireland I shall be hated as an Englishman. As a Protestant, I shall be denounced from every altar. My life may be in danger. Well, I am prepared to face that.

TIM: Never fear, sir. We know how to respict a brave innimy.

BROADBENT: What I really dread is misunderstanding. I think you could help me to avoid that. When I heard you speak the other evening in Bermondsey at the meeting of the National League, I saw at once that you were—You wont mind my speaking frankly?

TIM: Tell me all me faults as man to man. I can stand anything but flattery.

BROADBENT: May I put it in this way?—that I saw at once that you were a thorough Irishman, with all the faults and all the qualities of your race: rash and improvident but brave and goodnatured; not likely to succeed in business on your own account perhaps, but eloquent, humorous, a lover of

freedom, and a true follower of that great Englishman
Gladstone.

TIM: Spare me blushes. I mustnt sit here to be praised to me
face. But I confess to the goodnature: it's an Irish wakeness.
I'd share me last shillin with a friend.

BROADBENT: I feel sure you would, Mr Haffigan.

TIM [*impulsively*] Damn it! call me Tim! A man that talks
about Ireland as you do may call me anything. Gimme a
howlt o that whisky bottle [*he replenishes*].

BROADBENT [*smiling indulgently*]: Well, Tim, will you come
with me and help to break the ice between me and your
warmhearted, impulsive countrymen?

TIM: Will I come to Madagascar or Cochin China wid you?
Bedad I'll come to the North Pole wid you if yll pay me
fare; for the divil a shillin I have to buy a third class ticket.

BROADBENT: Ive not forgotten that, Tim. We must put that
little matter on a solid English footing, though the rest can
be as Irish as you please. You must come as my—my—
well, I hardly know what to call it. If we call you my agent,
theyll shoot you. If we call you a bailiff, theyll duck you
in the horsepond. I have a secretary already; and—

TIM: Then we'll call him the Home Secretary and me the Irish
Secretary. Eh?

BROADBENT [*laughing industriously*] Capital. Your Irish wit
has settled the first difficulty. Now about your salary—

TIM: A salary, is it? Sure I'd do it for nothin, only me cloes
ud disgrace you; and I'd be dhriven to borra money from
your friends: a thing thats agin me nacher. But I wont take
a penny more than a hundherd a year. [*He looks with restless
cunning at Braodbent, trying to guess how far he may go*].

BROADBENT: If that will satisfy you—

TIM [*more than reassured*]: Why shouldnt it satisfy me? A
hundherd a year is twelve-pound a month, isnt it?

BROADBENT: No. Eight pound six and eightpence.

TIM: Oh murdher! An I'll have to sind five timme poor oul
mother in Ireland. But no matther: I sad a hundherd; and
what I said I'll stick to, if I have to starve for it.

BROADBENT [*with business caution*]: Well, let us say twelve
pounds for the first month. Afterwards, we shall see how
we get on.

TIM: Youre a gentleman, sir. Whin me mother turns up her
toes, you shall take the five pounds off; for your expinses
must be kep down wid a sthrong hand; an—[*He is interrupted by the arrival of Broadbent's partner*].

*Mr Laurence Doyle is a man of 36, with cold grey eyes,
strained nose, fine fastidious lips, critical brows, clever
head, rather refined and goodlooking on the whole, but with
a suggestion of thinskinnedness and dissatisfaction
that contrasts strongly with Broadbent's eupeptic jollity.*

*He comes in as a man at home there, but on seeing the
stranger shrinks at once, and is about to withdraw when
Broadbent reassures him. He then comes forward to the
table, between the two others.*

DOYLE [*retreating*]: Youre engaged.

BROADBENT: Not at all, not at all. Come in. [*To Tim*] This
gentleman is a friend who lives with me here: my partner,
Mr Doyle. [*To Doyle*] This is a new Irish friend of mine,
Mr Tim Haffigan.

TIM [*rising with effusion*]: Sure it's meself thats proud to meet
any friend o Misther Broadbent's. The top o the mornin
to you, sir! Me heart goes out teeye both. It's not often I
meet two such splendid speciments iv the Anglo-Saxon
race.

BROADBENT [*chuckling*]: Wrong for once, Tim. My friend Mr
Doyle is a countryman of yours.

*Tim is noticeably dashed by this announcement. He draws in
his horns at once, and scowls suspiciously at Doyle under
a vanishing mask of goodfellowship: cringing a little, too,
in mere nerveless fear of him.*

DOYLE [*with cool disgust*]: Good evening. [*He retires to the
fireplace, and says to Broadbent in a tone which conveys
the strongest possible hint to Haffigan that he is unwelcome*]
Will you soon be disengaged?

TIM [*his brogue decaying into a common would-be genteel*

accent with an unexpected strain of Glasgow in it] I must be going. Ivnmportnt engeegement in the west end.

BROADBENT [*rising*] It's settled, then, that you come with me.

TIM: Ishll be verra pleased to accompany ye, sir.

BROADBENT: But how soon? Can you start tonight—from Paddington? We go by Milford Haven.

TIM [*hesitating*] Well—I'm afreed—I [*Doyle goes abruptly into the bedroom, slamming the door and shattering the last remnant of Tim's nerve. The poor wretch saves himself from bursting into tears by plunging again into his role of daredevil Irishman. He rushes to Broadbent; plucks at his sleeve with trembling fingers; and pours forth his entreaty with all the brogue he can muster, subduing his voice lest Doyle should hear and return*]. Misther Broadbent: dont humiliate me before a fella counthryman. Look here: me cloes is up the spout. Gimme a fypounnote—I'll pay ya nex Choosda whin me ship comes home—or you can stop it out o me month's sallery. I'll be on the platform at Paddnton punctial an ready. Gimme it quick, before he comes back. You wont mind me axin, will ye?

BROADBENT: Not at all. I was about to offer you an advance for travelling expenses. [*He gives him a bank note*].

TIM [*pocketing it*] Thank you. I'll be there half an hour before the thrain starts. [*Larry is heard at the bedroom door, returning*]. Whisht: hes comin back. Goodbye an God bless ye. [*He hurries out almost crying, the £5 note and all the drink it means to him being too much for his empty stomach and overstrained nerves*].

THE BULL OF BASHAN

Sean O'Casey

The plays of Sean O'Casey, one of J. M. Synge's successors, also suffered at the hands of certain outraged sections of his audiences: one, in particular, The Plough and the Stars *provoked similar riots when it was first performed at the Abbey Theatre in 1926. Like Synge, too, O'Casey found his inspiration among the poorer elements of Irish society—in his case the slums of Dublin—as well as the social upheaval resulting from the Easter Rising and the Troubles. His main characters are often a mixture of the tragic and the comic in much the same mould as those of J. M. Synge. Stephen Benson, the 'hero' of 'The Bull of Bashan' is just such a figure: the kind of man to be found propping up the bar in pubs all over Ireland. A disappointed, disillusioned man who makes his living driving a horse and cart and lives on stories of his past. In fact, he will tell anyone who will listen in the 'Black Bull' about the days when he was a cow-puncher in the Argentine and could handle even the most dangerous animals with practised ease. So he says—until the evening when a bull runs amok outside the pub and Stephen is called upon to be the man to save the day . . .*

Sean O'Casey (1884–1964), deservedly recognised as among Ireland's foremost playwrights, was born in one of the poorer districts of Dublin and only received a rudimentary education. He worked as a labourer and for nationalist organisations before becoming a dramatist, utilising elements of the city's low life in his early plays such as Shadow of the Gunman (1923) *and* Juno and the Paycock (1924) *with its unforgettable character, the boastful 'Captain' Boyle. Following the success of these plays at the Abbey Theatre, O'Casey became more experimental and impressionistic in later productions like* Cock-a-doodle Dandy (1949) *with its colourful action and stage trickery including a whiskey bottle whose contents will not spill, and* The Bishop's Bonfire (1955). *He also wrote a number of essays and a handful of short pieces of fiction among which 'The Bull of Bashan' first published in* Time and Tide *in December 1933, is an almost perfect 'pub play' told in short story form . . .*

*   *   *

The day had been very hot, but a delicious coolness had come into the evening air, as, work finished and over for the day, Stephen Benson sat and sipped his pint of beer in 'The Black Bull'. Stephen was a small, spare man, with a big moustache which flowed, rather than grew, over his upper lip, and trickled down both sides of his chin. He was bald to the back of his skull, where the hair still struggled to grow, getting a little thicker as it reached the neck. His arms were thin and sinewy, and his hands were as broad as the largest leaf on a chestnut tree. He stared dully out of the window of the tavern, gazing vacantly at every figure that passed by, and wondered how he could possibly brighten the next few days; for it was only halfway between the first of the week, and the uplift of payday.

'Huh,' he said, 'I'm fed up with life, finished and fed up with it all,' and he brushed off with his fingers the froth of the beer that lingered, like tawny drops of dew, on his shaggy moustache. 'Sitting on a lorry all day, and trying to get a dying horse to stick life out a little longer, and drag the lorry after him, isn't a life that would get a medal given to a man. Huh, that's it—I'm fed up with everything.'

He glanced over enviously at the barman washing the dirty glasses.

'He's pretty well placed,' thought Stephen, 'for he's never far from what can put a little sparkle into life.'

He noticed that the barman was now stretching his neck to look over the guard that covered half the window.

'Anything up?' he asked.

'There's a lot of people running to the top of the street,' said the barman.

'Raise your little finger here,' said Stephen, 'and you'll get a crowd. All of them hunting after a thrill, and never getting one,' and he took a great gulp of the beer that remained in the glass.

'I got my chance ten years ago, and I let it pass.'

'Yes?' queried the barman, trying to look as if he were interested in all that Stephen was saying. 'Ten years ago?'

'Argenteena,' murmured Stephen, 'pressed to go out with a friend as a cowboy. Great life, exciting, galloping over the pampas, and trotting along the paths we cut through the cardoon thistles rounding up the bullocks and the bulls.'

'Dangerous pastime,' murmured the barman.

'No more danger in corralling bulls than there is in housing hens,' said Stephen, 'provided you've got the right kind of grit in you, for bulls is naturally afraid of man. Steers, not cattle, is what we call them in Argenteena, and, if your nerves are steady enough, fix even a pawing bull with your eyes, walk slowly and firmly up to him, he'll get frightened, and when you're near him, he'll wilt and almost go down on his knees to you.'

'I'd rather you'd do it, than me,' said the barman.

'Then,' went on Stephen, 'just slip a cord around his horns and lead him home. But once let the slightest sign of fear, even for a second, slink into your eyes, and he's down on top of you.'

'Curious the power that must be in the eyes of a man,' murmured the barman.

'No,' replied Stephen, 'the weakness is in the eyes of the bull. They're bigger than ours, and a bull sees a man ten or twenty times bigger than he really is, so that a man looks a kind of god to a bull; it's the way the animal's eyes is fashioned. I've often tried it on bulls when I was down in the country, and it never failed once.'

'Different countries, different customs,' said the barman.

'Aw,' said Stephen, as he filled his pipe, 'work, excitement, and animation are only midgets of things here. Everything out there's on a big scale. Butterflies, red, black, green, blue and orange, some striped and some speckled, millions of them, ten feet from tip to tip, and feelers on them as big as broom handles with knobs on.'

'I'd like a holiday, but I wouldn't care to live out there,' said the barman.

'Soon get used to it,' answered Stephen. 'It's the heat that does it. Tropical head makes everything grow fast and furious. The bells of the blossoms out there are bigger than the funnels of Atlantic liners—a whole family could camp in one of them comfortable.'

'How do the bees manage?' asked the barman.

Stephen looked at him scornfully. 'There ain't no bees in Argenteena,' he said, and lay back on his seat to smoke thoughtfully.

Suddenly the swing door of the tavern opened and two corduroy-trousered men came in. Their faces lit up when they saw Stephen, and they made towards him at once. 'We've been looking for you, Steve, my boy,' said one of the men, 'and thought, at last, that we might find you here.'

'Ay,' said the second man, 'a quid waiting to be earned by you, Stephen, as easy as kiss hands.'

'The moment we saw what was happening, we set out in search of you,' said the first man.

Stephen wondered what was the cause of this anxiety to find him. He remembered that whenever he was wanted it was usually to tell him evil tidings, and his mind immediately became uneasy.

'Huh,' he muttered, 'let them want me, and let them wait— I'm having a quiet rest here after a hard day's work.'

The two men came over to him; each took hold of an arm, and tried to raise him from the seat; but Stephen sat firm.

'Drink up your beer and come along quick,' said one of them.

'Come along where, man?' asked Stephen.

'Think of the glorious hours of a night the pound'll give the three of us,' said the other man. 'The chance you've been waiting for years has come at last.'

'What chance, man?' asked Stephen.

'The same thing mightn't happen again for a century,' said the second man, 'so come along.'

THE BULL OF BASHAN 219

'What thing, what thing, what thing?' shouted Stephen.

The first man looked wonderingly into Stephen's eyes as he murmured, 'Surely to God you're not afraid to chance it?'

Why does he ask me shall I be afraid? thought Stephen. There must be danger lurking around somewhere, or he wouldn't ask me that—so go careful, go careful, Stephen, my boy.

'Thousands'll watch you, and thousands'll cheer you while you're mesmerizing it,' said the second man.

'Till the steady stare of your eyes forces the animal to go down on its knees in front of you,' said the first man.

Stephen jerked himself free from the coaxing pressure of the two men's hands.

'What are you holdin' me for?—what mesmerizin', what animal?' he shouted.

The first man bent down, and looked admiringly up into Stephen's face.

'The bull,' he said; 'the bull that's broken loose, and is bellowing and running about wild in the street beyond.'

'A bull,' stammered Stephen, 'bellowing and running about wild in the street beyond?'

A crowd began to gather at the door of the tavern and make remarks.

'We've found him,' said the first man to the crowd, 'and he's coming along now in a second.'

'Get him to hurry up,' said a man in the crowd, 'for the bull's getting a bit restless, and may injure somebody if he isn't put under control.'

'The police,' said another man, 'are keeping the crowd back so that Stephen can have plenty of room to work.'

Stephen felt faint. He had been too open-mouthed, blathering round the whole district of how well and effectively he could handle a bull. Many a time, in the parlour of a house, or the parlour of a pub, he had shown how the thing was done. What mad moment put it into his head to meddle with bulls? And Argenteena? What the hell did he know about Argenteena or care either? Find it hard to get it on the map, even though he had been talking about the country a few seconds ago. And now he was getting dragged out to get the better of a bull! He couldn't back out of it either, without becoming the laughing-stock of all who knew him and thousands who didn't. He felt his heart beginning to beat faster. He'd go as far as it was safe to go slowly, so that by the time he got there the bull might be under control.

'What sort of a bull is it?' he asked, as they were pushing him towards the door.

'Oh,' replied one of the crowd, 'it won't really take a lot of doing, Stephen, for it's only a young animal, and white.'

'A young animal, and white,' echoed Stephen, glaring vindictively at him who spoke. 'Shows how you know sweet damn all about it. Only a young animal, and white—it's the young bulls are the most dangerous, especially when they're white, man.'

Stephen felt himself being pulled along the street like lightning. Suddenly they all heard a deep, long bellow of a bull.

'Eh, don't rush me,' protested Stephen. 'None of you seem to realize that I may be going to my death. There's nothing easier for a young bull, when it's a white one, than to slip it across a man.'

The two friends who had come to fetch Stephen walked by his side, one on his left, the other on his right, carrying themselves with an air of importance and pride.

Damn easy for them to feel elated, thought Stephen, at another poor man's expense. He could hear the busy, joyous chatter of the crowd that followed.

'Stephen'll do it all right, he'll have the bull quietly tied up with a rope in the twinkling of an eye,' said one.

'I've seen, myself,' said another, 'a bull, bigger than this one, that was keeping a whole farm in under locked doors, downed by Stephen with only just a shake of his finger and a look from his eyes.' 'It was a lucky thing we thought of Stephen,' said a woman. 'An' a luckier thing we found him,' said another.

'A gang of cannibals, that's what they are,' murmured Stephen, 'a gang of cannibals.'

'Here we are,' said one of the men leading Stephen, with a gay note of confidence in his voice: 'here we are, at last,' as they began to mix with and push through a large crowd which had gathered at the end of a street. 'Gangway there, make way, gang-way, please.'

Stephen was shoved to the front, and somebody put a coil of rope in his hand. He looked round and saw, out of a mist, that he was in a long street, over each side of which towered huge, sombre-shaped stone warehouses, the walls broken at regular intervals by heavy wooden gates, all of which were now closed. Outside of one of the gates he noticed a low-decked lorry, from which the horse had been taken, standing idly there, the long, heavy shafts resting on the cobblestones of the street. Far away he saw a crowd of people gathered at the other end of the street, keeping close to the corners so that they might be able to dash off in different ways if the bull came too close. All the world like an arena, he thought; the warehouses, the dens; the heavy entrances, the gates that led the wild beasts in or out; the cobble-stones the place where the battles were fought; and the crowds at each end, the audience that watched, laughed, cheered or turned their thumbs down. His eyes swam, his ears buzzed, his stomach felt queer, his legs felt like heavy columns of steel, and his heart thumped so madly that he almost saw his breast swelling out in front of him, sinking back and swelling out again. He felt a terrible desire to yell, to turn and fly, to yell and yell and turn and fly away to God knows where.

'You'd better make a start, me man,' said a heavy-headed policeman, to Stephen, 'if you're goin' to do it before the stars come out.'

'Let no one cough or laugh or cheer, to startle the animal,' said Stephen, as he moved forward.

He wished that the rope he held in his hand was a pair of rosary beads; but it wasn't, and it was getting as heavy as a hawser. He winked his eyes to shake off the gossamer mist which covered them and peered ahead. Then he saw the bull. A young, supple, yellowish-white fellow, with long curving horns tipped with black; powerful, muscular neck strong enough to toss a man over the warehouses; elegant, twitching flanks that a gleam from the setting sun turned to bronze. There he stood gazing fixedly at the crowd gathered at the far end of the street, slashing his back with his twitching tail—now on the right side, now on the left. As Stephen went on, his pace grew slower. The bull, with a stronger and more vicious switch of his tail, suddenly turned round, and looked at Stephen. Stephen stood still. He felt himself sinking down into a small, little man as the head of the bull grew bigger and bigger, till the eyes were like huge red November suns, and the horns spread over the sky like the branches of an oak tree. Then Stephen heard a sound, like thunder, and knew that the bull had bellowed. He let the rope fall from his hands, turned swiftly on his heels and fled. His legs that had been as heavy as lead moved like the wings of a swallow. He would rush headlong into the crowd at the end of the street, bury himself deep in the midst of the people, and put a crowd of soft bodies between himself and the charge of the bull. Then he heard the thuh thuh thuh thud, thuh thuh thuh thud of the bull's hooves on the cobbles as the animal came along after him. He glanced ahead and saw that the crowd had scattered, and were flying off in different directions. A wave of hatred surged through his soul as he raised his voice and shouted, 'Stand your ground, there, stand your ground.' But they heeded him not, and ran for their lives. Dirty cowards, the people, thought Stephen, as he rushed along; dirty cowards the whole of them—they wouldn't risk a pinprick to save a man's life. That's the thanks I get for showin' them an example of what a man ought to be.

Closer and closer came the sound of the thuh thuh thuh thud, thuh thuh thuh thud of the bull's hooves on the cobblestones, and Stephen felt the hot, bitter breath from the bull's nostrils on the back of his neck.

His eye caught sight of the horseless lorry standing idly by one of the warehouse gates, a few yards away. He made for the lorry, swerving suddenly to the right as the bull swept past him. He heard the scratching of the bull's hooves on the cobbles as the animal checked his speed to turn and charge at him again. But as the bull was almost on top of him he dived under the lorry, sliding over the cobbles to the end farthest from the bull, tearing his trousers and tearing his knees as he did so. Thrusting its head under the lorry, the bull glared at him and bellowed.

Stephen crawled out by the other side, but the bull trotted round, and he had to dive under the lorry again. He looked from beneath the lorry and saw that the crowd were gathering again in their old places to watch. First they had watched to see what he would do to the bull; but now they watched to see what the bull would do to him. The moment he got under the lorry the bull thrust his head under, too, and tried to reach him with his horns, so that Stephen had to scurry on his knees to the other side of the lorry. The bull trotted round, and again Stephen had to hurry on his knees to the other side of the lorry. Not one of the crowd stirred to help him. Stephen was getting exhausted; he wouldn't be able to keep up the dodging much longer. Crawling swiftly to the end of the lorry, Stephen shouted over to the crowd: 'For God's sake, dear Christian people, do something to drive him away before he rips me open, 'n leaves me in sthrips lying on the road.' He had hardly finished the sentence before the bull was round poking at him, and he was forced to crawl rapidly back to the other end of the lorry. Then he cocked his ears in amazement, for he heard the sound of laughter; the crowd were laughing and enjoying his terrible predicament. They even began to make ironical comments on the situation. Stephen heard them all as he was scurrying from side to side and from end to end of the lorry.

'He'll get away from you, Stephen, if you're not careful.'

'Don't interfere, now—Stephen has his own way of tamin' bulls.'

'He's doin' all this dodging just to tire the animal out.'

'Hope he won't be prosecuted for cruelty to animals.'

'He shouldn't tease the animal too much, for he's not in Argenteena now.'

With a lunge of his head, the bull thrust his horns between the spokes of one of the wheels, listing an end of the lorry three or four feet from the ground, letting it down again with a thump which nearly cracked the skull of Stephen. He felt that he was done. But it was hard lines that he would have to slide into the unknown with his ears full of the hilarity of a cowardly, pleasure-seeking crowd. He'd make one last effort to get them to realize what a serious thing life was: lying on his belly, he put his hands to the sides of his mouth, making a rough megaphone of them, and shouted to the crowd: 'For the love of God, brothers, get the police to do something, or send for the fire brigade.' Then with his clothes torn and muddy, his hands and knees scratched, damp with sweat, he lay down flat and waited for the bull. He heard the rattling of the lorry as the bull savagely pulled it about, his horns caught in the spokes of a wheel. He heard the patter of feet and the murmur of many voices. He prayed that when the bull came, death might be swift and painless. Mother o' God, he felt the horns poking at his coat. A few seconds more, and the horns would be boring his vitals! He was roughly turned over on his back, and pulled and punched—the bull was going to worry him before he gave him the final prod. He heard laughter, and a loud voice telling him to get up an' be sensible. He opened his eyes, and saw a burly policeman bending over him.

'Where is he?' murmured Stephen. 'Is he gone; is he undher proper conthrol?'

'Here,' replied the policeman, 'get up ower that, man, an' don't be keepin' the crowd gathered to obsthruct the thraffic. If it's the bull you're thinkin' of, he's gone away long ago, roped liked a fly in a spider's web. We've had more than enough of your demonsthration of cow-punchin', so get up ower that an' go home—you an' your cocky walk an' your lassooin'.'

Stephen climbed painfully to his feet, dejected and crestfallen. With head bent down, he pushed his way through the crowd that murmured ironical praise as he passed.

'I'll be out of this disthrict,' muttered Stephen as he hurried away, 'before the week's out, for they're not Christians. They'd never get to the end of their jeerin' if I stopped among them— a nest of ignorant pagans, that's what they are.'

It was a sweltering hot evening, and Stephen was voluptuously drinking a foamy pint of beer as he sat in a pub at the other end of the town.

'I left the disthrict,' he was saying to the barman, 'because they weren't Christians. Savages with clothes on—that's what they were.'

'This must be the hottest evening yet this year,' murmured the sweating barman.

'Nothin' to the heat in Argenteena,' replied Stephen.

'Spent some of your time out there?' queried the barman.

'Best part of me life,' replied Stephen, 'cow-punchin'.'

'Dangerous job, that,' said the barman.

'Soon get used to it,' said Stephen carelessly. ''Course you have to keep your wits about you. I seen many a good man speared when he was off his guard.'

'Bulls are big out there, aren't they?' asked the barman.

'Big as bisons,' said Stephen. 'Everything's on a big scale out there. The bells of flowers out there are as big as the funnels of Atlantic liners—a whole family could camp in one of them comfortable.'

'How do the bees manage?' asked the barman.

Stephen emptied his pipe by tapping the bowl on the sole of his foot, and glanced scornfully at the barman.

'There ain't no bees in Argenteena,' he said.

THIRST

Flann O'Brien

Flann O'Brien is probably equally remembered as the author of a comic masterpiece, At-Swim-Two-Birds, *published in 1939, or as a brilliant satirical newspaper columnist who signed himself Myles na Gopaleen. But he also had a considerable impact on the world of the theatre and in 1943 wrote* Faustus Kelly, *a tale of the Devil involving himself in Irish politics with unexpected results (he prefers Hell) and which proved one of the funniest plays ever staged at the Abbey. 'Thirst' is a not dissimilar piece of writing in the 'pub play' tradition in which a landlord and two of his customers who are drinking after hours engage a policeman in a scathing little sketch which one critic claims shows that O'Brien had 'an ear for dialogue on a par with Joyce'.*

The name Flann O'Brien was itself just one of several pseudonyms used by Brian O'Nolan (1911–66) who was born in Strabane, County Tyrone, one of a family of twelve children. He was educated at University College, Dublin where his penchant for humour was first revealed in student debates and for allegedly publishing obscene stories in Old Irish in the college magazine— although no one in authority could actually read the Old Irish. From 1935, O'Nolan worked as a civil servant, but because no government employee was allowed to publish under his real name, issued At-Swim-Two-Birds *as by Flann O'Brien. The novel was recommended by Graham Greene and highly praised by Samuel Beckett and James Joyce. In 1940, employing another name, Myles na Gopaleen, he began a column in the* Irish Times, *'Cruiskeen Lawn' (meaning 'Little Brimming Jug' and full of the curiosa of everyday Dublin life) which appeared for nearly thirty years and won admirers far beyond the confines of Ireland. Among these fans were the American humourists, S. J. Perelman and James Thurber who rated it the funniest newspaper feature ever published.*

O'Brien was a familiar figure in a number of the Dublin pubs including Grogan's, the Dolphin and the Scotch House—to all of which he referred regularly in his column—although he is celebrated today in the Porter House on Parliament Street. This sells a creamy, bitter-sweet beer known as 'Plain', an old Dublin expression for porter, which O'Brien immortalised in a poem, 'A Pint of Plain is Your Only Porter'. Ill-health caused O'Brien to retire early from the civil service in 1953, but he continued to write 'Cruiskeen Lawn' as well as further novels, The Hard Life (1962), The Dalkey Archive (1964) *and* The Third Policeman, *published posthumously in 1967. He even had the last laugh on his many admirers by dying—appropriately—on April Fool's Day 1966.*

*   *   *

(The curtain goes up on the bar. It is after hours. Light from a distant street-lamp shines faintly on the window. The bar is lit (very badly) by two candles which are set on the counter, one of them stuck in a bottle. The Publican, MR C., *who is suitably fat and prosperous in appearance, is leaning over the centre of the counter talking to* PETER, *who is sitting on a stool side-face to the audience.* JEM, *who is in the nature of a hanger-on, is away in a gloomy corner where he can barely be discerned. Both customers are drinking pints; the Publican has a small whiskey. The curtain has gone up in the middle of a conversation between* PETER *and the Publican.)*

MR C. (*dramatically*): And do you know why? (*There is a pause.*) Do you know why?

PETER: Begor, Mr Coulahan, I couldn't tell you.

MR C. (*loudly, lifting a bottle and pouring*): Because he's no good—that's why—no bloody good at all! *(Finishes pouring bottle.)* And another thing—*(Dramatic pause.)*

(He finishes his drink in one gulp. Turns to the shelves for the whiskey bottle and noisily fills himself another. As the talk proceeds he is occupied with pulling two further stouts to fill up the customers' glasses. PETER *smokes and bends his head reflectively.* JEM *is silent save for drinking noises. He shows his face for a moment in the gloom by lighting a cigarette.)*

MR C.: He has a brother from the County Galway that comes up every year for the Horse Show, a hop-off-my-thumb that you wouldn't notice passing you on the stairs, all dressed out in fancy riding-breeches. Last year he turned up in the uncle's pub beyond in Drumcondra, complete with fountain-pen . . . and cheque-book. Gave your man as his reference. *(He pauses ominously.)* My God, the unfortunate bloody uncle. *(He laughs hollowly.)* The poor unfortunate bloody uncle. Twelve pounds fifteen shillings he was stuck for. Thirteen pounds you might say—thirteen pounds that he spent a good month of his life gathering together by the sweat of his brow! Now for God's sake—did you ever hear anything like it?

JEM *(who has a strong Dublin accent)*: Oh, the cheque-book is the man. Manny's the time I wished to God I had one of me own!

PETER *(slyly)*: Of course, that crowd digs with the other foot. It's a lot of money to be stung for, there's no doubt. Some publicans are very foolish.

MR C.: Digs with the other foot? If you was to ask me—they dig with both feet! Whatever suits their book at the time, they'll dig with that one. And they do all the digging in other people's pockets! *(Sips whiskey.)* Sure, I believe your man's wife was up for lifting stuff out of Slattery's.

PETER *(surprised)*: Is that so? I didn't hear that.

MR C.: Certainly, man. Certainly she was.

JEM: Begob, half the town's wheelin' stuff outa that place night and day, they do be bringin' hand-carts up there, some of them.

PETER (*reflectively*): It's funny how some families seem to go all the one way. It's some sort of a streak. It's in the blood, I suppose.

JEM: Aye, it's the blood right enough.

PETER: There's a bad ugly streak in that crowd—although every one of them got a good education. All at the Christian Brothers, no less.

MR C. (*turns to bottle behind him and pours himself another whiskey*): Don't be talking man! Sure it's up in Mountjoy jail I'd have every one of them, and that's where they'll be yet,—doing a stretch of seven years apiece for grand larceny and robbery and thievery and every crime in the calendar. And wasn't there another brother that skipped to America after sticking up a bank in the Troubles—all in the name of Ireland. (*He moves to cash register.*)

JEM: Begob, Mr Coulahan, and I forgot about the bank stick-up!

MR C.: Sure we put up with far too much in this country. (*Sighs.*) And there's a certain other gentleman comes in here for his pint that ought to be locked up too, a very . . . very . . . respectable . . . gentleman——(*He breaks off.*) What was that? (*Noise.*)

JEM: Eh, what's that?

PETER (*startled*): What? I heard nothing.

(COULAHAN *moves to shelves.*)

MR C.: Shhh! Shhh! For God's sake! It's the Guards!

PETER and JEM: The Guards! The Guards! Begob! We're ruined! (PETER *and* JEM *duck behind counter.*)

MR C.: Shhh.

(*He blows out one of the candles, completely obliterating* JEM. *He tiptoes to the window and listens with bent head.*)

MR C. (*in agitated whisper*): Shhh! Now for God's sake. I think that bloody Sergeant is on the prowl.

JEM: Begob! We're bunched! (*He blows out candle on table.*)

MR C. *and* PETER: Shhh! (*Three knocks on the door.*)

SERGEANT (*outside door*): Guards on duty! Guards on duty. Will you please open up, Mr Coulahan.

PETER: We'll keep very quiet.

MR C. (*loudly, in violent agitation*): SHHHHH.

(*There is complete silence.* PETER *leans over to the remaining candle and caps the flame in his hands to hide the lights.* MR C. *is bent nearly double in his intent listening and keeps on Shhh-ing and waving a hand for even further silence. There is no sound at all without. Thirty seconds pass. Suddenly* MR C. *leaps at the candle and blows it out, leaves nothing visible save the window that is lit by the street-lamp. Almost simultaneously three loud knocks are given on the door.*)

(*The knocks are repeated, more urgently. The three remain completely still. Then* COULAHAN *moves to the counter where he finishes his drink. The knocks are given again. The bottom of the door is kicked slightly and the thick brogue of the* SERGEANT *is faintly heard shouting something.* MR C. *is heard sighing heavily.*)

MR C.: Well, that's that, that's that. (*He is groping for his matches, finds them and carefully lights both candles.*) Yes, that's that.

(*The knocks are repeated even louder. He comes from behind the counter. Then moves to the door.*)

MR C.: Alright, Sergeant, I'm coming. (*He opens the door.*) Good night to you, Sergeant. That's a hardy cold one for you.

SERGEANT (*to invisible Guard*): That's all right, Guard.

(SERGEANT *enters.* COULAHAN *closes door, switches on light.*)

SERGEANT: It is, indeed, as you say, Mr Coulahan, a cowld, raw class of a night. 'Tisn't a seasonable time of the year at all for this time of year. 'Tis not indeed!

MR C. (*coming forward with a show of forced gaiety and going back behind the counter*): Well, we can't complain, we had an easy enough winter up till now. No, we can't complain. We can't . . . complain.

(*The* SERGEANT *has found his note book and pencil.*)

SERGEANT: It's in the wife's name, if I'm not mistaken, Mr Coulahan?

MR C.: Yes, Sergeant, the house is in the wife's name. *(Pause.)*

PETER: You know my name, I suppose, Sergeant?

SERGEANT: I do. I do. And if I'm not altogether mistaken, that's another old friend of mine beyant.

JEM: Oh, too true, Sergeant. Manny's the time we've met before. And will again, please God.

SERGEANT: O faith we will. We'll meet again, and many a time. Many a time.

JEM: I suppose, Sergeant, you wouldn't mind if I finished me bottle of stout? We don't want waste in these hard times, do we?

SERGEANT (*turning away from* JEM'S *direction with great deliberation*): What ye might do when me back is turned, is a thing I would know nothing at all about.

(All resume their drinks, which are nearly full, the SERGEANT *standing very aloof with his back to the counter. He appears to be engrossed in his notebook.)*

PETER: We might as well be hung for sheep as lambs, I suppose.

MR C. (*dismally*): Yes, indeed. We all know you have the terrible time of it, Sergeant, in the performance of your duty.

PETER (*moves to bar*): Begob and you're right, Mr Coulahan.

MR C.: It would be as much as my livelihood or your promotion in the force was worth for me to offer you a drink after hours in these premises. Or for you to accept it—even on such a blasted, blizzardy one like this when the flesh might be skinned off your bones and you in the pursuit of your duty. Think of that, gentlemen!

PETER: It's tough, right enough, Sergeant. *(He turns to* SERGEANT.*)*

MR C.: If I was caught offering you a drink after hours, Sergeant, I could be brought up on the gravest charges—bribery, corruption and attempted suborning of the police force.

*(*JEM *moves to bar.)*

JEM: God save us, Mr Coulahan!

MR C.: What would happen to you, Sergeant, I don't rightly know at all—not being fully acquainted with the rules, regulations and disciplinary measures governing the Civic

Guards or Gawrdah Skeekawnah, as now known. *(Sighs deeply.)* We both have the hard times of it, Sergeant, and that's the truth. *(He turns for bottles behind him.)* A strong ball of malt is what I'm badly in need of myself at this moment—what with being perished with the cold all day. *(Pours drink.)* And now, at night, with a breach of closed hours on me hands. *(Sighs heavily and takes drink.)*

JEM: True enough. The cold was somethin' fierce today. Desperate. You'd want mufflers round yer legs as well as round yer neck.

PETER: Well, the summer won't be long now.

COULAHAN: The summer? *(Sighs.)* D'you remember last August, Sergeant?

SERGEANT: I do and I don't, Mr Coulahan. I do and I don't.

MR C.: It was the grand month of summer weather, Sergeant. I was out swimming twice. The water was like soup. And begob the heat of the rocks would nearly burn the feet off you.

JEM: I never fancied the water at all, Mr Coulahan. Never had any time for it. It's not a natural thing to be getting into. It's alright for fish, of course.

MR C.: That month of August was so hot it—it put me in mind of the First War—when I was out beyond in Messpott!

JEM: Holy God, where's that?

MR C.: Messiopotamia! Did ye never hear tell of Messiopotamia? And there was me fighting the Turks and the Arabs— fighting for small nationalities! That's the quare one, Sergeant. That month of summer we had brought me back to the First World War.

SERGEANT: Them two Great Wars were desperate and ferocious encounters.

PETER: I suppose it was very hot out there?

MR C.: Hot did you say? I don't believe there was heat anywhere like it before or after. It was a class of heat that people in this part of the world wouldn't understand at all. Forty years ago and more and I can still feel that sun beyond in Shatt-el-Arab. That was where we landed.

(The SERGEANT *takes no notice and* MR C. *quietly refills his own drink and pulls three stouts, the third of which he places on the counter between himself and the* SERGEANT.*)*

PETER: Was there—much sunstroke?

MR C.: Sunstroke? We thought the heat in the ship was bad enough—and so it was—till we landed! Nearly three thousand of us! *(Gasps.)* The first thing I feels walking down the gangway is a big rush of hot air up me nose. The heat was beltin' up outa the ground like smoke out of an engine. The air was so thin and so hot that you wouldn't feel yourself breathing it. It was—stretched out, d'you know. Thinned out be the heat coming at it outa the ground and outa the sky and all sides. It was dried and no moisture in it at all— like a withered pea. *(Pause.)* It was like putting your head into an oven and taking a deep breath.

PETER: I wouldn't fancy that at all—bad as the weather is in Ireland, it's better than that.

MR C.: You haven't heard the half, so you haven't. We weren't finished gasping for breath, when another desperate thing happened! The lads were hours coming off the boat, and the rest of us was lined up there on the quayside. It was this way—I got tired standing on me feet—if you know what I mean—and went to change me weight from one foot to the other. Well, do you know what I'm going to tell you? My feet was stuck. *(They gasp.)* Stuck to the ground.

JEM: Begob, ya musta had spikes in them.

MR C.: Spikes be damned! Weren't we all standing there in our tropical rubber-soled shoes, and wasn't all the rubber melting under us.

JEM: I never heard the like of that. Never.

MR C.: A thousand men lined up there on the quay—and not one of them able to budge. My God, it was fierce! Fierce!

JEM: Did you ever throw a bit of rubber inta the fire by accident? Begob, the hum off it would destroy yer nose altogether.

MR C.: Of course, we were soldiers. No question of 'Please, Sir, I'm stuck to the ground, Sir! Me shoes is meltin', Sir,

what'll I do, Sir?' None of that class of thing at all. Oh, no.
It was just a question of standing there, waiting for the order
to quick march. You shoulda seen us when we got the order.
D'you know what it was like? Did you ever see a fly—a
fly trying to walk off a fly-paper?

JEM: I know what you mean—exactly! Buzzin' and roarin'
and twistin' and workin' away with the legs—up to his neck
in sticky stuff.

MR C.: Just like flies on a fly-paper we were.

JEM: Isn't that I was sayin'?

MR C.: It was a march of only two hundred yards to our quarters—but it was the dirtiest—sweatiest—stickiest—and
driest march we ever had. Every man in a lather of sweat,
his clothes stickin' to his skin, and his tongue hangin' outa
him lika dog's.

(Here both JEM *and* PETER *take long and resounding slugs
from their cool drinks. The sergeant fusses uncomfortably
with his book as if determined to take no interest in* MR C.'s
recital.)

PETER: Begob, Sergeant, and me own tongue's beginnin' to
hang out like a dog's as well!

MR C.: Well, begging the Sergeant's pardon and kind indul-
gences, I'm going to have a ball of malt meself because I
feel the want of it after thinking about me days as a soldier
out in Messpot. God help me. (COULAHAN *drinks.*)

SERGEANT (*ponderously*): I'm finishing up me notes here—
and when me notes is finished, we'll all have to say good
night and go home to our beds—and thank God we have
beds to go to.

JEM: You never spoke a truer word, Sergeant. Sometimes I do
be . . .

SERGEANT: There might be murders and all classes of illegal-
ities goin' on behind me back, but what I don't see I don't
know . . .

JEM: That's a fact, Sergeant.

SERGEANT: The Law is a very—intricate thing. And nobody
knows it better than meself.

MR C.: Spoken like a sensible man, Sergeant, and we're all very grateful. We know you're only doin' your duty. Just the same as we were when we were servin' in the King's uniform out in Messiopotamia before it was burnt off our backs with the heat.

PETER: I suppose you had many a bad time after the day you landed in the rubber shoes?

MR C.: Bad times? BAD TIMES did ye say? Did I not ... (*Gulps another drink.*) Did I not tell you about the desert?

JEM: You did not. (*Pause.*)

MR C.: We had some desperate times out in the desert. No man that lived through that will ever have the memory of it off his mind—not even if he had his brain washed—and that's a fact!

JEM: Begob, and I'd hate to have me brain washed! It's bad enough havin' yer ...

MR C.: There was a detachment of Arab madmen sighted away out in the desert near some oasis or other—There they were, musterin' together to get ready to come in and attack us ...

PETER: Begor ...

MR C.: Maybe there was a thousand of them in it, and others comin' in on camels to join them.

PETER: I'd be nervous of camels.

MR C.: So the order comes down that we're all to march out and go for them before they had a chance to get themselves into battle-order. (*Sips drink.*) That was the way it was. I'll never forget it—as long as I live—never! (*Pause.*)

PETER: Were they far out in the desert?

MR C.: I'd say—I'd say—about twenty-five or—mebbe thirty miles—as the crow flies.

JEM: Does there be crows in the desert?

MR C.: At six o'clock in the morning—sic ack-emma we called it—we got the order. (*In Sergeant-Major's voice.*) Get ready to march in two hours. (Normal voice.) On with the rubber shoes and the packs and the belts and the water-bottles, and the bloody big rifles! It was a load that would kill a man in his health. Then out on parade. (*Sergeant-Major voice.*) Quick March! Left, right, left, right! (*Normal voice.*) Away out into the wilds with us—a straggling string of men staggering out into the burning sand. *(He drinks.)* A twenty-four hours forced march. *(Puts down glass.)* But we were bet— bet to the ropes! It was the shoes again.

JEM: Didn't I tell ye?

MR C. (*drinks again*): Then the rubber began to melt again— and give out little puffs of smoke. Soon the feet began to be roasted like two joints with a fire under them!

PETER: The Lord save us!

MR C.: Don't be talkin', man! When I'd got an extra stab of heat in the feet, I'd give a lep inta the air with the pain of it.

JEM: I declare to me God!

MR C.: But when I'd come down on the sand again, I'd get worse roastin' from the weight of the lep—showers of sparks flying' right, left and centre. (*Drinks again.*) And d'you know what was happenin' all this time?

JEM: I suppose the enemy lads was lyin' in wait behind the trees?

MR C.: What trees?

JEM: Wouldn't there be all classes of palm trees about the place?

MR C.: Well, I'll tell you what was happenin' (*Drinks again.*) I declare to God the sun began to come down on top of us—outa the sky! Every minute that passed, it seemed to be lower—and lower—down—down—on top of our heads. The heat, gentlemen—the heat! (*Gulps hurriedly.*) I can nearly feel it still. Then after a while I felt a queer thing happenin'.

JEM: I was goin' to say that.

PETER: Would ye shut up, and let . . .

MR C.: After a little while I begun to dry up!

PETER: Dry up?

MR C.: Every bit of me begun to get dried up and withered. The first thing that went outa order was the tongue and the mouth. Me tongue begun to get dry and cracked! And then it begun to get—bigger!

JEM: Oh, Holy Hour!

MR C.: It swelled out till it nearly choked me and got as hard and dry as a big cinder. I couldn't swally with it! *(All three gulp drinks.)* The whole inside of me mouth got dry and cracked the same way—and so did me neck and all inside me.

PETER: The Lord between us and all harm!

MR C.: It was like bein' grilled—except there was no gravy.

PETER: I suppose the eyes were affected, too.

MR C.: Don't be talkin' man! The eyes—the eyes begun to get singed and burnt at the edges. And, as well as that, the watery part dried up in a way that was something fierce. *(Pause.)* Before I knew where I was—the eyebrows were gone!

PETER: No!

MR C.: Withered and scorched away be the heat they were— Hell itself. *(Gulps another drink.)* It was terrible. There we were, staggerin' through the bloody—brazen—boilin'— blanketty-blank heat. The skin chippin' and curlin' off our faces. Our bodies dryin' up and witherin' into wrinkles like—prunes! And the worst of it—a hot, dry thirst comin' up outa our necks, like the blast from a furnace. Oh, my God, it was desperate—desperate. *(He gulps again.)* D'you know the first thing the lads done—nearly every one of them? *(Pause.)* Took off their water-bottles—and threw them away. And do you know why? Do you know why? *(Pause.)* I'll tell you why—the water-bottles were made of metal. Some class of anumilliyum—anumilliyum as thin as paper. When that sun got to work on them bottles, I needn't tell you what happened. First of all, the water got up near to boiling-point. Even if you could hold the bottle in your hand and open it, the water would be no good to you— because it would scald the neck off you. There was only one thing to do with the bottles—get rid of them! Matteradam what else happens.

PETER: Wasn't it terrible, throwin' away bottles full of water in the middle of the desert.

MR C.: Well, there you are—there you are.

JEM: Of course you coulda buried all the bottles deep down in a hole and come back for them when the thirst was at you. The water'd be nice and cool then.

PETER: And what happened after that?

MR C.: What happened after that is not a thing I would like to swear to because—the heat began to have a very bad effect—up here—(*Tapping forehead.*)—in the attic.

PETER: I suppose so.

MR C.: There's a lot of moisture and blood and so on in the brain, y'know. The brain is like a wet sponge, and very queer things are goin' to happen. Very queer things.

PETER: I suppose you're lucky to be alive at all.

MR C.: Very queer things. (*Lowering voice.*) The first thing was—I lost me sense of direction! I didn't know whether me head was me heels or whether I was standin' or sittin', d'you know? I was fallin' all over the place.

PETER: I declare to me——

MR C.: So were the other lads—walkin' and crawlin' on top of each other—every man as dry as a brick, with his tongue swollen out in his parched mouth half-chokin' him. And—the—thirst!!! My God, the thirst!!!!

(SERGEANT *comes to counter and takes three drinks, one by one, and drinks them.*)

SERGEANT: Tell me, lads. Tell me—does anybody mind if I sing 'The Rose of Tralee'?

(*They all sing.*)

THE DIVINER

Brian Friel

*Brian Friel is Ireland's greatest living playwright and his work
has deservedly earned comparison with that of Synge, Shaw and
O'Casey. His characters are likewise the victims of history, social
disintegration and political brutality. Yet, even when they are
losers and failures, they still manage to summon up the power
of their imaginations in a search for meaning to their lives. Friel
uses this idea in 'The Diviner', one of his few short stories, about
Nelly Doherty, a woman recently widowed for the second time
in her life, and seeking the aid of a Diviner's powers to discover
what link—if any—there may be between her first drunken husband and the second who has just been found drowned in mysterious circumstances. It is also the moving tale of her struggle for
respectability in the face of her first husband's love of the bottle.*

*Born in Omagh, County Tyrone, the son of a schoolmaster,
Brian Friel (1929–   ) followed in this same profession for ten
years as a primary and intermediary teacher in Derry. But his
passion for literature and the stage led to him contributing work
to the Abbey Theatre and fame came in 1964 with the technically
daring production of* Philadelphia, Here I Come *in which two
actors play the upbeat outer and troubled inner selves of an
Irishman about to emigrate to America. The production proved
a big success on both sides of the Atlantic and was filmed in
1970. Another milestone in Brian Friel's career was* Dancing at
Lughnasa *(1990), about two poverty-stricken sisters, which
opened at the Abbey, transferred to Broadway, won three Tony
Awards, and was later filmed. This play, along with* Freedom of
the City *(1973) and, appropriately,* Making History *(1988) were*

among a group of the author's works revived at a special festival at the Abbey in 1999 to mark his seventieth birthday. Would that the great man of the Irish theatre might find time to write more stories like 'The Diviner' . . .

*   *   *

During twenty-five years of married life, Nelly Devenny was ashamed to lift her head because of Tom's antics. He was seldom sober, never in a job for more than a few weeks at a time, and always fighting. When he fell off his bicycle one Saturday night and was killed by a passing motor-cycle, no one in the village of Drumeen was surprised that Nelly was not heartbroken. She took the death calmly and with quiet dignity and even shed a few tears when the coffin was lowered into the grave. After a suitable period of mourning, she went out to work as a char-woman, and the five better-class families she asked for employment were blessed for their prompt charity, because Nelly was the perfect servant—silent, industrious, punctual, spotlessly clean. Later, when others, hearing of her value, tried to engage her, they discovered that her schedule was full; all her time was divided among the bank manager, the solicitor, the dentist, the doctor and the prosperous McLaughlins of the Arcade.

Father Curran, the parish priest, was the only person she told she was getting married again, and he knew she told him only because she had to have a baptismal certificate and letters of freedom.

'He's not from around these parts, Nelly, is he?' the priest asked.

'He's not, Father.'

'Is he from County Donegal at all?'

'He's from the West, Father,' said Nelly, smoothing down the hem of her skirt. 'Of course, Mr Doherty's retired now. He's not a young man, but he's very fresh-looking.'

'Retired?' the priest said promptingly.

'Yes, Father,' said Nelly. 'Mr Doherty's retired.'

'And you'll live here in Drumeen with—with Mr Doherty?'

'That is our intention, Father.'

'Well, I wish you every blessing, Nelly,' said Father Curran in dismissal, because he was an inquisitive man and Nelly was giving nothing away. 'I'll see you when you get back.' Then quickly—an old trick of his—'The wedding is in the West, did you say?'

'That has to be settled yet, Father,' said Nelly calmly. 'It will just be a quiet affair. At our time of day, Father, we would prefer no fuss and no talk.'

He took the hint and let her go.

Nelly Devenny became Nelly Doherty, and she and her husband moved into her cottage at the outskirts of the village. Drumeen's speculation on Mr Doherty was wild and futile. What age was he? Was he younger than Nelly? What part of the West did he come from? What had he been—a train driver, a skipper of a fishing boat, a manager of a grocery shop, a plumber, a carpenter? Had he any relatives? Had he even a Christian name? Where had they met? Was it true that she had put an advertisement in the paper and that his was the only answer? But Nelly parried all their probings and carefully sheltered Mr Doherty from their clever tongues. The grinding humiliation of having her private life made public every turnabout in bars and courthouses for twenty-five years had made her skilled in reticence and fanatically jealous of her dignity. He stayed in the house during the day while she worked, and in the evening, if the weather was good, they could be seen going out along the Mill Road for a walk, Nelly dressed entirely in black and Mr Doherty in his gabardine raincoat, checked cap, and well-polished shoes, the essence of respectability. And in time the curiosity died and the only person to bring up the subject now and again was McElwee, the postman, who had been a drinking pal of Tom Devenny, her first husband. 'I'm damned if I can make head or tail of Doherty!' he would say to the others in McHugh's pub. 'A big, grown man with rough hands and dressed up in good clothes and taking walks like that—it's not natural!' And McElwee was also puzzled because, he said, Mr Doherty had never received a letter, not even a postcard, since the day he arrived in Drumeen.

On the first Sunday in March, three months after their marriage, Mr Doherty was drowned in the bog-black water of Lough Keer-agh. Several of the mountainy Meenalaragan people who passed the lake on their way to last Mass in the village saw him fishing from Dr Boyle's new punt, and on their way home from the chapel they found the boat, water-logged, swaying on its keel in the shallow water along the south shore. In it were Mr Doherty's fishing bag, his checked cap, and one trout.

Father Curran went to Nelly's house and broke the news to her. When he told her, she hesitated, her face a deep red, and then said, 'As true as God, Father, he was out at first Mass with me,' as if he had accused her of having a husband who skipped Mass for a morning's fishing. (When he thought about her strange reaction later that day, he concluded that Mr Doherty most likely had not been out at first Mass.) He took her in his car out to the lake and parked it at right angles to the shore, and there she sat in the front seat right through that afternoon and evening and night, never once moving, as she watched the search for her husband. When Father Curran had to go back to Drumeen for the seven o['clock devotions—in an empty chapel, as it turned out, because by then the whole of the village was at Lough Keeragh—he had not the heart to ask her to get out. So he borrowed the curate's car, and the curate took the parish priest's place beside Nelly. Every hour or so, they said a rosary together, and between prayers Nelly watched quietly and patiently and responded respectfully to the curate's ponderous consolings.

Everyone toiled unsparingly, not only the people to whose houses she went charring every day—her clients, as she called them: Dr Boyle; Mr Mannion, of the bank; Mr Groome, the solicitor; Dr Timmons, the dentist; the McLaughlins—but the ordinary villagers, people of her own sort, although many of them were only names to her. Logan, the fish merchant, sent his lorry to the far end of Donegal to bring back boats for the job of dragging the lake; O'Hara, the taximan, sent his two cars to Derry to fetch the frogmen from the British Admiralty base there; and Joe Morris, the bus conductor, drove to Killybegs for herring nets.

The women worked as generously as the men. They condoled
with Nelly first, each going to where she sat in the parish priest's
car and saying how deeply sorry she was about the great and
tragic loss,. To each of them Nelly gave her red, washer-woman's
hand, said a few suitable words of thanks, and even had the
presence of mind to inquire about a sick child or a son in America
or a cow that was due to calve. Then the women set up a canteen
in Dr Boyle's boathouse and made tea and snacks for the workers
on the lake. Among themselves they marvelled at Nelly's calm,
at her dignified resignation.

'The poor soul! As if one tragedy wasn't enough.'

'Just when she was beginning to enjoy life, too.'

'And they were so attached to each other, so complete in
themselves.'

'Have his people been notified?'

'Someone mentioned that to Nelly, but she said his people are
all dead or in England.'

'He must have got a heart attack, the poor man.'

'Maybe that . . .'

'Why? What did you hear?'

'Nothing, nothing . . . Nobody knows for certain but himself
and his Maker.'

'Is it true that he took the Doctor's boat without permission?
That he broke the chain with a stone?'

'Sure, if he had gone to the Doctor straight and asked him, he
would have got the boat and welcome.'

'Poor Nelly!'

'Poor Nelly indeed. But isn't it people like her that always get
the sorest knocks?'

It was late afternoon before the search was properly organized.
The mile-long lake was divided into three strips, which were
separated by marker buoys. Each strip was dragged by a seine
net stretched between two yawls. The work was slow and frustrat-
ing, the men unskilled in the job. Ropes were stretched too taut
and snapped. The outboard motors got fouled in the weeds. Then
dusk fell and imperceptibly thickened into darkness, and every
available vehicle from Drumeen was lined up along the shore

and its headlights beamed across the water. Submerged tar barrels were brought to the surface, the hulk of an old boat, the carcass of a sheep, a plough, and a cart wheel, but there was no trace of Mr Doherty. At intervals of half an hour a man in shirt and trousers went to the parish priest's car to report progress to Nelly.

'Thank you,' she said each time. 'Thank you all. You are all so kind.'

And immediately the priest beside her would resume prayers, because he imagined that sooner or later she would break down.

Father Curran had just returned from devotions and released the curate when the two frogmen arrived. They were English, dispassionate, businesslike, and brought with them all the complicated apparatus of their trade. Their efficiency gave the searchers new hope. They began at the north end, one taking the east side, the other the west. Carrying big searchlights, they went down six times in all and then told Mr Boyle and Mr Mannion that it was futile making any further attempts. The bottom of the lake, they explained, had once been a turf bog; the floor was even for perhaps ten yards and then dropped suddenly to an incalculable depth. If the body were lying on one of these shelves, they might have found it, but the chances were that it had dropped into one of the chasms, where it could never be found. In the circumstances, they saw no point in diving again. They warmed themselves at the canteen fire, loaded their gear in O'Hara's taxis, and departed.

The searchers gathered behind the parish priest's car and discussed the situation. Nelly's clients, the executives, who had directed operations up to this point, now listened to the suggestions of the workers. Some proposed calling the search off until daylight; some proposed pouring petrol on portions of the lake and igniting it to give them light; some proposed calling on all the fire brigades in the county and having the lake drained. And while the Drumeen people were conferring, the mountainy Meenalaragan men, who had raised the alarm in the first place and had stood, silent, watching, beside the drowned man's waterlogged boat throughout the whole day as if somehow it would divulge its secret, now bailed out the water and, armed with long poles, searched the whole southern end of the lake. When they had no success, they returned the boat and slipped off home in the darkness.

The diviner was McElwee's idea. The postman admitted that he knew little about him except that he lived somewhere in the north of County Mayo, that he was infallible with water, and that his supporters claimed that he could find anything provided he got the 'smell of the truth in it'.

'We're concerned with a man, not a spring,' said Dr Boyle testily. 'A Mr Doherty, who lies somewhere in that lake there. And the question is, should we carry on with the nets or should we wait until the morning and decide what to do then?'

'He'll come if we go for him,' McElwee persisted. 'They say he's like a priest—he can never refuse a call. But whether he takes the job on when he gets here—well, that depends on whether he gets the smell of the—'

'I suggest we drag the south end again,' said Groome, the solicitor. 'The boat was waterlogged when it was found; therefore, it can't have drifted far after the accident. If he's anywhere, that's where he'll be.'

'We'll wait until the morning,' said McLaughlin of the Arcade. 'There's no great urgency, is there? Wait until we have proper light.'

'I vote for getting the diviner,' said McElwee. 'He likes to work while the scent is hot.'

'It's worth trying,' said one of Logan's men. 'Anyhow, what are you going to do tomorrow—try the nets again? After what the frogmen told you?'

Most of the men agreed.

'All right! All right!' said Dr Boyle. 'We'll get this fellow, whoever he is. But we'll tell Father Curran first.' They went round to the front of the car, and the Doctor spoke in to the priest.

'It has been suggested, Father,' he said, choosing his words as carefully as if he were giving evidence at an inquest, 'that we send for a diviner in County Mayo, a man who claims to be able to—to locate—'

'A what?' the priest demanded.

'A diviner, Father. A water diviner.'

'What about him?'

'It appears, Father, according to McElwee and some of the men here—it appears that this diviner has been successful on occasion in the past. We are thinking of sending for him.'

Father Curran turned to Nelly.

'They're going to send for a water diviner now,' he said, putting a little extra emphasis on the word 'now'.

'Whatever you say, Father,' said Nelly. 'I'll never be able to repay you for all your kindness this night.'

'Well, Father?' said the Doctor.

'It's up to yourselves,' said the priest. Then, in dismissal, 'Let us begin another rosary. ''I believe in God the Father Almighty, creator of Heaven and earth . . .'' '

McElwee and one of McLaughlin's apprentices set off after midnight for County Mao. None of Nelly's clients offered a car, so they travelled in a fifteen-year-old van belonging to McElwee's brother-in-law. After they left, the searchers broke up into small groups, sat in the cars and lorries and tractors lined along the shore, turned off the headlights, and waited. The night was thick and breathless. The men talked of the accident and of Mr Doherty. Each group knew something more about the man that had been known previously. In one car, it was known that his name was Arthur. Two lorries away, it was decided that Mr Doherty was not as retiring as one might have thought; one night a boisterous bass voice was heard coming through Nelly's kitchen window. In the Arcade delivery van, someone said that Dr Boyle was seen going into the cottage at least once a fortnight, and Nelly was never known to be sick. In one of the tractors, Nelly's frequent visits to the chemist were commented on. But these scraps of knowledge meant nothing; they were the kind of vague tales that might attach themselves to any stranger with a taste for privacy. The man at the bottom of the lake was still that respectable stranger in the good raincoat and the well-polished shoes.

The night was at its blackest when the pale lights of the returning van came bobbing over the patchy road. Immediately, fifty headlamps shot across the water and picked out tapering paths on the gleaming surface. Car doors slammed and the lakeside hummed with subdued excitement. Father Curran had been dozing. He opened his eyes and smacked his lips a dozen times. 'What? What is it?' he asked.

'They're back,' said Nelly, sitting forward in her seat. 'And they have him with them.'

The diviner was a tall man, inclined to flesh, and dressed in the same deep black as Nelly and the priest. He wore a black, greasy homburg, tilted the least fraction to the side, and carried a flat package, wrapped in newspaper, under his arm. The first impression was, What a fine man! But when he stepped directly in front of the headlights of one car there were signs of wear— faded, too active eyes, fingernails stained with nicotine, the trousers not a match for the jacket, the shoes cracking across the toecap, cheeks lined by the ready smile. He spoke with the attractive, lilting accent of the west coast.

McElwee and McLaughlin's apprentice, fluttering about the diviner like nervous acolytes, led him to Father Curran's car. He opened the door, removed his hat, and bowed to Nelly and the priest. His hair was carefully stretched across a bald patch. 'I am the diviner,' he said with coy simplicity.

Father Curran leaned across Nelly to get a closer look at him.

'What's your name? Who's your parish priest?'

He ignored the questions and addressed himself to Nelly, 'I will need something belonging to your husband, something that was close to his person—a tie, a handkerchief, a—'

'Will this do?' asked McElwee, thrusting the checked cap over the man's shoulder into the car.

'Yes, that will do,' the diviner said. 'Thank you.' Then, to Nelly, 'His name was Arthur Doherty.'

'Arthur Doherty,' Nelly repeated, almost in a whisper.

'And he was born and reared in the townland of Drung, thirteen miles north of Athenry.'

'Drung,' said Nelly. She licked her lips. 'Did you know him?'

'I travel the country and I meet many people. I will search for the stonemason, but I will promise nothing.'

'How did you know he was a stonemason? You must have known him.'

'In a manner of speaking. Just as I recognize you,' he said.

She leaned away from him. 'You don't know me! I never saw you before!'

'You are Nelly Devenny, a highly respectable and respected woman. You work for the best people in Drumeen.'

'That dirty toper McElwee,' McLaughlin of the Arcade broke in.

'I will do my best,' the diviner said, withdrawing from the car and smiling at her—a sly, knowing smile, a sort of wink without an eye being closed.

'Father!—' Nelly began. She clutched the priest's elbow, her face working with agitation.

Father Curran did not heed her; he was sniffing the air.

'Whiskey!' he announced. 'That man reeks of whiskey!'

'Father, what will he do? D'you think he's going to do anything, Father?'

'A fake! A quack! A charlatan! Get a grip on yourself, woman! We'll say another rosary and then I'll leave you home. They're wasting their time with that—that pretender!' And he blessed himself extravagantly.

Neither Dr Boyle nor Mr Groome nor Dr Timmons nor Mr Mannion nor McLaughlin of the Arcade volunteered to take the diviner out. McElwee and he went alone, the postman at the oars, the diviner sitting on the bench across the stern. The checked cap lay on his knees. He had removed the newspaper wrapping from his package, revealing a Y-shaped twig, and now he held it carelessly in his hands by the forked portion, the tail of the Y pointing away from him. The others gathered along the shore in the gloomy corridors between the headlights and watched them pull out. Before the boat was ten yards away from the edge of the water, Nelly left the priest's car for the first time that day and ran to join the watchers. The women gathered protectively around her.

The boat moved evenly up the lake. One minute it was part of the blackness, the next it was caught, exposed, frozen in a line of light projected by a headlight, then lost, then caught. Calmly, imperturbably, exasperatingly it went on revealing itself and losing itself, until the minutes of blackness seemed endless and the seconds of exposure mere flashes. But the pattern was regular—the vehicles were evenly spaced—and soon the eyes of the watchers knew to relax when the boat and blackness were one, but where it crossed a ribbon of light they devoured it, noted the new position of the oars, the slant of McElwee's back, the hunched, tensed shoulders of the diviner. No one spoke; no one dared speak. A word to a neighbour, a glance at one's watch, a look at Nelly's face and one might never find the punt again.

Then it disappeared. The watchers fastened on the next beam, waited, blinked, wondered had they missed it, stared again, murmured. Had it stopped? Where was it? Why the delay? Had it found something? Then it appeared again, moving slowly into the spotlight, first the bow, then McElwee, then the oars poised above the water, then the diviner, now standing rigid, his elbows bent, his hands at his chest, his head stiffly forward. Where it sat, a yellow picture projected against the night. Seconds passed. A minute. Two minutes. Three minutes. To watch was pain. The picture dissolved, men and boat merging in a blur, then took shape again.

'Come out! Come out! Bring out the boat hooks!'

McElwee was on his feet, his face screaming into the light, his arms gesticulating wildly to an audience he could not see. 'He's here! Bring out the boats! He's here!'

No one stirred. Then, after a minute, a youth broke away from the crowd and leaped into a yawl, and another followed him, and then everyone was moving and calling for oars and lighting cigarettes and wading heedlessly out into the water. The women held Nelly's arms, because she was trembling violently.

The body lay in twenty feet of water directly below the diviner's quivering twig. They brought it in to the shore and carried it up the gravel immediately in front of Father Curran's car. There they laid it on top of a brown sail.

McElwee got down on his knees beside the body. He closed

the eyes and the sagging mouth and knitted together the fingers of the rough hands. Then he adjusted the good gabardine raincoat and the trousers and placed the two feet together.

'He was a good man,' said the priest. He was standing beside the car door, close to the group of women that surrounded Nelly. He lifted his chin and allowed his eyelids to droop. 'He was a man who lived a quiet life and loved his God and his neighbours,' he said in his pulpit voice. 'At this moment, he is enjoying his just reward. At the hour of his demise, he was carrying his rosary beads—am I correct, McElwee?'

'I'll see, Father,' said McElwee.

He knelt again. While he worked, the men and women in the circle around the body looked away, gravely studying each other or staring off into the darkness beyond the cars. Then McElwee rose to his feet and moved quickly out of the circle, holding the dead man's belongings against his chest, his shoulders rounded as if to protect them. 'I—I—we'll have to look again, Father,' he said, facing away from the car. He took off his jacket and placed it on the ground and laid several objects on it. Then he folded the jacket around them.

'Did you find the beads?' the priest said.

'The clothes are soaking wet, Father. It's hard to get your hands into the pockets.'

'What do you have there?'

The postman straightened up and turned towards the light. 'There are these,' he said, holding something in his wet hands.

'Is that his wallet?'

'Yes. And the watch.'

'Give them to me.'

Someone handed the wallet and the watch to the priest, who gave them at once to Nelly.

'What else is there?' the priest asked.

'Nothing, Father.'

'There is something else in your jacket there, McElwee.'

'Show him, McElwee,' said the Doctor quietly.

McElwee looked at his jacket on the ground. Then he opened it. There were two dark-green pint whiskey bottles lying on it, side by side. One of them had no cork; and the other had been opened, but the cork was still in it.

'Ho-ho, so that's it!' said Father Curran. 'And what are you doing with two bottles?'

'I found them,' said McElwee quietly.

'He found them!' the priest cried. 'And what—' He saw the faces in the circle, and then realization hit him. He opened his mouth to speak again, but closed it without a word.

Imperceptibly, it was dawn, a new day vying with the priest's headlamps. No one spoke; no one moved. Then McElwee bent and folded his jacket over the bottles once more. He turned and glanced at the priest, and then, in a voice that was no more than a whisper but which carried clearly above the lapping of the water and the first uncertain callings of the birds, he said, 'We'll say a rosary for the repose of the soul of Arthur Doherty, stonemason, of Drung, in the County Galway.' He began the Creed, and they all joined him.

While they prayed, Nelly cried, helplessly, convulsively, her wailing rising above the drone of the prayers. Hers, they knew, were not only the tears for twenty-five years of humility and mortification but, more bitter still, tears for the past three months, when appearances had almost won, when a foothold on respectability had almost been established.

Beyond the circle around the drowned man, the diviner mopped the perspiration on his forehead and on the back of his neck with a soiled handkerchief. Then he sat on the fender of a car and waited for someone to remember to drive him back to County Mayo.

4

HOLDING THE HOUR

Drinkers' Tall Stories

THE GEOGRAPHY OF AN IRISH OATH

William Carleton

Heavy drinkers—be they entertainers or a nuisance—have been a recurring subject with Irish writers for centuries. This final section of the book is devoted to the imbiber in all his moods and begins with a classic story written in the early years of the nineteenth century. In the case of Peter Connell, it is the death of his wife that sets him on a downward spiral of indulgence, refusing to take the advice of either the local squire or his parish priest. But when the priest threatens to stop saying mass for Peter's wife, he agrees to sign an Oath restricting his daily consumption. The schemes and dodges Connell uses to circumnavigate this agreement are both amusing and ingenious. As a matter of note, variations of the 'Irish Oath' have been recorded throughout Ireland for many years.

William Carleton (1794–1869) whose real name was Uilliam O Cearbhallain, was one of 14 children of an impoverished farmer in Clogher, County Tyrone. Educated at several of the 'hedge schools' for poor children, he intended to become a priest, but gave this up in disillusionment after an unhappy pilgrimage to St Patrick's Purgatory in Lough Derg. For a time Carleton was a member of the Ribbonmen, a secret society fighting the English landlords, then worked as a private tutor before moving to Dublin where he adopted the Protestant faith and began to write a series of satirical caricatures of Irishmen and women based on his own experiences. These were published in the Christian Examiner *and later collected in two volumes as* Traits and

Stories of the Irish Peasantry (1830–34), making Carleton a household name. One critic of the time referred to him as 'a natural, inventive and untutored genius'. For his part, Carleton declared that, 'Secret societies, sloth and drink are the major faults of my countrymen.' The portrait of an Irish drunk that he provides in 'The Geography of an Irish Oath' is a prototype of many of the others who will be encountered in the remaining pages of this book.

*   *   *

Peter Connell felt the loss of his wife, Ellish, deeply and he unhappily had recourse to the bottle to bury the recollection of a woman whose death left a chasm in his heart which he thought nothing but the whisky could fill up.

His transition from a life of perfect sobriety to one of habitual, nay, of daily, intoxication was immediate. He could not bear to be sober; and his extraordinary bursts of affliction, even in his cups, were often calculated to draw tears from the eyes of those who witnessed them. He usually went out in the morning with a flask of whisky in his pocket, and sat down to weep behind a ditch—where, however, after having emptied his flask, he might be heard at a great distance singing the songs which Ellish in her lifetime was accustomed to love. In fact, he was generally pitied; his simplicity of character, and his benevolence of heart, which was now exercised without fear of responsibility, made him more a favourite than he ever had been. His former habits of industry were thrown aside; as he said himself, he hadn't heart to work; his farms were neglected, and but for his son-in-law would have gone to ruin. Peter himself was sensible of this.

'Take them,' said he, 'into your own hands, Denis—for me, I'm not able to do anything more at them; she that kep' me up is gone, an' I'm broken down. Take them—take them into your own hands. Give me my bed, bit, an' sup, an' that's all I want.'

Six months produced an incredible change in his appearance. Intemperance, whilst it shattered his strong frame, kept him in frequent exuberance of spirits; but the secret grief preyed on him within. Artificial excitement kills, but it never cures; and Peter, in the midst of his mirth and jollity, was wasting away into a shadow. His children, seeing him go down the hill of life so rapidly, consulted among each other on the best means of winning him back to sobriety. This was a difficult task, for his powers of bearing liquor were almost prodigious. He has often been known to drink so many as twenty-five and sometimes thirty tumblers of punch without being taken off his legs or rendered incapable of walking about. His friends, on considering who was most likely to recall him to a more becoming life, resolved to apply to his landlord. He entered warmly into their plan, and it was settled that Peter should be sent for, and induced, if possible, to take an oath against liquor. Early the following day a liveried servant came down to inform him that his master wished to speak with him.

'To be sure,' said Peter; 'divil resave the man in all Europe I'd do more for than the same gintleman, if it was only an account of the regard he had for her that's gone. Come, I'll go wid you in a minute.'

He accordingly returned with the flask in his hand, sayin, 'I never thravel widout a pocket-pistol, John. The times, you see, is not overly safe, an' the best way is to be prepared—ha, ha, ha! Och, och! It houlds three half-pints.'

'I think,' observed the servant, 'you had better not taste that till after your return.'

'Come away, man,' said Peter; 'we'll talk upon it as we go along. I couldn't do really widout it. You hard that I had lost Ellish?'

'Yes,' replied the servant, 'and I was very sorry to hear it.'

'Did you attend the berrin?'

'No, but my master did,' replied the man; 'for, indeed, his respect for your wife was very great, Mr Connell.'

This was before ten o'clock in the forenoon, and about one in the afternoon a stout countryman as seen approaching the gentleman's house, with another man bent round his neck, where he hung precisely as a calf hangs round the shoulders of a butcher when he is carrying it to his stall.

'Good heavens!' said the owner of the mansion to his lady, 'what has happened Smith, my dear? Is he dead?'

'Dead!' said his lady, going in much alarm to the drawing-room window—'I protest I fear so, Frank. He is evidently dead! For God's sake go down and see what has befallen him!'

Her husband went hastily to the hall-door, where he met Peter with his burden.

'In the name of heaven, what has happened, Connell?—what is the matter with John? Is he living or dead?'

'First, plase your honour, as I have him on my shouldhers, will you tell me where his bed is?' replied Peter. 'I may as well lave him snug, as my hand's in, poor fellow. The divil's bad head he has, your honour. Faith, it's a burnin' shame, so it is, an' nothin' else—to be able to bear so little!'

The lady, children, and servants were now all assembled about the dead footman, who hung, in the meantime, very quietly round Peter's neck.

'Gracious heaven! Connell, is the man dead?' she inquired.

'Faith, thin, he is, ma'am, for a while; but, upon my credit, it's a burnin' shame, so it is——'

'The man is drunk, my dear,' said her husband—'he's only drunk.'

'A burnin' shame, so it is—to be able to bear no more nor about six glasses, an' the whisky good, too. Will you ordher one o' thim to show me his bed, ma'am, if you plase,' continued Peter, 'while he's an me? It 'ill save throuble.'

'Connell is right,' observed his landlord. 'Gallagher, show him John's bedroom.'

Peter accordingly followed another servant, who pointed out his bed, and assisted to place the vanquished footman in a somewhat easier position than that in which Peter had carried him.

'Connell,' said his landlord, when he returned, 'how did this happen?'

'Faith, thin, it's a burnin' shame,' said Connell, 'to be able only to bear——'

'But how did it happen? for he has been hitherto a perfectly sober man.'

'Faix, plase your honour, asy enough,' replied Peter. 'He begun to lecthur me about dhrinkin', so, says I, "Come an' sit down behind the hedge here, an' we'll talk it over between us"; so we went in, the two of us, a-back o' the ditch, an' he began to advise me agin dhrink, an' I began to tell him about her that's gone, sir. Well, well! och, och! no matther!—so, sir, one story, an' one pull from the bottle, brought on another, for divil a glass we had at all, sir. Faix, he's a tindher-hearted boy, anyhow; for, as myself began to let the tears down when the bottle was near out, divil resave the morsel of him but cried afther poor Ellish as if she had been his mother—faix, he did! an' it won't be the last sup we'll have together, plase goodness! But the best of it was, sir, that the dhrunker he got, he abused me the more for dhrinkin'. Oh, thin, but he's the pious boy when he gets a sup in his head! Faix, it's a pity ever he'd be sober, he talks so much scripthur an' devotion in his liquor!'

'Connell,' said the landlord, 'I am exceedingly sorry to hear that you have taken so openly and inverately to drink as you have done ever since the death of your admirable wife. This, in fact, was what occasioned me to send for you. Come into the parlour. Don't go, my dear; perhaps your influence may also be necessary. Gallagher, look to Smith, and see that every attention is paid him, until he recovers the effects of his intoxication.'

He then entered the parlour, where the following dialogue took place between him and Peter:-

'Connell, I am really grieved to hear that you have become latterly so incorrigible a drinker; I sent for you to-day with the hope of being able to induce you to give it up.'

'Faix, your honour, it's jist what I'd expect from your father's son—kindness, an'dacency, an' devotion wor always among yees. Divil resave the family in all Europe I'd do so much for as the same family.'

The gentleman and lady looked at each other, and smiled. They knew that Peter's blarney was no omen of their success in the laudable design they contemplated.

'I thank you, Peter, for your good opinion; but, in the mean-

260 HOLDING THE HOUR

time, allow me to ask what can you propose to yourself by drinking so incessantly as you do?'

'What do I propose to myself by dhrinkin', is it? Why, thin, to banish grief, your honour. Surely you'll allow that no man has rason to complain who's able to banish the thief for two shillin's a day. I reckon the whisky at first cost, so that it doesn't come to more nor that at the very outside.'

'That is taking a commercial view of affliction, Connell; but you must promise me to give up drinking.'

'Why, thin, upon my credit, your honour astonishes me. Is it to give up banishin' grief? I have a regard for you, sir, for many a dalins we had together; but for all that, faix, I'd be miserable for no man, barrin' for her that's gone. If I'd be so to oblage anyone, I'd do it for your family; for divil resave the family in all Europe——'

'Easy, Connell—I am not to be palmed off in that manner. I really have a respect for the character which you bore, and wish you to recover it once more. Consider that you are disgracing yourself and your children by drinking so excessively from day to day—indeed, I am told almost from hour to hour.'

'Augh! don't believe the half o' what you hear, sir. Faith, somebody has been dhrawin' your honour out. Why, I'm never dhrunk, sir—faith, I'm not.'

'You will destroy your health, Connell, as well as your character; besides, you are not to be told that it is a sin, a crime against God, and an evil example to society.'

'Show me the man, plase your honour, that ever seen me incapable. That's the proof o' the thing.'

'But why do you drink at all? It is not necessary.'

'An' do you never taste a dhrop yourself, sir, plase your honour? I'll be bound you do, sir, raise your little finger of an odd time, as well as another. Eh, ma'am? That's comin' close to his honour! An' faix, small blame to him; an' a *weeshy* sup o' the wine to the misthress herself, to correct the tindherness of her delicate appetite.'

'Peter, this bantering must not pass. I think I have a claim upon your respect and deference. I have uniformly been your friend, and the friend of your children and family, but more especially of your late excellent and exemplary wife.'

'Before God an' man, I acknowledge that, sir—I do—I do. But, sir, to spake sarious—it's thruth, ma'am, downright—to spake sarious, my heart's broke, an' every day it's breakin' more an' more. She's gone, sir, that used to manage me; an' now I can't turn myself to anything, barrin' the dhrink—God help me!'

'I honour you, Connell, for the attachment which you bear towards the memory of your wife, but I utterly condemn the matter in which you display it. To become a drunkard is to disgrace her memory. You know it was a character she detested.'

'I know it all, sir, an' that you have thruth an' rason on your side; but, sir, you never lost a wife that you loved; an' long may you be so, I pray the Heavenly Father this day! Maybe if you did, sir, plase your honour, that, wid your heart sinkin' like a stone widin you, you'd thry whether or not something couldn't rise it. Sir, only for the dhrink I'd be dead.'

'There I totally differ from you, Connell. The drink only pro-longs your grief, by adding to it the depression of spirits which it always produces. Had you not become a drinker, you would long before this have been once more a cheerful, active, and industrious man. Your sorrow would have worn away gradually, and nothing but an agreeable melancholy—an affectionate remembrance of your excellent wife—would have remained. Look at other men.'

'But where's the man, sir, had sich a wife to grieve for as she was? Don't be hard on me, sir. I'm not a dhrunkard. It's thrue I dhrink a great dale; but thin I can bear a great dale, so that I'm never incapable.'

'Connell,' said the lady, 'you will break down your consti-tution, and bring yourself to an earlier death than you would otherwise meet.'

'I care very little, indeed, how soon I was dead—not makin' you, ma'am, an ill answer.'

'Oh, fie, Connell, for you, a sensible man and a Christian to talk in such a manner!'

'Throth, thin, I don't, ma'am. She's gone, an' I'd be glad to folly her as soon as I could. Yes, *asthore*, you're departed from me! an' now I'm gone asthray—out o' the right, an' out o' the good! Oh, ma'am,' he proceeded, whilst the tears rolled fast down his cheeks, 'if you knew her—her last words too— Oh, she was—she was—but where's the use o' sayin' what she was?—I beg your pardon, ma'am—your honour, sir, 'll forgive my want o' manners; sure, I know it's bad breedin', but I can't help it.'

'Well, promise,' said his landlord, 'to give up drink. Indeed, I wish you would take an oath against it; you are a conscientious man, and I know would keep it, otherwise I should not propose it, for I discountenance such oaths generally. Will you promise me this, Connell?'

'I'll promise to think of it, your honour—aginst takin' a sartin quantity, at any rate.'

'If you refuse it, I'll think you are unmindful of the good feeling which we have ever shown your family.'

'What?—do you think, sir, I'm ungrateful to you? That's a sore cut, sir, to make a villain o' me. Where's the book?—I'll swear this minute. Have you a Bible, ma'am?—I'll show you that I'm not mane, anyway.'

'No, Connell, you shall not do it rashly; you must be cool and composed; but go home, and turn it in your mind,' she replied, 'and remember that it is the request of me and my husband for your own good.'

'Neither must you swear before me,' said his landlord, 'but before Mr Mulcahy, who, as it is an oath connected with your moral conduct, is the best person to be present. It must be voluntary, however. Now, good-bye, Connell, and think of what we said; but take care never to carry home any of my servants in the same plight in which you put Smith to-day.'

'Faix, thin, sir, he had no business, wid your honour's livery upon his back, to begin lecthurin' me agin dhrinkin' as he did. We may all do very well, sir, till the timptation crasses us—but that's what thries us. It thried him, but he didn't stand it— faix, he didn't!—ha, ha, ha! Good mornin', sir—God bless you, ma'am! Divil resave the family in all Europe——'

'Good morning, Connell—good morning! Pray remember what we said.'

Peter, however, could not relinquish the whisky. His sons, daughters, friends, and neighbours all assailed him, but with no success. He either bantered them in his usual way, or reverted to his loss, and sank in sorrow. This last was the condition in which they found him most intractable; for a man is never considered to be in a state that admits of reasoning or argument when he is known to be pressed by strong gushes of personal feeling. A plan at length struck Father Mulcahy, which he resolved to put into immediate execution.

'Peter,' said he, 'if you do not abandon drink, I shall stop the Masses which I'm offering up for the repose of your wife's soul, and I will also return you the money I received for saying them.'

This was perhaps the only point on which Peter was accessible. He felt staggered at such an unexpected intimation, and was for some time silent.

'You will then feel,' added the priest, 'that your drunkenness is prolonging the sufferings of your wife, and that she is as much concerned in your being sober as you are yourself.'

'I will give in,' replied Peter; 'I didn't see the thing in that light. No—I will no be drunk; but if I swear aginst it, you must allow me a rasonable share every day, an' I'll not go beyant it, of coorse. The thruth is, I'd die soon if I gev it up altogether.'

'We have certainly no objection against that,' said the priest, 'provided you keep within what would not injure your health or make you tipsy. Your drunkenness is not only sinful, but disreputable; besides, you must not throw a slur upon the character of your children, who hold respectable and rising situations in the world.'

'No,' said Peter, in a kind of soliloquy, 'I'd lay down my life, *avourneen*, sooner nor I'd cause you a minute's sufferin'. Father Mulcahy, go an wid the Masses. I'll get an oath drawn up, an' whin it's done, I'll swear to it. I know a man that'll do it for me.'

The priest then departed, quite satisfied with having accomplished his object; and Peter, in the course of that evening, directed his steps to the house of the village schoolmaster, for the purpose of getting him to 'draw up' the intended oath.

'Misther O'Flaherty,' said he, 'I'm comin' to ax a requist of you, an' I hope you'll grant it to me. I brought down a sup in this flask, an' while we're takin' it we can talk over what I want.'

'If it be anything widin the circumference of my power, set it down, Misther Connell, as already operated upon. I'd drop a pen to no man at keepin' books by double enthry, which is the Italian method invinted by Pope Gregory the Great. The three sets bear a theological ratio to the three states of a thrue Christian. ''The waste-book,'' says Pope Gregory, ''is this world, the journal is purgatory, an' the ledger is heaven. Or it may be compared,'' he says, in the priface of the work, ''to the three states of the Catholic Church—the Church Militant, the Church Suffering, and the Church Triumphant.'' The larnin' of that man was beyant the reach of credibility.'

'*Arrah*, have you a small glass, masther? You see, Misther O'Flaherty, it's consarnin' purgatory, this that I want to talk about.'

'Nancy, get a glass—oh, here it is! Thin, if it be, it's a wrong enthry in the journal.'

'Here's your health, masther!—not forgettin' you, Mrs O'Flaherty. No, indeed, thin, it's not in the journal, but an oath I'm goin' to take aginst liquor.'

'Nothin' is asier to post than it is. We must enther it undher the head of—let me see!—it must go in the spirit account, undher the head of Profit an' Loss. Your good health, Mr Connell! Nancy, I drink to your improvement in imperturbability! Yes, it must be enthered undher the——'

'Faix, undher the rose, I think,' observed Peter; 'don't you know the smack of it? You see, since I tuck to it, I like the smell o' what I used to squeeze out o' the barley myself long ago. Misther O'Flaherty, I only want you to dhraw up an oath aginst liquor for me; but it's not for the books, good or bad. I promised to Father Mulcahy that I'd do it. It's regardin' my poor Ellish's sowl in purgatory.'

'Nancy, hand me a slate an' cutter. Faith, the same's a provident resolution; but how is it an' purgatory concatenated?'

'The priest, you see, won't go an wid the Masses for her till I take the oath.'

'That's but wake logic, if you ped him for him.'

'Faix, an' I did—an' well, too. But about the oath? Have you the pencil?'

'I have; jist lave the thing to me.'

'Asy, masther—you don't undherstand it yit. Put down two tumblers for me at home.'

'How is that, Mister Connell? It's mysterious if you're about to swear *aginst* liquor!'

'I am. Put down, as I said, two tumblers for me at home. Are they down?'

'They are down; but——'

'Asy!—very good! Put down two more for me at Dan's. Let me see!—two more behind the garden. Well!—put down one at Father Mulcahy's; two more at Frank Carroll's, of Kilclay. How many's that?'

'Nine!!!'

'Very good! Now put down one wid ould Bartle Gorman, of Nurchasy; an' two over wid Michael Morris, of Cargah. How many have you now?'

'Twelve in all!!!! But, Misther Connell, there's a demonstration badly wanted here: I must confiss I was always bright, but at present I'm as dark as Nox. I'd thank you for a taste of explanation.'

'Asy, man alive! Is there twelve in all?'

'Twelve in all; I've calculated them.'

'Well, we'll hould to that. Och, och!—I'm sure, *avourneen*, afore I'd let you suffer one minute's pain, I'd not scruple to take an oath aginst liquor, anyway. He may go an wid the Masses now for you, as soon as he likes! Mr O'Flaherty, will you put that down on paper, an' I'll swear to it, wid a blessin', to-morrow.'

'But what object do you wish to effectuate by this?'

'You see, masther, I dhrink one day wid another from a score to two dozen tumblers, an' I want to swear to no more nor twelve in twenty-four hours.'

'Why, there's intelligibility in that! Wid great pleasure, Mr Connell, I'll indite it. Katty, tear me a lafe out o' Brian Murphy's copy there.'

'You see, masther, it's for Ellish's sake I'm doin' this. State that in the oath.'

'I know it; an' well she desarved that specimen of abstinence from you, Misther Connell. Thank you!—your health agin! an' God grant you grace and fortitude to go through wid the same oath!—an' so He will, or I'm grievously mistaken in you.'

OATH AGAINST LIQUOR

made be me, Cornelius O'Flaherty, Philomath, on behalf of Misther Pether O'Connell, of the Cross-roads, Merchant, on one part—and of the soul of Mrs. Ellish O'Connell, now in purgatory, Merchantess, on the other.

I solemnly, and meritoriously, and soberly swear that a single tumbler of whisky punch shall not cross my lips during the twenty-four hours of the day, barring twelve, the locality of which is as followeth:—

Imprimis—Two tumblers at home 2
Secundo—Two more ditto at my son Dan's 2
Tertio—Two more ditto behind my own garden 2
Quarto—One ditto at the Reverend Father Mulcahy's ... 2
Quinto—Two more ditto at Frank Carroll's, of Kilclay . 2
Sexto—One ditto wid ould Bartle Gorman, of Nurchasy 1
Septimo—Two more ditto wid Michael Morris, of Cargah 2
                                                                      ——
                                                                       12

N.B.—I except in case any Docthor of Physic might think it right and medical to ordher me more for my health; or in case I could get Father Mulcahy to take the oath off me for a start at a

wedding or a christening, or at any other meeting of friends where
there's a drink.

                                                          his
       Witness present,   PETHER x O'CONNELL.
"CORNELIUS O'FLAHERTY, Philomath.   mark.
       June the 4th, 18—.

    ☞ I certify that I have made and calculated this oath for
Misther Pether O'Connell, Merchant, and that it is strictly and
arithmetically proper and corrent.

                            CORNELIUS O'FLAHERTY, Philomath.
       Dated this 4th day of June, 18—."

'I think, Misther O'Flaherty, it's a dacent oath as it stands.
Plase God, I'll swear to it some time to-morrow evenin'.'

   'Dacent! Why, I don't wish to become eulogistically addicted,
but I'd back the same oath, for both grammar and arithmetic,
aginst any that ever was drawn up by a lawyer—ay, by Counsellor
Daniel O'Connell himself!—but, faith, I'd not face him at a vow,
for all that; he's the greatest man at a vow in the three kingdoms.'

   'I'll tell you what I'm thinkin', masther—as my hand's in,
mightn't I as well take another wid an ould frind o' mine, Andy
Cavanagh, of Lisbuy? He's a dacent ould residenther, an' likes
it. It'll make the baker's or the long dozen.'

   'Why, it's not a bad thought; but won't thirteen get into your
head?'

   'No, nor three more to the back o' that. I only begin to get
hearty about seventeen; so that the long dozen, afther all, is best;
for God He knows I've a regard for Andy Cavanagh this many
a year, an' I wouldn't wish to lave him out.'

   'Very well—I'll add it up to the other part of the oath.

Octavo—One ditto out of respect for dacent Andy
    Cavanagh, of Lisbuy 1

Now I must make the total amount thirteen, an' all will be right.'

   'Masther, have you a prayer-book widin? Bekase if you have,
I may as well swear it here, an' you can witness it.'

'Katty, hand over the Spiritual Exercises—a book aquil to the Bible itself for piety an' devotion.'

'Sure, they say, masther, any book that the name o' God's in is good for an oath. Now, wid the help o' goodness, repate the words afore me, an' I'll swear thim.'

O'Flaherty hemmed two or three times, and complied with Peter's wishes, who followed him in the words until the oath was concluded. He then kissed the book, and expressed himself much at ease, as well, he said, upon the account of Ellish's soul, as for the sake of his children.

For some time after this his oath was the standing jest of the neighbourhood: even to this day Peter Connell's oath against liquor is a proverb in that part of the country. Immediately after he had sworn, no one could ever perceive that he violated it in the slightest degree; but there could be no doubt as to his literally fulfilling it. A day never passed in which he did not punctually pay a friendly visit to those whose names were dotted down, with whom he sat, pulled out his flask, and drank his quantum. In the meantime, the poor man was breaking down rapidly; so much so that his appearance generally excited pity, if not sorrow, among his neighbours. His character became simpler every day, and his intellect evidently more exhausted. the inoffensive humour, for which he had been noted, was also completely on the wane; his eye was dim, his step feeble, but the benevolence of his heart never failed him. Many acts of his private generosity are well known, and still remembered with gratitude.

In proportion as the strength of his mind and constitution diminished, so did his capacity for bearing liquor. When he first bound himself by the oath not to exceed the long dozen, such was his vigour that the effects of thirteen tumblers could scarcely be perceived on him. This state of health, however, did not last. As he wore away, the influence of so much liquor was becoming stronger, until at length he found that it was more than he could bear, that he frequently confounded the names of the men and the number of tumblers in the oath, and sometimes took, in his route, persons and places not to be found in it at all. This grieved him, and he resolved to wait upon O'Flaherty, for the purpose of having some means devised of guiding him during his potations.

'Masther,' said he, 'we must thry an' make this oath somethin' plainer. You see, whin I get confused, I'm not able to remimber things as I ought. Sometimes, instid o' one tumbler, I take two at the wrong place; an' sarra bit o' me but called in an' had three wid ould Jack Rogers, that isn't in it at all. On another day I had a couple wid honest Barney Casey, in my way acrass to Bartle Gorman's. I'm not what I was, masther, *ahagur*; so I'd thank you to dhraw it out more clearer, if you can, nor it was.'

'I see, Mr Connell; I comprehend, wid the greatest ase in life, the very plan for it. We must reduce the oath to Geography, for I'm at home there, bein' a surveyor myself. I'll lay down a map o' the parish, an' dhraw the houses of your friends at their proper places, so that you'll never be out o' your latitude at all.'

'Faix, I doubt that, masther—ha, ha, ha!' replied Peter. 'I'm afeard I will, of an odd time, for I'm not able to carry what I used to do; but, no matther—thry what you can do for me this time, anyhow. I think I could bear the long dozen still, if I didn't make mistakes.'

O'Flaherty accordingly set himself to work; and as his knowledge, not only of the parish, but of every person and house in it, was accurate, he soon has a tolerably correct skeleton map of it drawn for Peter's use.

'Now,' said he, 'lend me your ears.'

'Faix, I'll do no sich thing,' replied Peter—'I know a thrick worth two of it. Lend you my ears, *inagh!*—catch me at it! You have a bigger pair of your own nor I have—ha, ha, ha!'

'Well, in other words, pay attention. Now, see this dot—that's your own house.'

'Put a crass there,' said Peter, 'an' thin I'll know it's the crass-roads.'

'Upon my reputation, you're right; an' that's what I call a good specimen of ingenuity. I'll take the hint from that, an' we'll make it a hieroglyphical as well as a geographical oath. Well, there's a crass, wid two tumblers. Is that clear?'

'It is, it is! Go an.'

'Now here we draw a line to your son Dan's. Let me see—

he keeps a mill, an' sells cloth. Very good. I'll draw a mill-wheel an' a yard-wand. There's two tumblers. Will you know that?'

'I see it—go an—nothin' can be clearer. So far I can't go asthray.'

'Well, what next? Two behind your own garden. What metaphor for the garden? Let me see—let me cogitate! A dragon—the Hesperides! That's beyant you. A bit of a hedge will do, an' a gate.'

'Don't put a gate in, it's not lucky. You know when a man takes to dhrink, they say he's goin' a grey gate, or black gate, or a bad gate. Put that out, an' make the hedge longer, an' it'll do—wid the two tumblers, though.'

'They're down. One at the Reverend Father Mulcahy's. How will we translate the priest?'

'Faix, I doubt that will be a difficquilt business.'

'Upon my reputation, I agree wid you in that, especially whin he repates Latin. However, we'll see. He writes PP afther his name—pee-pee is what we call the turkeys wid. What ud you think o' two turkeys?'

'The priest would like them roasted, but I couldn't undherstand that. No—put down the sign o' the horsewhip or the cudgel; for he's handy an' argues well wid both!'

'Good! I'll put down the horsewhip first and the cudgel alongside of it, then the tumbler; an' there 'ill be the sign o' the priest.'

'Ay, do, masther, an' faix the priest 'ill be complate—there can be no mistakin' him thin. Divil a one but that's a good thought!'

'There it is in black an' white. Who comes next? Frank Carroll. He's a farmer. I'll put down a spade an' a harrow. Well, that's done—two tumblers.'

'I won't mistake that aither; it's clear enough.'

'Bartle Gorman's, of Nurchasy. Bartle's a little lame, an' uses a staff wid a cross on the end that he houlds in his hand. I'll put down a staff wid a cross on it.'

'Would there be no danger of me mistakin' that for the priest's cudgel?'

'Not the slightest. I'll pledge my knowledge of geography they're two very different weapons.'

'Well, put it down—I'll know it.'

'Michael Morris, or Cargah. What for him? Michael's a pig-driver. I'll put down a pig. You'll comprehend that?'

'I ought; for many a pig I sould him in my day. Put down the pig; an' if you could put two black spots upon his back, I'd know it to be one I sould him about four years agone—the fattest ever was in the country—it had to be brought home on a car, for it wasn't able to walk wid fat.'

'Very good—the spots are on it. The last is Andy Cavanagh, of Lisbuy. Now, do you see that I've drawn a line from place to place, so that you have nothing to do only to keep to it as you go. What for Andy?'

'Andy! Let me see—Andy! Pooh! What's come over me that I've nothing for Andy? Aye! I have it. He's a horse-jockey—put down a grey mare I sould him about five years agone.'

'I'll put down a horse; but I can't make a grey mare wid black ink.'

'Well, make a mare of her, anyway.'

'Faith, an' that same puzzles me. Stop, I have it—I'll put a foal along wid her.'

'As good as the bank. God bless you, Misther O'Flaherty. I think this'll keep me from mistakes. An' now, if you'll slip up to me afther dusk, I'll send you down a couple of bottles and a flitch. Sure, you desarve more for the throuble you tuck.'

Peter had, however, overrated his own strength in supposing that he could bear the long dozen in future; ere many months passed he was scarcely able to reach the half of that number without sinking into intoxication. Whilst in this state he was in the habit of going to the graveyard in which his wife lay buried, where he sat and wept like a child, sang her favourite songs, or knelt and offered up his prayers for the repose of her soul. None ever mocked him for this; on the contrary, there was always some kind person to assist him home. And, as he staggered on, instead of sneers and ridicule, one might hear such expressions as these:-

'Poor Pether! he's nearly off; an' a dacent, kind neighbour he ever was. The death of the wife broke his heart—he never ris his head since.'

'Ay, poor man! God pity him! He'll soon be sleepin' beside her, beyant there, where she's lyin'. It was never known of Pether Connell that he offinded man, woman, or child since he was born, barrin' the gaugers, bad luck to thim, afore he was marrid—but that was no offince. Sowl, he was their match, anyhow. When he an' the wife's gone, they won't lave their likes behind them. The sons are *bodaghs*—gintlemen, now; an' it's nothin' but dinners an' company. *Ahagur*, that wasn't the way their hardworkin' father an' mother made the money that they're houldin' their heads up wid such consequence upon.'

The children, however, did not give Peter up as hopeless. Father Mulcahy, too, once more assailed him on his weak side. One morning, when he was sober, nervous, and depressed, the priest arrived, and finding him at home, addressed him as follows:-

'Peter, I'm sorry, and vexed, and angry this morning; and you are the cause of it.'

'How is that, your reverence?' said Peter. 'God help me,' he added, 'don't be hard on me, sir, for I'm to be pitied. Don't be hard an me for the short time I'll be here. I know it won't be long—I'll be wid her soon. *Asthore machree*, we'll be together, I hope, afore long—an' oh! if it was the will o' God, I would be glad it was afore night!'

The poor, shattered, heart-broken creature wept bitterly; for he felt somewhat sensible of the justice of the reproof which he expected from the priest, as well as undiminished sorrow for his wife.

'I'm not going to be hard on you,' said the good-natured priest; 'I only called to tell you a dream that your son Dan had last night about you and his mother.'

'About Ellish! Oh, for heaven's sake, what about her, father, *avourneen*?'

'She appeared to him last night,' replied Father Mulcahy, 'and told him that your drinking kept her out of happiness.'

'Queen of Heaven!' exclaimed Peter, deeply affected, 'is that true? Oh,' said he, dropping on his knees, 'father, *ahagur machree*, pardon me—oh, forgive me! I now promise, solemnly and seriously, to drink neither in the house nor out of it, for the time to come, not one drop at all, good, bad, or indifferent, of either whisky, wine, or punch—barrin' one glass. Are you now satisfied? An' do you think she'll get to happiness?'

'All will be well, I trust,' said the priest. 'I shall mention this to Dan and the rest, and, depend upon it, they, too, will be happy to hear it.'

'Here's what Mr O'Flaherty an' myself made up,' said Peter; 'burn it, father—take it out of my sight, for it's now no use to me.'

'What is this at all?' said Mr Mulcahy, looking into it. 'Is it an oath?'

'It's the joggraphy of one I swore some time ago; but it's now out of date—I'm done wid it.'

The priest could not avoid smiling when he perused it; and on getting from Peter's lips an explanation of the hieroglyphics, he laughed heartily at the ingenious shifts they had made to guide his memory.

Peter, for some time after this, confined himself to one glass, as he had promised; but he felt such depression and feebleness that he ventured slowly, and by degrees, to enlarge the 'glass' from which he drank. His impression touching the happiness of his wife was that, as he had for several months strictly observed his promise, she had probably during that period gone to heaven. He then began to exercise his ingenuity gradually, as we have said, by using, from time to time, a glass larger than the preceding one; thus receding from the spirit of his vow to the letter, and increasing the quantity of his drink from a small glass to the most capacious tumbler he could find. The manner in which he drank this was highly illustrative of the customs which prevail on this subject in Ireland. He remembered that in making the vow he used the words, 'neither in the house nor out of it'; but, in order to get over this dilemma, he usually stood with one foot outside the threshold and the other in the house, keeping himself in that position which would render it difficult to determine whether he was either out or in. At other times, when he happened to be upstairs, he usually thrust one-half of his person out of the window, with the same ludicrous intention of keeping the letter of his vow.

Many a smile this adroitness of his occasioned to the lookers-on; but further ridicule was checked by his woe-begone and afflicted look. He was now a mere skeleton, feeble and tottering.

One night, in the depth of winter, he went into the town where his two sons resided; he had been ill in mind and body during the day, and he fancied that change of scene and society might benefit him. His daughter and son-in-law, in consequence of his illness, watched him so closely that he could not succeed in getting his usual 'glass'. This offended him, and he escaped without their knowledge to the son who kept the inn. On arriving there, he went upstairs, and, by a *douceur* to the waiter, got a large tumbler filled with spirits. The lingering influences of a conscience that generally felt strongly on the side of moral duty, though poorly instructed, prompted him to drink it in the usual manner, by keeping one-half of his body, as nearly as he could guess, out of the window, that it might be said he drank it neither in nor out of the house. He had scarcely finished his draught, however, when he lost his balance, and was precipitated upon the pavement. The crash of his fall was heard in the bar, and his son, who had just come in, ran, along with several others, to ascertain what had happened. They found him, however, only severely stunned. He was immediately brought in, and medical aid sent for; but, though he recovered from the immediate effects of the fall, the shock it gave to his broken constitution, and his excessive grief, carried him off a few months afterwards. He expired in the arms of his son and daughter, and amidst the tears of those who knew his simplicity of character, his goodness of heart, and his attachment to the wife by whose death that heart had been broken.

THE KEG OF POTEEN

Lynn Doyle

Pether MacDermott, the schoolmaster of Ballygullion, 'drinks like a herrin' ', never goes to bed sober and yet never fails to turn up in the morning to run his elementary school. Alcoholic he may be, but the kids and the people of Ballygullion all love him. Indeed he is one of the recurring characters in Lynn Doyle's nine volumes of tales about the town—apparently in County Down—which are all narrated by Pat Murphy, a Catholic farmer with a taste for sport and whiskey: legal or illegal. In this story, it seems the local police sergeant rather has it in for MacDermott after the teacher gets off a charge of drunkenness, and so the locals at Michael Casshidy's pub—Pether and the farmer among them—plan to teach the custodian of the law a lesson. It involves disguise, cunning and a keg of poteen. The subsequent events are as uproarious as any in the Ballygullion saga.

'Lynn Doyle' was the pseudonym of Leslie Alexander Montgomery (1873–1961) who spent his working life as a banker in Ulster while channelling his talent for comedy into the long running series about Ballygullion. Born in Downpatrick, he apparently invented his pseudonym while still a young man appearing with the Ulster Literary Theatre which had been set up as a rival to the better known Irish Literary Theatre. Just as the civil servant, Brian O'Nolan aka Flann O'Brien, had observed the proprieties of his profession by adopting a pen name, so banker Montgomery chose 'Lynn Doyle' as his theatrical name and, subsequently, his literary nom-de-plume. He published the first of the Ballygullion stories in 1908—undoubtedly drawing inspiration from the cross-section of humanity who

crowded the premises of his bank—and the last in 1957, by which time they were widely regarded as among the very best parodies of small town life. Doyle's command of spoken Irish is so acute as to virtually force the reader to laugh out loud, and the smell of 'The Keg of Poteen' in the following pages is almost tangible.

*   *   *

His full name was Pether MacDermott, but nobody iver called him anything but 'wee Mac', or maybe, sometimes, 'the masther'.

He was a wee, black-avised man wi' black side whiskers an' a white-lookin' face; an' his eyes was a kind av boiled lookin' wi' whiskey.

As long as I mind him, an' that's above twenty years, he had been schoolmasther at Ballygullion, an' all that time he'd been dhrinkin' like a herrin'.

If iver he wint to bed sober, 'twas because the pubs was shut before he got right full; an' even then it was hard to bate, for whin the dhrouth was on him he'd ha' faced turpentine itself.

Wan night there was a magic-lanthern show in the schoolhouse, an' they'd kep' him sober be hard watchin', he dhrunk the methyl-ated spirits for the lamp unbeknownst to the man that owned the lanthern, an' they had to put the show off, an' give the money back.

But they couldn't get him put out av the school. For all he'd be as dhrunk as a fiddler the night, he'd turn up brave an' respect-able in the mornin'; an' to see him goin' to the school wi' a black coat an' an ould tall hat, you'd niver ha' though it was the wee man that was threw out av Michael Casshidy's roarin' full the night before.

Mornin' or evenin', dhrunk or sober, he always wore the tall hat. They said he wint to bed in it.

There was wan bould bid made to shift him. 'Twas the time the sargint av polis found him lyin' in the sheugh on a Saturday night, an' brought him before the Bench on the Monday. They say he was more than ordinary full, be rayson that his uncle that was in Amerikay had sent him twinty pound.

Howiver, wi' Sunday comin' in, his head got well shired; an' on the Monday he was as fresh as a cricket in a ditch. He give the childher a half-holiday, an' wint off to the Coort like a tee-totaler, barrin' a breath you could ha' lit wi' a match.

An' for all the sargint's hard swearin', an' he swore like a veterinary surgeon on a horse case, the masther clane bamboozled him. There was nobody there but thim two selves, whin the sargint lifted him, an' the sargint was no great teetotaler himself; so, between that an' a bit av a lanin' towards him Major Donald-son, the Chairman, had, for ould neighbourship sake, he got off flyin'; an' the sargint was reprimanded for what the Major called 'excess av zale'.

From that day on the sargint's knife was in the masther up till the hilt, but he niver got a chance at him till the time I'm goin' to tell ye av.

Wan November night, as me an' four or five others was sittin' in Michael Casshidy's, big Billy Lenahan, a terrible man for a joke, calls us all round him.

'Boys,' sez he, 'if yez are game for a bit av fun. I could put yez on till a big set.'

'What is it, Billy?' sez I.

'Well,' sez he, 'I hear the sargint's gone to Dublin for a couple av days——'

'An' I hope he'll miss his way back,' sez Michael Casshidy across the bar.

There was a wee matther av prohibited hours betwen Michael an' the sargint that had stood Michael forty shillin's an' costs, an' a mark on his license as well.

'Wheesht, Michael,' sez I, 'an' let the man tell his story.'

'Well,' sez Billy, goin' on, 'yez know there's some wicked men does be keepin' a bit av a still up in the hills beyont.'

We ail had a bit av a laugh to ourselves at that; for the four men that run the same still was in the room, an' Billy was the boss man himself.

But Billy niver smiled. 'Supposin',' sez he, 'some av these men tuk the masther up the hills a bit, an' give him a wee keg av the rale stuff, an' wan av us dhressed up in the sargint's

278 HOLDING THE HOUR

clothes an' come on him carryin' it home, do yez think,' sez he, 'there's be a hunt?'

'Hunt,' sez Long James Heggarty. 'There'd be a hunt my legs would hardly keep up wi', for all they're brave an' long. But how'd ye get the sargint's clothes?'

'Niver mind that,' sez Billy, 'the two constables an' me is brave an' thick, an' I think I can work it. If you an' James, Pat,' sez he to me, ' 'll bring the masther up till the foot av the loanin' below the Whinny Hill the morrow night about nine, Pether an' John here'll bring down the potheen, an' I'll do the sargint. Him an' me's about a build,' sez he. 'Be there as soon afther nine as ye can, an' get the keg on his back, an' whin yez hear me comin' do you shout, "Here's the sargint!" The masther 'll not be long in the wan place aither that, I'm thinkin'.'

So 'twas all arranged, an' the next night about eight Long James an' me goes round for the masther, to catch him before he wint to Michael's.

'D'ye think he'll come?' sez James, as we were walkin' over to the house.

'Come?' sez I. 'Man, he'd go to hell for a dhrink, sure ye know that.'

'It's mighty little he'd get in the same place,' sez James. 'Howiver, he'll likely go the length av the hill, anyway.'

There wasn't much persuadin' to do. It was all we could manage to keep him from bein' at the spot at half-past eight, as soon as he heard av the potheen. Howiver, he kep' us well up to time, an' just on the bat av nine we come to the foot av the loanin'.

There we found John Kinner, an' Pether Larney, wi' a wee keg av potheen ready for slingin' on a man's shouldhers.

'Boys,' sez the masther, 'this is rale good av ye. Will yez have a wee dhrop before ye go?'

'No, thank ye, sir,' sez John. 'We'd betther waste no time. There's no knowin' but the sargint might come on us. He's always nosin' about here.'

'Come on then, boys,' sez the masther, all in a flurry; 'sling it on me back, an' we'll be out av this.'

So we got it on his back, an' just as we had it done, Pether Larney raises a shout. 'Run, boys, like the divil, here's the sargint!'

'The words wasn't out av his mouth till the masther was away down the loanin' like a hare, splashin' through the gutthers, wi' the wee keg dundherin' on his backbone cruel. James an' I afther him double quick.

'We'll take to the fields, boys,' sez he in a gasp, whin we got to the bottom av the loanin'. 'Stick to me, an' we'll bate that police divil yet. If he gets me, me school-teachin's over in Ballygullion. Aise the keg off me back till I get up the ditch.'

Just as he was up on it, we hears a yell from behind; an' the wee man gives a spang an' over. The keg pulls out av James's hands an' comes down on his back wi' a wallop. There was a terrible clatther av broken glass.

'Blood an' ouns!' sez James, 'what's that?' as we lept over afther him.

'Nothin',' sez the masther, 'just a wee dhrop I had in me pocket to keep me from havin' to open the keg. Niver mind it,' sez he, an' away he goes tearin' down the field.

'Will Billy miss us, d'ye think?' sez James, as we run along afther him.

'Not him,' sez I, 'he'll ha' seen us crossin' the ditch. If he has a nose at all, he could near thrack us be the scent, anyway. Sure the masther's lavin' a thrail av whiskey would do for a dhrag-hunt.'

Wi' that we hears another yell behind us closer than the first.

'He's not missed us,' sez I; 'there's he's over the ditch.'

'That's not Billy's voice,' sez James.

'It's not very like,' sez I; 'but who else could it be?'

'It's terrible like the sargint's,' sez James. 'There's two av thim too,' sez he, lookin' back.

There was another yell, closer still. We could ha' caught the words if we hadn't been runnin'.

'Be me sowl,' sez James, 'it's the sargint himself.'

An' right enough it was. We lost time in the nixt ditch, an' thin we could hear him quite plain, shoutin' on us to stop.

'Run, Masther MacDermott, dear, for the love av Hivin,' sez I; 'it's the sargint himself that's on us.'

'Av coorse it is,' sez he; 'didn't ye know that all along? Come on. If we were over the brook here, we're on betther ground, an' we'll bother him yet.'

'Dhrop the keg, masther,' sez James.

'Divil a bit av me,' sez the masther, between his teeth, 'if I burst myself. Now, boys, for the brook!'

He tuk off well from the brow av it, an' James an' me give him a shove that lit him on the far side on his mouth an' nose.

But the ould tall hat jumped off his head an' lit in the wather.

'Me hat!' sez he, gettin' to his feet.

'Damn your hat,' sez James. 'Come on, or we're catched.'

'If I'm catched,' sez the wee man, 'I'll be catched like a gintleman. Get the hat,' sez he, 'or I'll not budge.'

'Blast ye for a wee fool,' sez I, 'do ye want us catched too? Will ye come on, or we'll lave you an' your hat both.'

But be this time he was in the brook, gropin' for it.

'Come on, Pat,' sez James, 'an' lave him there, bad scran to him!'

'No, no, James,' sez I, 'we can't do that in any dacency. We brought him intil this, an' we'll ha' to stick to him. It's too late now anyway. Here's the sargint, an' wan av the polis. He's callin' us be name.'

Just on the word up comes the sargint blowin' and puffin', an' a constable wi' him, near as far through as himself.

'Aha! James Heggarty an' Pat Murphy,' sez he; 'ye're well caught this time. Ye thought I was away, did ye, an' ye could make potheen as ye plazed? An' who's this in the ditch? . . . Be the Lord,' sez he wi' a yell, 'it's the masther!'

'Good-night, Misther MacDermott,' sez he, as the wee man scrambled up the brook side. 'If it doesn't put ye about,' sez he, salutin' him very polite, 'maybe ye'd step up till a magisthrate's wi' me an' your friends here. An' we'll just go up to Major Donaldson's. He's a friend av yours, an'll be right glad to see ye.'

'It'll bother him to save ye this time,' sez he, very wicked all at once. 'He'll not call this "excess av zale," I'm thinkin',' an' he tapped the keg.

Nobody spoke; an' all the way to the Major's not a word was said.

The masther walked in front wi' his head down, an' the keg bobbin' up an' down on his back; for the sargint niver offered to take it off him.

'Whatever has come on Big Billy?' sez I to James, in a whisper.

'I don't know,' sez James, 'an' I'm not frettin' much. To hell wi' him an' his jokes. This'll sound well in Ballygullion in the mornin'; forbye that we'll be fined in about twenty pound apiece,—if we get off wi' a fine.'

The five av us were showed intil the Major's office, an' prisintly he came in himself in his evenin' dhress, smokin' a cigar.

Whin his eyes fell on the masther sittin' wi' the keg on his back, an' lookin' like a dog wi' a tin to his tail, he gives a whistle.

Thin he sees the sargint.

'What's this?' sez he, 'what's this, sargint?'

'Just a gang av shebeeners, your Worship,' sez the sargint. 'An' I'm sorry to say,' sez he, wi' a grin as far from a sorry man's as iver ye seen—'I'm sorry to say Misther MacDermott's at the head av it. I've caught him red-handed, as ye see. If ye'll make out the Committal ordher, I'll have thim to the barracks for the night, an' they can be returned for thrial at the Bench to-morrow.'

The Major looked terrible cut; but he says nothin', but goes for a pen an' ink.

'How did this come about, Sargint Thomas?' sez he, in a stern voice. 'But wait a minit, sargint,' breakin' off an' ringin' the bell.

'Mary,' sez he to the servant, 'bring in some whiskey an' wather.'

Whin it come he poured out glasses apiece.

'Give these unforthumate men a dhrink, sargint,' sez he; 'they look tired an' wet. An' maybe you an' the constable will take a little. You're nearly in as bad a state as they are.'

Afther we all were done, he left the bottle down beside the masther—for he knew his man—an' whin he turned round to his writin' desk, the wee man poured himself out a rozener would ha' have made a cat spake.

'Now, sargint,' sez the Major.

'Well, sir,' sez the sargint, clearin' his throat, an' spakin' as if he was in the witness box, 'I was in the barracks at eight o'clock p.m., this evenin', when William Lenahan came in.'

'William Lenahan?' sez the Major, in a bothered way.

'Big Billy av the Hills,' sez the masther. He was comin' roun' fast, wi' the second dhrink.

'Oh, yes,' sez the Major. 'Go on, sargint.'

'William Lenahan,' sez the sargint. 'I asked him what I could do for him. He seemed surprised to see me, an' said he thought I was in Dublin. Thin I begin to smell a rat,' sez the sargint, warmin' up, an' dhroppin' his witness box voice.

'Wondherful!' sez the masther. 'I thought ye had no nose except for whiskey.'

'I asked him what he wanted, seein' that I was there,' sez the sargint, goin' on as if he hadn't noticed the masther; 'an' he said he had heard there was a reward offered for the men that was makin' potheen, an' he had called to find out quietly. Thin I begin to see how the cat was jumpin',' sez the sargint, rubbin' his hands.

'Was she jumpin' afther the rat ye smelt, sargint?' sez the masther.

The Major choked a bit over his paper. 'Hold your tongue, MacDermott,' sez he. 'Well, sargint?'

'Well, sir, I don't know whether he had quite made up his mind to bethray his confidherates or not; but he hadn't bargained on encountherin' *me*,' sez the sargint, swellin' out his chest, 'an' afther interrogatin' him for some time, I got out av him that there was a convoy av potheen comin' down the hills to-night, an' if I'd be at the loanin' below the Whinny Hill, between nine an' half-past, I'd catch some av the dipridators.'

'I'll niver believe it,' sez the masther, thryin' to rise till his feet, an' sittin' down sudden, through the keg catchin' on the back av the chair. 'Billy niver sold the pass, I'll swear.'

'So I went to the spot,' goes on the sargint, still not noticin' him, 'an' afther a long chase I captured the villains. The ring-leader, MacDermott——'

'Misther, to you,' sez the masther.

'The ringleader, *Misther* MacDermott,' sez the sargint wi' a sneer on the 'misther,' 'wi' a keg av potheen on his back. It's there still, as ye may see.'

'There's nobody knows that betther than me, that's carried it since nine o'clock,' sez the masther. Sure the maker's name is branded on me shouldher blades be this time. But how do you know it's poteen?' says the masther. 'You'll have to prove it.'

The sargint looks at Major Donaldson.

'As a matther av form, ye must, sargint,' sez the Major.

'Just take the keg off me back an bore a bit av a gimlet hole in it, an' I'll test it meself,' sez the masther, 'I'm terrible dhry.'

'I'm surprised to hear it,' sez the Major, lookin' at his bottle. 'But we'll thry a dhrop av potheen for your complaint. Ring the bell, sargint.'

'Mary,' sez he to the girl, bring a gimlet an' a clane tumbler.'

So they got the keg off the masther's back, an' afther borin' it, they dhrew a glass, an' right enough, the Major handed it to the masther.

The wee man takes a good pull at it, an' all at wanst begins chokin', an' splutherin' an' coughin' as if he was in the last thraws.

'What's wrong, masther? What in Hivin's name is wrong?' sez the Major, takin' the glass out av his hand, an' smellin' it. He looked puzzled for a minit, an' then put it till his lips.

'Run for the priest, boys!' sez he, 'the masther's poisoned!'

'What is it, Major dear?' sez I. 'What is it at all, at all?'

'Wather,' sez he, 'be me sowl. Spring wather, as I'm a mag-isthate!'

'*What!*' sez the sargint, wi' a roar.

'Wather,' sez the Major, 'Divil a doubt av it. Taste it yourself, sargint, if ye don't believe me.'

The sargint just wet his lips wi' it, and put it down; an' then I knowed it was all right, for the sargint was no fonder av wather than the masther was.

'It seems to be wather,' sez the sargint, lookin' terrible foolish.

'Ye'll hardly commit me for carryin' a dhrop av wather home, Major Donaldson,' sez the masther between coughs.

But the Major couldn't spake. He was lyin' in the chair laughin' fit to break his heart, an' ivery man in the room was followin' suit—barrin' the sargint.

'Oh, sargint, sargint,' sez the Major, wipin' his eyes, 'they'll laugh ye out av Ballygullion for this.'

Divil a word the sargint spoke, but glowers round wi' the eyes standin' in his head. Thin he motions to the constable, claps the helmet on his head, an' out av the room like a madman, the constable afther him, thryin' to keep his face straight.

Whin we had our laugh out—'Boys,' sez the Major, 'take another dhrink, an' go home to your beds. I don't know who plotted this, but I'm niver likely to get a betther laugh, anyway.'

'Take a good dhrop, masther,' sez he; 'your stomach has got a surprise this night'll take it a long while to get over.'

Whin we'd done he showed us to the door himself, an' bid us 'Good-night.'

At the bottom av the avenue we come on Big Billy, sittin' on somethin', be the roadside, an' laughin' till the fat shook on him.

'Don't spake to me, boys,' sez he. 'Sure I know all about it. The sargint's away down the road as if the divil was afther him. Didn't I bamboozle him this night,' sez he.

'Ay, an' ye bamboozled me too,' sez the masther. 'I'm near dead wi' the runnin' an' the fright. You an' your jokes'll be the death av some dacint man.'

'Niver mind, masther,' sez Billy, risin' an' pickin' up a keg. 'Here's somethin'll console ye. This is the rale Simon Pure this time.'

'It's not wather again, Billy?' sez the masther, doubtin' like.

'Thry it,' sez Billy; 'a dhrop av as good potheen as ye iver lipped.'

'Come down to the house, boys,' sez the masther. 'We've had a hard night; but we'll warm our hearts before we go to bed. An' we'll dhrink Billy's health too; for he's dhrawn the sargint's teeth this time. He's made a common gull av him,' sez he; 'an' thim that doesn't laugh at it in Ballygullion in the mornin' 'll not cry anyway.'

THE DRUNKARD

Frank O'Connor

*Mick Delany has a reputation on the terrace as a big drinker.
He prides himself, though, on being a man who can 'keep steady
for months' when he wants to. However, his family know it only
takes one glass and then it is a case of 'The Drunkard's Progress',
says his son, Larry, the narrator of this story. In recent months,
however, life in the Delany home has been running fairly
smoothly—until the sudden death of Mr Dooley, a commercial
traveller, and one of Mick's friends. The funeral that follows is
an occasion fraught with danger for a man like his father, Larry
knows, but it is actually the youngster himself who is in for the
biggest shock when the mourners gather after the service in the
local pub . . .*

*Frank O'Connor (1903–66), whose real name was Michael
O'Donovan, was born in the city of Cork. His father was an
intermittently alcoholic labourer and his mother a domestic servant, yet despite living on the edge of destitution, an intense love
and an ability to treat all the problems thrown at them by life
with good humour kept the family together. After a very basic
education, Frank O'Connor drifted from one menial job to
another until he joined the Republican side and fought in the
Irish Civil War. After the hostilities, he obtained a job in the
Dublin library and began writing for various newspapers and
magazines. It was O'Connor's brilliant short stories, however,
that set him apart and these were soon being published in some
of the world's most prestigious magazines including* The New
Yorker, *which resulted in him being offered a teaching post at
Harvard. The influence of these tales—subsequently collected in*

volumes ranging from Guests of the Nation (1931) *through to*
More Stories (1954)—*caused historian Vivian Mercier to declare
him in 1964, 'the Old Master of the Irish short story'. The tale
of 'The Drunkard' bears evidence of more than a little personal
knowledge, in all probability drawing on O'Connor's own uneasy
childhood.*

*   *   *

It was a terrible blow to Father when Mr Dooley on the terrace
died. Mr Dooley was a commercial traveller with two sons in
the Dominicans and a car of his own, so socially he was miles
ahead of us, but he had no false pride. Mr Dooley was an intellectual, and, like all intellectuals the thing he loved best was conversation, and in his own limited way Father was a well-read man and
could appreciate an intelligent talker. Mr Dooley was remarkably
intelligent. Between business acquaintances and clerical contacts,
there was very little he didn't know about what went on in town,
and evening after evening he crossed the road to our gate to
explain to Father the news behind the news. He had a low,
palavering voice and a knowing smile, and Father would listen
in astonishment, giving him a conversational lead now and again,
and then stump triumphantly in to Mother with his face aglow
and ask: 'Do you know what Mr Dooley is after telling me?'
Ever since, when somebody has given me some bit of information
off the record I have found myself on the point of asking: 'Was
it Mr Dooley told you that?'

Till I actually saw him laid out in his brown shroud with the
rosary beads entwined between his waxy fingers I did not take
the report of his death seriously. Even then I felt there must be
a catch and that some summer evening Mr Dooley must reappear
at our gate to give us the lowdown on the next world. But Father
was very upset, partly because Mr Dooley was about one age
with himself, a thing that always gives a distinctly personal turn
of another man's demise; partly because now he would have no
one to tell him what dirty work was behind the latest scene at
the Corporation. You could count on your fingers the number of

men in Blarney Lane who read the papers as Mr Dooley did, and none of these would have overlooked the fact that Father was only a labouring man. Even Sullivan, the carpenter, a mere nobody, thought he was a cut above Father. It was certainly a solemn event.

'Half past two to the Curragh,' Father said meditatively, putting down the paper.

'But you're not thinking of going to the funeral?' Mother asked in alarm.

''Twould be expected,' Father said, scenting opposition. 'I wouldn't give it to say to them.'

'I think,' said Mother with suppressed emotion, 'it will be as much as anyone will expect if you go to the chapel with him.'

('Going to the chapel,' of course, was one thing, because the body was removed after work, but going to a funeral meant the loss of a half-day's pay.)

'The people hardly know us,' she added.

'God between us and all harm,' Father replied with dignity, 'we'd be glad if it was our own turn.'

To give Father his due, he was always ready to lose a half day for the sake of an old neighbour. It wasn't so much that he liked funerals as that he was a conscientious man who did as he would be done by; and noting could have consoled him so much for the prospect of his own death as the assurance of a worthy funeral. And, to give Mother her due, it wasn't the half-day's pay she begrudged, badly as we could afford it.

Drink, you see, was Father's great weakness. He could keep steady for months, even for years, at a stretch, and while he did he was as good as gold. He was first up in the morning and brought the mother a cup of tea in bed, stayed at home in the evenings and read the paper; saved money and brought himself a new blue serge suit and bowler hat. He laughed at the folly of men who, week in week out, left their hard-earned money with the publicans; and sometimes, to pass an idle hour, he took pencil and paper and calculated precisely how much he saved each week through being a teetotaller. Being a natural optimist he sometimes continued this calculation through the whole span of his prospective existence and the total was breathtaking. He would die worth hundreds.

If I had only known it, this was a bad sign; a sign he was becoming stuffed up with spiritual pride and imagining himself better than his neighbours. Sooner or later, the spiritual pride grew till it called for some form of celebration. Then he took a drink—not whisky, of course; nothing like that—just a glass of some harmless drink like lager beer. That was the end of Father. By the time he had taken the first he already realized that he had made a fool of himself, took a second to forget it and a third to forget that he couldn't forget, and at last came home reeling drunk. From this on it was 'The Drunkard's Progress', as in the moral prints. Next day he stayed in from work with a sick head while Mother went off to make his excuses at the works, and inside a fortnight he was poor and savage and despondent again. Once he began he drank steadily through everything down to the kitchen clock. Mother and I knew all the phases and dreaded all the dangers. Funerals were one.

'I have to go to Dunphy's to do a half-day's work,' said Mother in distress. 'Who's to look after Larry?'

'I'll look after Larry,' Father said graciously. 'The little walk will do him good.'

There was no more to be said, though we all knew I didn't need anyone to look after me, and that I could quite well have stayed at home and looked after Sonny, but I was being attached to the party to act as a brake on Father. As a brake I had never achieved anything, but Mother still had great faith in me.

Next day, when I got home from school, Father was there before me and made a cup of tea for both of us. He was very good at tea, but too heavy in the hand for anything else; the way he cut bread was shocking. Afterwards, we went down the hill to the church, Father wearing his best blue serge and a bowler cocked to one side of his head with the least suggestion of the masher. To his great joy he discovered Peter Crowley among the mourners. Peter was another danger signal, as I knew well from certain experiences after Mass on Sunday morning: a mean man, as Mother said, who only went to funerals for the free drinks he could get at them. It turned out that he hadn't even known Mr Dooley! But Father had a sort of contemptuous regard for him as one of the foolish people who wasted their good money in public-houses when they could be saving it. Very little of his own money Peter Crowley wasted!

It was an excellent funeral from Father's point of view. He had it all well studied before we set off after the hearse in the afternoon sunlight.

'Five carriages!' he exclaimed. 'Five carriages and sixteen covered cars!' There's one alderman, two councillors and 'tis unknown how many priests. I didn't see a funeral like this from the road since Willie Mack, the publican, died.

'Ah, he was well liked,' said Crowley in his husky voice.

'My goodness, don't I know that?' snapped Father. 'Wasn't the man my best friend? Two nights before he died—only two nights—he was over telling me the goings-on about the housing contract. Them fellows in the Corporation are night and day robbers. But even I never imagined he was as well connected as that.'

Father was stepping out like a boy, pleased with everything: the other mourners, and the fine houses along Sunday's Well. I knew the danger signals were there in full force: a sunny day, a fine funeral, and a distinguished company of clerics and public men were bringing out all the natural vanity and flightiness of Father's character. It was with something like genuine pleasure that he saw his old friend lowered into the grave; with the sense of having performed a duty and the pleasant awareness that however much he would miss poor Mr Dooley in the long summer evenings, it was he and not poor Mr Dooley who would do the missing.

'We'll be making tracks before they break up,' he whispered to Crowley as the gravediggers tossed in the first shovelfuls of clay, and away he went, hopping like a goat from grassy hump to hump. The drivers, who were probably in the same state as himself, though without months of abstinence to put an edge on it, looked up hopefully.

'Are they nearly finished, Mick?' bawled one.

'All over now bar the last prayers,' trumpeted Father in the tone of one who brings news of great rejoicing.

The carriages passed us in a lather of dust several hundred yards from the public-house, and Father, whose feet gave him trouble in hot weather, quickened his pace, looking nervously over his shoulder for any sign of the main body of mourners crossing the hill. In a crowd like that a man might be kept waiting.

When we did reach the pub the carriages were drawn up outside, and solemn men in black ties were cautiously bringing out consolation to mysterious females whose hands reached out modestly from behind the drawn blinds of the coaches. Inside the pub there were only the drivers and a couple of shawly women. I felt if I was to act as a brake at all, this was the time, so I pulled Father by the coattails.

'Dadda, can't we go home now?' I asked.

'Two minutes now,' he said, beaming affectionately. 'Just a bottle of lemonade and we'll go home.'

This was a bribe, and I knew it, but I was always a child of weak character. Father ordered lemonade and two pints. I was thirsty and swallowed my drink at once. But that wasn't Father's way. He had long months of abstinence behind him and an eternity of pleasure before. He took out his pipe, blew through it, filled it, and then lit it with loud pops, his eyes bulging above it. After that he deliberately turned his back on the pint, leaned one elbow on the counter in the attitude of a man who did not know there was a pint behind him, and deliberately brushed the tobacco from his palms. He had settled down for the evening. He was steadily working through all the important funerals he had ever attended. The carriages departed and the minor mourners drifted in till the pub was half full.

'Dadda,' I said, pulling his coat again, 'can't we go home now?'

'Ah, your mother won't be in for a long time yet,' he said benevolently enough. 'Run out in the road and play, can't you?'

It struck me as very cool, the way grown-ups assumed that you could play all by yourself on a strange road. I began to get bored as I had so often been bored before. I knew Father was quite capable of lingering there till nightfall. I knew I might have to bring him home, blind drunk, down Blarney Lane, with all the old women at their doors, saying: 'Mick Delaney is on it again.' I knew that my mother would be half crazy with anxiety; that next day Father wouldn't go out to work; and before the end of the week she would be running down to the pawn with the clock under her shawl. I could never get over the lonesomeness of the kitchen without a clock.

I was still thirsty. I found if I stood on tiptoe I could just reach Father's glass, and the idea occurred to me that it would be interesting to know what the contents were like. He had his back to it and wouldn't notice. I took down the glass and sipped cautiously. It was a terrible disappointment. I was astonished that he could even drink such stuff. It looked as if he had never tried lemonade.

I should have advised him about lemonade but he was holding forth himself in great style. I heard him say that bands were a great addition to a funeral. He put his arms in the position of someone holding a rifle in reverse and hummed a few bars of Chopin's Funeral March. Crowley nodded reverently. I took a longer drink and began to see that porter might have its advantages. I felt pleasantly elevated and philosophic. Father hummed a few bars of the Dead March in *Saul*. It was a nice pub and a very fine funeral, and I felt sure that poor Mr Dooley in heaven must be highly gratified. At the same time I thought they might have given him a band. As Father said, bands were a great addition.

But the wonderful thing about porter was the way it made you stand aside, or rather float aloft like a cherub rolling on a cloud, and watch yourself with your legs crossed, leaning against a bar counter, not worrying about trifles but thinking deep, serious, grown-up thoughts about life and death. Looking at yourself like that, you couldn't help thinking after a while how funny you looked, and suddenly you got embarrassed and wanted to giggle. But by the time I had finished the pint, that phase too had passed; I found it hard to put back the glass, the counter seemed to have grown so high. Melancholia was supervening again.

'Well,' Father said reverently, reaching behind him for his drink, 'God rest the poor man's soul, wherever he is!' He stopped, looked first at the glass, and then at the people round him. 'Hello,' he said in a fairly good-humoured tone, as if he were just prepared to consider it a joke, even if it was in bad taste, 'who was at this?'

There was a silence for a moment while the publican and the old women looked first at Father and then at his glass.

'There was no one at it, my good man,' one of the women said with an offended air. 'Is it robbers you think we are?'

'Ah, there's no one here would do a thing like that, Mick,' said the publican in a shocked tone.

'Well, someone did it,' said Father, his smile beginning to wear off.

'If they did, they were them that were nearer it,' said the woman darkly, giving me a dirty look; and at the same moment the truth began to dawn on Father. I suppose I must have looked a bit starry-eyed. He bend and shook me.

'Are you all right, Larry?' he asked in alarm.

Peter Crowley looked down at me and grinned.

'Could you beat that?' he exclaimed in a husky voice.

I could, and without difficulty. I started to get sick. Father jumped back in holy terror that I might spoil his good suit, and hastily opened the back door.

'Run! run! run!' he shouted.

I saw the sunlit wall outside with the ivy overhanging it, and ran. The intention was good but the performance was exaggerated, because I lurched right into the wall, hurting it badly, as it seemed to me. Being always very polite, I said 'Pardon' before the second bout came on me. Father, still concerned for his suit, came up behind and cautiously held me while I got sick.

'That's a good boy!' he said encouragingly. 'You'll be grand when you get that up.'

Begor, I was not grand! Grand was the last thing I was. I gave one unmerciful wail out of me as he steered me back to the pub and put me sitting on the bench near the shawlies. They drew themselves up with an offended air, still sore at the suggestion that they had drunk his pint.

'God help us!' moaned one, looking pityingly at me, 'isn't it the likes of them would be fathers?'

'Mick,' said the publican in alarm, spraying sawdust on my tracks, 'that child isn't supposed to be in here at all. You'd better take him home quick in case a bobby would see him.'

'Merciful God!' whimpered Father, raising his eyes to heaven and clapping his hands silently as he only did when distraught, 'what misfortune was on me? Or what will his mother say? ... If women might stop at home and look after their children themselves!' he added in a snarl for the benefit of the shawlies. 'Are them carriages all gone, Bill?'

'The carriages are finished long ago, Mick,' replied the publican.

'I'll take him home,' Father said despairingly ... 'I'll never bring you out again,' he threatened me. 'Here,' he added, giving me the clean handkerchief from his breast pocket, 'put that over your eye.'

The blood on the handkerchief was the first indication I got that I was cut, and instantly my temple began to throb and I set up another howl.

'Whisht, whisht, whisht!' Father said testily, steering me out the door. 'One'd think you were killed. That's nothing. We'll wash it when we get home.'

'Steady now, old scout!' Crowley said, taking the other side of me. 'You'll be all right in a minute.'

I never met two men who knew less about the effects of drink. The first breath of fresh air and the warmth of the sun made me groggier than ever and I pitched and rolled between wind and tide till Father started to whimper again.

'God Almighty, and the whole road out! What misfortune was on me didn't stop at my work! Can't you walk straight?'

I couldn't. I saw plain enough that, coaxed by the sunlight, every woman old and young in Blarney Lane was leaning over her half-door or sitting on her doorstep. They all stopped gabbling to gape at the strange spectacle of two sober, middle-aged men bringing home a drunken small boy with a cut over his eye. Father, torn between the shamefast desire to get me home as quick as he could, and the neighbourly need to explain that it wasn't his fault, finally halted outside Mrs Roche's. There was a gang of old women outside a door at the opposite side of the road. I didn't like the look of them from the first. They seemed altogether too interested in me. I leaned against the wall of Mrs Roche's cottage with my hands in my trousers pockets, thinking mournfully of poor Mr Dooley in his cold grave on the Curragh, who would never walk down the road again, and, with great feeling, I began to sing a favourite song of Father's.

> Though lost to Mononia and cold in the grave
> He returns to Kincora no more.

'Wisha, the poor child!' Mrs Roche said. 'Haven't he a lovely voice, God bless him!'

That was what I thought myself, so I was the more surprised when Father said 'Whisht!' and raised a threatening finger at me. He didn't seem to realize the appropriateness of the song, so I sang louder than ever.

'Whisht, I tell you!' he snapped, and then tried to work up a smile for Mrs Roche's benefit. 'We're nearly home now. I'll carry you the rest of the way.'

But, drunk and all as I was, I knew better than to be carried home ignominiously like that.

'Now,' I said severely, 'can't you leave me alone? I can walk all right. 'Tis only my head. All I want is a rest.'

'But you can rest at home in bed,' he said viciously, trying to pick me up, and I knew by the flush on his face that he was very vexed.

'Ah, Jasus,' I said crossly, 'what do I want to go home for? Why the hell can't you leave me alone?'

For some reason the gang of old women at the other side of the road thought this very funny. They nearly split their sides over it. A gassy fury began to expand in me at the thought that a fellow couldn't have a drop taken without the whole neighbourhood coming out to make game of him.

'Who are ye laughing at?' I shouted, clenching my fists at them. 'I'll make ye laugh at the other side of yeer faces if ye don't let me pass.'

They seemed to think this funnier still; I had never seen such ill-mannered people.

'Go away, ye bloody bitches!' I said.

'Whisht, whisht, whisht, I tell you!' snarled Father, abandoning all pretence of amusement and dragging me along behind him by the hand. I was maddened by the women's shrieks of laughter. I was maddened by Father's bullying. I tried to dig in my heels but he was too powerful for me, and I could only see the women by looking back over my shoulder.

'Take care or I'll come back and show ye!' I shouted. 'I'll teach ye to let decent people pass. Fitter for ye to stop at home and wash yeer dirty faces.'

' 'Twill be all over the road,' whimpered Father. 'Never again, never again, not if I lived to be a thousand!'

To this day I don't know whether he was forswearing me or the drink. By way of a song suitable to my heroic mood I bawled 'The Boys of Wexford,' as he dragged me in home. Crowley, knowing he was not safe, made off and Father undressed me and put me to bed. I couldn't sleep because of the whirling in my head. It was very unpleasant, and I got sick again. Father came in with a wet cloth and mopped up after me. I lay in a fever, listening to him chopping sticks to start a fire. After that I heard him lay the table.

Suddenly the front door banged open and Mother stormed in with Sonny in her arms, not her usual gentle, timid self, but a wild, raging woman. It was clear that she had heard it all from the neighbours.

'Mick Delaney,' she cried hysterically, 'what did you do to my son?'

'Whisht, woman, whisht, whisht!' he hissed, dancing from one foot to the other. 'Do you want the whole road to hear?'

'Ah,' she said with a horrifying laugh, 'the road knows all about it by this time. The road knows the way you filled your unfortunate innocent child with drink to make sport for you and that other rotten, filthy brute.'

'But I gave him no drink,' he shouted, aghast at the horrifying interpretation the neighbours had chosen to give his misfortune.

'He took it while my back was turned. What the hell do you think I am?'

'Ah,' she replied bitterly, 'everyone knows what you are now. God forgive you, wasting our hard-earned few ha'pence on drink, and bringing up your child to be a drunken corner-boy like yourself.'

Then she swept into the bedroom and threw herself on her knees by the bed. She moaned when she saw the gash over my eye. In the kitchen Sonny set up a loud bawl on his own, and a moment later Father appeared in the bedroom door with his cap over his eyes, wearing an expression of the most intense self-pity.

'That's a nice way to talk to me after all I went through,' he whined. 'That's a nice accusation, that I was drinking. Not one drop of drink crossed my lips the whole day. How could it when he drank it all? I'm the one that ought to be pitied, with my day ruined on me, and I after being made a show for the whole road.'

But next morning, when he got up and went out quietly to work with his dinner-basket, Mother threw herself on me in the bed and kissed me. It seemed it was all my doing, and I was being given a holiday till my eye got better.

'My brave little man!' she said with her eyes shining. 'It was God did it you were there. You were his guardian angel.'

THE GUINNESS GODDESS

Marian Keyes

Lucy Sullivan is a Nineties Irish girl. Likes a drink, likes to party, likes boys—but suffers from low self-esteem. She is driven by a desire to get married, despite the unhappy example of her mother and irresponsible father who are constantly warring. But though Lucy's mother is often scathing about her father's drinking—'To hear him tell it, Dad could out-drink Oliver Reed,' the older woman says—Lucy has a genuine sympathy for her unhappy, bewildered dad. Will her fate be to end up with a man like him? When she meets Gus—'call me Augustus for short'—at a party, Lucy senses herself falling under his prowess both as a charmer and a drinker.

Marian Keyes (1963–) has become an international bestseller with her stories of the lives and loves of today's single women—but, according to the Times, *'is much more than Ireland's answer to Bridget Jones'. She is a down-to-earth writer whose books are character-based rather than plot-driven and though unashamedly commercial—'I'm not going to win the Booker prize,' she has joked—they have earned her a huge and enthusiastic following. Her road to success has not been without its problems, though. She was born in Limerick, the eldest of five children of a local government worker. Educated at the Presentation Convent in Dublin—where she delighted in shocking the nuns with 'dodgy make-up and dangerously short skirts'—Marian Keyes then took a degree in law at University College, Dublin. However, realising she did not want to be a solicitor, she moved to London and found a job as a book keeper. A mixture of low self-esteem, boredom and excessive drinking—'alcohol was my constant companion, it was my prop and my dearest friend,' she admitted to the* Daily Telegraph *in 1998—led to a period of treatment in 1994, but at the same time provided her with the inspiration and raw material to write.* Watermelon, *her first novel, was published in 1995, followed the next year by* Lucy Sullivan Is Getting Married, *a powerful tale with alcoholism at the heart of a tangled love story. The huge success of this book and* Rachel's Holiday *(1997)—also above recovery from addiction—propelled Marian Keyes into the big league of today's most popular writers on a par with her own favourite author, Maeve Binchy.*

*   *   *

In the months that followed I replayed the scene in my head so often that I remembered absolutely everything about it, down to the smallest details.

I was just on my way out of the kitchen when I heard a man's voice saying admiringly, 'Behold—a vision in gold! A goddess. A veritable goddess.'

Naturally I kept pushing and shoving to leave the room because, although I was wearing a gold dress, I was also wearing my well-tailored inferiority complex so I didn't, for a second, think that I was the one being called a goddess.

'And not just any kind of goddess,' the voice continued. 'But my favourite kind of goddess, a Guinness goddess.'

The bit about the Guinness broke through my humility barrier so I turned around and there, wedged in beside an upright freezer, leaning against the wall, was a young man. Not that there was anything unusual about that because it was, after all, a party, and the place was full of people, even a couple of men, leaning against household appliances.

The young man—and it was hard to say just how young he was—was very cute with longish black curly hair and bright green, slightly bloodshot eyes, and he was smiling straight at me, as though he knew me, which suited me just fine.

'Hello.' He nodded in a civil and friendly fashion.

Our eyes met and I had the oddest sensation. I felt as though I knew him too. I stared at him and, although I knew I was being rude, I couldn't stop. Hot confusion swept over me and at the same time I was totally intrigued because, although I was certain that I had never met him, that I had never before in my life seen him, somehow I knew him. I don't know what it was but there was *something* about him, something very familiar.

'What's kept you?' he said cheerfully. 'I've been waiting for you.'

'You have?' I swallowed nervously.

My head raced. What was happening, I wondered? Who was he? What was this instant recognition that had flashed between us?

'Oh aye,' he said. 'I wished for a beautiful woman with a can of Guinness and here you are.'

'Oh.'

A pause where he lounged against the wall, the picture of relaxation, happy and good-looking, if a little bit bleary-eyed. He didn't seem to find anything unusual about the conversation.

'Have you been waiting long?' I asked. In an odd way it felt like a very normal thing to ask, as though I was making conversation with a stranger at a bus stop.

'The best part of 900 years.' He sighed.

'Er, 900 years?' I asked, raising an eyebrow. 'But they hadn't invented cans of Guinness 900 years ago.'

'Exactly!' he said. 'My point exactly! God knows, but wasn't I the sorry one. I've had to wait for them to come up with the technology and it's been so boring. If I'd only wished for a jug of mead or a pitcher of ale I could have saved both of us a whole lot of trouble.'

'And you've been here all this time?' I asked.

'Most of the time,' he said. 'Sometimes I've been over there,'—he pointed to a spot on the floor about a foot away from where he was standing—'but mostly I've been here.'

I smiled—I was totally captivated by him and his story-telling.

He was *exactly* the kind of man I liked, not dull or staid, but imaginative and inventive and so *cute*.

'I've been watching for you so long that it's hard to believe you're finally here. Are you real?' he asked. 'Or just a figment of my Guinness-starved imagination?'

'Oh, I'm perfectly real,' I assured him. Although I wasn't at all sure myself. And I wasn't sure whether *he* was real either.

'I want you to be real and you're *telling* me that you're real, but I might be imagining it all, even the bit where you're telling me that you're real. It's all very confusing—you can see my problem?'

'Indeed,' I said solemnly. I was *enchanted*.

'Can I have my can of Guinness?' he asked.

'Well, I don't know,' I said anxiously, forgetting for a moment that I was enchanted.

'Nine hundred years,' he reminded me gently.

'Yes, I know,' I said. 'I see your point perfectly, but they're Daniel's. I mean, he paid for them and I was just about to give him one, but . . . oh never mind. Have one.'

'Donal may have paid for them, but destiny says they're mine,' he told me in a confidential tone, and somehow I believed him.

'Really?' I asked, my voice wobbling, torn between a desire to just surrender to whatever supernatural forces were operating around this man and I, and the fear of being accused of not standing my round and making free with other people's Guinness.

'Donal would have wanted it this way,' he went on, gently removing something from under my arm.

'Daniel,' I said absently, casting a glance down the hall. I could see Daniel's head and Karen's head close together and I didn't think Daniel looked as if he cared about a can of Guinness, one way or the other.

'Maybe you're right,' I agreed.

'There's only one problem,' said the man.

'What's that?'

'Well, if you're imaginary, then, by definition, your Guinness will also be imaginary and imaginary Guinness isn't half as nice as the real stuff.'

He had such a beautiful accent, so gentle and so lyrical, it sounded familiar, yet I couldn't quite place it.

He opened the can and poured the contents down his throat.

He drank the whole lot in one go as I stood looking at him. I have to say I was impressed. I'd seen very few men able to do that. In fact the only one I'd ever seen do it was my dad.

I was delighted—completely captivated by this man-child, whoever he was.

'Hmmm,' he said thoughtfully, looking at the empty can and then looking at me. 'Hard to tell. It *could* have been real and then again it might have been imaginary.'

'Here,' I said, pushing the other can at him. 'It's real, I promise.'

'Somehow I trust you.' And he took the second can and repeated the performance.

'Do you know,' he said thoughtfully, wiping his mouth on the back of his hand, 'I think you might be right. And if the Guinness is real then that means that you're real too.'

'I think I am,' I said sorrowfully. 'Even though a lot of the time, I'm not sure.'

'I suppose you sometimes feel invisible?' he asked.

My heart leapt. Nobody, *nobody*, had ever asked me that before and that was *exactly* how I felt for huge chunks of my life. Had he read my mind? I was mesmerised. So much recognition! Somebody understood me. A total stranger had just looked straight into my soul and seen the essence of me. I felt light-headed with exhilaration and joy and hope.

'Yes,' I said faintly. 'I sometimes feel invisible.'

'I know,' he said.

'How?'

'Because so do I.'

'Oh.'

'There was a pause and the two of us just stood looking at each other for a little while, smiling slightly.

'What's your name?' he asked suddenly. 'Or will I just call you the Guinness Goddess? Or, if you like, I could shorten it to GG. But then I might mistake you for a horse and try to back you and let's face it, you don't look anything like a horse and although you have nice legs . . .' (At this point he paused and leant over sideways so that his head was level with my knees.)

'Yes, very nice legs,' he continued, straightening up, 'I'm not sure if you could run fast enough to win the Grand National. Though you might come in the first three, so I suppose I could do an each way bet on you. We'll see. We'll see. Anyway, what's your name?'

'Lucy.'

'Lucy, is it?' he said thoughtfully, looking at me with his green, green, slightly bloodshot eyes. 'A fine name for a fine woman.'

Although I was certain that it was the case, I had to ask him anyway—'You're not . . . by any chance . . . *Irish*, are you?'

'Sure, bejibbers and bejabbers and what else would I be, only Oirish?' he said, in a stage Irish accent, and did a little dance. 'All the way from County Donegal.'

'I'm Irish too,' I said excitedly.

'You don't sound it,' he said doubtfully.

'No, I am,' I protested. 'At least both my parents are. My surname is Sullivan.'

'That's Irish all right,' he admitted. 'Are you of the species Paddius, variety Plasticus?'

'Sorry?'

'Are you a plastic paddy?'

'I was born here,' I admitted. 'But I *feel* Irish.'

'Well, that's good enough for me,' he said cheerfully. 'And my name's Gus. But my friends call me Augustus for short.'

'Oh.' I was charmed. It got better and better.

'I'm very pleased to meet you, Lucy Sullivan,' he said, taking my hand in his.

'And I'm very pleased to meet you, Gus.'

'No, please!' he said, holding up his hand in protest, 'Augustus, I insist.'

'Well, if it's all the same to you, I'd rather call you Gus. Augustus is a bit of a mouthful.'

'Am I?' he said, sounding surprised. 'A mouthful? And you've only just met me!'

'Er, you know what I mean . . .' I said, wondering if perhaps we were slightly at cross-purposes.

'No woman has ever said that about me before,' he said, looking at me thoughtfully. 'You're a most unusual woman, Lucy Sullivan. A most *perceptive* woman, if I may say so. And if you will insist on formality, then Gus it is.'

'Thank you.'

'It shows that you were well brought up.'

'It does?'

'Oh yes! You've a lovely manner, very gentle and polite. I suppose you can play the piano?'

'Er, no, I can't.' I wondered what had sparked the abrupt change of subject. I wanted to tell him that I could play the piano because I was desperate to please him, but at the same time too afraid to tell a barefaced lie, in case he suggested that we play a duet there and then.

'It'd be the fiddle then?'

'Er, no.'

'The tin whistle?'

'No.'

'In that case it must be the accordion?'

'No,' I said, wishing he would stop. What was all this about musical instruments?

'You don't look like you've got the wrists to be a bodhrán player, but you must be one all the same.'

'No, I don't play the bodhrán.'

What was he talking about?

'Well, Lucy Sullivan, you have me well and truly beat. I give up. So tell me, what *is* your instrument?'

'What instrument?'

'The one that you play?'

'But I don't play an instrument!'

'What! But if you don't play, then you're surely a poet?'

'No,' I said shortly, and started thinking about how I could escape. It was too weird, even for me, and I had a very high weirdness threshold.

Flann O'Brien characters were all very well in Flann O'Brien books, but they were a different matter when you had to make small talk with them at parties.

But, as if he had read my mind, he put his hand on my arm and suddenly became a lot more normal.

'Sorry, Lucy Sullivan,' he said, humbly. 'I'm sorry. I've scared you, haven't I?'

'A bit,' I admitted.

'I'm sorry,' he said again.

'That's OK,' I smiled, relief filling me. I had no objection to people being quirky, slightly eccentric even, but when they started to display psychotic tendencies, I knew when to throw in the towel.

'It's just that I had a great feed of class A drugs earlier this evening,' he continued, 'and I'm not quite myself.'

'Oh,' I said faintly, not sure what to think now. So he took drugs? Did I have a problem with that? Well, not really, I supposed, so long as he wasn't mainlining heroin because we were short of teaspoons in the flat as it was.

'What drugs do you take?' I asked tentatively, trying not to sound condemnatory.

'What have you got?' He laughed. Then he stopped abruptly, 'I'm doing it again, aren't I? I'm scaring you?'

'Weeell, you know . . .'

'Don't worry, Lucy Sullivan. I'm partial to the odd mild hallucinogenic or mood-relaxant, nothing more. And in small quantities. And not very often. Hardly ever, really. Apart from pints. I have to admit to a fondness for a great feed of pints early and often.'

'Oh that's all right,' I said. I had no problem with men who drank.

But, I wondered, if he was currently under the influence of some narcotic, did that mean that normally he didn't tell stories and dream up things and was just as dull as everyone else? I desperately hoped not. It would be unbearably disappointing for this gorgeous, charming, unusual man to disappear along with the last traces of drugs from his bloodstream.

'Are you normally like this?' I asked cautiously. 'You know, er, imagining things and telling stories and all that? Or is it just the drugs?'

He stared at me, his shiny curls falling into his eyes.

Why can't I get *my* hair to shine like that, I wondered absently, I wonder what conditioner he uses.

'This is an important question, isn't it, Lucy Sullivan?' he asked, still staring at me. 'A lot depends on it.'

'I suppose,' I mumbled.

'But I've got to be honest with you, you know,' he said sternly. 'I can't just tell you what you want to hear, now can I?'

I wasn't at all sure whether I agreed with that. In an unpredictable and unpleasant world it was both unusual and very pleasant to hear what I wanted to hear.

'I suppose.' I sighed.

'You won't like what I'm going to tell you, but I'm morally bound to tell you anyway.''

'Fine,' I said sadly.

'I have no choice.' He touched my face gently.

'I know.'

'Oh!' He shouted suddenly and theatrically threw wide his arms. He attracted worried looks from all around the kitchen— people as far away as the back door turned to look. ' "O, what a tangled web we weave, when first we practice to deceive!'' Wouldn't you agree, Lucy Sullivan?'

'Yes.' I laughed. I couldn't help it, he was just so mad and funny.

'*Can* you weave, Lucy? No? Not much call for it these days. A dying art, a dying art. I'm no good at it myself—two left feet, that's me. Now, to tell you the God's honest truth, Lucy Sullivan . . .'

'I wish you would.'

'Here goes! I'm even worse when I'm a drug-free zone. There! I've said it! I suppose you'll be getting up and leaving me now?'

'Actually no.'

For a moment he was silent.

'But don't you think I'm a lunatic and an embarrassment and a holy show?'

'Yes.'

'You mean to tell me that lunatics and embarrassments and holy shows are your particular bag, Lucy Sullivan?'

I had never really thought of it that way before but now that he had mentioned it . . .

'Yes,' I said.

THE ROCKY ROAD TO DUBLIN

Shane MacGowan

Drinking and music are inseparable in Ireland. From time immemorial the one has prompted the other and the nation's great range of songs from traditional ballads to modern pop tunes bear wonderfully tuneful witness to this fact. Many an artist who has become successful began his or her career playing in pubs and bars, entertaining audiences who are mostly receptive but not above criticism. Singing in pubs is, indeed, as much a part of the craic *as conversation. Movie director Alan Parker said recently after filming in the country, 'The truth is if you ask absolutely anybody to sing in Ireland, they'll gladly oblige: often beautifully and sometimes even without a glass of Guinness in their hand.' Nowadays, after years of domination by the folk singers and showbands, the Irish scene has produced a group of artists and bands who have become international stars. Foremost among these are Van Morrison, admiringly remembered at the Portaferry Hotel near Belfast; U2's Bono and 'The Edge' who played the popular Baggots Inn in Dublin during their early years; and the anarchic punk rocker Shane MacGowan of the Pogues. His book,* A Drink with Shane MacGowan *(2001) is probably the most outrageous and revealing memoirs of any non-conformist rock star.*

Shane Patrick MacGowan (1957–   ) grew up on a small farm in County Tipperary. His mother was a successful model and award-winning traditional Irish singer, but his father, he says, was a renowned drinker, 'In our family, it was like: "If the kid likes a drink, let him have a drink,"' and the young MacGowan first tasted alcohol when he was given a baby bottle of Powers

Whiskey at the tender age of eight! He won a scholarship to Westminster School but was expelled after a year. It was while he was working as a barman in London that he saw a performance of the Sex Pistols and, inspired by this, rapidly became one of the central figures in the rise of punk, simultaneously creating his own legend as a drinker of vast quantities of alcohol. He formed his first group, the Nipple Erectors and sang under the name of 'Shane O'Hooligan'. MacGowan's second group were called Pogue Mahone, but they were forced to change this to the Pogues when the BBC discovered that the name was Gaelic for 'kiss my arse'. In A Drink With Shane MacGowan, *he has described the astonishing success story of the group and his own 'chaotic, breakdown-scarred, alcohol-fuelled lifestyle' which, by his own admission, is full of tales that are part fact and part fiction. MacGowan is, in truth, a compelling storyteller and in this episode about the evolution of the Pogues introduces one of his literary inspirations, Brendan Behan—among the others are Joyce, O'Casey, Flann O'Brien and Patrick McCabe—as well as revealing his astute knowledge of Ireland's musical heritage and its link to the nation's drinking culture.*

*   *   *

There was no decent live music around when the Pogues started. What I wanted to do was to go back beyond rock and roll, before rock and roll, and do Irish music but do it for a pop audience because I think Irish music is very like rock and roll, it's one of the musics that influenced rock and roll, it's one of the musics that makes up rock and roll.

A lot of Irish songs are rock and roll songs. 'The Rocky Road to Dublin', for instance, is a rock and roll song. People were doing all this World music shit at the time we started and I just found it really annoying and boring and I thought, It's there in our own backyard, Irish culture, Irish music is living and breathing here in England and all around the world. I didn't know how far around the world it spread at that stage, but wherever there are Irish people there is Irish music and they want to hear it. It was so obvious.

It wasn't really my idea to start the band, it was the other people, Spider and Jem and a guy called Ollie who was the first drummer. I got swayed into it because I was mixed up with the Nips and they thought the Nips were a good band ... I didn't ever think they were a good band but they were a very popular band, live, and if we had had the right breaks we could have had a great deal of success, we were a good pop band and we had a good following, a loyal following. I, or rather, we, created that again with the Pogues.

There was no generation gap with the Pogues, we weren't just playing to teenagers ... we were playing to everybody. We were a bar band and we played country music and rock 'n' roll and we played stuff like 'The Green Green Grass of Home' and 'Don't It Make My Brown Eyes Blue' as well as Irish stuff. We were doing a showband music, but putting a massive kick up the arse into it as well as traditional Irish music so we were taking seriously stuff that hadn't been taken seriously in pop music before. The suits, black suits with white shirts which we wore, were Brendan Behan uniform and that's why we chose them, not to look smart, but to look like as if we could have come from any decade, if you know what I mean. We could have looked like people from the fifties, sixties or seventies ... we just looked like classic Paddys.

I was really into Brendan Behan. We were all into him but I was heavily into him. I think I identified with him because I had a massive drink problem and because I liked his writing and because he was Irish. I liked all the Irish writers but he was the most hip Irish writer, the one who was the most popular. He was the one who was a hit, who had hits. He was a bit like Irvine Welsh. He was a writer who really lived, he was in the IRA, he'd been in jail. It appealed to me that he had really been there, that he wasn't making it up. That really appeals to me in anybody.

I wanted to make pure music that could be from any time, to make time irrelevant, to make generations and decades irrelevant. I wanted not to insult people's intelligence and not to pretend to be intellectual. I wanted the music not to be about angst and how terrible it is lying in your bedroom taking heroin and all that rubbish. I didn't want it to be about how bad drinking was, I wanted to celebrate taking drugs and drinking and life. I wanted to celebrate the seedy side of life which I enjoy. I like pubs and drugs and sex. I resented the eighties trend towards apathy and towards musicians being well behaved. I wanted to stop people right where they were and take them back, back, right back before the Beatles, before Elvis and start off there.

The Pistols and the Ramones also took the music back to a stage when it was simple, but they didn't take the lyrics back to being banal. I didn't want to take the lyrics back to being banal, either, which is always a danger. Irish music doesn't have banal lyrics, so I didn't want my own songs to have banal lyrics. And they didn't.

I never intended to write as many songs as I did. I didn't want to be known as a songwriter, I wanted the group and pop and rock 'n' roll and music to dance to and celebrate and all the rest of it, but not to insult people's intelligence. And I think I achieved that for a while, by just doing it without any bullshit. We stripped down the drumkit to one snare and cymbals and we only had one electric instrument—the bass.

We were heavily influenced, also, by the Dubliners who I thought were the band that demonstrated Irish pop music the best. So Behan wasn't actually as important an influence as the Dubliners were, because it was the music that was most important to me, always was. The fact that I wrote clever lyrics or, at least, that people thought my lyrics were clever, was irrelevant to me. I didn't want to become the one that everybody picked on to be a genius and when that started, I knew it was getting dangerous. Because once one person gets picked on and singled out, the group harmony is going to start breaking up. The rest of the group believed my press, even though I didn't believe it. And then they decided I was just a stupid drunk, after all, because they read it in the papers.

JUST VISITING

Bernard Mac Laverty

Paddy Quinn is an alcoholic dying in hospital. His only visitor is Ben, a teacher, who knows his friend is just allowed a couple of cans of Guinness a day, so he sneaks in a half-bottle of Scotch each time he calls. Their friendship has been an on-off one for years, but in the sad, companionable old boozer, Ben sees a kind of substitute father figure for the one he never knew. It may be against the rules to give the patient whiskey, but Ben is under no illusions that Quinn has not got long to live and sees no reason why he should not enjoy a last tot or two. Their talk is sparse and ironical as the drinks sees them both through to the inevitable conclusion—though not one without its moments of frustration and anger for Ben . . .

Bernard Mac Laverty (1942–) was born in Belfast and attended St Milligan's Catholic Grammar School before working for ten years as a laboratory technician at Queen's University. In 1974 he decided to leave Ireland for Edinburgh with his wife and four children where he found employment as a teacher. In his spare time, he worked on his first novel, Lamb (1980), *about a priest's tortured love for a vulnerable boy. The success of this book—later filmed in 1985 with Liam Neeson—enabled Mac Laverty to write full-time.* Cal (1983) *about the hopeless love of a man for the woman whose Protestant husband he helped murder, brought him to international attention, and was followed by* Grace Notes (1997) *which was short-listed for the Booker Prize. Although Mac Laverty has only returned to Northern Ireland a few times, he enjoys revisiting the pubs of his youth and has used the nation's drinking culture in several of his short stories as well as the novel* Grave Notes *which features a hilarious drunken scene in the Crown bar, Belfast. Mac Laverty says that his favourite form of writing is the short story and 'Just Visiting' is both typical of his work and in its mixture of pathos and resolution provides an appropriate finale to this collection.*

*   *   *

The pub, almost opposite the hospital gate, had an off-licence attached. He waited a long time for the green man before crossing. The rain was falling constantly and the wind darkened the pavements as it gusted. He ran with his coat collar up. A bell chinked when he opened the door and a girl came out from the back to serve him. There was not a great range of Scotch in half bottles so he bought, not the cheapest—because that would look bad—but a middle-priced one. The girl began to wrap it in brown paper.

'Don't bother,' he said. 'It'll do like that.' He slipped the half bottle into his jacket, making sure the pocket flap concealed it.

In the lift to the wards a Sister with winged spectacles stood opposite him. He thought he heard the liquid clink in the bottle when they stopped at any floor but she didn't seem to notice. When the lift doors opened on the fourteenth floor he smelled the antiseptic—but there was another smell—a perfume he couldn't quite place. A sweet, intense—uneasiness. He walked along the corridor.

He hadn't seen Paddy for three years—not since he himself had moved to the city. Through the ward windows he could see men in various propped positions, in beds, on beds. A sign above one—NIL BY MOUTH. Was that him? How much had the illness changed him? Would he recognise him easily? A nurse in her forties sat at a desk mid-way along the corridor. She continued writing her report, then looked up.

'Just visiting,' he said. 'I'm here for a Mister Quinn. Mister Paddy Quinn.' She stood up and escorted him. The name tag on her lapel said *Mrs MacDonald*. Again he was aware of the liquid clinking in the bottle in his pocket.

'He's in a room by himself—he's still very weak after his operation. So please—if you don't mind—don't be too long.' She opened the door and called out, 'Visitor for you, Paddy.'

A figure lay flat in the bed with his back to the door facing the window. The visitor moved round the bed to face him.

'Paddy—how are you?'

The nurse closed the door. Paddy gave a groan and heaved himself onto his elbow.

'I hate that bitch, MacDonald. She is so fucking patronising,' he said. 'Good to see you, Ben.' Ben reached out and touched the older man on the shoulder. 'Watch me—or I'll fall apart.' Ben plumped up the pillows and wedged them behind Paddy's back.

'So—how are you?'

'Some fucker unseamed me from the nave to the chaps.' Paddy lay back on the pillows and blew out his breath. His beard and hair were now completely white. When he opened his pyjama jacket to display his wounds Ben tried not to let anything show on his face. There was an incision beginning at Paddy's neck which zig-zagged down his side to the bottom of his ribs.

'Jesus, it's like the map of a railway track.' There were junctions and off-shoots and either there was extensive bruising or else the whole wound had been painted with iodine.

'It's hand-stitched,' he said. 'Nothing but the best.'

'Is it sore?'

'Naw . . .' Paddy looked at him. 'What the fuck d'you think?'

Ben nodded, not knowing whether to smile or not.

'Did you manage to run the cutter?'

Ben glanced over at the small window in the centre of the door. There was no one looking.

'In my wash-bag,' said Paddy. Ben slipped the bottle from his pocket into the wash-bag, covered it with a damp facecloth and zipped it up.

'Crinkle-free,' he said. 'The girl was going to wrap it but I said no. I didn't know the lie of the land up here.' The wash-bag was now stowed at the bottom of the bedside cabinet. Ben sat down on a chair. Paddy leaned back on his pillows.

'It's good to know that's there.'

'Are you not allowed *anything*?'

'Two cans of Guinness a day. Three if someone's brave enough to buck the system.'

'Slim rations,' said Ben.

'I'm on that many bloody drugs . . .'

'When did you arrive?'

'The night I phoned. They operated the next day.'

'I'm sorry I couldn't get up sooner but you know how it is.' Ben shrugged, making out he had no control over anything. 'So—how have you been since I last saw you?'

'Apart from cancer—okay.'

'Sorry—but you know what I mean. How's the town I love so well?'

'The terrible town of Tynagh. It's not been the same since you left. Morale has taken a nose dive.' There was a long silence. 'Where green peppers wrinkle on the Co-op shelf.' Ben rested his elbows on his knees and stared down at the terrazzo floor. Paddy stared at the white coverlet. 'What's the teaching like here?'

'For fuck's sake, Paddy . . .' Ben leaned back in his chair and appeared to concentrate on the ceiling. There was another pause—the wind buffeted the window and the rain sounded like hailstones against the glass. 'I mean—they wouldn't operate . . . to that extent if they didn't think they could . . . I mean the signs are *good*. My own father—they just took one look and closed him up again. Told my mother the only thing left was to take him to Lourdes. Are you getting radiotherapy?'

'Chemotherapy. They say it's worse.'

'But they wouldn't put you through all that if they thought . . . if they didn't think you had an . . . excellent chance.'

'Did she take him? To Lourdes?'

'Yeah.'

'And?'

'He died the week he came back. We were just kids—didn't even know he was ill.'

'Fuck it—pour me some orange juice. In that glass.' There

was a carton on the grey metal locker and Ben stood and began
to pour out of the torn spout of the cardboard. 'Stop—go easy.
Just enough to colour it.'

'What?'

'The whiskey.'

'Are you sure? Paddy, I'd hate to be the one . . .'

'I'll do it myself then.'

'Stay where you are.' Ben crouched and took the half bottle
out of the wash-bag. There was a series of small metallic snaps
as he broke the screw-top, then the hollow rhythmic clunking as
he poured whiskey into the tumbler of orange juice.

'Say when.' Ben kept his body between the tumbler and the
door. He stopped pouring. Paddy said,

'When.'

He put the bottle back in the wash-bag and handed the glass
to Paddy. Paddy sniffed at it.

'Terrible fucking smell—orange juice.' He raised the glass to
his mouth, quickly tipped it back and swallowed half its contents.
Then the remainder. He lay for a moment with his eyes closed.
'Oh that's good. What about yourself?'

'No, it's too early for me. Thanks all the same.'

'That's how it all started. Difficulty swallowing. It went on
for a couple of months—and then it got so bad I went to Doctor
Fuckin Jimmy. And now I'm here.'

'Doctor Fuckin Jimmy.' Ben shook his head, stood up and
sniffed at the air. 'Maybe I'd better open that window for a
bit.'

'Jesus, you'll have it as cold as the caravan in here.'

'It's the smell—if the nurse comes in.' The lower section of
the window hinged in at the bottom. The wind gusted up into
his face when he opened it. 'It didn't stop us having some good
nights.'

'Plenty of internal central heating. Days in the *Seaview*, nights
in the caravan.'

'Good times, Paddy.'

'Laughing to piss point.'

'*Mine's a whiskey,*' said Ben, imitating Paddy's voice, '*and*

I'll leave the measure up to yourself. And when it came to your round, you oul bastard—*What kind of beer can I buy you a half pint of?'*

'That's a lie.' They laughed and nodded.

'Do you still live in it?'

'The caravan? Yeah. If it hasn't blown away. It should be tied down a day like that. But I can't be bothered any more.'

'Come on Paddy . . .'

'The doctors were saying—when I get out the District will *have* to house me. They say they'll not release me *until* I get a place to recover in.'

'You see—they expect you to get better.' Paddy nodded but he didn't seem sure. He said,

'How's the wife and weans?'

'Fine—everybody's fine.' Ben looked at the racing grey sky and then down at the leafless trees in the grounds.

'I liked the kid who thought wind was made by the trees waving.' Ben looked round and Paddy was lying back on his pillows with his eyes clenched shut. 'Maybe I'd better go,' he said. 'Is there anything you want?'

'Yeah—you could run the cutter for me again. In fact, if you don't I'll break your legs for you.'

'Okay—okay. But it'll be Friday before I can come.'

'And close that fucking window.'

Ben snapped the wood frame back and snibbed it.

'The windows must be like that to stop you jumping out. When it all gets too much.' Just then Mrs MacDonald tapped the glass of the door with a fingernail. 'I'm overstaying my welcome here.'

'Fuck her. I remember seeing it written up in big six-foot letters once—on a wall. *Do what you're told—REBEL.'*

'So you keep telling me.'

'She's nothing but a saved oul bitch,' said Paddy. 'Before you go I want you to do something for me.'

'Yeah sure.'

It seemed important and he leaned forward to listen attentively. He thought of wills, of funeral arrangements, of last wishes.

'See the wardrobe—there's a dead man in my dressing-gown pocket. Dispose of it.'

On the way out in the main corridor he smelled the sweet intense perfume again. It was so strong it almost caught the back of his throat like cigarette smoke. Mrs MacDonald was now sitting at her desk in the light of an anglepoise. He stopped and waited for her to pause in her writing.

'Yes?' Mrs MacDonald looked up from her work and Ben felt he had to point vaguely in the direction he'd come from.

'I've just been visiting Paddy Quinn.'

'Of course.'

'And I wanted to give you my number—just in case. He hasn't anybody. Here, that is.' She wrote down Ben's particulars.

'You're a friend of his?'

'Yes—we've known each other for about ten years now. We were neighbours—sort of.'

'In Tynagh?'

'Yes—when I was teaching at the High School there.'

'Lucky you. What a beautiful place. It's my favourite seaside town.'

'How do you know it?'

'Mr MacDonald and I drive through it most years. On our way somewhere.' Ben nodded but decided to say nothing. He cleared his throat.

'How is he? I mean I know he's weak but . . . how is he?'

'Mr Milne—sorry, the surgeon—is convinced that he caught it in time. They are all quite hopeful.'

'That *is* good news.'

'But he's almost sixty—and hasn't treated himself as well as some.'

'Thank you—thank you anyway for all you are doing.'

Then he saw the source of the perfume—behind Mrs Mac-Donald's desk—two bowls of hyacinths. Big bulbs sitting proud of the compost, flowering pink and blue and pervading the wards and corridor with their scent. It was a smell he hated because he associated it with childhood, with the death of his own father. A hospital in winter brightening itself with bowls of blue and pink hyacinths—a kind of hypocrisy, the stink of them everywhere. His mother crying, telling them all to be brave.

It felt like the first day of summer—warm with the sun shining out of a cloudless sky and the trees in the hospital grounds in full leaf.

When Ben went into the ward it was empty. Mrs MacDonald said with a repressed sigh that Paddy was probably in the smoking-room. Ben walked to the far end of the corridor and looked through the small window of the door. There were four or five men inside. He went in.

'How're ya,' he said. Paddy was in his wheelchair sucking his pipe.

'On fortune's cap I am not the very button.' They laughed. After the treatment the hair on the right-hand side of his face had fallen out and gave his beard a lop-sided look. He was fully dressed in trousers and jacket and sat apart, looking out the window. The others were in a group, smoking cigarettes. 'Have you put on some weight?'

'According to the scales,' said Paddy. The room was bluish with smoke and smelled stale. There was a green metal waste bin quarter filled with cigarette butts. 'And how are you?'

'Great—the first week of the holidays. Like the first couple of hours on a Friday night.'

'You can hardly see out this fucking window for nicotine. Look at it.' The glass was yellowish, opaque. 'It hasn't been cleaned for months. Nobody *ever* sweeps the floor in here. The message is, if you smoke in this hospital we're gonna make you feel like shit because we're going to treat you like shit.' He knocked his pipe out into the bucket and began to roll some tobacco between his hands. Ben sat down. The white-painted window sill had tan scorch lines where cigarettes had been left to burn.

'Take it easy—maybe in a . . . a ward of this nature they have a point.'

'Fuck off, Ben. People get hooked on things.' He tamped the

tobacco into the bowl of his pipe and began lighting it with a gas lighter. 'Addiction is a strange bastard. It creates a need where no need existed. And satisfying it creates a pleasure where no pleasure existed.'

Ben looked at the cigarette smokers. At least two of them looked like winos, with dark-red abused faces. They wore hospital dressing-gowns over pyjamas and had open hospital sandals. Ben stared down at their feet. They were black like hide with pieces of cotton wool separating the toes. Their toes looked dried, encrusted and brittle. His eyes flinched away.

'Let's go outside. I'll take you for a spin in the wheelchair.'

'Did you run the cutter?' Ben nodded and indicated his pocket. 'Let's stash it in my room first. And I'll get you the money.'

'Don't worry about it. It's a gift—this time.' Ben wheeled him along the corridor. Mrs MacDonald was on the desk and she spoke to Ben as they passed.

'He's fair putting on the pounds,' she said. Ben felt obliged to stop the wheelchair. He nodded.

'It'll be food—you must be giving him food.'

Paddy sat staring ahead.

'Why don't you go out—that lovely day. Get a breath of fresh air.'

'It's not fresh air I want,' said Paddy, 'but the good fug of a pub somewhere.'

'Don't you dare,' said Mrs MacDonald and Ben and she laughed. Paddy's knuckles were white on the armrests of his chair.

Ben slipped him the half bottle and Paddy stood up and went into the toilet with it. He tried to vary the places he stored it. Ben stood waiting, staring out the ward window. Mrs MacDonald passed the door with a slip of paper in her hand. She smiled and stopped. She put on a whispering voice.

'I'm serious about that.'

'What?'

'The pub business. It would be terrible to undo all the good work. I'm holding *you* responsible.' She grinned and walked away in her flat shoes, flicking at her piece of paper with her finger.

When Paddy came out of the toilet Ben smelled the whiskey off his breath as he got back into wheelchair.

'How much weight have you put on?'

'A couple of pounds but I'm still lighter than when I came in. It's that fucking chemotherapy-therapy that goes for you. And the no drink laws. They stop you drinking and then ask you to put on weight—for fucksake. Drink's full of calories.'

'I've been thinking about half bottles—the shape of them. There's something Calvinist about them. They're made flat like that *for* the pocket. No bulge, no evidence. A design to fit the Scots and the Irish psyche.'

'Shut up and drive.'

There were many patients outside in the hospital grounds, sitting on benches in pyjamas and dressing-gowns tilting their faces up to the sun, or being wheeled abut. A couple of female nurses in white uniforms lay on the grass. There was a blackbird over by the railway cutting singing constantly.

'It even feels like summer,' said Ben. They stopped at an empty bench beside a laburnum tree and Paddy got out of the chair onto the bench. He sat filling his pipe, staring at the cascades of yellow blossom.

'This bastard's poisonous. You've no regard for my health at all.'

'What was wrong with those guys' feet—in the smoking room?'

'Gangrene—smoking makes your legs drop off.'

'What?' They both laughed. 'That's crap. Why doesn't it happen to you?'

'I guess I'm just lucky. Naw—it happens mostly to cigarette smokers. It's called . . . some big fuckin name. It stops the circulation to your feet. They go black and drop off.'

'And those guys are still up there smoking?'

'You've never smoked Ben, so shut your mouth.' He lit his pipe with the gas lighter and exaggerated every gesture and sigh of satisfaction. 'It gives a selected few of us a little pleasure as we funnel our way down the black hole to oblivion. Speaking of which . . .'

'What?'

'Why don't we go for a drink?'

'Naw—'

'At the clinic where they used to dry me out they *taught* me to drink. They said . . .'

'Never drink on your own.'

'And now *you* are here. It can't be too far to the nearest pub, for fucksake. Isn't there one just at the gate?'

'Naw—'

'What the fuck's wrong. Are you on the wagon or something?'

'No—it's inadvisable. It's very pleasant here.' A train rattled through the cutting but they could not see it. The blackbird changed trees and began singing from the opposite side of the tracks. 'So—any word of a house yet?'

'No.'

'Or any word of them letting you home?'

'No.' His pipe wasn't going well and he knocked it against the spokes of the wheelchair. 'Fuck it.' He sucked and blew but couldn't free the blockage.

'There's no need to go into a huff, Quinn.'

'The first time in twelve fuckin weeks that I get a chance to have a drink without those nurses breathing down my neck— and you won't take me.'

'That's right.' There was an ornamental flower-bed with bushes and grasses screening them from the front of the hospital.

'Pull me a bit of that stuff,' said Paddy, pointing to stalks of wheat-like grass. Ben glanced in the direction of the hospital then did what he'd been asked. Paddy pulled his pipe apart and pushed the stalk through the plastic mouthpiece. When it was cleared he blew through it and reassembled the pipe. He threw the grass stalk on the ground at his feet. It was black with tar.

'*WHY* will you not take me?'

'Because you're not allowed. The doctors do not allow you.'

'What doctors have you been talking to, for fucksake?' He

turned away from Ben in irritation and looked towards the hospital gate. For a moment Ben thought the old man might attempt to make it on his own.

'They serve coffee on the ground floor. We could go over there.'

'What doctor said I wasn't allowed to go to the pub?'

'Look, Paddy—do you want to get better or not?'

'That is not what we are talking about—we are talking about going for a fucking pint and maybe a chaser in a nice atmosphere with maybe a barmaid.'

'Paddy—catch yourself on. Do you not think I know you of old? Nights spent in the terrible town of Tynagh. Once you get into a pub there's no way of getting you out.'

'You're chicken. A coward. A man who can't break the rules no matter *who* lays them down.'

Ben stood up and ushered Paddy back into the wheelchair.

'Come on. I'll buy you a coffee.'

Paddy got unsteadily to his feet and almost fell into the chair. He was shaking his head in disbelief.

Ben got the coffees in wobbly plastic containers and brought them down to Paddy by the window. Outside was a small lawn with more off-duty nurses, both male and female, sprawled on it.

'Aw fuck,' said Paddy, staring out. 'Lift your knees a bit more, darling.'

'Stop it. Would you like a biscuit or anything?'

'No.'

The formica table-top was covered in brown sugar spilled from a half-used paper sachet. The plastic container was too hot for Ben's fingers and he left it to cool. A baby was crying somewhere and two children were running up and down between the tables chasing each other. A mother stood and called them to order. Paddy stared out the window, his hands joined across his midriff. Ben began wiping the spilled sugar into a neat pile with a paper napkin.

'I sometimes do what they told you not to,' he said.

'What? Who?'

'The drying-out clinic. I drink on my own. At night.'

'Thank God you fucking drink sometimes.'

'When everybody's gone to bed.'

'You mean your wife.'

'I *like* to relax with a dram.'

'It'll not do you a button of harm. There are worse things,' said Paddy. The nurses on the lawn got up simultaneously and moved back into the hospital. Paddy looked up at Ben. 'I believe you're the undercow of that wife of yours.'

'Nonsense, Paddy.'

'Do you drink more or less when she's there?'

'Probably less. But I only have one or two.'

'Or three? Or more? When you're drinking you can only count to three.'

Ben smiled.

'Sometimes it's frightening to see the level on the bottle the next day.'

'You're not too bad then—if there's any left in the bottle. But it'll get worse—you know that. You're no fool, Ben.'

'Thanks for the advice, Holy Father.'

'I want you to remember this—you can only give advice to fools.'

'I don't understand.'

'If you feel the need to give someone advice you're *assuming* that they are a fool.'

'That is advice.'

'What?'

'What you're giving now—to me.'

'It's not advice. We're having a fucking conversation.'

Paddy pulled out his pipe and lighter. He pressed the plug of tobacco deeper into the bowl and aimed the flame at it. Ben fanned his hand in front of his face to keep the smoke at bay.

'Problem drinking,' he said, 'is a thing that builds up gradually.'

'Problem drinking? What are you talking about *problem* drink-

ing for?' Paddy laughed out loud. 'Drinking's the solution, for
fucksake.'

'Paddy, you're right beneath a *No Smoking* sign.'

'Fuck it. People like the smell of a pipe.'

'In a hospital?'

'*Especially* in a hospital.'

Ben finished his coffee and made movements to stand up.
'Look I'll not be able to make it three times a week from now
on. I have stuff for summer school. I'll come Tuesdays and
Saturdays, if that's okay with you.'

'Yeah, sure. It's good of you to come at all.'

'Naw—. It's good to hear your crack again.'

'It's not the way it used to be. More's the fuckin pity. Ben,
you're the best friend I ever had.'

'Easy on, Paddy. Statements are in danger of being made here.'

'No—it's true.'

'Okay—okay. But I've gotta go.' Ben stood up and spun Paddy
round in the wheelchair and headed for the lift. There was no
one else going up. When the doors closed Ben asked,

'Any dead men you want me to get rid of?'

'Naw—there was a fella got out yesterday. He took them away
in his suitcase. They sent him home to die. But he took the
empties all the same.'

There was snow on the hills which turned to sleet as Ben drove
down into Tynagh. It was more a village than a town—a collection of shops, five pubs and as much churches all gathered around
a harbour which had silted up over the past two decades. The
school where he'd taught looked even more dilapidated and
cement grey than he remembered. Because of the holiday the
car-park and playground were deserted. On the football field in
the drifting rain a flock of seagulls stood just inside the penalty
area.

The hospital was on the far side of the town—on the outskirts.
It shared a building with an Old People's Home. He recognised
the nurse on the front desk; she had been a pupil of his. He
remembered her as a bright girl—she had written a good

argumentative essay on *The Nature of Tourism*. When she recognised Ben she blushed.

'Hello, sir. I presume you're here to see Paddy. He talks a lot about you.'

She led him down the corridor, speaking over her shoulder to him. He felt she was embarrassed at having made the slip and called him *sir*.

'So how are you liking the big smoke, then?'

'Oh fine—it suits me fine.'

She stopped outside a room and dropped her voice. 'They sent Paddy back here to . . . recuperate . . .'

'And how's he doing?'

'Not as well as we would like.' She gestured to the room and continued walking along the corridor. She had an Elastoplast between her Achilles tendon and her shoe.

Paddy was lying on his bed against a pile of pillows with his eyes closed. There was a drip above his bed and a tube taped to his arm. His cheek bones stood out and he was a very bad colour.

Hearing someone in the room he opened his eyes.

'For fucksake Ben, what are you doing here?' His voice was hoarse and he seemed to have difficulty swallowing.

'Visiting you.' Ben reached out and shook hands. He was aware of the sinews in the older man's handshake. The arm with the drip attached lay flat, wrist upwards on the covers. 'You're looking okay—for a man that's been through the mill.'

'Do you think so?'

'I *know* so.'

'Jesus, I don't feel it.'

'What's it like here?'

'Fuckin terrible.'

'But you're surrounded by people you know . . .'

The room was on the seaward side of the hospital and the windows had been dulled by the salt blowing off the Atlantic so that the grey-green of the hills looked even greyer.

'Is your wife with you?'

'No—it's just a quick visit. I didn't know whether you wanted me to . . . y'know, run the cutter.' Ben tapped his jacket pocket and pulled the neck of a half bottle into view.

'All very acceptable,' said Paddy. 'The more the merrier. Put it there.' He indicated the open shelf on the bedside cabinet. Someone has brought him a basket of fruit which was still covered in cellophane. The white grapes were beginning to go brown. Ben reached over.

'Where?'

'Anywhere.'

It was only then that Ben noticed the full tumbler standing on the bedside cabinet. He bent over and sniffed it. It was whiskey.

'They allow you it in here?'

'A little,' said Paddy. Then he smiled. 'As much as I can drink.'

'Is that a . . . That must be a good sign.'

'They say if it helps put on some weight it'll do no harm. Would you like a snifter?'

'Nah—Paddy. Never during the day. Anyway, I'm driving the car.'

'How long are you staying?'

'I'll go back tomorrow. All things being equal.'

'What the fuck kind of an expression is that? From an English teacher? *All things being equal.* When was any fucking thing ever equal?'

'Sorry. Sloppy speech.' Ben smiled. 'Any word of a house?'

Paddy shook his head. 'They say I've got to put the weight back on before I go anywhere.'

'Are you eating much?'

Paddy looked up at the drip and licked his lips. 'Lancashire Hotpot.'

Ben didn't know what to say. 'Sorry?'

'You remember we once talked about problem drinking? Well I've got it now.'

'What?'

'A problem drinking. My fucking throat's given up. I can't swallow anything any more. This is high protein, high fibre, high fucking God knows what—but it might as well be Molly Magill's pish as far as my weight's concerned.'

'Paddy—don't be so impatient. You're looking . . . okay.'

'Okay?'

'Okay is good enough—at this stage.'

'Angela says they put the apple tart and custard through at the same time as the hotpot. And a cup of tea.'

'Angela. That's it. I'd forgotten her name. Angela Stewart. She was a pupil of mine.'

'So she tells me.'

'Is there anything you want? Anything I could get you from the town?'

'Naw, thanks. When I was in the best of health there was nothing you could get me from this town.' He picked up the glass and took a tiny sip then lay back on his pillow. He held the whiskey in his mouth but some of it leaked out at the corner of his lips.

'What brought you to this godforsaken dump in the first place?'

'It's where I ended up. After the war. As good a place as any. As bad a place as any.'

'Oh aye—the Morse Code business.'

'For the North Atlantic. The trouble with drinking cronies is— remembering what you're told them. *Drink is a great provoker of four things*—the one Shakespeare left out was amnesia.'

Ben had to lean forward a little to hear what Paddy was saying. He took the glass from Paddy's hand before it spilled and replaced it on the bedside cabinet.

'I still like the taste of it,' Paddy said. 'So you've met Angela?'

'Yeah.'

'She's a great kid. She does things for me. I suppose it's her way of telling the matron to get stuffed. The rules do not apply to a man in my position.' His breathing was becoming difficult. He reached out for his pipe which lay in a tin-toil ash-tray. He sucked the mouth-piece but did not light it. 'Could you maybe call her for me?' Ben rose quickly to his feet.

'Are you okay? Is anything wrong?'

'Don't fuss, Ben.'

He found Angela at the front desk and told her that Paddy wanted her. This time he made sure to use her name.

'I'm very busy,' she said. 'Tell him I'll be along as soon as I can.'

'Thanks, Angela.' Ben sat with Paddy for another fifteen minutes. The older man was tired or drugged and kept dozing off. Ben didn't like to disturb him and sat saying nothing. The hospital was full of noises—there was a distant rattling of dishes, someone whistling, a plastic door flapped shut, in the next room someone dropped a pair of scissors in a stainless steel sink. When Angela arrived breathless, Paddy said,

'Here comes the upwardly nubile.'

'Paddy—what do you want this time?' She turned to Ben. 'He's a terrible bloody man. You see what I've to put up with?' Ben nodded and smiled.

'I want to have a drink with my friend here,' said Paddy. He indicated the bedside cabinet.

'What do you take me for? A bloody waitress?'

'You know what I'm talking about, sweetheart. And I want you to pour one for that teacher of yours. A large one.'

'Honestly, Paddy, I've got the car.'

He sat bolt upright in the bed and his eyes bulged. His voice was as loud as he could make it.

'Fuck you and your fucking car.'

Angela winked at Ben and poured him a glass of whiskey.

'Do you take water in it?'

'Indeed I do. The same again.'

The nurse handed him the glass and said to him, 'The toilet is on the left at the bottom of the corridor.'

'Sorry?'

'Just a little walk—for a few moments.' She raised her eyebrows and smiled.

'Oh yes—?' He walked down the corridor and went to the toilet even though he didn't really need to go. When he came out Angela passed him, hurrying back to her post.

'He'll be in better form now,' she said.

Ben went back into the room. With one hand Paddy was combing back his white hair.

'There's your drink,' he said. Ben took it and toasted him.

'Cheers,' he said. He was looking for Paddy's glass to chink. The tumbler stood empty on the bedside cabinet. Paddy saw him looking and said,

'It's in the Lancashire Hotpot.'

Ben looked up at the drip. 'You old fuckin bastard.'

Paddy laughed. His eyes seemed brighter. 'All my life I've been looking for bad company to fall into and it's only recently I've realised I'm it.' They laughed a bit. 'I should've got Angela to fix one of these up in the caravan years ago. With a catheter out the window. You wouldn't have to budge for weeks.'

They talked about the good times—remembered the after-hours drinking, the windowsilling their way home, the parties with no food and 'the night of the starving fisherman' when they found bite marks in a bar of Echo margarine. When Paddy laughed it turned into a phlegmy cough which was difficult to stop so Ben tried to change the conversation and keep it as low-key as possible. After a while Paddy said,

'When you see people like her—Angela—it makes everything worth it. She doesn't give a fuck what anybody says.' He seemed to doze a bit, then jerk awake. He was beginning to slur. 'There was a thing about Wittgenstein on last night—on the radio—his last words were—*Tell them it was wonderful*. I think he was probably talking about the rice pudding.'

After about an hour Paddy fell into a deep sleep. Ben put his almost full whiskey where Paddy's tumbler had been. Then he left on tip toe.

Ben walked along the school corridor into the carpeted office section. The red light was on outside the Principal's office so he went into the Secretary's room.

'Hi Ben.'

'Who's in with him?'

'A parent—I think.' She checked a notebook. 'Yes, Lorimer of 3D—his father.'

'Can I see him next?'

'Doubt it, love. There's a Revised Arrangements in Geography Higher Grade meeting at eleven.'

'Lunch time?'

'Come down again at one—I hope you had a good night some-where, Ben?'

'Why?'

'You look like you're a bit hung over.'

'I was at home. I'll explain sometime.'

'Cheers.'

Ben wasted most of his lunch hour waiting for the red light to be switched off. He went again to the Secretary.

'Who's in?'

'Nobody, love—just knock. He's probably at his lunch.'

Ben knocked.

'Come in.'

The room was filled with the scent of a single hyacinth in a pot by the window. It was that time of year again. The Principal was sitting behind his desk which faced the door. He was eating a sandwich and a cup of tea steamed on the polished surface of the desk. Beneath the cup was a wooden coaster, so crude it was obviously made by a pupil. The slats of the venetian blinds were half closed. Outside the harsh sunlight created a glare.

'Ben—what can I do for you?' The Principal was a dark sil-houette. There was a distant yelling from the play-ground.

'Em—I got the news last night that a friend—a very close friend of mine . . . Well, that he died.'

'Oh, I'm sorry to hear that.'

'Yes, we got to know each other in the terrible town of Tynagh.'

'Oh yes—when you were teaching up there.'

'He was a great man.'

The Principal set his half bitten sandwich on a serviette on the desk. 'And . . . ?'

'I just wanted permission to go to the funeral.'

'When it is?'

'Tomorrow.'

'In Tynagh?' The Principal considered this for a moment. 'What you're really looking for is leave of absence.'

'Yes.'

The Principal sighed, 'It's sad but you know the rules as well as I do. The Region will only allow it for *close* relatives.'

'This man was a close friend. Maybe he's the father I'd like to have had.'

The Principal folded the paper napkin over the sandwich. He put it in the desk drawer and closed it. He cleared his mouth of food.

'I'm very sorry, Ben. It's not up to me. I can only make recommendations to the Region. The decision is not mine. And I can only make recommendations with regard to *close* relatives. If you like you can submit a request to the Regional Director.'

'And if he refuses?'

The Principal lifted his shoulders in a long shrug. 'Then you can't go.'

'He was important to me. More than a relative.'

'I'm afraid it can't be helped.'

'What would happen if I went anyway?'

'If you went awol?'

Ben nodded. He was still standing in the middle of the floor. The faint yelling from the playground seemed to grow in volume.

'That would not be a good thing—at all. Because we are very short-staffed at the minute.' He looked up at Ben, then swivelled a bit in his chair. 'With this flu that is going about.'

'He was called Paddy Quinn. And he was one of the best read people I ever met. He was sharp and he had very little luck.'

The Principal stood up. 'They say it's not a particularly bad flu.' He went to the window and changed the tilt of the venetian blinds so the room was flooded with light. 'Ben, if you'll excuse me, I have a lunch to finish.'

The funeral service was at ten o'clock and there was to be a gathering in the public bar of the Seaview Hotel afterwards. A piper had been engaged and paid for by the owner of the hotel as a mark of respect for a valued customer and friend. There was no point in Ben sending condolences—who would he send them to? Paddy would understand—he never did have any regard for ritual or the niceties of any situation. He would have said, 'Fuck it—do what you want to do.' At 9.45 Ben set his third-year class a comprehension exercise to keep them quiet.

'Sir, why do we have to do this crap?'

'Lorimer—you are supposed to be on your best behaviour. You do it because I say you do it.'

Ben sat, glad of the silence he could impose. When it came to ten by the clock and the class were working quietly he got up and went into the book cupboard. Although he preferred whiskey he had filled his hip flask with vodka—he knew it couldn't be detected on the breath—and he drank a toast to Paddy. Then another one. It was the first drink he had ever had during working hours and it made him feel good that he was, in some small way, giving them the fingers. He closed his eyes and leaned his head against a stack of *Art of English IV* and tried to visualise what was happening two hundred miles away in the town of Tynagh.

ACKNOWLEDGEMENTS

The editor and publishers are grateful to the following authors, publishers and agents for permission to reprint copyright stories in this collection. The O'Brien Press Ltd for 'After The Wake' by Brendan Behan; David Godwin Associates for 'Irish Revel' by Edna O'Brien: A. M. Heath Limited for 'Gold At Night' by Peter Tremayne and 'Thirst' by Flann O'Brien; Pan Macmillan Ltd for 'The Hen Party' from *Waiting For The Healer* by Eamonn Sweeney, 'The Boils of Thomas Gully' by Patrick McCabe, 'The Bull of Bashan' by Sean O'Casey and 'The Rocky Road to Dublin' from *A Drink With Shane MacGowan* by Victoria Mary Clarke and Shane MacGowan; John Johnson Ltd for 'Teresa's Wedding' by William Trevor; The Random House Group for 'We Are Green! We Are White!' from *The Van* by Roddy Doyle, 'The Guinness Goddess' from *Lucy Sullivan Is Getting Married* by Marian Keyes and 'Just Visiting' by Bernard Mac Laverty; The Samuel Beckett Estate and The Calder Educational Trust for the extract from 'Ding Dong' by Samuel Beckett; Jonathan Williams Literary Agency for 'Peter McCabe's Bargain' by Patrick Kavanagh; Constable Publishers for 'The Heat of the Sun' by Sean O'Faolain; Transworld Publishers for 'An Unusual Request' from *The International* by Glenn Patterson; HarperCollins Publishers Ltd for 'The First Singles Bar' from *A Monk Swimming* by Malachy McCourt; The Society of Authors for 'Tim Haffigan' from *John Bull's Other Island* by Bernard Shaw; Gillon Aitken Associates Ltd for 'The Diviner' by Brian Friel; A. P. Watt Ltd for 'The Key of Poteen' by Lynn Doyle; PFD for 'The Drunkard' by Frank O'Connor.